THE SECRET OF THE BARBICAN

And Other Stories

BY

J. S. FLETCHER

AUTHOR OF
THE ANNEXATION SOCIETY,
THE WOLVES AND THE LAMB,
KING *versus* WARGRAVE, ETC.

GROSSET & DUNLAP
PUBLISHERS NEW YORK

THE SECRET OF THE BARBICAN

—Q—

PRINTED IN THE UNITED STATES OF AMERICA

CONTENTS

THE SECRET OF THE BARBICAN

AGAINST TIME

CHAPTER I

At five minutes to one o'clock on that spring Saturday afternoon, Ledbitter, senior clerk at Watson & Metcalfe's, contractors, of Walford, had no other idea in his mind than that of joy that the week-end interval was near at hand. He was a hard-working, cheerfully energetic young man, who never shirked his job from Monday to Saturday—but he was always thankful when Saturday arrived. Saturday meant so much. Ledbitter was a husband of three years' standing, and there was a youthful Ledbitter at home, who was just beginning to walk and talk. On Saturday afternoons Ledbitter took him out in the Park, guiding his tottering steps, and conversing with him about the ducks and wild-fowl on the ponds. Moreover, Saturday heralded Sunday. On Sunday you could stay in bed an hour longer and eat all your meals without hurrying; on Sunday Mr. and Mrs. Ledbitter took the rising hope to his grandparents. Oh, yes, Saturday and Sunday were oases in the desert of labour—splendid days of rest and leisure. No fear, said Ledbitter, of a man like himself failing to appreciate them. Three minutes more, and the clock would strike one, and he would be free to race home, and——

Sharman, the manager, came across to Ledbitter's desk as the clerk was locking it up.

"You posted that tender of Steel & Cardyke's all right yesterday?" he asked.

"Yesterday, yes!" answered Ledbitter. "Last night it was."

"Registered it, of course?" said Sharman.

"Yes, it was registered," replied Ledbitter.

Sharman took up a book that lay on the desk and turned it over.

"I don't see the receipt," he remarked. "Haven't you pasted it up?"

"It's in another waistcoat pocket at home," answered Ledbitter. "I'll bring it Monday."

"Don't forget," said Sharman. "You should always paste these receipts up at once. It's all we've got to show the governors that a tender's been sent."

He turned away to his own desk, and Ledbitter said good-morning and hurried out. He was glad to get out, glad that Sharman had not kept him talking—had not looked at him. For in the very act of telling Sharman that he had posted the tender to London, and that the receipt for it was at home, Ledbitter suddenly remembered that he had neither posted it nor had any receipt for it, and he went away from the office curiously afraid.

Ledbitter was one of those wise young men who know when they have got a good job, and who would rather do anything than lose it. He had been with Watson & Metcalfe seven years, and his salary was four pounds a week, and it was steadily increasing. He was a good servant, and he had good masters, and up to now he never remembered making a mistake since he picked up a pen in Watson & Metcalfe's service. But here was a bad one. He had forgotten to post a tender which involved a sum of half a million of money! It was no formidable document in appearance, to be sure. The tender, a mere matter of round figures, was written—by Watson himself—on an ordinary sheet of office notepaper and enclosed in an ordinary office envelope, sealed and blue pencilled.

If it had only been a big, heavy document, Ledbitter would never have forgotten it. But, being as small as it was, he had slipped it within an inside pocket of a winter waistcoat which he was wearing on the previous morning, intending to register it when he went home to dinner—and it had escaped his memory. How he could have been so forgetful he could not think. But he did remember that on going home he had found that winter waistcoat becoming much too warm, and had changed it for a lighter one. Of course, the tender was safe enough—he would hurry home and get it off. And, after all, it would be in time. The tenders which Steel & Cardyke were inviting had to be delivered, by post or by hand, at their office in London by four o'clock on the following Monday. Heaps of time—if he got the tender off at once, as he would take care to do. The only thing he was afraid of was that Sharman, if he inspected the post-office receipt, might notice that the letter had not been handed in on Friday, but on Saturday. However, Sharman would be satisfied, most likely, to hear that the receipt had been pasted up in the book kept for that purpose, and would not even glance at it. And the great thing was to get the tender off so that it would be in London first thing on Monday morning.

Ledbitter lived in a small bandbox of a house, just outside the centre of the town. There was a pleasant odour of beefsteak and onions in the hall when he opened the door, and his wife, on hearing his step, immediately called to him that dinner was ready.

But Ledbitter self-denyingly shouted an entreaty for delay, and darted up the stairs to his bedroom. He dashed at a wardrobe wherein he kept his garments, and a moment later began to yell over the top of the staircase:

"Fanny, where's that winter waistcoat of mine?" he vociferated. "Where's it got to? You know, the one I took off yesterday noon when I came home to dinner."

Mrs. Ledbitter looked out of the back-parlour door.

"Bless me, Herbert," she exclaimed, "you must be losing your memory! Don't you remember that you told me a fortnight ago, that you'd about done with that old waistcoat, and that when you left it off this spring I could sell it with a lot of other old clothes of yours? I sold a whole bundle of stuff yesterday afternoon. And, by the by——"

Ledbitter let out a groan that seemed to shake the house. He made two leaps down the stairs. His wife opened her lips to scream, but the scream died as she caught a full sight of his white face.

"You—you sold it!" he stammered hoarsely. "Good heavens! To whom?"

"Milson's, of course!" answered Mrs. Ledbitter. "But, as I was saying——"

Ledbitter was already at the door. He was quite deaf and half blind as he dashed at the gate of the little garden and darted into the street. His wife's cry might as well have been addresed to the paving-stones.

"Herbert, Herbert, come back! I say, Herbert!" she called after him. "If you're wanting——"

But Ledbitter was utterly obsessed by one idea, and he ran madly away towards the town.

Milson was well known in Walford. He dealt—extensively—in second-hand clothing. He would buy every and any article, no matter what its age and condition. He gave good prices for what he bought. That was one side of his business. The other was his selling side. It was a mystery to the curious what Milson did with the cast-off garments that he purchased. But there was this fact, that he had always in stock an enormous quantity of second-hand clothes, at ridiculously cheap figures, which looked almost as good as new. Cast-off garments went into one department at Milson's, passed through some extraordinary transformation in another, and emerged in a third looking quite spick and span, carefully cleaned and pressed, and ticketed at prices which encouraged purchasers to buy half a dozen suits at once.

Ledbitter dashed into Milson's main shop and ran up against Milson himself—a little podgy man with a goatee beard and a large cable chain of heavy gold across his ample girth. He buttonholed him without ceremony, and made an effort to get his breath.

"You bought some cast-off clothes from my wife yesterday!" he gasped. "Mrs. Ledbitter, Acacia Terrace—you know."

"Quite right, my boy," answered Milson affably. "Price quite satisfactory, I hope?"

"Hang the price!" said Ledbitter. "I want a certain winter waistcoat that was amongst those things—a dark red ground with black spots in it, flannel-lined. Must have it. She shouldn't have sold it."

"Very sorry, my boy, but it's impossible," replied the second-hand clothes dealer, rubbing his beringed hands. "Odd, now, but I sold that there waistcoat as soon as I'd bought it. I put your wife's little lot down on that very counter to sort 'em out when I came in from calling on her, and just then there was a feller walked in as took a fancy to that waistcoat, and bought it straight off—with other warm things what he'd come special for. He was a feller, my boy, as was just going to emigrate, d'ye see, to Canada."

"Canada!" exclaimed Ledbitter. "Is—is he off?"

Milson removed a large cigar from the corner of his lips and waved it in the air expansively.

"I should say he might by now, my boy," he answered. "It runs in my mind that he said he was going to-day. He was a feller, d'ye see, that was going what they call going prospecting, in the cold regions of ice and snow, where the bitter winds do blow, my boy, and he thought it 'ud be a good notion to take a nice bundle of warm stuff out with him. Which," concluded Milson, digging his hands into his pockets and rattling his money—"which, my boy, I sold him with pleasure. And with profit—mutual, of course."

Ledbitter had grown deadly calm. For the first time in his life he began to know what book-writing folk mean when they talk about the calmness of despair.

"You don't know where this man lived in Walford?" he asked.

"You're wrong, my boy, for I do!" replied Milson. "Or I should say did, for, as I observed previous, I should think he's gone. He was a navvy feller, d'ye see, and his name was Terry, and his address was Barcoe's lodging-house, round the corner in Mill Street. I sent him his parcel there last night. And what might you be wanting that particular waistcoat for, Mr. Ledbitter, now? Because——"

But Ledbitter was out of the door and running

across the road towards Mill Street. That was a narrow alley in the poorest quarter of the town, and it was celebrated for its registered lodging-houses. Ledbitter looked for Barcoe's as he might have looked for something of inexpressible value. He caught sight of the name at last, in white letters on a black board, and he dashed through a group of men, sitting on the door-steps, into a white-washed passage, to find himself confronting the deputy, a big, bullying-looking fellow who scowled at him as if he took him for an unwelcome visitor.

"Now, then, mister?" demanded this person.

"Have you got a man named Terry here?" panted Ledbitter. "He was here yesterday, I know. Milson, the clothes-dealer, says he was here. I want him—at once."

"Do yer?" sneered the deputy. "Don't you wish yer may get him, then! He's off, mister."

"Where?" demanded Ledbitter.

"Canada," retorted the deputy. "That's where he's gone. 'Taint exactly next door, neither."

"But—which way?" entreated Ledbitter. "Where—you know what I mean—what place is he sailing from?"

The deputy folded his enormous arms, bared to the shoulders, and scratched his elbows. He sized Ledbitter up.

"What do you want to know for?" he growled. "I ain't going to give my customers' private business away to no strangers. You ain't a 'tec.—I knows that, but you might be a lawyer's clerk by the look of yer."

Ledbitter rose to the occasion—gladly.

"That's it!" he exclaimed. "We want this Terry—something to his advantage—bit of money, you know. If I can catch him before he sails, eh?"

He slipped a half-crown into the deputy's hand, and the deputy relaxed.

"Oh, if that's it, mister!" he said. "Well, he went off to Liverpool this morning—him and a mate of his name of Scaby. They expected to sail late to-night or early to-morrow, didn't know which, so they went in good time. On the Starnatic they was going, so I heard 'em say—steerage, ov course. You ain't ever seen this Terry? Big, red-haired chap—"

But Ledbitter was off again. He leapt through the idlers at the door, ran down the street, and made for the Central Station. As he ran three names beat themselves on his aching brain like unappeasable steam-hammers: Terry—Liverpool—Starnatic! Starnatic — Liverpool — Terry! Liverpool — Terry — Starnatic! Everything else in the world was blotted out. He had no home, no wife, no baby, no nothing! He never would have anything until he seized that infernal letter.

He dashed into the booking-office of the big station and clapped a sovereign on the ledge of the ticket window, hoarsely demanding to be booked to Liverpool.

"How—how soon is there a train?" he faltered. "Soon?"

The clerk turned an unconcerned eye at the clock.

"If you do double time up No. 6," he answered, as he pushed ticket and change across the ledge, "you'll just catch or just miss one."

Ledbitter ran. He was dimly aware of colliding with various moving bodies in his progress. Some of them were soft and yielding, and they cried out. Some were hard, and they hurt him. Then a guard used severe language, and threw him into some receptacle, where he fell into a corner. Presently he looked up, and found himself in an otherwise empty carriage. The train was moving. Outside its windows he caught a glimpse of the big dome of Walford Town Hall. It slid away. So did the spire of the parish church. So did the roofs and chimneys of the last outskirts of Walford. Then Ledbitter realised matters, and he put his throbbing head in his hands and groaned heavily.

CHAPTER II

LEDBITTER'S first proceeding, on recovering his breath, was to form an accurate idea of where he was and what he was after. That took rather more time than might be thought. He got a clear conception at last. He was at the beginning of a hundred mile run between Walford and Liverpool. It would take nearly three hours; he would reach Liverpool, then, by say, five o'clock. Once there, he had to find a ship called the Starnatic. She would probably have a few hundred passengers on her books—he had to find a man named Terry, a steerage passenger. There might be a score of Terrys. Also, by the time he found the Starnatic, or, rather, got to hear of her, she might have sailed. In that case, he, Ledbitter, was ruined for life, and might as well drown himself in the Mersey. But the deputy had said, "Late to-night or early in the morning." There was hope—much hope. Let him hope—and meanwhile he counted his money

Ledbitter realised that money would be an immense factor in the successful prosecution of this enforced campaign against fate; he did not know where he might not have to go before he recovered that letter. So he turned out his purse. He had had seven shillings in it when he went to the office that morning, and to that he had added his week's salary—four pounds. He had given the lodging-house man half-a-crown, and paid eight shillings and ninepence for his ticket to Liverpool. So he had three pounds fifteen shillings and ninepence on him. He could do a lot on that. And then he suddenly remembered that he had left his wife without anything. Instead of handing over the usual house-keeping money to her—his invariable proceeding on Saturdays—he had rushed away after that beastly waistcoat. Well, it was no great matter. She would be all right, perfectly all right—she had money in a box. But he realised that he must send her a wire as soon as he reached his journey's end.

Ledbitter by this time was enormously hungry. He had had nothing to eat since eight o'clock that morning. Now that he had nothing to do but sit still and be carried on to events at which he could only guess, his hunger asserted itself to the exclusion of all other feelings. He began to wonder if the train—an express—would run right through. Some trains, he knew, did make a non-stop run between Walford and Liverpool. But fortunately the train did stop—for a few minutes—at Manchester, and he ran to the nearest refreshment room, swallowed a glass of ale, and grabbed a bag of sandwiches. And as the train moved off again Ledbitter satisfied his hunger in some degree and concocted the necessary telegram.

That telegram, Ledbitter decided, must be sent as soon as he set foot on the Liverpool platform. He foresaw that he might not be able to present himself at the office first thing on Monday morning. His notion was that if he recovered the tender that night, or on Sunday, he would make sure of its delivery by taking it to London himself. His money would just enable him to do that. But until he could assure his employers that he had repaired his failure to post the tender, and that it had been duly handed in, he did not want them to know what was happening. Therefore, he must wire careful instructions to his wife.

The train ran into the Exchange Station on time—5:15—and Ledbitter immediately made his way to the telegraph office. And after further cogitation he got off the longest private message he had ever sent in his life:

"After waistcoat. If not home by breakfast-time Monday morning, send excuse to firm. Say suddenly called away, family affliction. No account mention where I am nor what after. Love.

"HERBERT."

That, with the address, came to thirty-six words, and cost Ledbitter one and ninepence. He picked up the coppers which remained out of a two-shilling piece, and went forth from the big station—a compound of misery and hope. The active part of his quest had begun.

Ledbitter had never been in Liverpool before. He had never had occasion to think of Liverpool, or to formulate any idea of it. He was troubled to find it was such a big place. Nevertheless, he kept his wits. And, picking out a man who looked like a seafaring person, he asked him if he could tell him where he would be likely to find a ship called the Starnatic.

"Starnatic!" said the man. "That'll be the North Canada Line. Go down Water Street, and you'll see their office—big place; you can't miss it."

He obligingly showed the way to Water Street, and Ledbitter set forward. And presently he found himself in a palatial building amid much plate glass and mahogany counter, and he began to realise that a shipping office in these days is something more than a mere shed on a quay-side.

A clerk came forward to attend to Ledbitter's requirements, and Ledbitter, having been a clerk himself ever since he left school, and seeing good-humour in this fellow-clerk's face unburdened himself—fully. He told of his unaccountable lapse of memory, of what it meant to him to recover that letter and its important enclosure—told it all. And the shipping clerk comprehended, and smiled, and sympathised—and shook his head.

"You've a nice job on, old man!" he said, with evident fellow-feeling. "There are five or six hundred emigrants going out on that boat. Like looking for a needle in a bottle of hay!"

"But I know the man's name!" said Ledbitter.

"Pooh!" answered the clerk. "Names! Some of 'em are Smiths when they leave home and Brown by the time they strike Liverpool. And if you boarded the Starnatic and the word was passed for Terry, ten to one Terry wouldn't respond—he'd think he was wanted. See?"

"What's to be done?" asked Ledbitter miserably.

"The Starnatic," answered the clerk, who was obviously anxious to assist, "is in the river. She's lying off the landing-stage—black funnels with green bands. She won't go out before one o'clock Sunday afternoon—probably about twelve-thirty, as a matter of fact. You can board her this evening, if you like. But I don't think that'll be much good, you know."

"For heaven's sake, why?" demanded Ledbitter. "I understand the man's going to sail on her."

The clerk shrugged his shoulders.

"Ay, just so," he answered. "And, like many or most of 'em, he'll join her at the last minute! If they like, these emigrants can sleep on board to-night. Some of 'em will—they'll be the lot that have no money to waste on shore. But most of 'em'll have a last night of it in old England, and they'll be scrambling aboard up to the very last second. Some, of course, never will get aboard. See?"

Ledbitter saw—and groaned. He had never anticipated this awful possibility.

"What's to be done?" he asked again. "I thought I should have nothing to do but walk on to the ship, ask for this man, and——"

"No doubt, but you thought wrong," said the clerk. "Well, I'll tell you what you must do. I'll give you a line to the purser. You board the boat pretty late to-night, and tell the purser all you've told me. If the man's aboard then, he'll find him. If not, go back at noon to-morrow. I tell you this man you want mayn't board the Starnatic till last thing!"

Ledbitter thanked his informant gratefully, took the note he gave him, and went away. It was scarcely six o'clock, and he had nothing to do for hours. He wandered about. He went down to the landing stage and picked out the Starnatic by her black funnel and green bands. He turned into a cheap restaurant, and fed himself—cheaply. All the evening he hung about the landing-stage, examining every likely-looking face, to see if he could recognise the description of Terry. And at ten o'clock he hired a boat and was rowed across to the ship. It had begun to rain; it was very cold—Ledbitter had no overcoat; he was thoroughly miserable.

The purser, a fat man, who was drinking rum in his cabin, asked Ledbitter if he and the writer of the letter thought he was going to spend the whole night and all Sunday forenoon asking the names of every Tom,

Dick, and Harry who was then in or would come into the steerage. But, when Ledbitter had pressed half a sovereign into his palm and had told his woeful story, the purser relented. He treated his shivering visitor to a glass of good Jamaica, and told him that he would give him the best of advice. Let him go ashore and get a bed and a good night's sleep. Let him come aboard at precisely twelve o'clock next day. By that time he—the purser—would have ascertained if Terry was aboard; if not, Ledbitter could watch the gangway and scrutinise every arrival until the Starnatic tooted a farewell to the Mersey.

Ledbitter had no option but to do as he was told. He went ashore again. He got a cheap bed at a riverside inn; he indulged in more Jamaica before retiring, but his spirits were very low when he sought his couch. He was doubtful, anxious, miserable. And all night the steamers in the river hooted and whistled, and kept him awake. When he did sleep a little, in the early morning, it was to dream that the Starnatic had escaped him, that she was steaming at fifty knots an hour down the Mersey, and that a big red-haired man was standing in the stern, waving a waistcoat at him with shouts of derisive laughter.

The riverside inn folk, cheap as they were, gave Ledbitter a good, solid breakfast that Sunday morning. It cheered him up. He went out into a beautiful sunshiny day and felt mightily encouraged. And from half-past nine until half-past eleven he haunted the landing-stage, watching.

He saw various boatloads put off to the Starnatic, but he saw no big, red-haired man. And at twenty minutes to twelve he himself bargained with a boatman, and went off on his forlorn hope.

The purser shook his head at Ledbitter.

"There ain't no such man on board—yet," he said. "I've seen to it myself. Now I'll put you in touch with every steerage passenger that sets foot on our decks from this out—and I can't do more!"

He stationed Ledbitter at a certain railed-in place near the gangway, and left him. And Ledbitter, whose heart was beating as fiercely as the engines were about to beat, watched and watched. Scores of men and women came from tenders and tugs and boats—had to pass him—and not a man had red hair!

The purser came along, too, and whispered:

"We're off in ten minutes!" he said. "You'll have to go presently. If he isn't here with this last lot——"

Just then Ledbitter was aware of a big, Milesian-looking, roughly-dressed fellow, who came swaggering and smiling along the deck, one big bundle under his arm, another slung over his shoulder. His hair was—but red was a modest term to apply to it.

Ledbitter seized his man with the grip of despair.

"You're name's Terry!" he exclaimed. "You're from Walford?"

The fiery-haired one looked down from his six-foot three with all the ease of conscious innocence.

"And phwat's if that's me name, misther?" he asked gaily. "Ye have it very pat on yer tongue, I'm thinkin'!"

"You bought a waistcoat from Milson on Friday," said Ledbitter hurriedly, but with extraordinary clearness. "A dark red ground with black spots. My wife sold it to Milson. There's a letter in it—of importance. I've followed you to get that letter. Have you found it—have you got it? Get the waistcoat out of your bundles. I'll give you half a sovereign for that letter!"

The red-haired giant dropped his bundles and scratched his head.

"I'd give ye the letther for nothing, misther, if I had it!" he exclaimed. "But I never seen it, and I haven't the weskut. 'Twas this way, d'ye see," he went on, as Ledbitter almost fainted. "When I got here to Liverpool yisterda' afthernoon, I overhauled me kit. And some of it I sold to a fellow at the lodgin' house, and the weskut among the rest. Shure, it was too small! So—I haven't it!"

"What lodging-house? What fellow?" gasped Ledbitter. "Quick!"

"Brannigan's Lodgin'-House, Orange Court," said Terry. "But the feller's name—ah, I niver heard no name of him! A little weeshy feller——"

"Now, then, come on, you!" bawled a man in Ledbitter's ear. "All ashore! We're off!"

"With a bad squint in one eye of him, misther!" shouted Terry, as Ledbitter was forced down the gangway. "Ye'd easy find him by the squint he has on him. Good luck to ye, misther!"

When Ledbitter became fully alive again, he was on the landing-stage once more. He glanced across the river—the Starnatic had already gone half a mile on her way towards Canada. And Ledbitter was still on his way in search of the waistcoat. But which way now? He turned towards the city muttering.

"Brannigan's Lodging-House, Orange Court," he repeated over and over again. "A little weeshy feller with a bad squint on him! Great Scott!"

CHAPTER III

LEDBITTER strolled along, almost aimlessly, sick at heart, until, on the wide, open space beyond the landing-stage, he ran up against a policeman. That gave him an idea.

"Can you tell me where Orange Court is?" he asked.

The policeman immediately pointed along the road which flanked the line of docks.

"Third to your right, second to the left o' that," he answered. "Nice place, too!"

"Dangerous?" asked Ledbitter, almost indifferently.

"Roughish part down there," said the policeman. "What might you be wanting, now, if it's a fair question?"

Ledbitter was so hungry for human sympathy that he gave this casual acquaintance a brief account of his trouble. The policeman whistled.

"Nice job!" he remarked. "Well you might find this man. And, again, you mightn't. Some of 'em's there for a night, and then the world swallows 'em up again. Come and go, d'ye see, in a manner of speaking. But I'll give you a tip: Don't you go pulling your money out inside Brannigan's. If you find this man get him to walk up into the main road there with you. Don't let him see what you've got about you—in Brannigan's at any rate."

Ledbitter thanked his informant and went off in the direction indicated. He was presently plunged into a network of unsavoury courts and alleys, and when he eventually found Brannigan's he felt uncommonly timid about crossing its threshold. But a man who stood at the door in his shirt sleeves, smoking his pipe and reading the Sunday newspaper, eyed him as with authority.

"Wanting somebody in here, Mister?" he demanded cautiously. "You ain't a police chap, I know, 'cause yer wouldn't be alone if you were. What's your game? Scripcher reader? Mission'ry?"

"Are you the lodging-house keeper?" asked Ledbitter.

"That's me, guv'nor" admitted the man. "And I asks again—what might you be?"

Ledbitter thought it best to be candid. He told his story, carefully insisting on the fact that the letter contained nothing of any value, not even a postal-order. But—"was that man there?"

The lodging-house keeper pocketed Ledbitter's half-crown, and nodded.

"Shifty!" he said. "That's the bloke! Shifty so called 'cause he squints. Don't know no other name for him. He's here now, asleep. Make it another half-dollar, guv'nor, and I'll have him out to you in a jiffy!"

Ledbitter parted with a further two-and-sixpence, and waited on the flags outside the lodging-house. And presently there emerged a little, suspicious, furtive-eyed rat of a man, who looked his visitor well over from top to toe before he drew near him. Ledbitter had to reassure him at some yards distance before he would approach. It was for all the world like coaxing a wild animal who fears a trap.

But eventually he persuaded the man to walk up the court with him, and to convince him that all he wanted was the waistcoat which he had bought from the red-haired stranger the day before. And then, for the second time that morning Ledbitter nearly fainted when Shifty replied that he hadn't got the much-desired garment.

Ledbitter stood like a statue of despair while Shifty explained matters. He, Shifty, had been in funds when Terry was overhauling his kit and offering some of its contents for sale, and he had bought a few articles, the waistcoat amongst them. But later he and some of his mates had got playing pitch-and-toss, and he had lost his money. Therefore to see him over the Sunday, he had bundled up his purchases, repaired to the pawnbroker's, and raised four bob on them.

Accordingly, the waistcoat was now at Mr. Mordecai Aaron's establishment round the second corner.

"Which, guv'nor, is a safe place," concluded Shifty. "So your bit of a letter can't come to no harm. Only" —here he paused and regarded his interviewer with a squint of extraordinary strength—"pawnbrokers isn't open on Sundays. And I'm off Wigan way to-night. Got a job there at six to-morrow morning."

"I must have that waistcoat," said Ledbitter firmly. "Can't you stop?"

"There's a way, guv'nor," interrupted Shifty, squinting more than ever. "I can't stop, nohow. But you buys that pawn-ticket off of me! See? Then to-morrow morning you goes and takes them things out o' pawn, and you gets your letter. How's that guv'nor?"

Supplementing this, Shifty put his hand somewhere inside his clothing and drew out a pawn-ticket. He held it before Ledbitter's eyes, pointing to various items.

"Pair o' cloth trousers," he said, "weskit—that's your'n, guv'nor—knitted cardigan—three on 'em. Pawned for four bob. Now, as yer p'r'aps don't know, guv'nor, a pawnbroker never lends more nor one-fourth the vally of a article. Accordingly, them things is worth sixteen bob. Then, of course, there's my loss of 'em. I should ha' took 'em out next time I was in Liverpool. So make it a quid, guv'nor, and the ticket's yours."

Ledbitter had to give way. He extracted a sovereign from his decreasing store, took the pawn-ticket and hurried off to more salubrious regions. And when he reached a respectable street he turned into the first respectable tavern he saw, and spent fourpence on a bottle of ale, with intense joy. He would get it first thing Monday morning; he would catch the next train to London with it.

At this point he suddenly thought of his financial resources, and he sat down in the corner of the saloon bar into which he had wandered, and with a bit of pencil and a scrap of paper did a little reckoning. He had set out from home with £4 7s. Up to that moment, what with various expenses—boatman, the tips to the purser and to the lodging-house keeper, and the sovereign paid for the pawn-ticket—he had laid out £2 15s.; he had accordingly £1 12s. left. Out of that he had to find himself in food and lodgings until next morning; there would be four shillings and a copper or two to pay at the pawnbroker's; he would have to reserve at least a sovereign for his fare to London. So it came to this—he had about four shillings whereon to live, to eat, drink, sleep until next day. Of course he could do it—he would have to do it—he must do it. Only let him get that letter; only let him get to London and to Steel and Cardyke's office, there, by four o'clock on Monday afternoon, and all would be well. As to getting home again from London to Walford—well, he would trust to luck. Nothing mattered but the handing in of the tender by the specified time.

That was the most miserably Sunday Ledbitter had ever spent in his life. The sea air blowing off the Irish Channel made him hungry, and he dared not eat—at least to satisfaction. He lunched off bread and cheese and beer; he spent the afternoon wandering about Liverpool. He indulged in a meat tea in a cheap restaurant when evening came. He wandered about again, and went supperless to bed in a place where you could stop the night for a shilling. He had another sleepless night. Next morning he breakfasted at a coffee-stall for threepence. And at nine o'clock he was at Mordecai Aaron's establishment, and by five minutes past had explained matters, produced the pawn-ticket, and put down the necessary principal and interest. Two minutes later the much-desired waistcoat was in his hands. Trembling with excitement, he plunged his fingers into the inner pocket.

Empty!

"Th'elp me if I thought ath how you'd find anythink, mithter," said the Jew youth to whom Ledbitter had explained matters. "Afther pathing through all them handth wathn't likely ath how you would find it, wath it, now?"

Ledbitter made certain. Then he flung the redeemed articles down and turned on his heel.

"Wath to be done with theeth, mithter?" asked the Jew youth.

But Ledbitter walked out without answering, and he had gone a good mile away from that shop before he realised that he had really left it. Then he suddenly woke up from his abstraction and saw that he was at the Exchange Station.

It was all over now. Of course he was ruined. The firm would sack him at once. He would never get another job. He and his wife and the kid would all have to go to the poor-house. All right. It was fate. No, it was his own confounded carelessness. No, something had gone wrong with his beastly head. No, it was—he did not know what it was. But it had happened. It was all over. He was down—deep, deep, deep down—and out.

And suddenly he realised that there would be no going to London and that the sovereign which he had reserved for that purpose was in his pocket. He realised something else, too; he was ravenously hungry. And the fare home to Walford was only eight-and-nine.

Without a word he walked into the station restaurant. Magnificent in his acceptance of defeat, he ordered a waiter to bring him two boiled eggs and a couple of thick mutton chops. Then he picked up a newspaper, and for an hour ate and drank and trifled with the news. There was an account in the newspaper of the execution of a criminal—the unfortunate man, it said, ate a hearty breakfast before walking to his doom. Ledbitter understood him.

He felt better after that breakfast, but he had to go home. And after trifling about a bit, and wondering whether he had better not sneak into Walford at night, he took heart and boarded an express.

At three o'clock that afternoon he quietly walked into his own parlour, and found his wife calmly sewing a new pinafore for the baby.

Mrs. Ledbitter screamed, and threw her arms round him. Ledbitter gently disengeged her, sat down and fixed her with a look.

"Fanny," he said, "we're ruined! There was a letter in that waistcoat which I'd forgotten to post. I've been to Liverpool after it, and it's—lost. Tomorrow morning I shall get the sack. I——"

Mrs. Ledbitter, not to be repressed, threw her arms round him again.

"Herbert!" she exclaimed. "Oh, if you'd only waited one second when you rushed off! I called you back, and you wouldn't look round. Milson called you back when you ran away from his shop. He came up to tell me, guessing what you were after, but you wouldn't listen to him. I found the letter when I sold him the things, Friday, and I went out and posted and registered it at once. Here's the receipt. I forgot all about it on Friday and Saturday, too, because of baby's teeth. And you needn't bother at all about the firm. I sent them a note this morning, saying you were in bed with a sick headache."

Ledbitter took the scrap of paper, looked at it to reassure himself, and then lifted his hand and shook his fist. He was about to swear that he would have Milson's blood for not pursuing him to the station, when he suddenly remembered that out of the wreck of his week's money he had bought his wife and the baby a box of chocolates. In that remembrance the recollection of his week-end misery floated into thin air.

II: THE EARL, THE WARDER AND THE WAYWARD HEIRESS

CHAPTER I

THE Earl of Normanstowe flung away the newspaper which had just been handed to him, and looked defiantly round the semi-circle of faces, all eager and youthful as his own, which surrounded his armchair, set in a corner of the smoking-room which at that, his pet club, was regarded as the peculiar preserve of himself and his set.

"I will lay any man an even ten thousand pounds," he said in calm but forceful accents, "that I walk out of this club to-night and hide myself in London for the space of one month without being found, let whatever efforts to find me be made by whoever likes to make 'em! Who takes me?"

The attendant faces slowly withdrew themselves from the contemplation of Lord Normanstowe's healthy countenance and gave themselves to turning elsewhere. From the lips of one came a deep sigh.

"Wish I'd got ten thousand to lay at that game," said their owner. "I guess I'd ferret you out in less than a month, Normanstowe."

"I repeat that I'll lay any man ten thousand pounds," said Lord Normanstowe. "But—there'll be conditions."

"What conditions?" asked a member of the group. "Stiff 'uns, of course."

"No, easy ones. All I would ask is 16 hours' start. To be plain and matter-of-fact, I'll put it like this: I'll engage to walk out of this room at precisely 8 o'clock this evening and disappear in my own way. Whoever takes my bet engages not to do anything in the way of searching for me until 12 noon to-morrow. That's giving me the 16 hours' start I asked for, isn't it?"

"And when the search begins, is the searcher to have a free hand? Can he do what he pleases? Employ the police, for instance," asked somebody else. "Can he offer a reward? Can he stick up bills, placards?"

"He can do whatever he jolly well likes! He can offer a reward in hundreds or in thousands. He can subsidise all the private detectives, inquiry agents and investigation offices in London. He can get the whole of Scotland Yard at his back if it's possible. All I say is that I'll lay ten thousand to his ten thousand that I disappear at 8 o'clock to-night, and that I'm not found until I walk into this room at 8 o'clock in the evening precisely one month hence."

"And you wouldn't go out of town."

"I wouldn't go out of town."

"What's town to mean?" inquired a dark-visaged young gentleman who sat in a tilted chair in the corner. "Radius of one mile from St. James's Street, say?"

"Rot!" answered Lord Normanstowe. "Radius of five miles from Charing Cross."

"That's a lot of country to cover," remarked the young man in the corner. "There are thick coverts and deep woods within that bit."

"It's London, anyhow," said Normanstowe. "What is it we've been talking about? Here's an account in the newspaper about a chap walking out of a club in

Pall Mall and disappearing so effectually that he can't be found. You fellows say it's impossible for any man of note to disappear in London except by collusion and design. I say that's nonsense. I believe I'm pretty well known in more ways than one. Very good. But I say that without any help from anybody I will disappear for the space of a month. That's my conviction. And I'll back it to the extent of ten thousand."

The dark-visaged young gentleman tilted his chair a little more.

"I'll take you," he said.

The semblance of a gentle sigh ran round the semicircle. Normanstowe, phlegmatic as ever, half-turned towards a table furnished with writing materials.

"Good!" he said. "We'll put it down in formal fashion. Chisholm, how did they do these things in the days of our grandfathers?"

"In the days of our grandfathers," replied the man addressed, who was also the eldest of the group, "they kept a book in these places and entered up individual bets. As we don't possess such an iniquitous thing here, we must make a half-sheet of the club notepaper suffice."

He reached over to the table, and took paper and pen and laid a blotting pad on his knee.

"I'll write it down," he said. "I think I remember the phrasing of the old-time wagers. This is about it." And he read slowly, as he wrote:

" 'Lord Normanstowe bets Sir Charles Wrigge ten thousand pounds that he, Lord Normanstowe, walks out of the Melatherium Club at 8 o'clock p. m., on October 20, 1904, disappears, and is not found by Sir Charles Wrigge nor by any person Sir Charles

Wrigge employs to search for him, before he walks into the club at 8 o'clock p. m. on November 20, 1904. Lord Normanstowe engages not to go out of a radius of five miles from Charing Cross during the time of his disappearance.' How's that?" concluded Chisholm.

"All right, as regards me," replied Normanstowe. "But now for Wrigge."

"Oh, that's similarly worded, with small differences," said Chisholm, continuing to write, "This is it: 'Sir Charles Wrigge bets Lord Normanstowe ten thousand pounds that he, Sir Charles, or persons employed by him, will find Lord Normanstowe, dead or alive, within the time and under the conditions specified in the bet made by Lord Normanstowe with him. Sir Charles Wrigge engages to give Lord Normanstowe 16 hours' start dating from 8 o'clock p. m. on October 20, 1904.' Now, if you'll both initial this sheet of paper," concluded Chisholm, "I'll put it in my pocket-book, and the thing's done."

Wrigge laughed as he took and carefully put away his bit of paper.

"I shall find you before a fortnight's up, Normanstowe," he said, confidently.

"I'll lay you another ten thousand you don't," exclaimed Normanstowe, with equal confidence. "Won't have it? All right." He pulled out his watch. "It's 6:30. I'm going to make my preparations. When they are made, I shall dine here, comfortably, quietly. At precisely 8 o'clock I shall walk out of the dining-room and the house and into the street. And you will see me no more for one month."

"During which time all London will ring with your name and fame," remarked Chisholm. "Get your preparations made and we'll all dine together."

CHAPTER II

LORD NORMANSTOWE'S preparations were of a simple and an elementary character. He went over to a quiet corner and wrote a note to his sister, Lady Trementower, who enjoyed a widespread reputation as being the most gossipy woman in London. It was a brief and a characteristic epistle.

"My dear Gabble: For reasons of my own, I am about to disappear from the world—I mean our world—for the space of one month from to-night. My disappearance will naturally cause much comment. It will also give you something new to talk about. You may expatiate on several hypotheses—that I may have gone into retreat, to meditate on my sins, or be writing an epic poem in a Bloomsbury attic, or have disguised myself as a crossing sweeper in order to study life. The only reason I have for writing this note, is to privately assure you that I shall be quite well and happy, and that I shall reappear to a much-concerned world at 8 o'clock on the evening of November 20 next.

"Your affectionate brother,

"CARROTS."

This communication Lord Normanstowe laid aside for posting later in the evening. Meanwhile he proceeded upstairs to a bedroom, which was perpetually reserved for him, and wherein he kept various suits of clothes, changes of linen, and articles of toilet. Before dressing for dinner he looked out a small and well-worn kit-bag and into this he packed an old tweed suit of a nondescript grey which he had carefully preserved from the hands of his valet because it possessed certain sentimental associations. Also he packed in the kit bag a shaving outfit, a pair of brogues and a couple of fairly heavy dumb-bells. Locking up the bag he made his evening toilet. And that accomplished, he went downstairs to take an early dinner.

It was remarked by those who dined with Lord Nomanstowe that evening, that his appetite was noticeable. He ate with great gusto; he was particular in selecting a certain burgundy for which the cellar of the Melatherium is justly famous. Yet while he ate and drank with such relish, he was careful to leave himself time to smoke an excellent cigar after dinner. He sighed once or twice as he sniffed its fragrance and sipped his coffee. But at precisely five minutes to 8 o'clock he jumped to his feet with alacrity, threw away the cigar, and left the room. At one minute to eight he reappeared at the door, wearing a dark coat over his evening dress, and carrying the small kit bag. The men who were in the secret, headed by Sir Charles Wrigge and Chisholm, joined him in the hall.

"It seems, somehow," said one, "as if we were about to assist at an execution. You are really off, Normanstowe?"

Normanstowe smiled affectionately upon the group, gripped his kit bag, and, as the hall clock struck eight, walked down the steps into St. James's Street. The men whom he left behind saw him disappear in the shadows. One of them remarked, quite unnecessarily: "He's gone!"

CHAPTER III

NORMANSTOWE, carrying his kit bag, walked up the street in leisurely fashion until he reached Piccadilly. At the corner he signalled to the driver of a passing taxicab.

"Take me," said Normanstowe, as he entered, "to Paddington railway station."

The driver observed nothing in his fare's manner or speech that could cause him to hesitate. To him the young earl seemed to be no more than an ordinary young gentleman of the superior classes who might be inclined to put half-a-crown into his hand at the end of the journey, without any unnecessary words or reference to the state of the metre. In this pleasant conjecture the driver proved to be right; when he pulled up at the first-class booking office at Paddington, his fare duly presented him with the coin in question before lounging slowly into the station. A porter standing near suddenly started, and, touching his cap, made for the small kit bag.

"No, thank you, my man," said Normanstowe.

He passed forward, and the rebuffed porter looked at the driver, who was pouching his half-crown before attending to his metre.

"Know 'im?" asked the porter.

"Not from Adam," answered the driver.

"Lord Normanstowe, thet is," said the porter with pride. "Hearl of Normanstowe, y'know—'im wot done thet there charge with the Imperial Yeomanry at one of them scraps of the Boe-er war. Know him well 'ere, we do—got a plice dahn the line."

"Oh—that 'im?" said the driver. He pulled out the half-crown and spat on it before returning it to his pocket and moving off. And the porter, looking round, and into the booking office, saw Lord Normanstowe approach the ticket window.

Normanstowe had purposely thrown open his overcoat as he entered the booking office.

The clerk who dispensed first class tickets, and knew him well, recognised him as he demanded a first single for a certain station beyond Newbury, which was in close proximity to Normanstowe Park. He saw him stroll off in the direction of the train—he remembered all this two days later, when the news of the young peer's unaccountable disappearance began to be noised abroad. It was the opinion of that clerk that his lordship went to join a train which was about to leave for the West of England.

Normanstowe, however, joined no trains. He went out of the booking office by its western exit, lingered a moment at the bookstall, passed along the platform, and going downstairs to the dressing rooms, engaged one, paid for it, and locked himself within its privacy. That done, he set down his bag on the toilet table, and took a careful look at himself.

What Normanstowe saw in the glass was the apparition of a very ordinary type of young man. He had neither grace of figure nor distinction of feature. His hair was inclined—very much inclined—to be red; his face was a homely one; he possessed a snub nose and a wide smile, and his eyes were of that indefinite blue which is commonly associated with people who are called Smith or Robinson. He wore a moustache which was rather lighter in colour than his hair; he also wore small side whiskers—a vulgar habit which he had adopted out of sheer contrariness. And as he looked at himself in the dressing mirror, he grinned with what might have seemed to a beholder (had there been one present) a fatuous and a foolish delight.

"Common!" he murmured. "As common as ever they make 'em! The sort of young man who calls with a note book and a pencil to inspect the gas meter or take orders for the grocer. And the whiskers and moustache—or, rather, the disappearance of them—will make all the difference in the world."

These conclusions led him to divest himself of his dinner jacket, waistcoat, and dress shirt, and to shave his face as clean as that of a schoolboy who has been asked out to dinner. The disappearance of the moustache and the whiskers made him a very inconspicuous person indeed; with them all suggestion of a long line of ancestors seemed to disappear. He grinned again—more fatuously than before. That done, he drew off his trousers, kicked off his elegant boots, and took the old tweed suit, a coloured shirt, and a noncommittal necktie from the kit bag.

In ten minutes Normanstowe, looking at the results of his labours in the mirror, saw the reflection of a good, typical specimen of the very ordinary young man. He had kept his eyes open in his journey through his twenty-eight years of life, and he knew that you could meet just such a young man as he now looked to be by the thousand; you passed them in the streets, you saw them in the pits of the theatres, they were massed together in the shilling enclosures of the football fields; they huddled against the railings on the racecourses. He grinned again with increased delight.

"A very ordinary type indeed!" he said. "Excellent!"

Then, with a last glance at himself, he turned to the garments which he had discarded. He packed every one of them into the kit bag. There was money in the pockets of the trousers—gold, silver and copper. He took it in his hand and gazed thoughtfully at it. In the end he selected a shilling, a sixpence, four pennies and a halfpenny, and put them in the watch pocket of his vest; the rest of the money he restored to his dress clothes. Then he packed up the shaving outfit and the discarded white shirt and tie; finally he crammed the overcoat and the two dumb-bells into the kit bag, which he proceeded to look. He glanced around him; no, he had not overlooked anything. Normanstowe's idea had been to walk out of Paddington Station to the canal which runs at the side of it and to drop his weighted bag into that part of the dismal waterway which is spanned by a bridge at the end of Warwick Avenue. He had once or twice been up that way, seeing home a sprightly lady who was associated with musical comedy, and who lived in that neighbourhood, and it had struck him as being a likely spot for getting rid of his present encumbrances. But, upon reflection, he thought that he might go one better—he would deposit his bag at the cloak room. They had a trick, these fellows, he said to himself, of dragging canals for dead bodies, and though the kit bag had neither name nor initials upon it, he knew that its contents would speedily be recognised. But it would remain in the cloak room, comfortably lost, for a long time.

Through sheer habit Normanstowe pulled out his watch. At the sight of it he whistled, not from any surprise in connection with the time, but because he suddenly recognised his own stupidity. Go where he meant to go with a valuable watch on which his initials and crest were enamelled! That would never do! He hastily took it off, and, unlocking the bag once more, put the watch safely inside. Then he remembered that the sleeve links in the cuffs of his coloured shirt were also ornamented with his initials, and he took them off, too. But when he had relocked the bag, he breathed freely, for he remembered that his undergarments and his shirt and his handkerchief and collar were ail unmarked—he had once sent out for a supply of such things from the club in a hurry and these were part of that supply, and there was nothing upon them that could betray him. He was denuded of everything.

He presently opened the door, looked cautiously around him, and, seeing nobody about, seized the bag and marched off. He passed two men and one lady on the platform with whom he was on intimate terms of friendship—not one of them knew him. So he marched still more confidently forward and slammed the bag down on the counter of the cloak room.

"Name?" demanded the person in attendance, beginning to fill out the ticket.

"Smith—John," answered Normanstowe, readily enough. He put down sixpence and presently took up fourpence in coppers, and walked off. "Now for it!" he muttered, and turned out of the station into the covered entrance-way.

Normanstowe knew exactly what he was going to do. For a young gentleman of his rank his knowledge of London was extensive and peculiar. Knowing what he wanted, he went straight to his object. That was the police station in the Harrow Road, close to Paddington Green. Five minutes' walk brought him to it. He put his hands in his pockets and looked at its lighted windows. He sauntered past the open door and saw uniformed individuals moving about inside. And, having thus prospected, he walked around the corner by Paddington town hall and filled the pockets of his jacket with stones which he kicked out of the road surface with the help of toe and heel.

Then Normanstowe went back, ready to carry out his nefarious design upon the innocent tenants of the police station. Just then the Harrow Road was fairly quiet at that point. There was no great stream of traffic; only a few people were about on the pavements. But amongst the few were two police constables, one on duty, the other off, who were exchanging remarks in close proximity to the door of the station. That was precisely what Normanstowe wanted; he desired to draw attention to himself as quickly as possible. Wherefore, having carefully selected three of his largest stones, he took a deliberate aim and threw one of them through a window of the charge office. As the crash aroused the attention of everybody who was near he threw a second stone through another window.

The two constables started into sudden activity, caught sight of the aggressor, saw him cast the second stone, and made a heavy dart for him. And Normanstowe, drawing back with a laugh, threw the third stone, with even more effect, just as various uniformed individuals came tumbling over each other out of the front door and down the steps of the station. Then, for the first time in his life, Normanstowe knew what it was to be forcibly grasped by the hands of authority. He became aware that they were no very gentle hands, and his ideas grew mixed and confused. It reminded him, this event, of a rough-and-tumble loose scrimmage in a hotly-contested football match, in which he appeared to be taking all the kicks and bruises. He came out of it mauled and breathless, to find himself within the building which he had so shamelessly attacked, the cynosure of many pairs of indignant eyes and the object of attention by a particularly truculent-looking inspector, who glared at him as if he meant to order his immediate execution.

"Now, then," demanded this awful being, "what did you do that for?"

"Fun!" answered Normanstowe unblushingly, and not without impudence.

The high official glared at him still more fiercely. In a purely official voice he asked his name and address. Normanstowe rudely bade him to find out these particulars for himself.

"Not that they matter," he added, still more impudently.

The inspector motioned to those who held the prisoner in a firm grip.

"Go through him," he commanded.

Somebody went through Normanstowe in thorough and systematic fashion, but they found nothing but the very small amount of small change which he had placed in his pocket at the railway station. For Normanstowe had kept his wits about him all through his adventures, and having made a tiny hole in the lining of his jacket, he had thrust into it the cloak room ticket which he had taken out for his kit bag. Wherefore there was not a scrap of paper upon him. All that was upon him, as an official voice presently announced, was one shilling and eightpence halfpenny, in silver and bronze, and five stones, obviously picked up from the road outside.

Three minutes later Normanstowe, seventh earl of his line, and owner of one of the finest estates in England, to say nothing of a town house, a Highland shooting-box and a stud of race horses, found himself in a police station cell. In the light of a feeble gas jet, placed where he could not interfere with it, he looked around him and grinned in his characteristic fashion, and his mind turned to sundry experiences in South Africa, not unconnected with want of food and with shelter that a respectable dog would have shaken its ears at.

"All a matter of taste," he observed calmly.

Then he sat down on the plain wooden bench, and, folding his arms, listened attentively to an inebriated lady, who, in the next cell, was cheering her present circumstances with hearty song.

CHAPTER IV

In the grey gloom of a dull October morning Normanstowe entered the dock of the police court, and afforded its habitues some occasion of interest and merriment. Officialdom could make nothing of him. He pleaded guilty with alacrity. He refused to give any name or address. The police were unanimous in testifying to his sobriety; nothing but his extraordinary conduct of the previous night suggested any doubts as to his sanity. Incidentally, it was reported, that when he was asked why he had done this thing, he answered that he had done it for fun. But at that the magistrate shook his head, and looked at the prisoner with a certain amount of speculative inquisitiveness.

"Did you break these windows for fun?" he asked.

"No," answered Normanstowe, "not at all!"

The magistrate looked down at the charge sheet, and then at Normanstowe.

"Why did you break them, then?" he inquired mildly.

"Why did I? Oh, by way of protest!" replied Normanstowe. "Protest, of course!"

"Protest against what?" inquired the magistrate.

Normanstowe looked at the edge of the dock, and then at the ceiling of the court, and then at a point somewhere between the top and bottom buttons of the magistrate's waistcoat.

"Oh, I don't know!" he answered. "Anything—everything! The Government, you know!"

The magistrate looked at the policeman who had brought Normanstowe to the seat of justice.

"Have you noticed anything about this man?" he inquired.

"Nothing, your worship," answered the policeman. "Excepting that, when he had eaten his breakfast this morning, he asked if he couldn't have another."

"Well, I offered to pay for it," interjected the prisoner. "You have one-and-eightpence-halfpenny of mine."

The magistrate favoured Normanstowe with a look which a very observant person would have taken to mean many things.

"Fined twenty shillings and costs, and you will have to pay for the damage you have done," he said tersely, "or you will go to prison for twenty-eight days."

"I am much obliged to you," said Normanstowe. "I will go to prison for twenty-eight days. Unless you like to take my one-and-eightpence-halfpenny as a first instalment, and——"

The magistrate made a slight motion of his pen, and Normanstowe found himself ushered out of the dock by a gruff-voiced person who asked him pertinently how long he wanted to keep the next gentleman waiting.

After that, Normanstowe himself waited at other people's pleasure in a comfortless, whitewashed receptacle, until such time as a cargo of evil-doers was ready for conveyance to Wormwood Scrubs. Some of his fellow passengers sang as Black Maria carried them westward. Normanstowe occupied himself in speculating on the best method of profitably spending the moments of what he was determined to regard as a rest cure.

For the various little preliminary rites of prison life Normanstowe was rigidly resolved to feel no distaste; certainly he would die before he would show any. He cheerfully did all that he was ordered to do. He looked confidingly, and in quite a polite manner at the various officials with whom he now commenced acquaintanceship. And suddenly he saw a face of which he had some curious recollection. It was the face of a warder; a youngish, good-looking, smartly-set-up fellow, who moved about with alert steps.

"Where have I seen that man before?" asked Normanstowe of himself. "I certainly remember his face. Suppose, now, that he remembers mine."

But then he comforted himself by his shorn-off moustache. Oh, no, not even Wrigge nor Chisholm would know him now, attired as he was. For at that moment he was wearing no more than a shirt, and the obligatory bath was literally at the end of his toes.

"In with you!" commanded the voice of authority.

That particular voice happened to be the voice of the warder whom Normanstowe was sure he had seen somewhere, and who was just then in charge of the ablutions. He was about to make some further remarks or orders when they were suddenly arrested. And, if Normanstowe had looked around he would have seen the warder's eyes fixed, as if they were fascinated, upon a certain mark which showed distinct and conspicuous upon the prisoner's left shoulder. But Normanstowe was just then engaged in a punctilious discharge of the duty required of him, and if he had thought to spare it was in the direction of thankfulness that the water was fresh and clean. He obeyed the prison regulations with scrupulous fidelity. When he had accomplished them in that instance he glanced at the warder of the somewhat familiar face, and became aware that he was looking at his prisoner with puzzled eyes.

"I hope to goodness that chap doesn't think he recognises me as somebody he's known!" thought Normanstowe. "It may be awkward if he gets ideas of that kind into his head."

It fell to the lot of that particular warder to march Normanstowe to his cell, and to instruct him as to rules and routine. All the time that he talked, the warder was staring at the prisoner in disconcerting fashion; and it required much self control on Normanstowe's part to refrain from requesting him to look elsewhere.

When the man had departed, Normanstowe sat down on his stool and considered matters. Supposing he was recognised! It would be unpleasant. It might lead to complications which would result in his losing his bet. But renewed confidence came to him.

"No, he can't know me," he decided. "It's impossible. All the same, I'm sure I've seen that chap before somewhere. In which case, he may have seen me."

During the next two or three days Normanstowe caught that warder looking at him narrowly. He looked at him as a man looks at something which puzzles him very much. Sometimes he looked at him when Normanstowe was on his way to and from the prison chapel; sometimes when he was taking the air in the exercise yard; sometimes when he visited his cell. Normanstowe began to feel as a highly sensitive insect may feel which is kept in a glass-covered receptacle by an inquisitive scientist who takes uncertain and speculative glances at it from time to time, wondering what it really is. He grew a little uneasy under these searching looks, and he got to be afraid of meeting the warder's eyes.

And on the fourth day, at a quiet hour of the afternoon, Normanstowe being busily engaged in sewing stout sacks together, the warder stole gently into the cell, and closed the door behind him. Normanstowe bent his head over his work; the warder coughed lightly.

"Er—my lord!" he whispered. "My—er—lord!"

Normanstowe looked up. The warder was winking mysteriously, and his right hand held out to the prisoner a scrap of paper. Once more his lips shaped themselves to emit another tremulous whisper:

"Your—er—lordship!"

CHAPTER V

NORMANSTOWE possessed the family temper. He forgot where he was, and he snarled angrily.

"Don't talk damned rot!" he said, snappily.

The warder shook his head.

"Beg pardon, my lord, but I felt sure I knew your lordship from the very first," he said. "It was the—the birthmark, my lord. When your lordship was—beg pardon for mentioning it—stripped."

Then Normanstowe remembered the birthmark, and felt inclined to kick himself for having forgotten it. It was a birthmark that ran in the family—a definite strawberry mark, and Normanstowe had always affirmed that it meant that he was some day to get two steps in the peerage, and be a duke. But how should this man know he had it?

He suddenly dashed his sacking and his needle on the floor of his cell.

"Who the devil are you?" he demanded. "Why do you come and interfere in this way? You're exceeding your duties, my man!"

The warder made signs which besought hushed conversation.

"Beg your pardon, I'm sure, my lord, but—the birthmark! Your lordship doesn't remember me—I was in your troop, my lord, during the war. Doesn't your lordship remember that awful hot day when we all bathed in the Orange River, near Bethulie? I saw the birthmark then. My name's Copper, my lord—ex-Trooper Copper."

Normanstowe resignedly picked up his work. That had got to be done, at any rate.

"Oh, all right, Copper," he said. "Sorry I spoke sharply. Thought I knew you, too, only I couldn't place you. Well, what do you want, Copper—I mean, sir?"

For he suddenly remembered what he was, and that it was his duty to address warders with respect.

"Sir—of course," he repeated. "I'd forgotten, of course, Copper—I mean, sir."

"Just so, my lord," said Copper. "Er—I'm a bit mixed, my lord."

"So am I," said Normanstowe, stitching away at his sack.

Copper looked all round him, as if he sought inspiration.

"To see you here!" he murmured. "Sewing sacks!"

"Seems a bit odd, doesn't it?" replied Normanstowe. "Ups and downs of life, you know. What's that scrap of newspaper?"

Copper brightened. He handed the scrap over.

"That's just it, my lord," he whispered. "That's what I came for. Read it."

Normanstowe read. What he read was just what he would have expected to read had newspapers come in his way. It was an excited announcement of his own disappearance. Half the world seemed to be searching for him. Also, three thousand pounds were being offered for news of him.

"That's Wrigge!" he muttered to himself. "He might have made it five. Well, Copper," he said aloud, "you see I'm at your mercy. Between ourselves, this is all because of a bet. I thought I should be safe here. But I never foresaw that anyone who could recognise that birthmark would be here!"

"But—but the life, my lord!" exclaimed Copper.

"It is quiet, certainly," said Normanstowe. "I like it. It's a rest cure."

"And this grub, my lord!"

"Plain—very, Copper. But wholesome and regular—and there were times in South Africa, Copper—when——"

"Yes, I know," said Copper. "I've not forgotten, my lord. Well, this is a rum go. And your lordship really means to stick it out?"

"I mean to stick it out, Copper, and I shall stick it out, unless——"

But the warder suddenly opened the door of the cell, poked his head out into the corridor, looked up and down, withdrew his body after his head, and vanished as rapidly as he had come. Normanstowe sighed.

"An entirely unforeseen contingency," he murmured.

Two days later Copper again appeared, bearing a second scrap of newspaper.

"The reward's gone up to five thousand pounds now," he whispered. Then his face became gloomy. "Five thousand pounds is an awful lot of money," he said.

Normanstowe laid down his needle.

"Copper," he said, "let's talk business. As our opportunities are limited, let us be business-like. I don't want to leave this peaceful retreat until my time is up. Now, then, can't I square you to hold your tongue?"

Copper flushed.

"I—I shouldn't like to do anything low, my lord," he said. "I wouldn't give your lordship away for anything. I'm sure. But five thousand——"

"I stand to win ten thousand if I'm not found for a month," said Normanstowe. "You hold your tongue and I'll set you up for life. Look here, do you think there's anybody else in this hole who might recognise me? Has anybody any suspicion?"

Copper shook his head with decision. No, he was certain there was no suspicion and no danger. If it hadn't been for the birthmark——

"All right," said the prisoner. "Now we come to business." He cocked a shrewd and whimsical eye at Copper, and the warder began to fidget under its inspection. "What's your idea, Copper?" he asked.

Copper suddenly grew bold and found his tongue.

"To get a better job than this," he answered promptly and firmly.

"What, for instance?" asked Normanstowe.

"Well, I'd like to go back to South Africa with money in my pocket," replied Copper. "I could make a fortune out there, if I'd capital."

"You shall have it," replied the prisoner. "Only keep your mouth shut until my time is up, and I'll see to you. Anything else, Copper?"

The warder rubbed his chin and smiled.

"Well," he said, half coyly, "there is a little of something else. The fact is, I've always had a sort of desire to see a bit of high life, just to—to see what it's really like, my lord. If your lordship could give me a taste of it, now——"

Normanstowe laid down his needle and his sack, and after staring at the warder, laughed, as loudly as he dared.

"Social ambitions, eh, Copper?" he said. Then he looked the man over. "You're an uncommonly good-looking chap, too," he continued. "You look much more like a peer of the realm than I do. All right—before you depart for South Africa I'll show you round a bit. And now go away, Copper, and let me get on with my daily task. There was one thing that I learnt in my soldiering days, Copper, and that was to obey orders. And while I'm here I mean to do my duty like a man. Well, that's settled. Hold your tongue, and hand in your notice, or resignation, or whatever it is."

So the warder went away and the prisoner resumed his stitching as if his life depended on it.

CHAPTER VI

THE reappearance of the Earl of Normanstowe in the merry world of Mayfair roused almost as much commotion as his sudden quitting of that fascinating stage had aroused precisely a month before.

His disappearance had set up a nine-days' wonder; the newspaper reporters, the police, the private inquiry agents, had racked their brains and used up all their energies in their attempts to find him. Certainly, said those who were acquainted with the youthful nobleman's career, there was nothing surprising about Normanstowe's sudden disappearance; it was like him to set everybody talking. His whole life, from his Eton days onward, had been a succession of episodes of the noticeable order.

It was he who painted the Provost's door a brilliant vermilion. It was he who drove a zebra and a dromedary, tandem fashion, round the park, himself attired in Arab costume, and accompanied by a gigantic Zulu, clothed to the manner, desperately armed. It was he who made a daring parachute descent at Ranelagh. It was he who, dressed up in wonderful garments of the East, and accompanied by a suite of singularly disguised friends, presented himself at the Mansion House, and introduced his person and company to the Lord Mayor as an Oriental potentate from the undiscovered regions of Asia. It was he who organised the famous hoax on the Prime Minister, whereby Downing Street and Whitehall were filled one afternoon with the equipages of all the ambassadors, diplomatists, and political luminaries of London. It was he who sent four Punch and Judy shows, a merry-go-round, and a travelling circus to the garden party at Lambeth Palace, which garden party was being given by the Archbishop of Canterbury to the Colonial bishops and their ladies.

Most people who kept themselves acquainted with things knew of Lord Normanstowe and his eccentricities: his disappearance merely seemed to them to be another of his little ways. The probability was, said they, that he was enjoying himself in Paris or Vienna, and would return again, with more mischief in his head, when he was least expected.

But Normanstowe presented himself at the Melatherium to the moment, loudly demanding his £10,000 as soon as he had greeted the select coterie which awaited his coming with suppressed excitement. They stared at him, wonderingly. That he had shaved off his famous whiskers, and even got rid of his moustache, was at once apparent; it was also apparent that he was a little thin. But he brought in with him an alert manner and bright, clear eyes, and he looked uncommonly fit, as if he had been in strict training. And then everybody wanted to know where he had hidden himself.

"That," replied Nomanstowe, carefully putting Wrigge's cheque away in his pocket, "is my secret. I have, of course, remained within the circumscribed area provided for in the terms of our wager. But as to where I have been, how I got there, what I did there, how I came away from there—that, my friends, is a secret which will never be revealed by me from now to Doomsday."

"Well, you've done it anyway," said Chisholm.

"Didn't I say I'd do it?" replied Normanstowe. "Of course I've done it. I'll do it again next year on similar terms. It's easy as lighting this cigar. But in the meantime I return to the calm and quiet routine of my usual life."

It was speedily noticed that in pursuing this routine Lord Normanstowe was accompanied almost everywhere by a quiet young man whom he introduced to his set and circle as Mr. John Copperthwaite. According to Normanstowe he had made the acquaintance in South Africa, and had been greatly delighted to renew it. Mr. Copperthwaite proved to be a quiet, well-behaved person, who united modest manners with eminently good looks; it was evident that on his recent arrival in this country he had patronised the best tradesmen in Saville Row and Bond Street, and his well set up, irreproachably garbed and groomed figure, handsome features, and quiet air impressed everybody who met him. And Normanstowe, who was entertaining him royally in the family mansion in Mount Street, used to laugh heartily when they were alone at night.

"'Pon my honour, Copper," he would say, "this is great fun! You're a consummate actor, by gad!"

"No," answered Copper, "I'm only perfectly natural—I never could act. I just take things as they come."

Whereupon Normanstowe would laugh more than ever in his high falsetto voice, and slap his guest on the back and declare that he was the best fun he had had for ages, and that they would keep things up. For Lord Normanstowe was never happy unless he was playing some mischievous game, and it delighted him to take the ex-trooper, ex-warder, out to dinners and dances—all to see him solemnly "playing pretty," as Normanstowe phrased it.

"Gad!" he used to say, "it's better than a play!" And he enjoyed it all the more—a characteristic of his—because he had the secret all to himself.

But one morning when Normanstowe was alone, occupied in the engrossing task of seeing how much his racing establishment had cost him that year, there entered to him his sister, Lady Trementower, who was some twelve years older than himself, and in addition to being an incurable gossip, was also a lady of observation and penetration. She closed the door of her brother's study, sacred to the serious reading of Ruff's Guide to the Turf and the latest French fiction, and dropped into a chair by his desk. Normanstowe took a sly glance at her, and saw signs of bad weather.

"Look here, Normanstowe," said her ladyship abruptly, "who is this man Copperthwaite?"

"Chap I knew in South Africa," answered Normanstowe, promptly and truthfully.

"I dare say you knew a lot of chaps, as you call them, in South Africa," observed his sister. "But who is he?"

"Name's John Copperthwaite," said Normanstowe. "Come from Windebusch, Orange Free State."

"That conveys nothing to me. I want to know who he is. Is he a gentleman?" demanded Lady Trementower.

"What's he look like?" asked Normanstowe.

"He is certainly a very well-mannered young man," replied his sister thoughtfully. "And much more modest than most of you young men are nowadays. But that doesn't explain him, and such strange people come from South Africa."

"Yes, live in Park Lane, most of 'em," said Normanstowe.

"I'm not talking of that sort," said Lady Trementower. "I want to know who this man is."

"What's the matter?" asked Normanstowe.

Lady Trementower coughed.

"Well, of course you introduced him as a friend of yours——"

"Excellent friend, thoroughly dependable, keeps his word," murmured Normanstowe. "Yes, go on."

"And so, of course I received him as such," continued her ladyship. "And he's come to us and we've been here, and we meet him at a great many places to which you take him, and, well, I'm uneasy about Alma Stuvesant."

Normanstowe lifted his hands in the air, opened his large mouth to its widest extent, and then pursed his lips in a shrill whistle.

"Whew! What—the heiress?" he exclaimed.

"That's just it," replied Lady Trementower. "Alma Stuvesant has a quarter of a million in her own right, Normanstowe. Not even her father can touch it. And think of what she expects to get from him—one of the richest men in Chicago!"

"But I thought you and she were fishing for nothing under a Marquis?" said Normanstowe. "You both gave me the frozen eye, anyhow."

"What girl do you suppose would marry you until you've settled down?" demanded Lady Trementower. "But, really, Normanstowe, I do believe the girl is in love with this Copperthwaite. And she's of age, and her own mistress, and you know what these American girls are!"

"Well, not quite, but I don't want to know any more," answered Normanstowe. "You—you surprise me greatly, I had no idea that Alma's amorous propensities——"

"When is this young man going back to South Africa?" asked Lady Trementower hastily.

"Don't know. I'll ask him," replied Normanstowe. "I think—yes, I believe—soon."

"Well, I hope so," said his sister, rising. "I hope so. The fact is that he and Alma are meeting every day—in the park, or in Kensington Gardens, or at one or other of the museums. I know. I've had her watched."

"What horrible depravity!" exclaimed Normanstowe. "Ah, these American manners. Sad, aren't they? So different to ours. However, I'll speak to Copper—I mean Mr. Copperthwaite."

That night in the privacy of the smoking-room, Normanstowe addressed his guest in fatherly fashion.

"I say, Copper, I had my sister here this morning,"

he said. "She was on to me like a thousand of bricks—about you."

"I trust I have done nothing to give her ladyship pain," answered the guest modestly.

"You'll give her ladyship an apoplectic fit if you don't mend your manners," answered the host. "You've been playing the meet-me-by-moonlight-alone game with the packed-pork maiden."

Copper drew himself up.

"My father was more than equal in rank to Miss Stuvesant's father," he said. "He was a clergyman, though a poor one—and if family reverses——"

"Oh, chuck that," said Normanstowe. "Miss Stuvesant is over here to marry a duke, or something of the sort. Why, man, she wouldn't have me! And don't you see, my sister would get into an awful hole if—but there, what's the use of talking? When do you think of leaving England to start that South African game, Copper?"

"I'm leaving England almost at once," replied Copper, tersely.

"That's all right," said Normanstowe. "Well, you've kept, and I'm sure you'll keep, your word to me. You're never to let it out about where we met, you know. Half the fun of my recent adventure is that all these fellows who were in at it are biting their tongues with vexation because they can't find out where I put myself. And here's the five thousand I promised you, Copper, and I hope you'll turn it into a million. And now let's have a turn at billiards, and you leave the Chicago beauty to espouse strawberry leaves."

Copper pocketed the cheque with a single word of thanks, and said no more. He went out of the house very early next morning, and Normanstowe formed the opinion that he had gone to book his passage to South

Africa. But just about noon, as he was thinking of strolling out to one of his clubs, Lady Trementower rang him up on the telephone, and as soon as she had got his ear, poured out a breathless flood into it.

"Normanstowe!" she screamed, "is that you? That headstrong girl has married that Copperthwaite person—married him, I tell you! At the Kensington Registry Office this morning. She's just sent me a note. Stay in, Normanstowe, do you hear? I'm coming round to see you at once. You must do something to have it annulled or——"

Normanstowe calmly dropped the receiver and rang off. Presently the bell again rang sharply; he took no notice. Instead he rang another bell for his valet.

"Beevers," he said, "we go to Paris, on our way South, by the 2.20 from Charing Cross. Pack all I shall immediately want, and all that you want, and meet me at the train. And oh, Beevers, tell Johnson that if anybody calls this morning—Lady Trementower, for instance—I'm out, and nobody knows when I shall be in."

Then Normanstowe walked out of the house, and began to shake the dust of Mayfair off his feet.

III: THE FIFTEENTH-CENTURY CROZIER

CHAPTER I

LINKWATER, senior and most trusted of the half dozen vergers of the Wyechester Cathedral, was having a day to himself on a job which could only be placed in the hands of a thoroughly responsible man. Abutting upon the chancel of the Wyechester Cathedral there is, as every tourist in those parts knows, an ancient building in which is housed the library of the Dean and Chapter. The walls are lined with old books and manuscripts, from enormous folios to tiny duodecimos; where there is any space between the bookstands there are pictures and engravings of nearly as venerable an antiquity as the books. And there are also glass-topped cases set up in the room, wherein are displayed the curiosities and treasures which gather about our old buildings—some of them at Wyechester are unique and all of them are of considerable value.

Rarely as those cases are unlocked, dust penetrates into them and settles there. And the librarian—a reverend member of the Chapter—noticing that dust one day, suggested to Linkwater that he should close the library against everybody some morning and get to work with a feather brush and a duster.

Linkwater was now at work. The one door of the library, which gave access to the north aisle of the choir, was locked; nobody could enter. The large centre table had been denuded of the objects which usually rested upon it; upon the space thus cleared Linkwater was laying out one by one the various objects which he carefully removed from the unlocked glass cases, all in order. They were many and curious —bits of Roman pottery and glass, dug up under the cathedral, old minerals, books of hours, fragments of manuscripts in uncial characters: each was sufficient to make an antiquary's mouth water. And most conspicuous amongst them, if not apparently most valuable, was the fifteenth-century crozier which had belonged to Bishop John de Palke, holder of the see 1411-1431, and somehow had escaped when the cathedral was robbed of its treasures in the time of Henry VIII. Maybe somebody had hidden it at that time, and had in later years restored it; anyway, there it had been, taken care of more or less, and now, more than ever, for the last two or three centuries, the most notable object in the larger of the two glass cases.

Linkwater lifted the crozier from the two metal rests on which it reposed, and—being a man of some taste—admired its workmanship for the hundredth time. It was certainly a fine specimen of medieval art work, of a period in which craftsmen took vast delight in their labours and great pains in their detailed perfection. The shaft was of ebony, the ornaments and the light and graceful crook at the head of parcel-gilt, which was scarcely tarnished with age. Linkwater took up his cleanest duster, and gave the crozier a loving rub along its entire length. And whether it was that he used more force than was necessary, or that the passage of four centuries had made woodwork and metal work loose, the crozier suddenly parted into two pieces in his hands, and he found himself holding the crook in one and the shaft in the other.

Linkwater, his first moment of surprise over, immediately saw what had happened. Where the crook and the shaft met there was a jointure, which had been concealed by a band of metal. It was odd that no one—in his time, at any rate—had ever noticed that the shaft could be detached from the crozier; and yet easily detached it could be, and there it was. He laid the two sections gently on the big table, and in doing so noticed that the shaft was hollow. Some time, perhaps when it was made, perhaps at a later period—a bore had been cut through it of a size big enough to admit a man's thumb. And that bore was filled up with wadding of some sort—wadding which looked like lint of cotton wool. Linkwater's curiosity was aroused by that. Why should anyone want to plug that bore with cotton wool? Why should the bore have ever been cut through the solid ebony of the staff? Here was certainly some mystery which he must solve.

And forthwith he drew out his penknife. The penknife had a thin corkscrew attached to it. With this he delicately disturbed the surface of the compressed wadding. It was wool—the softest wool taken from the under part of a fleece, where it is softest and silkiest. And Linkwater began to draw it out of the hollow shaft, strand after strand of it, which had been forced in until it had been firmly packed in the cavity. But suddenly something quite different to the wool appeared. There dropped from the hollow, and lay on the table before the verger's astonished eyes a great blazing ruby. And following it came a stream of sawdust, and in that stream more rubies, and with the rubies sapphires, and with the sapphires diamonds. This shower of precious stones tinkled on the table, caught the shafts of midday sun which poured in through the old stained window of the library, and

Linkwater drew a deep breath and rubbed his eyes.

After that, being essentially a man of common sense, he reassured himself that the one door of the place was securely locked. Then he counted the stones. Nine magnificent rubies, seven sapphires, eighteen diamonds. They were all of considerable size, especially the rubies. He swept them together into a little heap, which flashed back red and blue and white light; then he took from his pocket a wash-leather bag, in which he usually carried his money, and, having emptied it of its silver, he placed the strangely discovered treasure in it. Then he put the bag in his pocket, cleared away the sawdust and the wool, and calmly applied himself to fitting the shaft and the crook of the crozier together. It would be a long time—a very, very long time—he thought, before anyone ever discovered that little matter again, for he took special care to effect the new jointure in such a fashion that the two sections would not readily come apart. And while he thus worked, Linkwater thought.

Like everybody else who was connected officially with it, Linkwater knew that Wyechester Cathedral had been possessed of an extraordinary amount of treasure in medieval times. He had heard learned men talk of the possessions of the church—heard them many a time, in that very library. He had heard descriptions of the jewels which ornamented the shrines and altars, the reliquaries and vestments, in the pre-Tudor days—and he had also listened with vast interest to those learned men, wondering where all those rare things went to. Much of the treasure, of course, had been appropriated by the crown, under Henry VIII, but Linkwater remembered that he had heard more than one eminent antiquary express the opinion that a great deal of it had been secretly hidden. And now he inclined to that belief—for here was a fine proof of its value as a theory! Someone, four hundred years ago, had, without doubt, hidden those precious stones in the old crozier, cunningly hollowed out for part of its length to make room for them. And he, Linkwater, after all these years, had had the rare good luck to find them.

And—nobody knew!

The ancient library was very spick-and-span, free of dust, all in order, when Linkwater quitted it that afternoon. The fifteenth-century crozier lay in its usual place within the big glass-topped case and Linkwater duly handed the key of that case to the librarian, said nothing to the librarian about the contents of his wash-leather bag, and once he reached his own cottage in Friary Lane he locked the bag safely up in a certain box which he kept screwed down to the floor, under his bed. Linkwater was one of those men who can keep a secret. He was a confirmed bachelor—always had been, always meant to be. But if he had possessed a wife he would still have had secrets—and this was one which no wife would ever have got out of him.

CHAPTER II

LINKWATER made ready, and consumed his tea-supper, and while he ate and drank his mind was busy. In spite of the fact that he was almost as much a part of the ecclesiastical establishment of Wyechester as the Dean himself, Linkwater was impassive on questions of strict commercial morality as any one of the gargoyles on the cathedral tower. It was his principle that every man should do the best he can for himself. The more a man does for himself, said he, the less other folks will have to do for him. Therefore, whenever, and if ever, an extraordinary piece of good luck comes in a man's way, he is a fool, and worse, if he does not take full advantage of it. Besides, who had a better right to these precious stones than himself? The venerable folk to whom they had belonged were dead and gone over 400 years ago—their bones were somewhere under the pavements of the cloisters. Dead and gone! Yes, centuries ago, but Linkwater felt warmly and kindly towards them just then—they had put by a nice little store for him. And—he would use it to the best advantage.

His tea-supper over, Linkwater washed up his crockery, mended his fire, and went out. He repaired to the adjacent Mechanics' Institute, and asked the librarian for the best encyclopædia on the shelves. He selected three volumes from this—those beginning with D. R. and S. and, carrying them over to a quiet corner he began to read all about diamonds, rubies and sapphires. Now Linkwater was a highly intelligent man, and this was very good reading. He became deeply interested. He was himself a mine of information by the time he had finished his task. He learnt that diamonds have been known for a very, very long period; that they are mentioned by the earliest historians; that they are pure carbon in a crystallized form—that did not interest him greatly; that India was believed for a long time to be the only diamond-producing country; that all the diamonds known to be ancient came from India; that nowadays diamonds came from South America and South Africa. He learnt, too, with some surprise and great satisfaction, that the diamond is not the most precious of precious stones, and that the ruby is. This made him turn to the articles on rubies with added zest. He got somewhat puzzled over the chemical and scientific terms, but he found it established that rubies are of all stones the most precious, and that the best come from Burma and Siam. And when he had further learnt that the sapphire is also a stone of great value, and that the most valuable variety is the cornflower-blue one, Linkwater restored the encyclopædia to its place and went home highly satisfied.

"Nine rubies, seven sapphires, eighteen diamonds!" mused Linkwater, as he sat over his fire a little later, comforting himself with a pipe of tobacco and a glass of rum and water. "I ought to get a very nice thing out of the lot. And now—how to dispose of 'em to the best advantage."

That, however, was only one out of many questions which Linkwater addressed to himself that evening. For there were many things to think about. He meant to dispose of his find for his own benefit. Very good; but having done so—satisfactorily—he would be a man of much increased wealth. He would have to give some account—to somebody—of how his increase of wealth had come about. Of course, he could, if he liked, leave Wyechester altogether, and go clean away where he was not known.

But Linkwater had no desire to leave Wyechester. He was very comfortable. He had a good salary—and in spring and summer, when the tourists and Americans came around, his tips ran to a handsome total. Besides, in a few years he would be entitled to a pension. No: Linkwater desired to stay where he was—until his pension fell due anyway. And he also desired to have a good and plausible reason for suddenly becoming a better-off man. For you cannot become better off, said Linkwater, without letting people know it, unless you are a miserly hermit, and hide all your money where it does no good to you.

And Linkwater was not the sort to hide his money; his notion was that money makes money, and he had already decided that, as soon as he had converted those precious stones into cash, he would buy some property—house property—in Wyechester which would bring him a nice amount in rents. Now, you cannot buy property without its becoming known—you have to employ lawyers and so on, and in a small cathedral town everybody knows everybody else's business. Therefore it was necessary that Linkwater should presently invent some good plausible story in explanation of his sudden influx of riches.

But Linkwater was a man of resource and ingenuity. By the time he rose next morning he had hit on a plan which seemed to him a remarkably good one. Secure in his knowledge that he himself was not a Wyechester man, and had never set foot in the place until his first coming to it twenty years before, he invented a brother. He even gave this imaginary brother a name—Nelson. Nelson Linkwater sounded very well, and quite nautical. And it was necessary, for the purpose of Linkwater's story, that the brother should be a man who had gone down to the sea in ships.

Next day, Linkwater took his weekly half-holiday, and got in the train for Salport, twenty miles away on the coast. It was not often that he visited that famous town of ships and sailors, but he knew it well enough to make a bee-line for what he wanted. In the queer little streets off the Hard, and in the nooks and corners of the Hard itself, there were shops of a sort which are never found in any but seaport towns—shops in which all sorts of odds and ends, from bits of old metal to pieces of rare ivory, accumulate. It would be difficult to give a fitting name to these shops; when you have said that their proprietors are general dealers you have said little, for the word "general" is too narrow a term. Linkwater spent half an hour in examining the windows of these establishments, staring at the curious things which generations of seafaring men had picked up in all quarters of the globe and sold on coming home—usually for about a hundredth part of their value. And, finally, stepping into one kept by Issachar, a Semitic gentleman, he asked if there was such a thing in the store as a second-hand ditty box.

Now, the ditty box, as most folks are aware who know anything about nautical matters, is a small chest, often no longer than a cigar box, in which sailors are wont to keep their private belongings. Into this ditty box Jack puts all manner of queer things which he picks up in his travels. And Mr. Issachar had several in various states of repair. Linkwater picked out one that smelled strongly of the East, a square box made of some fragrant wood and fitted with a lock and key. It was by no means a new box, though it was in excellent repair; it looked as if it had been made by some Oriental craftsman at least a hundred years previously. This was precisely what Linkwater wanted, and he did not haggle about the price.

But his subsequent proceedings puzzled the vendor, who was well aware, from his semi-ecclesiastical rig, that Linkwater was not a seafaring man. For Linkwater began to buy things indiscriminately. He bought two or three old medals from a tray in the window, some Eastern coins, a string or two of beads, some pieces of embroidery, some carvings in bone, and at least one in ivory, a worked tobacco pouch and some queer pipes, a bit of canvas or two, two or three

Indian images the size of his thumb, an ancient purse of black leather, ornamented with a skull and cross-bones in silver—these were but items amongst other matters. As he purchased each he stored it in the ditty box; when the ditty box was full he paid the reckoning, had the box wrapped in canvas and brown paper, and went away. He had spent between four and five pounds, and he considered that he had laid out his money to good purpose.

Linkwater was very busy when he got home that night. Having locked up his cottage and drawn his blinds, he got out the precious stones from the chest beneath his bed, and stored them away in the queer old purse, wrapped the purse in one of the pieces of canvas, and deposited the parcel in the ditty box beneath all the other odds and ends. This done, and the box safely locked, he proceeded to wrap the oldest of his scraps of canvas round it, and afterwards to seal everything with wax. He used two or three sticks of wax in this sealing process. But if any second person had been present he would have been greatly surprised at Linkwater's next proceeding.

For as soon as all the seals were firmly set and quite hard Linkwater deliberately broke them. He broke them just as any recipient of the parcel would have broken them—by tearing the canvas wrapping off the box. And as soon as this was done, he wrapped the canvas loosely round the box again, put the lot under his arm, turned down his lamp and set off to call on the sub-dean.

CHAPTER III

THE sub-dean, a bachelor clergyman for whom Link-water had a great respect, lived in rooms in the High

Street, and he was toasting his toes at his fire, and reading a new pamphlet which had just been issued on a debatable point of Greek grammer, when the verger, carrying his parcel, was shown in to him. He stared over his spectacles as Linkwater set the parcel on the table.

"Hallo, Linkwater!" he said. "What have you got there? What's that mysterious looking object?"

"Sorry to intrude upon you, sir," replied Linkwater in his suavest tone. "I ventured to call, sir, desiring your advice. The fact is, sir—I don't think you knew I had a brother—Nelson Linkwater, sir?"

"No," answered the sub-dean. "Hadn't any idea of it."

"This is his ditty box, sir," continued the verger, with a side glance at his parcel. "He was a seafaring man. A ditty box, sir, is what they keep their little belongings in. The fact is, sir, my brother is—deceased. I had not seen him for many years. But he remembered me, sir. I have been over to Salport to-day, to receive this box from the hands of another seafaring person, to whom my brother entrusted it—on his death-bed, sir, for conveyance to me. Just arrived from Bombay, sir, this person I speak of. And—there are matters in that box, sir, on which I should be glad of your advice."

"Nothing—nothing alive, I hope?" suggested the sub-dean a little anxiously. "No snakes—nor centipedes—eh, Linkwater?"

"Nothing of that sort, sir," said Linkwater, producing the key. "No, sir—far different matters; you needn't be afraid, sir. Just the little things, curiosities and the like, sir, that a sailorman picks up and keeps," he continued, as he threw back the lid, and began to lay before the sub-dean's astonished eyes the odds and ends which he had bought of Mr. Issachar. "You see the sort of thing, sir. No great value, sir; but this purse, sir, contains something very different."

He took the strip of canvas from the purse, unfastened the clasp and shook out the jewels. The sub-dean gasped, as the light from his lamp caught the gleam of diamonds, the blood-red of the rubies, the delicate blue of the sapphires.

"Bless my heart, Linkwater!" he exclaimed. "Why, those stones must be worth a fortune! And—your brother's left them to you?"

Linkwater coughed behind his lifted hand.

"The seafaring man's words, sir—name of Sprigg, sir, Silas Sprigg—quite a stranger to me until this afternoon, sir—were that my brother entrusted this box to him with a message," he said. "All that was in it was for brother, James Linkwater—with his blessing, sir. So I suppose these are rightfully mine, sir. You consider them valuable, sir?"

The sub-dean polished his spectacles, and looked carefully at the stones, turning them over gingerly with the tip of his little finger.

"I am no great hand in judging these things, Linkwater," he said presently. "But I should say these stones are very valuable. Why, look at the size—and the fire of these diamonds! And those rubies! Rubies are exceedingly valuable, you know."

"Indeed, sir?" remarked Linkwater. "Ah, I wasn't aware of that, sir. Naturally I haven't any knowledge of these things. Do you think Mr. Waterman, the jeweller, would buy them from me, sir?"

"Waterman!" exclaimed the sub-dean. "Dear me! I don't suppose Waterman could afford it, Linkwater! Why, my good friend, these stones may be worth thousands! Where do you suppose your brother got them?"

Linkwater shook his head solemnly.

"I couldn't say, sir," he replied. "Nelson was a rolling stone, sir. He saw many strange places in his time. He was a great deal in India—and in Burma, sir."

"Burma, I believe, is a great place for rubies," remarked the sub-dean. "Dear me, this is very interesting! Well, I know what I would do if I were in your place, Linkwater—I should offer them to one of the great London firms. There must be—there are —great London jewellers who buy precious stones. I'll tell you what I'll do if you like. I have to go to town the day after to-morrow and I shall stay there for two or three days. I'll make inquiries for you."

Linkwater, always the politest of men, bowed his thanks.

"If I might be allowed to suggest, sir," he said, "and if it would be no trouble to you, perhaps you wouldn't mind showing these things to one of those firms you speak of? You would know better what to say to them. If it is not trepassing too much on your time, sir?"

"All right, all right, I will," replied the sub-dean, who was a very good-natured man. "I remember now—there's Morkin's of Bond Street. They're very famous people. But it's rather a responsibility having those stones on hand, Linkwater. Won't you be anxious about them?"

Linkwater smiled in a confidently superior manner.

"Not at all, sir," he answered. "So long as you have them. I believe you have a safe, sir—if you wouldn't mind putting the jewels in there until you go up to town."

The sub-dean pulled out his keys. Then he and the verger counted the stones and locked them up. After which Linkwater went away with the ditty box and the clergyman returned to his pamphlet, and found himself wondering between every line however Nelson Linkwater came to posesss those diamonds and rubies.

CHAPTER IV

THE obliging sub-dean, who was celebrated for his kindness of heart and disposition, and who had no other business in London than to pay a visit to his tailor and to look around a few old book shops, made his way to Morkin's, of Bond Street, the very morning after his arrival. And to a very solemn and grave gentleman, who from his appearance might have been a Harley Street specialist rather than a seller of precious stones and metals, he explained his errand. There was no reason why he should not tell Linkwater's story of his brother Nelson's remarkable legacy, so he told it in full in the jeweller shop. And the jeweller, listening within the privacy of a parlour behind with great attention, seemed to see nothing at all remarkable in the story. But when he came to examine the diamonds and the sapphires and the rubies, he appeared to find the contemplation of them extremely interesting; so much so, indeed, that he remained looking them over in silence for some minutes.

"You find those stones interesting?" suggested the sub-dean.

"Very interesting, indeed, sir," replied the jeweller, "remarkably so!"

"And—er—valuable?'" asked the sub-dean.

"I should say—from a first inspection of them—

that they are valuable," answered the jeweller cautiously.

"Of considerable value?"

"They may be of considerable value. Naturally, they need very careful inspection."

The sub-dean, as anxious on Linkwater's behalf as if the stones had been his own, ventured a direct question.

"Are you disposed to purchase them, then?"

"I think we should be disposed to purchase them," replied the jeweller. "But I should like an expert's opinion on them. The fact is," he continued, giving the sub-dean a candid look, "although I have had twenty-five years of experience, I have never seen stones like these before! They appear to be of—well considerable antiquity. You are staying in town?"

"Until to-morrow at any rate," replied the sub-dean.

"If you will leave these stones with me," said the jeweller, "and will call here again at four o'clock this afternoon I will in the meantime have them carefully examined by the greatest expert of the day—Mr. Levandine—and will give you his opinion upon them."

"You are very kind," assented the sub-dean. "That will suit me very well. At four o'clock, then?"

When the sub-dean went back at four o'clock he found the jeweller in his little parlour in company with a stoutish, shortish gentleman who was gazing at the jewels laid out on the table before him with an expression of deep interest. He looked up at the newcomer with keen eyes which were full of curiosity.

"This, sir, is Mr. Levandine," said the jeweller. "He has examined these stones very carefully and with great attention."

"You find them of interest?" remarked the sub-dean, seating himself and looking at the expert with curiosity. "They are unusual?"

Mr. Levandine pulled out a queer looking old snuff box and helped himself to a pinch of its contents.

"Um," said he. "Unusual! Interesting! I am not much of an expert in words, sir, but I am an expert in precious stones. Everybody knows me—wherever these things are bought and sold. Mr. Morkin, there, has told me your story about these things. Sent by a man in India to a man in England. Um! Well, I will tell you something. These stones are very old. They have all been at some time taken out of settings. I will stake my professional reputation that it is hundreds of years since they were so taken—hundreds of years since they were cut, polished, prepared! Fact, sir!"

"Dear me!" exclaimed the sub-dean, "I am deeply interested!"

"These diamonds, now," continued the expert, moving the stones about with his delicately tipped fingers. "Perhaps you don't know, but those who do know can tell something—a good deal—about the age of diamonds by the way they are cut. For many a hundred years nobody knew how to cut diamonds. Then somebody found out that you can cut and polish a diamond with—another diamond! They called that 'bruting,' and it was the only method they had—rubbing one diamond against another, for many a century. Then they began better methods—in India, and in China, and in Alexandria. But the man who invented the proper method—the polishing wheel, to be used with diamond dust—was Louis de Berquem, a Bruges man, who lived about 1450, or so.

"And so, sir, I will stake my professional reputation

that these very diamonds that we see here were cut and polished about that time—probably by de Berquem's cutters in Bruges under the Dukes of Burgundy in the fifteenth century—and nobody's ever cut, polished, or interfered with these diamonds since. Except," concluded Mr. Levandine, significantly, "except—to take 'em out of their settings. And that was done long, long, long ago!"

The sub-dean was listening with wide, wide open eyes.

"Dear me," he exclaimed, "that is interesting. It would appear, then, that these stones must have gone from Europe to India, eh?"

Mr. Levandine sniffed—and took another pinch of snuff.

"If you want my honest opinion, sir," he answered, "these stones—all of them—have at some time been taken from ecclesiastical ornaments. We all know that there were vast stores of precious stones in our old cathedrals before the Tudor times. They were set in shrines, in reliquaries, in vestments, in mitres, in copies of the Sacred Book. Old Harry the Eighth got lots of them, but a great many completely disappeared. Perhaps the cathedral clergy hid them. There were two or three English cathedrals which were particularly rich in treasure—York was one, yours of Wyechester was another. And," concluded Mr. Levandine, as he arose and picked up his umbrella and made for the door, "my opinion, sir, as an expert, is that all these stones originally belonged to your cathedral, and have been found in some place where they had been hidden—four hundred years ago! Good day, sir."

The expert marched out, and the sub-dean turned wonderingly to the jeweller.

"That is really remarkably interesting," he said, "and a little disconcerting. I have no reason whatever for doubting our senior verger's story. He is a most exemplary, well-conducted, thoroughly reliable man, and—er—not at all a man of any imagination. He could not—literally could not!—have invented the story which he told me. Besides, I myself saw, with my own eyes, the box which had been sent to him from his dead brother in Bombay. Of course, we don't know how the brother became possessed of these stones. They may have been cathedral property once, and then gone on their travels, as it were, eh?"

"Precisely," said the jeweller, a little drily. "But I have never known Mr. Levandine to be wrong. Do you still wish to dispose of these stones on your man's behalf, sir?"

"Well—er—I should be glad to know what you are disposed to offer for them," replied the sub-dean.

"We are willing," answered the jeweller, "to pay four thousand pounds for them. Cash, of course."

"Hem!" observed the sub-dean. "Four thousand pounds! That is their value, then?"

The jeweller coughed discreetly.

"Oh, well, not perhaps their value," he answered, smiling a little. "That is what we are prepared to put down for them. We should look to profit by our dealing, you know, sir."

"Frankly," said the sub-dean, "what is their value, between ourselves now?"

"Well, perhaps, from five to six thousand pounds," answered the jeweller. "Perhaps, rather more. But, as I said, we are willing, if your verger wants to sell, to pay four thousand—cash."

The sub-dean thought a minute and then rose.

"I will communicate with him," he said. "In the

meantime perhaps you will lock the stones in your safe?"

He went away after that and began a course of mental speculation which lasted the entire evening. It was really very remarkable. He had often heard the local antiquaries talk of the pre-Reformation treasures of Wyechester Cathedral and of the gems and jewels which had blazed in its chapels and shrines. Could it really be possible that the respectable Linkwater had come upon some hidden hoard, appropriated its contents and invented the story of the seafaring brother's legacy? Dreadful! Dreadful! But he would not think it. A vision of Linkwater's solemn face and grave mien rose up before him—almost reprovingly.

"No, no!" he muttered. "No, I cannot doubt Linkwater's probity. He is the image of propriety in every way. And yet——"

And yet he was doubtful and disquieted. He went to bed feeling unhappy. But in the night a brilliant idea came to him. He suddenly remembered that he himself was a very wealthy man and that he had just then a great many thousands of pounds lying at his banker's. Good, excellent! He would buy the jewels and keep the fact a secret, even from the good Linkwater. That would be most satisfactory. Linkwater could have his money; and he would have the jewels—well worth the money—and if they were ever proved to belong to the cathedral—well, he would give them to the cathedral with great pleasure. Next morning the sub-dean left his hotel early and hurried into the nearest telegraph office. A few minutes later he dispatched a message expressed in plain, if concise, terms:

"Will you take four thousand pounds cash?"

Then he went back to his hotel for breakfast, and while he ate and drank Linkwater's reply arrived:

"Offer accepted, with much gratitude for your kind services."

The sub-dean heaved a sigh of relief. This was really the best way of doing things. He heartily disliked the notion of an inquiry and of the scandal which might perhaps result. And so, during the morning, he took the jewels away from Mr. Morkin, repaired to his bank, drew four thousand pounds in notes, finished his business in London and went home. That night he handed the banknotes over to the verger. Linkwater took them, with more expressions of gratitude. He asked no questions and the sub-dean gave him no information. As for the jewels, the sub-dean locked them safely away in his private safe.

CHAPTER V

FROM that evening onward the sub-dean of Wyechester watched the senior verger with close observation and a curiosity which was almost whimsical. It seemed to him that Linkwater became graver, more serious, more solemn. He went about his duties with an added dignity. Visitors to the cathedral said that one of the most impressive things to be met with in the course of a tour around England was to be conducted over Wyechester and its cloister by Linkwater. Everybody who attended the cathedral services said that it did one's heart good to see Linkwater and his silver mace head the procession of choristers and clergy—not even the bishop himself was more stately. Linkwater indeed was an ornament to his profession. He was the fine ideal of vergers and a great institution.

The sub-dean had wondered if Linkwater's legacy would lead to his retirement. But Linkwater soon let him know otherwise. He had always been confidential with his sub-dean; recent events made him more so. And one day, meeting the sub-dean in the Close, he stopped him with a quiet smile.

"I did very well with the four thousand, sir," he said. "I had a chance of buying very good house property in the city, sir—those six houses known as Acacia Terrace, sir; you know them. The rentals come to two hundred and forty a year, sir. I hope you approve?"

The sub-dean approved cordially, and he became more interested than ever in Linkwater. He knew what the verger's salary was and he had a shrewd idea that he received handsome sums in the annual aggregate from tips—why, Linkwater must be quite well off! And he began to wonder if the deceased Nelson Linkwater, mariner, and the solemn verger had any nieces and nephews.

Next summer the sub-dean went to Switzerland for a holiday. He had been away a month when going into the Schweitzerhof Hotel at Lucerne one night, he found a bundle of letters awaiting him. And, turning them over, he at once recognised the handwriting of a Wyechester friend—Mr. Parkinstowe, the solicitor. He laid all the other letters aside and tore that open.

"Dear Sub-Dean," he read, "you will be sorry to hear that the senior verger, Linkwater, is dead. The poor man developed pneumonia and died within forty-eight hours. He was interred this afternoon in the precincts, in the corner reserved for cathedral officials.

"I am writing this to let you know that Linkwater, who had no living relatives, has left his entire property to you. I made the will for him immediately he was taken ill. There is no occasion for you to cut short your holiday on this account. I will attend to everything until your return. Hoping you are enjoying yourself amongst the Swiss hills and valleys, yours truly,

"JOHN PARKINSTOWE.

"P.S.—Linkwater's estate, real and personal, amounts, roughly speaking, to about £6,000."

The sub-dean read this letter twice before he slowly folded it up and put it in his pocket. He put his other letters with it, unread, and went in to table d'hote. And by the time he had taken a couple of glasses of very good burgundy he had come to a resolution. He would sell the jewels, add what they fetched to Linkwater's legacy, and devote the whole amount to restoring the west front of the cathedral. Perhaps Linkwater's ghost would come and look on and admire and approve. It was a comfortable thought, anyway. So the sub-dean settled himself down to dinner.

IV: THE YELLOW DOG

CHAPTER I

THE moment for which Hankinson had made such anxious and careful preparations during three weary weeks of watching and waiting had come at last. There, within a yard of him, was the old jeweller whom he meant to stun and to rob; there, in Hankinson's hand, was the sandbag with which he intended to strike him down. And all about the two men, the one unsuspecting, the other quivering with intent, hung the heavy silence of midnight, broken only by the metallic tinkle of the valuables which the old man was slowly transferring from counter to safe.

Hankinson, thief and criminal from his youth upward, had at that time been out of prison for precisely a month. He had no particular desire to return to prison; but, on the other hand, he had no leaning towards the path of rectitude. Upon emerging from durance he had possessed himself of a small stock of money which he had safely hidden in view of emergencies; when it was in his pocket, he had left his usual haunts in North London and betaken himself to new ones in the purlieus of the Mile End Road. He took a cheap lodging there, and began to look around him in Whitechapel and its neighbourhood. And in time he saw what he considered to be a good chance. Lurking about in the busy streets, always with eyes alert, he saw at last a prospect of replenishing the gradually emptying purse. Thereafter he gave all his thought and attention to that prospect. The prospect quickly became a scheme.

There was an old-fashioned, dingy jeweller's shop in a small side street off Houndsditch; it was also a pawnbroker's establishment. Three gilded balls overhung a passage entrance at the side. In that passage there was a sort of sentry box, in which the shutters of the front shop were kept. A curly-headed, hook-nosed boy put up those shutters every night before going home. He was utterly indifferent to the shutters, that boy, when he had once put them up; but when he had gone away, whistling, Hankinson, under cover of the dusk, took a mighty interest in them. For long years of trained observation had made Hankinson's eyes unusually sharp, and it had not taken him more than one glance to see that in one of these shutters there was a noticeable, an appreciable crack. You could see the light in the shop through it. Therefore, through it you could see into the shop.

Hankinson contrived to see into the shop through that slit a good many times. It was always at night that he made these observations, and he made them with delicacy and with speed. But within a week he learned a good deal. Much of what he learned was obvious in other ways—namely, that the shop was closed on Saturdays all day long; that from Monday to Thursday it was closed at nine o'clock in the evening; that on Friday nights it was kept open until eleven. But his observations through the crack in the shutter informed him that every night after closing hours, whether at nine o'clock or at eleven, Mr. Isidore Marcovitch, the old proprietor, a grey-haired, stooping figured Hebrew, busied himself, alone, unaided, in transferring his most valuable wares from his window and his counter to a large safe, which stood in the shop. And, dingy and old-fashioned as the shop was, there were valuables in it which made Hankinson covetous.

Hankinson made his preparations carefully. First of all, he convinced himself that this hiding away of goods was a nightly performance. Secondly, he made sure that the old man was always alone when the performance was gone through. Thirdly, he came to know that the only other occupant of the house was a girl—quite a young girl, presumably Mr. Marcovitch's granddaughter—who appeared to live in the upper regions. Hankinson formed the opinion on good grounds—that this young woman retired to bed long before closing hours on Friday nights; at any rate, there was a window in the very upper room in which a light shone for awhile every night at half-past nine. He grew to be positively certain that, beyond this girl, there was nobody on the premises save Marcovitch himself, and that Marcovitch was the only waking thing in the house when he put his goods in the safe on Friday evenings. Obviously, then, Friday was the day of excellent choice.

But Hankinson did not content himself with outside observation only. He felt it necessary to see the inside of that shop at close quarters. Therefore he invented a good excuse for visiting it twice—by taking something to mend and calling for the mended article a few days later. On these occasions he inspected this new hunting ground with due care. After the second inspection he told himself that it was all right. The big safe in which old Marcovitch stowed his best things stood detached from the wall; between the wall and it there was a space in which a man could easily bestow himself unnoticed. The only difficulty was to secure an unobserved entrance to the shop. For long vigilant observation had shown Hankinson that when Marcovitch was not behind his counter the curly-headed Jew boy was there; and when the boy was not there, Marcovitch was.

Hankinson watched for his opportunity for two Friday nights. At ten minutes to eleven on the second the opportunity came. For some reason or other the old jeweller sent the lad out of the shop. A moment later he himself quitted the counter and disappeared into the rear premises. And thereupon Hankinson slipped in, and a second later had hidden himself between the safe and the wall. There were old coats and cloaks, dusty and musty, hanging there, and they made good cover. If Marcovitch, when he came back, had narrowly inspected these ancient garments, he might have found Hankinson's nose protruding at one place and his feet at another. But Marcovitch suspected nothing, and Hankinson was well skilled in holding his breath.

The usual routine of the establishment went on placidly. The curly-headed boy presently put up the shutters and went away, pocketing his wages. Marcovitch locked, chained and bolted the door. He disappeared into the pawnbroking part of his shop. Hankinson heard more bolting and barring. Then, from some inner part of the premises he heard the sound of a withdrawn cork and a little gurgling and splashing; the old man, said Hankinson to himself, was about to refresh himself with a drink. Then came the scent of a strong, pungent cigar, and presently Marcovitch returned into view, a cigar in one corner of his bearded lips, a steaming tumbler in his hand. An odour of rum, strong, insidious, penetrated to Hankinson and overcame the nasty smell of the old garments. Because of his previous vigils, Hankinson was well acquainted with the accustomed routine.

Old Marcovitch began by unlocking the safe. Then he took out certain goods from the locked showcase on his counter. Better things came from a sort of wired-in enclosure which filled the centre of the window —an enclosure of stout wire, closely meshed and clamped. There were trays in that which contained rings and necklaces and ornaments set with diamonds and pearls. Some of these things were ticketed, some were not.

But Hankinson, having often glued his nose to the thick plate glass windows, had a good idea that he could easily stow away a few hundreds of pounds' worth of stuff out of those trays in one of his pockets. Good stuff, he said to himself, lies in little room.

It was Hankinson's intention to hit Marcovitch when the trays from the window and the counter-cases had been laid on the counter previous to transferring them to the safe. He had everything ready for the attack; the sandbag was already grasped in his right hand; in a left-hand pocket he had a gag all ready to insert in the old man's jaws; in another pocket a length of cord wherewith to secure Marcovitch's wrists. And the moment was drawing near, was almost there, when Marcovitch turned from his tray to the safe, took out of a drawer a small packet done up in brown paper with a tissue paper lining, and with a low chuckle of delight, shook out on the counter a quantity of loose diamonds.

Hankinson grew hot and cold and hot again as the light fell on those sparkling stones. Here, indeed, was luck! Such luck as he had never expected. He was not learned in the lore of precious stones, but he knew diamonds from paste; and he had no doubt that these sparkling things were genuine products of the South African diamond fields.

And there was pretty nearly a handful of them. They must be good, for nothing but the thought of their extreme goodness would account for the self-satisfied way in which the old Jew chuckled as he bent over them, turning their shining facets over with his claw-like finger. And—now was the time.

Hankinson glided out of his cover, and brought the sandbag crashing down on Marcovitch's bald head.

Marcovitch instinctively, spasmodically, threw up his hands. He emitted one groan, reeled, and was falling over on his side when Hankinson caught him. It was not part of Hankinson's game that Marcovitch should fall heavily on the floor. He let the old man slide gently down; in two minutes he had securely gagged him; in two more minutes he had drawn his hands behind his back and fastened his wrists together.

And it was as he rose from the accomplishment of these things that he suddenly heard a strange sound—the sound of something alive, drawing in its breath in a queer sniffing, snuffling fashion, somewhere close at hand. Hankinson recognised that sound. It was the sound made by an imprisoned animal which snuffs at the crack of its prison door.

"Lumme!" whispered Hankinson to himself. "A blinkin' dawg!"

He lost no time after that, and as he transferred the most valuable things to his pockets—diamonds here, gold there, he wondered how it was that he had never seen any dog about Marcovitch's premises. Presently the sniffing sound died away; all became quiet again. And, without as much as a glance at the fallen man, Hankinson made round the counter to the door. In his opinion the man who has done his work effectually should go away as soon as his job is done. But going, he took care to turn out the gas.

Hankinson had manipulated the key, the chain and the bar, and was about to open the door in gingerly fashion, when he heard a sound at the rear of the shop. He turned, muttering a curse. A door had noiselessly opened, and there, holding a lamp above her head, stood Marcovitch's granddaughter. She was in her nightgown, her hair—long, black, lustrous—fell far below her waist; her great eyes, dilated with alarm, shone like stars. And at her side, muzzling against her knee, was the strangest, ugliest-looking beast of a dog that Hankinson had ever set eyes on.

It was queerly shaped, it was of no known breed, it was a vile yellow in colour, and it had only one eye. It was borne in upon Hankinson, amidst the rush of thoughts which this new situation forced on his consciousness, that he would have bad dreams about that dog, and he cursed it without knowing that he was even thinking of it.

There were other things to think of just then. Hankinson realised his danger. He made a sudden dash back. The girl set up a loud scream, dashed the lamp in his face, drew back with the agility of a snake and locked the door behind her.

Hankinson went, too, then. He groped his way to the street door and let himself out. As he crossed the threshold he had an unpleasant feeling of a sinuous wiry body that cannoned against his legs, and he kicked out at it in sheer frenzy of hatred. But when he reached the pavement and looked round him there was no dog there. And, with another curse, he made off.

There was nobody about just at that point, but

there were people twenty yards away on either hand, and Hankinson's chief desire was to mingle with and get beyond them. He turned to the right and sped swiftly away, and just then the Jewess girl darted out into the street from the side entrance and let out a yell that startled every midnight stroller within the eighth of a mile.

"Murder!"

Hankinson shot into the nearest entry. It was light where he entered it; it was black where he traversed it; it was light again where he left it. And flinging a glance over his shoulder as he turned at the end of it, he saw figures dart after him; also he heard a queer padding sound not so far away from his heels. He then knew that here was a serious business and he set his teeth and ran. There was a network of alleys and courts and queer places thereabouts. Hankinson dodged from one to the other as a rabbit dodges about in its warren when the ferrets are after it. But wherever he went he heard the queer padding sound, and he cursed that one-eyed, yellow dog to the depths of a dog's tail.

And yet—once, twice, thrice, he looked round—at least once with his revolver in his hand—and never saw any dog at all, not even when there were patches of light which the pursuit, brute or human, must cross.

Eventually Hankinson, spent of breath, made two or three desperate twisting and twinings, and darted into a dark court. The next minute something seemed to catch him by the ankle. He made a violent plunge forward, dashed his head against a wall, saw thousands of stars flash and coruscate before his eyes, and felt a great buzzing and humming rise up somewhere behind his ears. And immediately after that

Hankinson, for the time being, felt and saw nothing more.

CHAPTER II

When Hankinson came back to consciousness he gradually realised that he was in surroundings of an undeniably strange sort. Save for a dull aching in his head, occasionally varied by a sharp stab of pain, he was not uncomfortable. He was lying on something very soft and warm; his head was properly pillowed; he felt that some hand had carefully tucked a covering around his limbs. He judged from these things that he was not, at any rate, in the detention cells of a police station; experience had taught him that in those places small consideration was shown to visitors. But it was no use opening his eyes, for he was in a queer sort of darkness—not an absolute black darkness, but a sort of deep, misty blue darkness, in the midst of which, high above him was a faint spot of ruby-coloured light. He could make that out, and he could tell that the darkness was blue and not black; more than that it was impossible to say.

But if Hankinson's eyes could do little, his nose was able to do more. His nostrils began to expand and to titillate under familiar odours. There was a queer, clinging, permeating scent all around and about; a scent of saffron and musk and sandalwood; it was heavy, thick, almost oppressive; it made him cough. There had been an unearthly silence about that place until then; Hankinson's cough sounded like a report of a revolver let off in a vault. And when it died away and silence fell once more, Hankinson heard the sniffling and snuffling of a dog somewhere close by. Then he remembered everything and a cold sweat broke out all over him. And at that moment a flood of light was turned on, silently, and Hankinson, blinking upward, saw standing at his side, a gigantic Chinaman, clad in the costume of his own country, who looked down upon him with an expression which would have sat well on the face of a sphinx. This extraordinary vision so frightened Hankinson that he immediately closed his eyes and shut it out. Then he felt a cool hand laid on his forehead and heard a voice speaking in perfect English and soft, mellifluous tones.

"How do you feel now?" asked the voice.

Hankinson made so bold as to open his eyes again. He took another, a longer look at the Chinaman. The Chinaman wore spectacles, and it was impossible to see his eyes clearly, but his tones were propitiating, and Hankinson's spirits revived.

"Bloomin' queer," he answered. He tried to move and for some reason found movement difficult. " 'Ow," he continued—" 'ow did I come 'ere, guv'nor?"

"I carried you into my house," said the Chinaman quietly. "I was taking the air at my door when you darted by me, followed by a dog. The dog suddenly caught you by the ankle and you stumbled and fell, and dashed your head against the wall. That," he added, laying a delicate fingertip on a lump of wet lint which decorated Hankinson's right temple—"that is where your head came into contact with something harder. It is well for you, my friend, that your frontal bones are of more than usual strength."

Hankinson stared. Then he referred to the only part of the speech which seemed to him to be really pertinent.

"That there dawg, now?" he asked anxiously. "Wot about 'im, guv'nor?"

The Chinaman pointed to a door at the foot of the couch on which Hankinson was lying.

"The dog," he answered, "is safely bestowed in there. He followed us in—and I took good care that he should not go out. He appears to be an animal of undoubted sagacity."

Hankinson moved again, and again found that movement was difficult, if not impossible.

"I'm obliged to yer, guv'nor," he said, "I—I'll be movin' now, if you ain't no objetcion?"

The Chinaman shook his head gravely.

"Not yet," he said. "It will not be well for you to move just yet. Let me advise you to rest quietly where you are."

"An' why?" demanded Hankinson suspiciously. "There ain't nothink serious, is there, guv'nor? A crack on the 'e'd, now—that ain't nothink. I got business, yer see, and——"

"And there are those who have business with you," remarked the Chinaman. "The police."

Hankinson felt cold again. But he managed to look surprised.

"Perlice?" he exclaimed. "Wot about the perlice then? I ain't——"

The Chinaman stretched out an arm and pulled a small, wheeled table from behind Hankinson's head. He silently directed Hankinson's eyes to it.

" 'Eavens!" muttered Hankinson.

The surface of the table was covered with an array of objects, pleasing enough in themselves, but not welcome to Hankinson under present circumstances. These objects were laid out in order neatly and systematically. There was a row of gold watches, there was another row of gold chains—good and solid. There were pendants, ornaments, bracelets—all of gold, for Hankinson had scorned anything of less value. And there were precious stones—some fine pearls—some excellent rubies—and in the centre of everything, on a rag of blue velvet, lay the diamonds over which the old jeweller had chuckled. Also, in one corner of the table lay Hankinson's revolver.

Hankinson felt very sick as he looked at these things. Yet—it was about what he had expected. And all he could do was to glare resentfully at the bland features of the spectacled face. The Chinaman, however, remained unmoved.

"That," he said, indicating the table, "will explain much. If you wish for further explanation—Mr. Marcovitch is dead."

Hankinson jumped—as much as that curious inertia would permit.

"Garn!" he said, in a low voice. "Yer don't mean it! It can't be, guv'nor. W'y I on'y——"

"He was quite dead when the police entered his shop," said the Chinaman. "You hit him too hard. And perhaps you are not very experienced in the use of the gag. However, he is dead, and the police are in pursuit of you."

Hankinson began to whimper.

"Yer've trapped me!" he whined. "Yer meanin' to 'and me over! Yer'd a deal better 'ave let me lie where I was. An' you've done somethink to me, an' all—I can't move."

"That," replied the Chinaman, "is the effect of a medicine with which I have treated you. Rest awhile, and the effect will pass off. I am not going to hand you over to the police. You are quite safe—quite safe, I repeat—so long as you do what I tell you."

Hankinson stared. He was suspicious as ever, but there was a calm confident assurance about the Chinaman which went far to allay suspicion. And suddenly his eyes brightened and his voice lost its whine and became almost cheery.

"You see me right, guv'nor, an' I'll make it all right wiv you," he said insinuatingly. " 'Struth, I 'adn't no intentions o' finishing the old man! An' wotever you likes out o' that little lot, it's yours."

The Chinaman pushed the table out of sight again. "We can discuss that matter later on," he said. "At present you must take some food, and after that you must sleep until evening, and then we will see about getting you away.

Hankinson's small eyes looked a sharp inquiry.

"Strite?" he asked. "No fetchin' the perlice in while I'm here?"

"You can trust me," answered the Chinaman. "It would not suit me to have police in my house. I have my own affairs."

That reassured Hankinson. He set down his host as being one of his own kidney. And presently he ate the soup—good rich soup, with strength in it—which the Chinaman brought him, and after that he went to sleep quite calmly.

CHAPTER III

WHEN Hankinson woke again there were two Chinamen in the room with him. One was the big man of the previous interview, the other, also garbed in Chinese dress, was a younger man of about his own size and weight—an almond-eyed, stolid-faced fellow who was regarding Hankinson with an inscrutable expression on his immobile features. The big man was talking to the small one in gibberish which Hankinson did not understand. Catching sight of Hankinson's opening eyes he broke off the conversation.

"You are quite better now," he said, not questioningly, but in positive assertion. "You—now you may get up. There is food and drink ready for you in the next room. Come this way."

Hankinson got up and stretched himself. Certainly he was all right then—not a trace of injury remained in him. And with this realisation of recovery, a desire for action came upon him. He wanted to be out of that. Instinctively he looked round for the little table on which his loot had been laid out. But the little table was not there.

"In the next room," said the big Chinaman with a grin. "Come."

Hankinson followed the two men into a plainly furnished apartment, which evidently did duty as living-room and kitchen. There was a table set out in English fashion. Hankinson was motioned to seat himself. The smaller Chinaman sat down in a corner and stared at him; the big one served him with hot roast fowl. Never had Hankinson eaten such tender food in his life. And he gave him a bottle of stout to drink; it seemed to Hankinson that he had never tasted such nectar. He stuffed himself, he guzzled freely, wondering all the time what it all meant. And when at last he could eat and drink no longer, he shoved away his plate and looked his host full in the face with half-impudent inquiry. For Hankinson was very sure that the big Chinaman was not playing the Good Samaritan for nothing; he would want his fee, like everybody else.

"An' now what, guv'nor?" asked Hankinson familiarly. "If it's all the same to you, yer know, I should like to 'op it. I dessay it's all right, but this 'ere neighbourhood ain't what you'd call healthy, is it, now?"

The big Chinaman, who had taken a seat by his compatriot during the final stages of Hankinson's repast, produced an evening newspaper and laid it before the guest. His long tapering fingers indicated bold headlines and other uncomfortable things about midnight murder and burglary. Hankinson's pale cheeks grew paler as he read.

"Yer said as 'ow yer could get me away," he muttered at last. "An' I said as 'ow yer was welcome to what yer liked to take out o' what I got—eh? How's it to be, guv'nor?"

"I can get you away," answered the Chinaman. "But—it will have to be out of England."

"Out of — England!" exclaimed Hankinson. " 'Struth! W'y I ain't never been out of England! I don't know no lingo but English. Where would it be now, guv'nor? Not—not to where you come from, would it? 'Cause I understand that's a longish way off."

The big Chinaman leaned forward as if to attract strict attention.

"Now listen," he said. "There is a Chinese ship in the river, lying off Wapping, which sails to-night for Amsterdam. Her captain will take you, on my recommendation, to Amsterdam. And in Amsterdam you can sell your—diamonds. When you have sold your diamonds you can take ship to America—or wherever you please to go."

Hankinson silently ran over his inventory of the stolen goods.

"Diamonds, eh?" he said musingly. "There are other things than diamonds, yer know."

"I have estimated the value of what was on you,"

said the Chinaman gravely. "The diamonds are worth about two thousand pounds. You will get one-third of their value in Amsterdam. The other things are worth about four or five hundred pounds. You can leave those with me—my share."

"Done!" exclaimed Hankinson. "But how am I to get down to that there ship?" he asked anxiously. "Seems ter me as 'ow there'll be a pretty sharp look-out for me, guv'nor, and no error! How's it to be done?"

The big Chinaman motioned to the smaller one.

"This gentleman," he said, "will lend you some garments. You will go down dressed as a Chinaman after dark. I will prepare you—make you up with a little paint and other matters. And we will begin now —time presses."

Hankinson cheerfully submitted to the proposed transformation. He stripped to his underclothing. He put on Chinese trousers and soft-soled Chinese boots; he was fitted with upper garments which amused him by their strangeness, and comforted him with their silky feeling. And then he sat down, and the big Chinaman produced a box of coloured pigments and delicate brushes and set to work on Hankinson's head and face. He worked with the zest of a true artist, and the other Chinaman stood by and admired without moving a muscle of his features.

At the end of half an hour Hankinson was bidden to look in a mirror, and he stood up and looked and stared. It did not amaze him that he did not know himself; what astonished him was that the craftsman's cunning had transformed him into the double of the other Chinaman! The big man, with a sly smile, had twisted his compatriot round so that he stood side by side with Hankinson, facing the mirror—and Hankinson gasped as he gazed at the two yellow faces.

"Gawd!" he said. "Why—it's 'im!"

The big Chinaman allowed himself to laugh. He put a few finishing touches to his work, adjusted the cap and false pigtail, finally produced a truly Chinese umbrella. And then, in short, plain fashion, he gave Hankinson his instructions. He was to make his way to a certain wharf in the neighbourhood of London docks; there he would be met by a boat's crew and taken on board the Chinese vessel. In his progress through the streets he was to preserve a sober, grave demeanour—above everything, he was not to hold converse with anyone, especially a policeman; if anybody accosted him he was to smile blandly and shake his head.

"Right, guv'nor?" said Hankinson. "I'm on—mum's the word. Now them shiners!"

The big man produced a small bag, open at the mouth; within it Hankinson saw gleams of sparkling fire. He made haste to stow it away in the pocket wherein he had already put his money. Then he gave the big man a firm look.

"There's another thing," he said. "I'm goin' into strange parts and amongst strange folks. And I ain't a-goin' wivout my revolver. Hand it over, guv'nor. As it was, mind."

The big Chinaman produced the revolver, showed Hankinson that it was fully loaded, and calmly dropped it into his own pocket.

"I will hand that to you in the street," he said. "I am going to walk a little way with you. Now let us go."

Without more ado he led Hankinson out of the

house into the night. And as they passed out the younger Chinaman hastened to a window which commanded the way by which they went. He saw them pass in and out of the lights of the lamps—and suddenly he saw a couple of vague shadowy figures emerge from a dark place and steal after them. In his eagerness and excitement to see that part of the proceedings, he threw up the sash of the window and leaned out. And in that instant the yellow dog, which had been tied up in that room, completed its day's task of eating through the stout cord that had prisoned it. The young Chinaman, leaning through the window, was conscious for a second of a sinuous body hurling itself past him. Before he had time to comprehend matters he saw that body vanishing round the corner. He shut the window then and retired to resume his usual sphinx-like demeanour.

The big man came back and grinned at his compatriot.

"They are after him," he said briefly.

"I saw them," replied the other.

The big man grinned again.

"It is fortunate that this fellow fell at my door," he said. "He has served us well. Certainly he will never fall there again. We benefit very well. We have what he brought in—and he has some worthless bits of paste. It is good!"

The younger man made no anwer to this. Nor did he mention that the dog had escaped.

"It is time that I go now," he observed.

And without further remark he proceeded to divest himself of his Oriental garments and to put on the inconspicuous suit of grey tweed which Hankinson had recently taken off.

CHAPTER IV

TEN minutes later a figure dressed in Hankinson's clothes much muffled about the neck and face, and having Hankinson's cap pulled down over its nose, slipped out of that quiet house and went away by devious paths to other and safer parts. No figure followed it; the two figures that had lurked in waiting for it since dark were following Hankinson.

And Hankinson went on, knowing nothing. He was beginning to feel himself safe, and he did not care how much people stared at him as he walked in the glare of the gas. He had what he believed to be diamonds in his pocket. It had never even occurred to him that the big Chinaman might or would substitute paste for the genuine articles. He had a prospect of selling them to advantage. And he had his revolver. Therefore, being a bit of an actor, he went onward, always smiling blandly. Hankinson knew the nearest way to the wharf of which the big Chinaman had spoken, and it took him little time to get down there. All his thoughts were of his own business, and he had no idea that two yellow-faced, slit-eyed fellows, clad in slop suits of blue serge, were dogging his every footstep. Nor did he know that an ugly, uncanny-looking one-eyed mongrel was slinking behind him, keeping close to walls and to the fronts of shops, that one eye perpetually fixed on its object of pursuit.

Hankinson never saw that dog until he had walked on to the wharf—a deserted, desolate, cold expanse of timber, on which there was no business doing at that hour of the evening. There was a pale gleam of yellow from the window of a waterside inn at the other end of the wharf; a half-moon was far up in the cloudy sky; here and there a faint gas flame burned. In this poor light Hankinson suddenly saw the yellow dog's one eye—baleful, malevolent. It turned him hot and cold, and he could do nothing but stare at it.

He saw nothing of a boat putting off from any vessel; thereabout, indeed, nothing of any sort seemed to be doing. There was, in fact, no sign of life on the wharf but in his own and in the dog's presence. And the dog had sat down now, and did nothing but watch him. When the clouds cleared off the moon, Hankinson saw the dog's one eye—and he cursed it under his breath in plain Cockney English.

It was in the midst of these muttered curses that the two slinking figures suddenly leapt out on Hankinson as he passed the stack of timber. There was a flashing of steel in the moonlight, and the soft silks in which Hankinson was masquerading. He fell over on his back as the knives were withdrawn, and convulsively twisted up and on to his side. He knew that blood was running from him like the spurts from a suddenly pricked wine-skin, but his brain was clear enough yet, and he mechanically snatched at his revolver and fired, left and right, at the two figures which were drawing back from him. And as his own eyes began to glaze he saw the two figures sway and fall—fall in the unmistakable fashion.

"Lor'!" gasped Hankinson as his head dropped. "Got—'em—both!"

Then Hankinson died, and the yellow dog came near and looked at him.

Where you find the bodies of three dead men lying in the moonlight on a Thames-side wharf, one of them an Englishman dressed in Chinese garb, two of them Chinese men attired in reach-me-down slop suits, the Englishman stabbed, the Chinese shot, the Englishman with a collection of paste diamonds on him, the Chinese with next to nothing, and all three watched by a miserable one-eyed yellow dog, you have all the elements of a first-class mystery. There were two Orientals in different places who could have solved that mystery, but your true Oriental knows how to keep a still tongue, and the yellow dog, unfortunately, was unable to make humans comprehend him.

V: ROOM 53

CHAPTER I

BEATRICE, chambermaid in Corridor C. of the Grand Harbour Hotel at Wychport, found it incumbent upon her in the faithful discharge of her duties to sit up three nights out of the six which belong to the working week until one o'clock in the morning. At twenty minutes after midnight the boat came in from the Continent, and for forty minutes after that the hotel was busy. The amount of business varied; sometimes quite a lot of people came into the hotel; sometimes only a few entered; the whole thing depended very largely on the sort of crossing that had been experienced. When the waters of the North Sea were in tractable mood, travellers, instead of tarrying at Wychport for what remained of the night, preferred to go straight on to London by the express which stood ready alongside the quay; it was, after all, only a ninety minutes run. But when the North Sea was in one of its bad tempers—which were somewhat frequent—many folk were only too glad to stagger into the hotel and seek the comfort of a quiet room and well-aired sheets, as quickly as possible. Therefore, Beatrice in hers, and several of her sister chambermaids in theirs, were on duty in the corridors until business, big or little, was definitely settled for the night.

Corridor C. was a very quiet and retired one. It was a short annex, running out of Corridor B.; it ought really to have been Corridor B. I. There were only six rooms in it—three on either side; they were numbered 48, 52 and 54 on the right-hand side; 49, 51 and 53 on the left-hand side. At the end of the corridor was one of those luxurious bathrooms for which the Grand Harbour Hotel is justly famous, and in the corridor itself, set between the doors of the various apartments were several very comfortable deep-backed, softly cushioned couches; Corridor C., indeed, with its old engravings of marine subjects, was quite a lounge. From half-past eleven every night, by which time the regular inhabitants had retired, Beatrice used to rest herself on one of these couches, under a convenient electric light and pass the time of waiting for the incoming boat by reading novels. She borrowed these novels from the circulating library at the harbour bookstall—twopence a volume—and in spite of her occupation, she got through two in a week and—especially for a very pretty one—Beatrice's taste in fiction was, to say the least of it, peculiar. For love stories she had no liking whatever. Problem novels she did not understand. The novel which is really an essay or a sermon made her yawn. Adventure stories she had a faint liking for, but the adventures were never strong enough. What Beatrice rejoiced in was the full-blooded, thoroughly sensational detective story, beginning with a first-class murder and ending up with the arrest of the last person in the world to be suspected. And after a somewhat lengthy course of this sort of reading she had come to be a connoisseur and an expert, and had learnt a good deal more about law, and medical jurisprudence, and New Scotland Yard and coroner's inquests, and the procedure at murder trials, than young women in her position are supposed to know.

Beatrice was in the middle of a particularly exciting novel, one midnight in March, when certain familiar sounds in the lower regions warned her that the Continental boat was in, and that some of its passengers had come across to the hotel. She laid aside her book (for she was a dutiful girl, who never neglected her obligations) and walked into Corridor B. There was a lift entrance there, and presently its ironwork lattice swung open with a clatter, and one of the hotel porters emerged carrying suitcases and bags and followed by two men. After her usual fashion Beatrice made a quick but thorough inspection of both. One was a little, somewhat stout gentleman, very much wrapped up in a fur-lined overcoat and a shawl, and decidedly foreign in appearance; the other was a tall, loose-limbed, good-looking man, just as English in manner and style as the other was un-English. Beatrice, out of her great experience, set him down as a military man. He gave her a glance as the three approached and she thought that he had a humourous and meaning eye.

"Fifty-three and fifty-four," said the porter.

Beatrice turned, and preceding the little procession along Corridor C. threw open the doors of opposite rooms and switched on the electric light. The porter hesitated, looking at the two men.

"Well," said the tall man, with a laughing glance at his companion, "which will you have? Both look alike, no doubt."

The foreign-looking person spread his gloved hands.

"Oh, it is no matter," he said, in good English, badly pronounced. "As you say—alike. It is all the same—yes. You that—I this. But—you come see me presently?"

"All right!" laughed the big man. "I'll see to it."

He turned into 54; the little man went into 53. And Beatrice went off to fetch hot water for both.

When she returned a few minutes later both men were in 53. They had taken off their coats and wraps. The tall man revealed himself in a smart, grey tweed travelling suit, of unmistakable English cut; the little man was in a frock-coat with silk lapels. He had a big cigar case in his hand and was inspecting its contents; the tall man had an unopened bottle of whisky on the dressing table, and was just about to extract its cork with a pocket corkscrew. He turned to Beatrice with a whimsical, illuminating smile.

"Now, I'm sure you're the sort of girl that would do anything for anybody," he said. "So I'm sure you'll be able to find a couple of tumblers, some sugar, a lemon, and a jug of boiling water—and it'll be all the better if you find 'em quick.

"Yes, sir," responded Beatrice. "At once, sir."

But outside Beatrice found interruption. The porter was up again with another gentleman—to be put in 51. He, too, appeared to be a foreigner, a dark-eyed, swarthy-skinned man of thirty or so. Fortunately, he wanted nothing whatever, and was quickly bestowed in his room, and Beatrice went after the matters required in 53. That did not take long; within a few minutes she was back with her tray. The two men were smoking cigars; the big one nodded at her with approval.

"Good girl!" he said. "I'll remember you in the morning. And, speaking of that, shall you be on duty in the morning, and at what time, if you are?"

"Yes, sir," answered Beatrice. "Six-thirty, sir."

"Bring me some tea and two or three biscuits as soon as ever you rise," commanded the tall man. "I want to catch a train at seven-twenty. Don't forget me. And this gentleman——" He turned to the foreigner. "Any liking for the early cup?" he asked with a laugh. "If so, tell her."

But the little man shook his head, with emphatic decision.

"No!" he declared. "Me—I stay in bed to-morrow morning till I feel inclined to get myself out of bed. No hurry! I ring my bell when I want something. Just now, I want that punch you promise to make me."

"Nothing more, then, gentlemen?" asked Beatrice.

"Not a thing!" answered the tall man. "Except to wish you a good-night."

"Good-night, gentlemen," replied Beatrice, politely.

She went away down the corridor and picked up the exciting novel. Could she have done just what she liked she would have read a few more chapters, for the hero was in deadly peril in his attempts to track down a peculiarly clever criminal. But it was now nearly one o'clock, and she had to be up again at six. Beatrice accordingly went to bed. And at twenty minutes to seven she knocked at the door of 54, laden with tea and dry biscuits.

The tall man was dressed and evidently ready for departure. He favoured Beatrice with another of his semi-whimsical looks.

"Good girl!" he said, as she set down the tray. "Nothing like punctuality! See how punctual I am! I shall catch my train in comfort. And there's the little remembrance I spoke of."

He dropped two half-crowns into Beatrice's palm, and laughed as he did so. Beatrice thanked him with her usual politeness, and went off. Ten minutes later she saw him going off, too, carrying his suitcase. She saw so many gentlemen in the course of her duties that they were all as so many nine-pins to her, but for some reason or other she wondered if she would ever see this particular one again; certainly he was a very pleasant-mannered gentleman.

The early morning wore on in its usual fashion. People got up, breakfasted, and went away or lounged about the hotel. Of such as were within Beatrice's jurisdiction, the lady and gentleman in 49 went downstairs at 8 o'clock; they had been in the place a week, and their habits were regular. The young lady in 50 departed for good at half-past eight; the foreign-looking man in 51 kept about the same time. But No. 53 had not shown himself when 10 o'clock came, and Beatrice wished he would get up, for she wanted to do his room.

It was not until 11 o'clock, however, that she heard anything of 53. Then, all in a sudden minute, she heard plenty. First came a ringing of 53's bell; then as she went down the corridor with hot water, 53's door was violently thrown open, and 53 himself, a wildly excited figure in a vividly coloured dressing-gown, appeared on the threshold waving both arms.

"The manager!" he shouted. "Fetch the manager! The police! Fetch the police! But stop. That fellow you saw in my chamber last night—him that was in there, 54—where is he?"

"Gone, sir!" replied Beatrice, but in amazement. "He left at seven o'clock. Is something the matter, sir?"

The little man groaned.

"I am robbed!" he said, in a deep voice. "Robbed! It is him—that man, there! He must have drugged me with his punch! Oh, I am a fool! But fetch the manager. I am robbed!"

He folded his arms dramatically, and turned into his

room, and Beatrice, setting down her hot water can, fled for the office. She was palpitating, mentally as well as physically, by the time she reached it, but she palpitated much more—in the mentally excited way—when, following the manager back to 53, she heard the foreign gentleman's dismal story. For here, for the first time in her experience, she was face to face with actual crime.

The manager wanted to know what it was all about; the foreign gentleman, making a praiseworthy effort to calm himself, endeavoured to explain.

"It is like this," he said, waving his hands. "I come over from Amsterdam; I am a merchant in diamonds. I bring with me some valuable, very valuable, diamonds for a client in London. Well, I am very poorly on the boat; it is a bad crossing. I make friends with that gentleman who comes in here with me last night; very pleasant, kindly fellow. He says stay at this hotel, get a good sleep, go on to London next day. He says, too, he will make me some good, old-fashioned punch; he has the real, proper stuff in his portmanteau. Very well, I come—this girl, she see him and me in my room here—she gets in the hot water and the other little things. He makes the punch—very good, very nice; we smoke our cigars, my cigars. We spend a pleasant hour—then good-night. And I wake—it is much later than I think. I get up, I ring. And then I feel beneath my pillow for the small case in which I have my diamonds, and behold, it is gone! I am robbed! It is that so very pleasant man—he drugs me and robs me! You will fetch the police; they must arrest him!"

The manager looked at Beatrice.

"Does he mean the tall gentleman who was in 54?" he asked. "Yes? Well, he's gone, hasn't he?"

"He went at seven o'clock this morning, sir," replied Beatrice. "He said he was going to catch the seven-twenty."

The Amsterdam man stamped his slippered feet and raised his eyes to the ceiling.

"Gone?" he cried. "Ah, the renegade, the evil one! But you know him; you will help to catch him? Is it not so?"

The manager rubbed his chin. Those were the days before compulsory registration came in; chance comers, staying for one night at an hotel, could please themselves whether they registered their names and addresses or not; so long as they were respectable, had luggage, or paid in advance, nobody cared who they were; they were numbers, not personalities, in the eyes of the hotel folk.

"Haven't the least notion who the gentleman was," he said. "I just caught a glimpse of him when you and he came in last night, sir, but I don't know him. We get hundreds of people who just come in for a night, or even for a few hours in the night, in the course of a month. But he seemed a highly respectable gentleman. Military-looking person, I thought."

"I am robbed!" said the Amsterdam merchant, more dramatically than ever. "Fetch to me your police!"

"Certainly, sir!" assented the manager. "But one question; have you left your room at all since you went to bed?"

"Oh, well, yes!" he admitted. "I leave him for, perhaps, ten minutes about eight o'clock this morning to fetch something up from a bag that I put in your stock room last night. But I lock him and put the key in my pocket."

The manager looked grave. He was well aware, though he took care not to say so, that there was nothing very difficult about entering any of his bedrooms.

"Um!" he said. "But you didn't put your little case containing the diamonds in your pocket?"

"What for?" demanded the Amsterdam man. "No; I leave him under the pillow, as I think. I lock my door, go away down the corridor, come back after ten—perhaps fifteen minutes—get into my bed again, go to sleep once more, till just now. And then my case is not there at all! No, I see it! This man drug me and enter my room in the night. Fetch me your police!"

"Um!" repeated the manager. "Certainly, I'll telephone for a detective, sir. But there were several strangers in the hotel last night who came by your boat. It may be that you were followed from Amsterdam by someone who knew you had these valuable things on you."

"No, it is that man!" asserted the despoiled, with acerbity. "He drug me with his very nice hot punch. You see, while we talk, friendly and pleasant, I make myself such a fool as to show him my diamonds."

"Oh!" exclaimed the manager. "Ah! well, that's quite another matter. I'll telephone to the police immediately. No other loss, sir; your purse, pocketbook, for instance?"

"He neither steal my purse nor my pocketbook, nor nothing. I have all my moneys, rings, watch; it is only my diamonds he have run off with, the bad one!" answered the Amsterdam merchant. "But he shall be found. Bring me a posse of police, detectives, fine clever fellows; we go to work!"

"I'll get one who's a smart hand, anyway," said the manager.

The smart hand arrived by the time the Amsterdam

merchant was dressed, and the proceedings began. Beatrice heard news of them now and again during the morning. She herself was subjected to a long examination by the detective, who she thought was a singularly dull, tedious, unimaginative person, totally unlike the detectives whom she met so regularly in fiction. She learned from him that the tall, good-humoured gentleman had taken a first-class ticket for London on the seven-twenty; he would arrive in London at nine o'clock, or thereabouts.

"So he'd be safely lost in that sparsely populated little village a good two hours before this Dutchy found out he'd been robbed!" grumbled the detective. And he expects me to find him in five minutes! I don't think! However, Dutchy's game to fork out five hundred quid to get his shiners back, so it's worth putting in for."

"Five hundred pounds reward!" gasped Beatrice.

"That's so," assented the detective. "And little enough. He's just told me and the manager that there was thirty thousand pounds' worth of diamonds in that little case—a case no bigger than my tobacco pouch. Lor! Well, my dear, you don't know anything more?"

"I don't know anything more," said Beatrice.

And herein Beatrice, dutiful girl though she was, departed sadly from the truth. For in doing up 54 that morning, after the tall gentleman's departure, she had found upon his dressing-table a visiting card. It was covered with pencilled figures on its blank side, but on the other was a beautifully engraved name and address:

"Captain H. A. Mervyn, 221st Lancers, Army and Navy Club, Pall Mall, S. W.

CHAPTER II

THAT was Beatrice's afternoon out; her time of liberty began at one o'clock. Half an hour later those of her sister chambermaids who saw her at all in their quarters were surprised to see her go forth in her best attire, a neat tailor-made walking costume of black habit cloth, on which Beatrice had laid out more of her last year's wages than she would have cared to admit. This, finished off by a pair of neat shoes, equally neat gloves, and a picture hat, made Beatrice look very quietly smart, and many men on the platform of the harbour station regarded her neat figure and demure air with admiration. But Beatrice regarded no one, she had other things in mind. She carried money in her purse and a third-class return ticket to London, and at ten minutes to two she stepped into an express, and at a few minutes after three found herself set down amidst the bustle of the Metropolis.

Beatrice knew London very well. She was, in strict fact, a Londoner, born and bred within sound of Bow Bells. Also, she had at one time or another been chambermaid in one or other of the big London hotels. So, in a manner of speaking, her foot was on her native heath. And, under ordinary circumstances, she would have taken an omnibus to Trafalgar Square, for she was a saving young woman who knew the value of even twopence. But these circumstances were anything but ordinary, and Beatrice chartered a taxicab and instructed its driver to set her down at the corner of St. James's Square. Having been accustomed to keeping her eyes open in her peregrinations, Beatrice was well acquainted with clubland, and knew the Athenæum from the Carlton, and the United Services from the Army and Navy; and in due time she was set down close by the Army and Navy, and, after remunerating her driver, turned towards that exclusive establishment as self-possessed and demure as when she quitted her usual haunts at the Grand Harbour Hotel.

The janitors within the portals of the Army and Navy felt unusual surprise and something almost approaching emotion when a very well-dressed young woman, very quiet and self-assured, descended upon their grandeur and asked in modest but firm fashion, if she could see Captain Mervyn, of the 221st Lancers. They were smart enough to see that this was no ordinary occasion; discerning enough to perceive that Beatrice, though certainly not a woman of rank and fashion, was no ordinary being. There were two of them in the portals, and they looked hard at her, and speculatively at each other.

"Captain Mervyn?" said one. "Um! I haven't seen the Captain for two or three weeks. Where's the 221st quartered now?"

"Aldershot!" replied the other functionary. "But Captain Mervyn's on the Continent—Holland or somewhere—been away for a fortnight. He was in the club the morning he left."

"Captain Mervyn returned to England last night," remarked Beatrice. "I saw him, at Wychport, just after he landed. That's why I want to see him again—on very important business."

The two janitors inspected her again, and made another inspection of each other.

"Well, he's not been in here to-day, miss," said one. "That is, as yet. But if he's in town he will be coming in. And, of course, if you saw him last night, he's in England again, and for him England means London or Aldershot."

"He came to London this morning by the seven-twenty," said Beatrice. "Do you know where he lives when he's in London?"

"Um!" admitted one of the janitors. "I do—but it's against all rules to give addresses. But," he added, seeing Beatrice to be disappointed, "if he is in town, he'll be in here by five o'clock, safe as houses, If you leave a message——"

"No," answered Beatrice, "the business is very important—for him. I'll call again. In the meantime I shall go and get some tea."

She had tripped off before the functionaries could say another word, and she went away unconscious that she had left a world of speculation behind her. For it is rarely that young women come asking for officers of crack cavalry regiments at their clubs, and when they do, the myrmidons wonder what they come for.

"Smart, quiet girl!" observed one janitor to the other. "Rum go, though! Looked serene enough, to be sure."

"Deep!" said the other. "Deep as they make 'em! Well, I reckon she'll look in again. Not to be put off, that sort!"

But Beatrice did not look in again. On leaving the Army and Navy she turned along Pall Mall intending to go into St. James's Street, where she knew of a place at which afternoon tea was procurable under refined surroundings. And she had just advanced as far as the corner when she suddenly caught sight of the man she wanted. Having the trick of remembering faces, Beatrice knew him again at once, though he was now attired in the height of fashion and wore the glossiest of silk hats, the shiniest of patent leather boots, and looked a very grand personage indeed. He was crossing the roadway from the direction of Cleveland Row, and Beatrice, waiting for him on her side of the street, planted herself directly in his path and looked at him out of her violet-tinted eyes. He gave a mighty start.

"Good Lord!" he exclaimed, instinctively raising his magnificent hat. "The little chambermaid! What on earth brings you here, young lady?"

Beatrice produced the card which she had found on the dressing table of 54.

"I came to find you, sir," she answered. "I have just called at your club. You were not in. They thought you might be in about five o'clock. So I was going to call again."

The cause of Beatrice's journey, now leaning both hands on the handle of his carefully rolled umbrella, and bending towards her from his considerable height, looked more mystified than she had ever seen a man look in his life. Yet already there was the birth of a whimsical smile about his lips, and the carefully brushed moustache was beginning to quiver.

"But—why?" he said. "What—what's it all about?"

"It is all about that gentleman, sir, who came in with you to the hotel early this morning," replied Beatrice. "He awoke at 11 o'clock to discover that he had been robbed."

Captain Mervyn gave another mighty start—almost a jump.

"No!" he exclaimed, his voice almost rising to a shout. "What—of his diamonds?"

"Yes, sir," assented Beatrice. "Thirty thousand pounds' worth. And—and he believes you stole them, after drugging him. And he has a detective at work, and——"

Heedless of whoever might be looking on, Captain Mervyn interrupted Beatrice with a burst of laughter which made her jump. Just as suddenly as it rose, it died away, and laying a hand on the girl's shoulder, he turned her round towards St. James's Street.

"Come along up here," he said. "You shall have some tea and tell me all about it. Now this is really the very biggest lark I ever heard of! This way."

In the quietest little corner of a smart little teashop Beatrice carefully narrated the doings of that morning at the Grand Harbour Hotel. Her companion found it hard work to restrain his laughter; evidently the adventure was one which suited his sense of humour. But when Beatrice had made an end, even down to the last detail, his whimsical face became grave and business-like.

"Now, you listen to me, young lady," he said, "I dare say you know the old proverb—that it's an ill wind that blows nobody any good? Very well—this little affair is going to do you some good. First of all, are you certain, absolutely certain, that this Dutch chap is going to make good his offer of five hundred pounds reward? Because that's highly important in view of what I'm going to tell you."

"The detective said so, sir," said Beatrice. "And I heard the foreign gentleman promise it to the manager, and more than that, the news was all over the hotel before I left, and a typewritten notice, mentioning the five hundred pounds, had been put upon the notice board.

"Good!" exclaimed Captain Mervyn. "Excellent! Very well—now you listen very carefully to what I'm about to tell you."

He bent forward across the little tea table and began to whisper, interrupting his story now and then with suppressed laughter. And though, up to then, Beatrice—who was strong on the point of humour—had remained remarkably grave, she, too, began to smile, and at least once she laughed outright.

"So there it is," said Captain Mervyn, in conclusion. "There's the plain truth—and it's for you to profit by. There are two lessons to be learned from it, too. One is, don't suspect innocent folk too quickly; the other, don't drink strong punch on an empty stomach, especially after a bout of seasickness. But that's neither here nor there—the thing is for you to get back."

"There's an express just after 5 o'clock, sir," remarked Beatrice.

"Then you've just nice time to catch it," said the Captain. "Come along, and I'll put you into a taxi. I wish I could go back with you. I'd give a year's pay to meet that little chap five minutes after you've done with him!"

When Beatrice was safely seated in the taxi-cab, Captain Mervyn put his hand in at the door.

"Well, good-bye, young lady," he said. "You're a smart girl, you know. Are you thinking of getting married?"

"I am engaged, sir," replied Beatrice, demurely.

"I hope he's a good chap. You deserve an extra good one," observed the Captain.

"Thank you, sir," said Beatrice. "He's is a very estimable young man—a rising tradesman, sir, and likely to do well, being thoroughly steady and painstaking."

The Captain raised his hat as he drew back.

"Bless you!" he said, and waved his hand. "Bye-bye!"

Dinner was just over at the Grand Harbour Hotel

when Beatrice, somewhat weary, but still cool and self-possessed, reentered its portals. As she passed the manager's room in the hall, she saw through its open doors the manager, the Amsterdam merchant, the detective, and an inspector of police, all in strenuous debate. She saw, too, that the typewritten notice had been replaced by a printed bill, with "Five Hundred Reward" set in very big black type at the head of it; copies of this bill were on every door of the hotel. But Beatrice paid little heed to them; she went quietly to her own quarters, changed her smart attire for her chambermaid's gown, apron and cap, and that done, repaired to room 53, into which she admitted herself by her master-key. Two minutes later she went downstairs and tapped at the door, still half open, of the manager's room. Inside, the voices were loud and excited.

"And I say that the whole thing has probably been the work of a gang of Continental thieves who followed you!" declared the manager. "There were several people came off that boat, and you say yourself you were out of your room for a quarter of an hour this morning, leaving the stuff there, so——"

"And I say it was that fellow that gave me the punch!" vociferated the Amsterdam merchant. "I turn my back on him once or twice while he mix it, and——"

Beatrice tapped again, and walking in, extended her hand and a small morocco-bound case to the despoiled one.

"Your property, I think, sir!" she said quietly.

The Amsterdam merchant gave a howl of delight which would have done credit to any hyena. He seized upon the case and tore it open.

"My diamonds!" he shouted. "Oh, I am saved! My diamonds is here!"

"Good heavens!" exclaimed the manager, staring at his chambermaid. "Where on earth did you find that, my girl!"

"Just where I should think the gentleman put it, sir," answered Beatrice. "Between the two mattresses of his bed. It suddenly struck me that he might have hidden his case somewhere and forgotten where, so I made a search—and found it."

The Amsterdam merchant suddenly smote his forehead, and groaned.

"She is right!" he said miserably. "I forgot! It is that so strong punch! I remember—now! Before he leave me, that big fellow, he say to me, 'Mind your precious stones.'

"'All right,' I say, 'I show you what I do with them—I sleep on them.' And I did put them between the beds—mattresses—not my pillow. Now I remember it all—yes! It is the punch, so strong, so good, put it out of my head this morning. But—what matter? I have them, my sweet, beautiful diamonds! And you are a good clever girl—the very cleverest girl!"

"Yes, sir," said Beatrice. "Thank you, sir. Five hundred pounds, if you please, sir."

The Amsterdam merchant's jaw dropped and his eyes bulged. His face paled, and he turned from one man to the other of those around him, and met with firm looks.

"But—they were not lost, after all!" he expostulated. "They were in my bed, what I pay for! Come, my dear, beautiful young lady, let us say a little present——"

The manager shut the door and stood against it.

He gave the Amsterdam man a look and pointed to a copy of the reward bill which hung on the wall. Five minutes later Beatrice withdrew, carrying her money with her. She was still quite cool and self-possessed, but when she read her usual amount of fiction that evening it seemed to her to fall a little flat. The actual events of the past twenty-four hours had been really exciting.

VI: THE SECRET OF THE BARBICAN

CHAPTER I

MR. SEPTIMUS HELLARD, an elderly and eminently respectable North Country solicitor, brought down to a West of England town on important business, found that business unexpectedly concluded on the second morning of his visit and himself faced with four spare hours before he could get an express train to London. He was not the sort of man to spend any time in idleness; accordingly, having lunched at his hotel and paid his bill, he inquired of the venerable head waiter if there was anything remarkable in Wilchester which he could go and see. And the head waiter, sizing up the general aspect of his questioner, suggested that Mr. Hellard should cross the market square to the Wilchester and County Museum, an ancient building, which he pointed out from the window of the coffee room.

"The very thing!" exclaimed Mr. Hellard, and immediately set out.

The head waiter could have made no better suggestion. Mr. Hellard had all his life been interested in antiquarian and archæological matters; his was the sort of mind that would contentedly spend hours in poring over an old document, and days in an endeavour to decipher an inscription on some moss-grown monument. He accordingly entered the portals of the Wilchester Museum with feelings of pleasurable anticipation, and for the next half hour was absorbed in a general contemplation of the various exhibits. After which, being a man of method, he proceeded to devote himself to his own patricular hobby—coins.

There were several cases of coins in that Wilchester Museum, all neatly arranged and set out—gold, silver, bronze—ranging from the earliest times of Roman occupation of this country to the later days of the Stuart period. Mr. Hellard was interested in all of them, but his interest was suddenly transformed into amazement as he stopped before the centre of one case, peered at it for a moment, started violently, and let out a sharp, uncontrollable ejaculation.

"Heaven bless my life and soul!" he exclaimed, careless whether anybody heard him or not, "What do I see? Can I really believe my eyes?"

In order to assure himself that his eyes did not deceive him, Mr. Hellard produced a magnifying glass of strong power from his inner pocket, polished it with his silk handkerchief, and looked, half fearfully, half hopefully, at the exhibit which had raised in him these violent emotions. To most people that exhibit would have seemed a very simple, very ordinary thing. In mere outward appearance it was nothing but a stout card, on which, secured by stout clips, were three old silver coins, each about the size of a modern two shilling piece. They were in remarkably fresh and good condition, the lettering and mounting was sharp and clear, as if they had just come from some mint. And on the bottom half of the card was inscribed in clear, bold handwriting, these lines:

"Fine Set of Famous Sarklestowe
Siege Coins.
Lent by F. Paver-Crompton, Esq., F.S.A."

Mr. Hellard looked through his magnifying glass—

once, twice, thrice. Then he put it back in his pocket, took his silk handkerchief out and mopped his forehead.

"Heaven bless me!" he muttered. "'Tis they without a doubt! Extraordinary."

With that he hurried out of the room and into a lobby in which a caretaker sat toasting his toes by the fire and reading a newspaper.

"I say!" said Mr. Hellard, grappling with his excitement and striving to be calm. "There are some exhibits in there—several, described as being lent by Mr. Paver-Crompton. Can you tell me where Mr. Paver-Crompton lives, now? Is it near here? Is it——"

The caretaker arose in silence, laid down his paper, moved heavily to the door, opened it, and beckoned the visitor outside into the market square. He extended a thick forefinger.

"You see that old red brick mansion a-standing under them trees where the rooks is a-flying?" he said. "That there is Mr. Paver-Crompton's residence. Little door in the garden wall, with a small brass plate on it—way into the front entrance. Thank'ee sir."

Mr. Hellard had pressed a shilling into his informant's hand, and was half-way along the market square before the caretaker could regain his fire. As he hurried he pulled out his card case; he had a card all ready for the trim parlour-maid, who presently responded to his ring, and he almost cried aloud with joy when he heard that Mr. Paver-Crompton was at home.

Two minutes later Mr. Hellard found himself in Mr. Paver-Crompton's presence, in a room so filled with folios, octavos, old prints, old curiosities that

Mr. Paver-Crompton himself, an elderly gentleman of a twinkling eye and pleasant smile, seemed as if he had been taken prisoner there, and would never be able to get out again. Mr. Hellard executed a deep bow; Mr. Paver-Crompton bowed, too, and glanced at his visitor's card.

"Mr. Hellard?" he said. "And from Sarklestowe? A long way off, and a deeply interesting place. I possess——"

"Sir," exclaimed Mr. Hellard excitedly, "you possess a set of our famous siege coins, struck in 1647, when our ancient castle was beleaguered. I have just seen them—in your museum. Where, I beg you to tell me—where did you get those coins?"

"Bought 'em!" answered Mr. Paver-Crompton with alacrity. "Last year."

Mr. Hellard gasped, dropped into the only chair that was not filled with massive tomes or curiosities, and, staring steadily at his host, rubbed his knees.

"Sir," he said in a low, concentrated voice, "that set of coins is the property of the Sarklestowe Corporation, to which body I am legal adviser. We lost that set—which is almost unique, and, indeed, is unique in one way, for it was the very first set ever struck—some years ago, under the most extraordinary and mysterious circumstances. Which," he concluded impressively, "have never been explained or accounted for from that day to this."

Mr. Paver-Crompton reseated himself at his desk and stared at his visitor.

"But," he said, "how do you know that set's yours? There are more sets than one in existence. I saw another set sold at Sotheby's many a year ago, when I was a lad, so——"

"Sir," answered Mr. Hellard, "I know your set is

our set, because each coin bears a very tiny private mark upon it, which I myself placed there some years since. Sir, there is no doubt. Wonderful—wonderful!" exclaimed Mr. Hellard. "That mere accident should have taken me into that museum, and that—"

"Look here!" interrupted Mr. Paver-Crompton, rising and going to a cupboard in the recess of his encumbered library. "Have a glass of my old port and tell me all about this mystery. Was this set—if it is yours, which, of course, I'm not going to grant, you know, just yet—stolen, then?"

Mr. Hellard spread out his hands and shook his head.

"Heaven knows what happened!" he answered. He took the glass which his entertainer handed to him, sipped its contents, murmured his praise of the wine, and returned to the absorbing subject. "I'll tell you all about it," he went on. "You're aware, of course, that when Sarklestowe Castle was besieged by the Parliamentarians, in 1647, the Royalist garrison struck these siege coins in silver. There were three separate coins, each differently worded. They are now extremely scarce, especially in sets. I question if there are four sets known to collectors; there are very few separate examples known. But our Corporation has always had, from the very first, and has most carefully treasured, the first set struck—the set, which, I say, is down your street there. It was always carefully kept in a safe by our town clerk, for the time being—until some eleven years ago—and thereby hangs my tale!"

"Go on with it, my dear sir," commanded Mr. Paver-Crompton. "Deeply interesting."

"Eleven years ago," continued Mr. Hellard, "the town clerk of Sarklestowe was one Mr. Frank Marshfield. He was a smart, rather dashing young fellow, a member of my profession, of course, and of a few years' experience before he came to us. He did his work excellently; he was, in short, a model town clerk, and everybody thought a great deal of him. And then, all of a sudden, a most distressing and remarkable thing happened."

"Disappeared with some of the town's goods and effects, I suppose?" suggested Mr. Paver-Crompton with a grim chuckle.

"It was all very distressing—and most peculiar," answered Mr. Hellard. "The circumstances were queer—most queer. I don't know if you remember it, my dear sir, but just eleven years ago there was an exhibition in London of old Corporation plate. You bear it in mind? Very good. Now, to that exhibition we were invited to lend certain objects—our 14th century mace, our famous loving cup presented to us by Richard III., and one or two other unique and valuable objects. To these we voluntarily added our set of the siege coins—a very handsome exhibit altogether. And, in order to insure their perfect safety, it was arranged that Marshfield himself should take them up to London and hand them over in person. Upon a certain morning—to be precise it was the 7th of December, a very dark, foggy winter day, as I remember very well—Marshfield left his rooms in Spurgate, in our town, carrying his valuable articles in a hand bag, in order to catch the 9 o'clock express to London. He said good-bye to his landlady at her door; he spoke to a couple of well-known townsfolk at the end of Spurgate; he was seen by another credible man of the town to turn the corner of Finkle Gate on his way to the station—and since that moment, my dear sir, Marshfield has never been seen or heard of! At any rate," added Mr. Hellard with great emphasis, "not by any Sarklestowe people—who would be uncommonly glad to either see or hear of him—uncommonly glad!"

"Ah!" observed Mr. Paver-Crompton knowingly. "Just so! Of course, there was something wrong?"

"I will continue this narrative in order," replied Mr. Hellard, sipping reflectively at his old port. "The course of events was in this wise: Mr. Alderman Mardill, chairman of our finance committee, was going up to town by that train, and had arranged with Marshfield that they should travel together. When Marshfield did not turn up at the station Mardill left a message for him with the station master, telling Marshfield where to meet him that evening in London—at some hotel or other, you know. Mardill, of course, thought that Marshfield had missed his train and would come on by the next. But the next went without Marshfield, and the afternoon one, too, and so the station master went up to the town to find him. And then, of course, the hue and cry began—and at the end of all these years Marshfield is still missing!"

"Never heard anything?" asked Mr. Paver-Crompton. "Literally anything!"

"Not a word, my dear sir!" answered Mr. Hellard. "The man who saw Marshfield turn the corner of Finkle Gate was the last person who ever set eyes on him in our town. He vanished. It's most remarkable. From Finkle Gate he had only to pass down the side of the castle and descend a flight of old stone stairs to the station. But nobody saw him. And the theory now is that he just went straight on to a low-lying part of the town, where the fog lay heavy that morning, made his way into the neighbouring woods and went clean away. Odd that no person saw him anywhere, but there were reasons for his flight."

Ah!" exclaimed Mr. Paver-Crompton with another grim chuckle. "I thought you'd come to that! Something wrong, of course?"

"Seriously wrong," admitted Mr. Hellard, shaking his head. "I'm afraid we were very, very lax at Sarklestowe in those days—we know much better now—and we allowed some of our officials, and notably our town clerk, far too much latitude. But, to cut matters short, we found that Marshfield had perpetrated serious defalcations. He had got hold of some valuable securities which have never been heard of since, and he had converted some others into cash. We also discovered that, making the most plausible and satisfactory excuses for doing so, he had been converting bank notes into gold at some of the banks in neighbouring towns. He must have had quite a quantity of gold—a thousand pounds' worth of gold, anyway, somewhere. So you understand why he vanished!"

"What I don't understand for one thing," remarked Mr. Paver-Crompton, "is this: You say he took some valuable securities which have never been heard of since. That implies that, wherever he got to, he never made use of them."

"Quite so," assented Mr. Hellard. "He never did. As a matter of fact we eventually regained our rights in them. But they were of such a nature that Marshfield, had he liked, could have converted them into cash in London as soon as he got there. There was nothing to stop him. And it's a marvellous thing that he didn't."

"Um!" remarked Mr. Paver-Crompton. "Well, you say he had the unique set of siege coins with him—my set?"

"He had," replied Mr. Hellard. "And I am positive, absolutely positive, that your set is our set. I tell you, my dear sir, I marked each coin in that set—I can show you the marks."

"Then through that set of siege coins you think you can trace something of this man?" asked Mr. Paver-Crompton, eyeing his visitor keenly.

Mr. Hellard threw up his hands.

"Oh, my dear sir," he said, "I wish you would tell me where, how, when you bought these coins!"

Mr. Paver-Crompton rose and rang the bell. He maintained a thoughtful silence until the trim parlourmaid appeared; then he spoke:

"Mary," said he, "get my usual portmanteau ready and have a cab called in half an hour. Now, my dear sir," he went on, when the girl had gone, "I will tell you what I will do. Your homeward way to your far-off northern town lies, of course, through London. I will go to London with you and take you to the man from whom I purchased that set of coins—and, by George, sir, I am so interested that I will stir heaven and earth to solve what's just as much a mystery to you as it is to me!"

CHAPTER II

At ten o'clock that night Mr. Paver-Crompton and Mr. Hellard arrived at Paddington. At ten o'clock next morning, arm in arm, they walked out of the Great Western Hotel and chartered a taxicab.

"Drive," commanded Mr. Paver-Crompton, "to the middle of Mortimer Street."

Mr. Hellard, a stranger to that part of middle London, looked round him with considerable curiosity when he and his companion left their vehicle and walked a little way along a street, which, to Mr. Hellard's eyes, seemed remarkably cosmopolitan. He was staring at the French names, the Italian names, the Jewish names, the antique shops, the old furniture and odds-and-ends shops, when Mr. Paver-Crompton touched his elbow and pointed him to a small brass plate very much in need of polish, which stood on the lintel of a shabby-looking door at the side of what was a tenement house. Upon this plate appeared the words: Mr. Issachar, Antiques.

" 'Cutest man in London in his line," observed Mr. Paver-Crompton as he and his companion began to make their way up a very dirty staircase. "And, I always think, the biggest antique and curiosity in his collection. Never mind the grime and cobwebs, my dear sir—but take care of your neck coming down."

There was still a long way to climb. At its end Mr. Paver-Crompton pushed open a door of what was evidently an attic, and ushered Mr. Hellard into the midst of an assemblage of venerable things which at any other moment would have completely absorbed his attention. But for that time his attention was at once concentrated on an old man, hook-nosed, skull-capped, long-bearded, who, clad in a nondescript garment, which covered him from head to foot, rose from a desk set in the midst of his accumulations and came forward with a deep bow.

"Well, Mr. Issachar," said Mr. Paver-Crompton cheerily, "here I am again, you see. But not to buy this time—merely to ask a little question. The fact is," he went on, tapping the old dealer's shoulder confidentially, "I want you to tell me something. You remember selling me that set of Sarklestowe siege coins and assuring me that you knew that they had recently been dug up in the neighbourhood of Sarklestowe Castle?"

"I assured you of what I myself was assured, sir," answered Mr. Issachar, who was rubbing his hands as he blinked at his visitors through a pair of big spectacles. "What I told you I should be told by the person from whom I bought."

"That's just it, sir," said Mr. Paver-Crompton. "Now, from whom did you buy? I'm particularly anxious to know. And—do you think the person who sold was a principal or an agent? It's important."

"An agent, sir," replied Mr. Issachar. "Otherwise I could not have imparted any information. I make it a strict rule never to divulge the names of principals in any of my transactions—it would be against my interests. But this man was certainly an agent."

"Ay, and who is he and where is he to be found?" demanded Mr. Paver-Crompton eagerly. "I want to find him at once."

"I only know him by a sort of nickname," answered the dealer. "He is known to our trade as Snuffy—Snuffy of Towler's Rents. I never knew him by any other name."

"Am I to hunt London for a man called Snuffy of Towler's Rents?" exclaimed Mr. Paver-Crompton. "Why——"

"Not at all sir," said Mr. Issachar. "Towler's Rents is a side street or alley, off Holborn; this man Snuffy keeps a curiosity shop there. You will easily find him. But," he added with a sly look, "whether you will get any information from him is another matter. And now, sir, allow me to draw your kind attention to this truly remarkable and interesting Louis Quatorze snuffbox, which——"

Mr. Paver-Crompton fled temptation—for that moment—and carefully piloted Mr. Hellard downstairs again and into another cab.

"Snuffy of Towler's Rents," he exclaimed as they sped along. "What a name, and probably what a place! And to think that such priceless antiquities pass through such hands and are haggled in such places."

Towler's Rents, duly arrived at, was certainly not the sort of locality in which the unthinking would expect to find objects of vertu. It was a narrow alley running out of Holborn in the direction of Bedford Row; there was just room in it for Mr. Paver-Crompton and Mr. Hellard to walk abreast; even then their elbows almost jostled the queer old windows of the dirty shops and half-wood house fronts on either side of them. One of the dirtiest of these windows contained some terribly dusty but good antiques, and Mr. Paver-Crompton paused and tried the door.

"This is our man, I'll be bound," he said. "And hang it all, the door's fast."

A slatternly woman looked out of the opposite house and caught Mr. Hellard's eye.

" 'E ain't in," she said, "Never is in at this time o' day. But if yer wants to know where 'e is, 'e's in the Partridge and Pelican, up there—that pub. Goes in there every morning reg'lar for a drop o' rum."

The two searchers glanced at the exterior of the Partridge and Pelican and then at each other. It was not the sort of place that broadcloth coats and silk hats could enter—without great loss of dignity.

"My very good woman," said Mr. Hellard, extracting a shilling from his pocket and dropping it gingerly into the ready hand extended to receive it, "we are in search of a person named Snuffy. If he is the man you refer to, will you have the goodness to fetch him to us? Tell him—er——"

"Tell him we want to see him about some of his old things," said Mr. Paver-Crompton.

The woman hurried towards the Partridge and Pelican and disappeared within one of its doors. And from the door presently emerged a man who was much more curious to look upon than Mr. Issachar—a tall, burly, paunchy man, whose bulk was tightly enveloped in a greasy fronted frock coat, the sleeves of which were much too short and the lapels of which were liberally ornamented with snuff, who was disreputable and unholy to look at, whose face was inflamed with spirits and whose eyes, small and pig-like, were crafty and suspicious. He rolled himself down the alley and touched the frayed brim of a doleful hat to the two strangers, whom he was evidently sizing up.

"Servant, gentlemen," he said. "Is there ought I can have the pleasure of showing you this morning? Some nice Chippendale and extra good Sheraton——"

"You're a Yorkshireman," incautiously remarked Mr. Hellard, thrown off his mental guard. "I know that by your accent."

Snuffy, of Towler's Rents, turned as he opened his shop door, and he threw a not too pleased glance at the speaker.

"It's a long time since I saw Yorkshire," he growled. "And what if I am Yorkshire?"

"Oh, nothing, my friend!" answered Mr. Hellard, as they followed him into the shop. "I merely remarked that you were—I'm one myself, for that matter."

"And it's about a Yorkshire matter that we've come to see you," said Mr. Paver-Crompton. "Mr. Issachar directed us to you. The fact is—and we'll make it worth your while to give any information you can—we want to know something, that you, no doubt, can tell us. Do you remember selling a set of Sarklestowe siege coins to Mr. Issachar of Mortimer Street some little time ago?"

Mr. Hellard, who was watching his fellow Yorkshireman's face with all the keenness of the legal observer, saw a faint twitch pass over Snuffy's unlovely features. He also saw a deepening of the gleam of suspicion which had been in the man's eyes ever since his North Country origin had been suggested to him. And when he replied, an added suspicion made itself manifest in his tones.

"Well, and what then?" he demanded.

"We want to know if you can tell us where, how and when you got those coins," answered Mr. Paver-Crompton. "And if you'll tell us, we'll give you——"

"Ahem," interrupted Mr. Hellard, with a deprecatory cough and a jog at his companion's elbow. "My dear sir—I—do not let us be in too much haste to offer pecuniary reward," he whispered. "Let us hear first if—eh?"

Snuffy, of Towler's Rents, had made no answer, and he betrayed no consciousness of Mr. Hellard's interruption. He rolled silently away amongst the litter of his untidy shop until he came to a desk in the corner, from which he extracted a dirty, much-thumbed ledger, the leaves of which he began to turn over with his claw-like fingers.

"Don't remember naught particular about 'em," he growled. "Might have summat set down here as would remind me. Siege coins, eh? How many of 'em now?"

"A set of three," replied Mr. Paver-Crompton. "Come now, you can't have forgotten a transaction like that! Why, you must know they're famous!"

Snuffy suddenly closed his book with a bang and looked up with a readiness which struck Mr. Hellard as being a piece of acting.

"Ay, I remember 'em now!" he exclaimed. "No, I don't know as they were famous—not so much in my line, you know. If I had known it I'd ha' made that old Jew pay more for 'em."

"What did he pay you then?" asked Mr. Paver-Crompton, who knew very well what a substantial cheque he had drawn for Mr. Issachar in this transaction. "How much, now?"

But Snuffy eyed his questioner sourly and shook his head.

"That's my business—and his," he growled. " 'Tain't yours, mister. Well, now, where did I get 'em? How much are you going to give for the information?"

Mr. Paver-Crompton turned to his companion. And Mr. Hellard thought it time to assert himself. "I think we'd better speak plainly," he said. "I may as well tell you, my friend," he went on, addressing the old dealer, "that these coins were abstracted from the possession of the Sarklestowe Corporation, to which I am solicitor. I——"

"Ay, I thought you were summat o' that sort," interrupted Snuffy. "Ye look it! Well, but I know naught o' that. All I know is that them coins were brought to me and that I bought 'em. Gi' me a fiver and I'll tell you all I know."

"No," said Mr. Hellard, "certainly not!"

Snuffy threw his memorandum book into the open desk and banged the lid.

"Then I shall say naught and ye can get out o' my shop!" he said. "I've naught to do wi't t' matter."

"We'll see about that," said Mr. Hellard. "This is a serious affair and you'll be made to give evidence."

"My dear friend," whispered Mr. Paver-Crompton, who had his hand in his pocket. "Allow me!—a little judicious expenditure, you know——"

"Make it a couple o' quid, then," growled Snuffy. "Not a ha'penny less!"

Mr. Hellard protested, but there was an exchange of coins between his companion and the old dealer, who pocketed his gains and sneered openly at the solicitor.

"Well," he said, "all I can tell you is this here—them coins was brought to me at a time when I had a dish full o' such like things in the window. A chap brought 'em and wanted to know if I'd buy 'em. So I bought 'em. And that's all!"

He grinned maliciously at Mr. Hellard, but Mr. Hellard shook his head.

"No," he said, "you know a lot more than that, my friend. Who was this man? What was his name?"

"D'ye think I ask my customers' names?" roared Snuffy. "Know naught about the man's name."

"What sort of man was he, at any rate?" persisted Mr. Hellard. "You know that!"

"Working sort o' fellow—gardener or summat o' that sort," growled the old man. "Said he were up in London on a holiday and that he'd dug them coins up in an orchard. Now then!"

"Where?" demanded Mr. Hellard. "At Sarklestowe?"

"Where else?" retorted Snuffy. "And that's all I know. And now away wi' you both, 'cause that's all I know and I want to lock up and go to my dinner. Ye'll get no more out of me!"

Mr. Hellard touched his companion's arm and they

withdrew into Towler's Rents and went away talking in confidential whispers. As for the old man they left behind them, he watched their disappearing figures until they had merged with the crowds in Holborn. Then he locked the shop door, rolled swiftly into Holborn himself, looked up and down, saw his two visitors cross the street and walk slowly westward, whereupon, with a grim chuckle, he turned away and made for the nearest telegraph office.

CHAPTER III

MR. HELLARD and Mr. Paver-Crompton went along in deep confabulation. Now and then so engrossed were they that they mutually paused, to the annoyance of other passengers on the sidewalk, who first ran into and then grabbed at them.

"This will never do," said Mr. Hellard, when a man carrying a heavy parcel had cursed them openly; "we are making ourselves a public nuisance." He looked up and around and noticed the Holborn Restaurant. "Let us go in there," he said. "It is almost time for lunch and we can sit down and converse quietly. My dear sir," he went on, when they had found a quiet corner and ordered their chops, "that man, I am confident, is deceiving us. He knows much more than he told us. And—most significant—he's a Yorkshireman."

"Why significant?" asked Mr. Paver-Crompton.

"Isn't Sarklestowe in Yorkshire?" replied Mr. Hellard. "Ah, my dear sir, as soon as I heard that man's voice I began to suspect something. How do we know that he hasn't had dealing with someone in Sarklestowe—that he isn't in touch with someone there—hasn't been there himself of late years? Certainly, I don't remember ever seeing the man there, but, small town as it is, he might have been there without my knowledge. I wish I knew that man's name."

"That ought not to be a difficult matter to discover," observed Mr. Paver-Crompton, with a commendable touch of worldly wisdom. "He lives in Towler's Rents. He's a furniture dealer. Surely his name will be in a trades directory. They'll have such a thing here—waiter!"

The waiter presently produced a London street directory, and Mr. Paver-Crompton, adjusting his glasses, began to turn over its pages. Before long he clapped his finger to an entry.

"There you are, that'll be the man—only furniture and curiosity shop in Towler's Rents, d'you see?" he exclaimed. "Thomas Capstick."

Mr. Hellard who was bending eagerly forward from the other side of the small table at which the two gentlemen sat, jumped up with such energy that the waiter, standing directly near, was obliged to spring forward to save the glass and china.

"Capstick!" exclaimed Mr. Hellard. "Capstick! You don't mean it! Capstick! Heaven bless my heart and soul. My dear sir, we must go to Sarklestowe at once—this instant!"

"No, a bit later," promptly responded Mr. Paver-Crompton. "The chops first, I think, my good friend. Now, why this eagerness?"

Mr. Hellard gave one more glance at the directory and relapsed into his chair again.

"Capstick! by all that's wonderful!" he groaned. "Capstick! Why, that's the name of the woman who acts as caretaker of Sarklestowe Castle. She lives in the old Barbican—ruined, of course. She has rooms in it. My dear sir, this Snuffy individual must be her relation."

"I daresay we're getting at something," said Mr. Paver-Crompton. "And since we've learned this much, we'll go around to Towler's Rents and see the old sinner again. Then you must plump him straight out with two questions: Is the woman at Sarklestowe Castle his relative? Did he get these siege coins from her? That'll be a stage further. In the meantime—waiter, hand me your wine list."

Fortified in body and more alert than ever in mind, Mr. Hellard and Mr. Paver-Crompton retraced their steps to Towler's Rents, but the dirty and frowsy shop was securely locked up and Thomas Capstick was not to be seen. Once more the woman who lived opposite thrust herself out of her doorway.

" 'E's gone awye, has old Snuffy," she said. " 'E come back soon after you was gone down the Rents and he set off hisself wiv a bag and 'e said to me, 'e said as 'ow he was going to the country on business and if anybody came a-wanting of 'im 'e'd be awye a week or more. Which 'e often goes awye like that."

The searchers after Snuffy of Towler's Rents went away into Holborn again, took a cab and drove back to their hotel.

"The question is," said Mr. Hellard meditatively, as they drove along—"the question is, has that old scoundrel—for I am convinced that he is an old scoundrel—set off for Sarklestowe?"

Mr. Paver-Crompton chuckled.

"No, no, my good friend!" he said. "Pardon me, that is not the question. The immediate question is what time can we ourselves get a train to your historic town? For what we want to do now—knowing what we do—is to betake ourselves to Sarklestowe as quickly as steam can propel us."

"You mean to see Mary Anne Capstick?" asked Mr. Hellard.

"Mary Anne, or Mary Jane, certainly," assented Mr. Paver-Crompton. "She is, in my opinion, the next link."

"Soon answer that question," said Mr. Hellard. "There's a splendid train from King's Cross at three-fifteen."

"Then we'll catch it and get down there," responded Mr. Paver-Crompton. "For there I am sure is the source of the stream we are trying to trace."

Eight o'clock that evening saw Mr. Hellard and his companion breathing the keen air of the wind-swept moorlands, over which the great Norman keep of Sarklestowe Castle still stands watch. They glanced at its mighty bulk as they walked through the darkness towards it.

"I suppose we'd better go straight to the Barbican?" asked Mr. Hellard. "A direct question unexpectedly put, eh?"

"Excellent!" agreed Mr. Paver-Crompton, "and if I may suggest what the question should be, I should advise you as soon as this woman opens the door to us to plump her with a plain inquiry, devoid of any preface, such as, 'Now, Mrs. Capstick, do you know of one Thomas Capstick, of Towler's Rents, in London?' "

"Good!" murmured Mr. Hellard, "I will."

But for the second time since noon Mr. Hellard and his companion found a door locked against them. The old Barbican, transformed into a dwelling-house of two or three rooms, was in darkness; not a gleam of candle or of fire came throught its diamond-pane windows. Mr. Hellard thumped loudly at the door; no answer came. But the door of a cottage close by presently opened and a man came out.

"John Green—a worthy fellow!" whispered Mr. Hellard, advancing towards the man. "Good evening, John, do you know where Mrs. Capstick is? She hasn't gone to bed at this hour, surely?"

John Green turned and looked back into the cottage, calling to his wife. That good woman came bustling out.

"Oh, it's Mestur Hellard, is it?" she said in broad Yorkshire. "Why, sir, Missis Capstick, she went away this forenoon. She's gone to Kettleby to see their 'Lizer—she's badly. She went at eleven o'clock did Mrs. Capstick, to catch t' train, and about two hours after she were gone, there wor a tallygraft come for her—t' tallygraft lad left it wi' me. An' as she'd left her door key wi' me I put t' tallygraft on her table—I thowt, happen, it wor to say their Lizer wor dead. But, of course, I don't know."

"Oh, she left her key with you, did she?" remarked Mr. Hellard, nudging his companion in the darkness. "Well, now, there's something I want out of the Barbican house, so just give me that key, will you, Mrs. Green? By the bye, did Mrs. Capstick say whether she'd return to-night?"

Mrs. Green stepped back within her cottage, took down a key from a nail and handed it over.

"She said she might, and she might not, sir," she replied. "It all depended on how their 'Lizer wor. If she found her right bad, she said she'd stop all t' night there."

Mr. Hellard opened Mrs. Capstick's door, let his visitor within, closed the door and struck a match. A candle stood in its stick on the centre of the table in the little room they had entered, and close by lay the buff envelope of the telegram. Mr. Hellard looked at it and then at Mr. Paver-Crompton.

"My dear sir," he murmured, with the half sinister expression of the conspirator, "I—the fact is, I'm going to open that telegram!"

Mr. Paver-Crompton nodded acquiescence.

"Precisely what I should do myself, under the circumstances," he said, "for in my opinion that wire is not from 'Lizer, but from London!"

Mr. Hellard's fingers trembled a little as he slowly opened the buff envelope. He gave one quick glance at the message, and then, with something between a groan and an exclamation of relief, handed the flimsy paper to his companion.

"You're right," he said. "It is from London, and from that hoary old trickster."

Mr. Paver-Crompton slowly read out the message:

"Mrs. Capstick, Barbican Cottage, Sarklestowe: Hellard here this morning. You had better go away at once.—COUSIN TOM."

"Handed in at twelve-fifty," said Mr. Paver-Crompton musingly. "Just after we left him, eh? But the woman across there said that Mrs. Capstick went away at eleven, and never got this wire?"

"A fortunate circumstance," remarked Mr. Hellard. "She'll come back—all unsuspecting. Well, my dear sir, what do you think?"

"Plain enough," replied Mr. Paver-Crompton. "There's no doubt whatever that the man Snuffy got those coins from this woman. But—where did she get them? And what does she know about—Marshfield?"

For a moment the two gentlemen stared at each other, a question in the eyes of each. A heavy step outside startled them, and Mr. Hellard tip-toed to the door and cautiously looked out.

"One of our constables," he whispered. "A thoroughly reliable man—we'll have him in; he may be useful."

The policeman duly summoned into the cottage, stared at Mr. Hellard with amazed eyes.

"Anything wrong, sir?" he asked, looking from one to the other, and then glancing round as if he missed something. "Aught about Mother Capstick?"

"There may be a good deal wrong, Johnson," answered Mr. Hellard gravely. "We don't know yet," he turned to Mr. Paver-Crompton. "Would it be any good to make a sort of preliminary search now?" he suggested. "There might be some indication——"

Mr. Paver-Crompton shook his head. He was about to express the opinion that measures of that sort would not be of much use at that stage, when the policeman, who had sharp ears, turned to the door, looked out, and closed it again.

"There's Mrs. Capstick a-coming along now," he said. "She's close at hand, sir."

Mr. Hellard's strategy developed itself.

"Stand back there, Paver-Crompton," he said sharply. "Get into that corner, Johnson—put yourself behind the door. Get between her and the door, once she enters. Now then."

A moment of breathless suspense; then the door was pushed open, and a big, elderly, raw-boned woman entered; behind her appeared the wondering faces of Green and his wife. It seemed to the watchers, from a strong scent of spirits which came in with her, that Mrs. Capstick had been drinking a little, and the eye which she turned on Mr. Hellard was distinctly fiery and aggressive.

"Now then, Mr. Hellard," she demanded loudly, "what right have you to get my key and walk into my house, I would like to know? Poor folk's houses is as good as rich folk's, and I'll not be put on by you nor nobody, let me tell you that, Mr. Hellard! What right——"

At that moment Mrs. Capstick's eloquence was cut short by a sight of the policeman, who, at a signal from Mr. Hellard waved the Greens away, shut the door, and placed himself against it. Mrs. Capstick suddenly caught her breath, glanced from one to the other of her visitors, and collapsed into a chair.

"Oh, what is it?" she exclaimed, with a curious drop from the indignant to the frightened. "What——"

"Now, Mrs. Capstick," said Mr. Hellard firmly. "you've got to tell the truth. We know more than you think. Come, now, where did you get those things you sold to your cousin, Thomas Capstick, in London? Out with it, now."

It was a shot made at a venture, but the watchers saw that it went home. And Mr. Hellard drove it further in by waving the telegram.

"Come now," he went on, in his sternest manner. "It's useless to keep anything back. You got those things—and more—from Mr. Marshfield years ago! Tell the truth about it—and about him. You've got a secret, and we'll have it out of you, if we have to pull every stone and stick of this old Barbican to pieces! So come on!"

Mrs. Capstick had begun to moan and sob, rocking herself to and fro in the chair into which she had dropped. Her eye went to a black bottle which stood flanked by a glass on a chiffonier.

"For mercy's sake gi' me a taste o' that!" she

moaned. "I'm fair upset, and my heart's bad! Gi' me a drop, you Johnson, and I'll tell you the truth, gentlemen, and be done with it—it's been a sore weight this many a year."

"Give her what she wants," commanded Mr. Hellard. He watched his prisoner sip and sip again, until the colour came back into her cheeks.

"Now, then, no nonsense," he said. "Tell me the whole truth."

Mrs. Capstick untied the strings of her bonnet and sighed deeply.

"I've allus been afraid it 'ud come out," she moaned. "I allus said so to Cousin Thomas, but he would have it 'at it were a safe thing. Well, it's like this, Mr. Hellard. It were when Marshfield, as you've just mentioned, disappeared. It was a very foggy morning, that—which made it all t' easier what happened. My Cousin Thomas were stopping a few days wi' me, and him and me had just finished our breakfasts, when there came a tap at the door, and it opened, and Marshfield looked in—that white and queer i' face 'at we jumped to our feet. 'For heaven's sake, Mrs. Capstick,' he says 'let me sit down a minute and get me summat—I'm overcome,' he says. 'I've been hurrying to t' station, and my heart's affected—I'm done,' he says. An' he staggered in, dropping a bag 'at he carried, and then fell into that theer chair. An' I rushed one way for summat, and my Cousin Thomas he rushed for a drop of sperrits 'at were in that cupboard, but afore we could do owt, Marshfield he gev' a queer groan and he went."

"Died!" exclaimed Mr. Hellard.

"He was dead as a doornail when we touched him," solemnly asserted Mrs. Capstick. "May I never bite nor sup again if he worn't dead! We knew that as soon as we touched his hand. And, of course, I were for running for help and a doctor. But as you know, Mr. Hellard, there wasn't a house nor a cottage near the old place at that time—they've all been built since—so there was no neighbours to call. And Thomas, he stopped me. 'Doctors is no use for dead men,' he says. 'Bide a bit and let me see what he has in that theer bag.' And, of course, Thomas did what he pleased. He opened t' bag, and theer was a lot o' gold money in it, and some papers, and them Corporation things 'at were afterwards reported as missing. And when he saw that, my Cousin Thomas fastened t' door and made me help him to carry t' body into that inner room theer. And later on in t' day he went out and made some inquiry in t' town, cautious like, you know, Mr. Hellard, and he came back and said to me 'at nobody 'ud never know aught about it, for theer weren't a soul i' t' place 'at had any idea 'at Marshfield had ever come near t' Barbican, and they were already saying 'at he'd fled t' town altogether. And so—well, we agreed 'at we'd stick to t' gold for ourselves. Thomas, he took charge of it, and carried it away to London wi' him and t' rest o' t' things, too—all excepting some papers 'at were in t' bag. An' them papers——"

Mrs. Capstick paused and looked fearfully at her audience.

"Them papers," she went on at last in a hushed voice, "is wi' t' body. And t' body's safe buried in one o' t' owd cellars down t' bottom o' them stairs. An' Lord ha' mercy, I've thowt many a time 'at I heerd Marshfield walking up them stairs i' t' dead o' night, but I knew it wor fancy, 'cause we niver laid a finger on him. An'—that's all. Mr. Hellard—what about my Cousin Thomas?"

Mr. Hellard looked grimly at his two companions before he turned to Mrs. Captsick.

"I hope we shall get your Cousin Thomas as easily as we've got you, my woman," he answered. "Bring Mrs. Capstick up to the police station, Johnson, and we'll get to work."

VII: THE SILHOUETTE

CHAPTER I

Of the many thousands of utterly ordinary-looking individuals who journeyed into the city from various suburban retreats every workday morning Limmis was, by a long way, the most ordinary and least likely to attract attention. He was the sort of young man whom no one would have ever troubled to look at twice. If you happened to look at Limmis once you knew—if you really happened to think about the thing at all—that you could see his like a hundred times in the next half mile of crowded street. He was inconspicuous, colourless, common—as common as peas or potatoes. His face was amiably honest; his eyes were inoffensively intelligent; his hair was neither one thing nor another; everything about him, even to his business suit of serviceable tweed, was of a type and pattern so well known that it could not possibly excite more interest than is excited by one blade of grass in a ten-acre meadow. You said of Limmis—if you wasted time by saying anything about him—that he was just one of the crowd and nothing more.

But one may easily fall into grave error by generalising too speedily about first impressions. Limmis—Horace Sinclair Limmis—was a young man of dual personality. He was not a Jekyll, it is true, nor a Hyde, which is equally true, but he led—very successfully—a double life.

From his hour of rising in the morning until that of

his tea-dinner in the evening Limmis passed a day of strict conventionality. He ate his breakfast, he caught a city train, he performed the duties of a clerk in a mercantile house from nine-thirty to five-thirty; he did all the things which are pertinent to this walk of life with thoroughness. But when he had returned home to the small house in the quiet street in the Kew district, wherein he resided with his parents and two sisters, and had eaten his chief meal of the day, Limmis became a changed character. He began, then, to enjoy himself—and his pleasure was all the greater because it was secret. Nobody knew anything about it. From the time that Limmis went out of an evening until the hour of his return none of his home circle knew what he did with himself.

What Limmis really did with himself would probably have seemed of a deadly dulness to most people. But it was a peculiar excitement to him to be perpetually on the lookout for adventure. He was not at all certain how adventure was to come, or what shape it would take, but he kept eyes and ears open for it. He frequented the river bank—being a capable swimmer, it seemed to him that he might some day have the chance of rescuing from drowning a rich man who would leave him all his money, or a beautiful girl who would reward him with her hand. He sat in dark corners in obscure bar parlours, hoping that he might overhear the details of some plot—expressed, of course, in cryptic language which he would translate for himself. He hung about lonely places in Richmond Park, and Wimbledon Common, and Putney Heath—there was always the chance of a murder, or, at any rate, an assault. It was as the breath of life to Limmis to see two suspicious-looking characters putting their heads together in a corner, and he got into insignificant trouble more than once by hanging around such characters—who, of course, invariably turned out to be a couple of citizens enjoying a quiet confabulation over a pipe of tobacco. And at least once he became an object of suspicion to the police, and had much difficulty in persuading an incredulous constable that his sole object in looking rather narrowly around a detached residence, whose proprietor was away at the seaside, was to make certain that it was not at that moment being investigated by a burglar.

"You leave them things alone," said the constable sourly and severely, eyeing Limmis with distinct disfavour. " 'Tain't none of your business to find out if the property's safe or if it isn't. You follow your nose 'ome, and leave our affairs to us, d'yer see? We don't want no bloomin' amachoor 'tecs round here. 'Op it!"

Limmis hopped it, smiling to himself. Having been bred on what is commonly called detective fiction he had a very low opinion of the intellectual powers of the average policeman. When this particular officer so rudely interrupted him he was theorising on what he should do if he found that a burglar really was in that house, and he smiled because he knew that no member of the force, uniformed or in plain clothes, could possibly theorise as he himself could.

"Amateur, indeed!" chuckled Limmis. "Ah, wait till I get a proper chance! Then——"

Limmis suddenly got a proper chance. Walking across one of the loneliest glades in Richmond Park one bright moonlighted night he became aware that something which looked like the body of a man lay a few yards ahead of him. It was suggestively motionless—so motionless that Limmis felt himself tremble a little as he stole forward to look at it. But he did not wonder at the immobility any more when he saw that over the whiteness of the glazed shirt, revealed by a low-cut waistcoat, a dull stain of crimson was slowly spreading before his very eyes.

CHAPTER II

THE sight of that crimson stain produced in Limmis certain emotions which he would have found it very difficult to define. He recognised that here, at last, actually at his very toes, was the adventure that he had often sought—it was there, veritably there, and in the very grimmest form in which adventure can come. This, he was sure, was a murder—only a murdered man could lie in that curious, sudden-stricken attitude. With a curious celerity of apprehension Limmis realised the whole scene. He was staring at a man, obviously a foreigner, well dressed, who lay in the grass, his white face reflecting the moonlight, his arms thrown wide on either side, in a dreadful stillness. That stillness suddenly weighed on Limmis's nerves—it was so heavy, so deep. He started a little when his own foot, timidly moving forward, pressed a dried twig and cracked it.

He went up to the still figure at last, bent over it, finally knelt at its side. Eventually he touched the dead man's forehead—a dark, swarthy forehead, around which masses of dusky hair were tossed. There was the slightest trace of warmth there, and the limp hand, on which Limmis presently laid his own, was also slightly warm. And Limmis suddenly lifted his eyes from the dead and gazed around him in futile search of something living.

"Must have been—just now!" he muttered. "Still warm! Gad! They can't be far off!"

It was at that moment that Limmis saw the shadow. At his back, a yard or two away, was a coppice, one of the many which make oases of foliage in the wide expanses of Richmond Park. It was fenced in by rails; immediately behind the spot on which Limmis knelt at the dead man's side there was a stretch of railing unbacked by any woodland; from beyond it the vivid moonlight poured its full, silvery radiance upon the close-cropped turf which lay around the body. And as Limmis looked up and about he saw, for one brief second, the sharply-cut silhouette of a shadow—the shadow of a man's head and shoulders. There was a high-crowned, foreign-looking hat, there was its steeple, dented at the top, there were its wide, stretching brims. And beneath the brims were two other projections, which Limmis knew to be the shadows of a pair of unusually long and pointed moustaches.

Even as Limmis looked this silhouette wavered, moved, disappeared. He sprang to his feet, rushed to the fence, looked over, and saw nothing beyond a rabbit, which scuttered away in the bracken. He heard the slight noises which the rabbit made, but he heard no other noises. The stillness fell again, and all he heard was the thumping of his own heart.

"Queer! Queer!" said Limmis. "I saw it—saw it!"

He drew away from the fence and looked right and left along it. It extended a good eighty yards in one direction, a good sixty in another; for the most part it was thickly packed with wood and undergrowth. Limmis knew, moreover, that that particular coppice extended deeply in the rear, eventually dropping into a widespread dell, from which there were a hundred ways of passing out into the loneliest parts of the park. He shook his head.

"Might as well look for a needle in a haystack!" reflected Limmis. "I can't tackle the job single-handed!"

Then it struck him that it was impossible to deal with any feature of the job single-handed; it was one of those things which a man cannot well keep to himself. He would have to go and tell the police of his discovery, that he was certain. And he moved off to the nearest gates to find a constable, and, having gone a yard or two, turned back to have another look at the corpse.

It was during this second and more searching inspection that Limmis saw that whoever had stabbed the dead man had subsequently used the point of the dagger or stiletto to scratch upon the forehead a curious mark—a couple of straight, upright lines, topped by another, more deeply cut. The blood was congealing in this disfigurement, and on the high, marble-white brow it made the figure of a letter T. Limmis puzzled over that as he rapidly crossed the lonely park. But he suddenly received illumination.

"That's it, of course!" he exclaimed. "That's it. T for traitor! Good!"

CHAPTER III

DURING the next fortnight Horace Sinclair Limmis was a good deal heard of. His name became quite familiar to the public; his photograph was reproduced in the newspapers. The police authorities, a magistrate, a coroner and his jury, a whole crowd of officials of one sort and another knew Limmis as the principal witness in the Richmond Park Mystery. He suddenly developed into a centre of attraction. People made excuses for calling upon his father and mother.

At the milk and bun shop in the city where Limmis took his noontide refreshment, crowds of wide-eyed fellow clerks gathered about him, and trim-waisted waitresses grew tired of pointing him out. He upset the office. Everybody, from the manager to the youngest boy, wanted to hear and rehear all the details. Finally the heads of the firm gave him a holiday, grimly remarking that he could come back when the coroner and the magistrate had quite done with him. Thenceforward, during a couple of glorious weeks, Limmis was seen in the coroner's court and in the magistrate's court. When he was not there he exhibited himself elsewhere.

But Limmis, whether he was being examined by coroner or magistrate, did not tell all he knew. The case, as presented before the authorities, resolved itself into this: the murdered man—who had been killed instantaneously by a dagger thrust—was found, upon being searched, to have nothing whatever upon him that could lead to identification. The publication of his photograph, however, established the fact that he was an Italian who had arrived in London on the day of the murder, had taken a room in Soho, dined at a Soho restaurant, and had left that restaurant at 7 o'clock in the evening, in company with another Italian, who, according to the evidence of a waiter, had introduced himself to him. This man the police arrested, and found on him certain matters which might have belonged to the dead man. But the accused quickly cleared himself. It was quite true, he said, that he introduced himself to the stranger; he did so because he saw that he was a compatriot who had a poor knowledge of English. It was also true that certain Italian money found on him had belonged to the dead man; he had given him English money in exchange for it. Certain picture post-cards of Genoa, unused, also found on him, had been given to him by the dead man; it so happened that they both came from near Genoa. But as regards his further concerns with the victim, they were short. He had walked from Soho to Charing Cross Metropolitan Station with him, and had there put him into a train for Richmond Park—after which he had never seen him again. All this the arrested man proved easily and conclusively, bringing irrefutable evidence as to his own movements on the evening of the murder. And when he was discharged, the mystery of that murder remained as great as it had been when Limmis first announced it. Nothing transpired, nobody came forward; the coroner's jury returned a verdict against some person or persons unknown, and the public began to itch for a newer sensation. And Limmis resumed the even tenor of his way, secretly conscious—and proudly so—that he was in possession of a secret. For neither to police nor to press representative, to coroner, nor to magistrate had Limmis said one word about the mysterious shadow silhouetted on the grass. That—that was has own affair.

Limmis cherished a deep design. He meant to solve this mystery himself. He had been obliged, the law being what it is, to call in the police, so to speak, but the mystery was his. In Limmis's opinion, the police would never find out any more about this affair; what was more, he felt sure that they would be all the better pleased if it came to be forgotten. But Limmis did not intend to forget. He was going to get at the truth—quietly, secretly, surely. When he had got at it—why, then he would make the most of his glory. Perhaps he would write a book about it; at any rate the newspaper people would write a good deal about him. And possibly—it had always been a dream of his—he would chuck clerkship in the city and start business on his own as a crime expert.

In Limmis' opinion, the murder of the unknown Italian—you could call him that, thought Limmis, though as a matter of fact, the dead man had left a name, Marco Ciappi, behind him at the lodging he had taken, where, however, he had left nothing else—was the climax of a vendetta; he possessed a shelf full of sensational stories about it. Or it might be the work of the Black Hand—he had also read largely on that subject. That mark on the forehead clearly proved that whoever killed Ciappi had afterwards branded him as a traitor—this was all in proper accordance with the traditions of the secret societies. The man whose shadow he had seen projected on the sward was, of course, of some secret society. And the obvious thing to do was to find him.

Limmis knew that before you can find anything you have to seek for it. He would have to seek for this man. And—also obviously—he must seek for him in a likely place. That likely place seemed to be in Soho, or, at any rate, Soho mixed up with Hatton Garden and Clerkenwell, and perhaps a bit of Tottenham Court Road. Thus it came about that Limmis, instead of going home respectably when office hours were over, went along to the streets which lie between Shaftesbury Avenue and Oxford Street, to keep his eyes open for a man who sported an unusually fierce moustache and wore a steeple crowned sombrero.

This was a new life for Limmis. He became familiar with a number of things which he had never heard of before. He discovered that it is possible to live quite a continental sort of existence in the very heart of London. He began to frequent queer little cafes and restaurants, where you heard very little English, but a great many strange languages and dialects, from Czech to the patois of the Levant: he ate strange dishes, he drank cheap wines; he watched curious-looking men and many women of a sort he had never seen before. He began to wonder how on earth London had come to be the dumping ground of all sorts of suspicious-looking foreigners, hailing from Bordeaux or Constantinople. But at the end of many weeks of this he had still not seen anything approaching the similitude of what he sought for.

It never occurred to Limmis that he himself might become an object, not perhaps of suspicion, but of interest. It never crossed his mind that because he regularly patrolled Greek Street and Dean Street, spent an hour or two in one or other of the many foreign restaurants in that neighbourhood, somebody might begin to wonder what he was doing there, he who was so obviously out of place. For that quarter, as everybody knows who knows London, has, outside its own folk, no denizens or frequenters who are not of the artistic sort—poets with long hair, actors with short hair, painters who affect grotesque clothing and odd manners, ladies of the ballet, chorus girls and young men from Fleet Street in search for an hour of giddy delight of a Paris-and-water sort. Now, Limmis looked anything but a follower of the arts; also he looked anything but a follower of youthful actresses. Nevertheless he was vastly surprised and taken aback, when as he sat in a quiet corner of a quiet restaurant one evening, a girl, who had, as it were, casually dropped into a seat on the other side of his table, and immediately dispatched the waiter for some small matter of refreshment, suddenly bent forward and addressed him.

"I sat down here because I want to speak to you," she whispered. "Please talk to me as if you know me. I have been watching you for some time—weeks."

Limmis, whose homely, freckled face had flushed under this abrupt address, stared and started.

"Me!" he said. "Me!"

"You," she answered. "You are Mr. Limmis. You were a witness in the Richmond mystery crime. You found Ciappi in Richmond Park—dead. And since then you have spent a lot of time about this district. You have been looking for somebody. Isn't it so?"

Limmis, instead of immediately answering the direct question, looked at the questioner. She was a pretty girl, dark, olive-skinned, with beautiful hair and eyes. She was quietly but becomingly dressed, and she was certainly not English, though she spoke the language readily, if with a slight, rather attractive accent. And Limmis, who had never in his life spoken to a foreign woman, and scarcely to a foreign man, instantly felt all a true-born Englishman's suspicion of anything hailing from beyond the Channel. In spite of the girl's prettiness, his manner became somewhat surly and his speech ungracious.

"What about it?" said Limmis. "I don't talk of my affairs to people I don't know."

The waiter returned just then with an ice, and the girl trifled with it until he had gone away again. Then she treated Limmis to a smile which would have melted the heart of an anchorite.

"Don't be offended," she said. "Just think for a moment. A woman's assistance is always worth having."

"Don't know as I made any remark about being in

need of any assistance," replied Limmis. "No recollection of it, anyhow."

"All the same, you'd be glad of it," said the girl, calmly. "You see, I'm pretty sure of what you're after."

"Oh!" exclaimed Limmis, loftily. "Indeed! Wear my thoughts painted on my forehead, I suppose? Ah, I ain't so sure of what you're after!"

He was becoming emboldened by that time, and he now dared to look his self-constituted companion full in the face—no mean feat for Limmis, who had never sought after women. He even smiled at her, confidently and loftily. But he soon found out that in the matter of exchanging glances or smiles the mysterious young lady could give him points.

"Aren't you?" she said, bringing the full power of her eyes upon him. "Then I'll tell you. I'm after what you're after!"

Limmis stiffened with suspicion. He nervously glanced around, fearful of listeners. But that was a quiet corner, and no one was within earshot.

"Perhaps you'll tell me what I'm after, since you're so knowing?" he said, half defiantly, half angrily. "Some people do know other people's business, I'm well aware, and——"

"You're after the man who killed Ciappi," she said, quietly interrupting him. "And—so am I."

That answer, so readily and confidently given, reduced Limmis to silence. He could only sit and stare. The girl went on eating her ice.

"Of course!" she said, calmly. "Hit it in one—haven't I? You see what good reason I had for speaking to you—eh?"

Limmis suddenly found his tongue. He bent forward and his eyes became bright with interest.

"What might you be wanting to find him for?" he whispered. "What—for what?"

The girl licked up the last of her ice, put down her spoon, and advancing her pretty face nearer to Limmis' nose, spoke one word with silky sweetness.

"Revenge!" she whispered.

CHAPTER IV

An hour later Limmis was still in that quiet corner of the restaurant, and the girl of the liquid eyes and seductive voice was still with him. There was a bottle of Italian wine on the table between them, and the girl sipped a little of its contents and Limmis drank it generously, but even at the end of the hour he still kept his secret to himself. As for the girl, she had told him everything—everything, that is, that she cared to tell. It sounded to Limmis very like a chapter out of one of the sensational romances which he kept on a carefully arranged shelf in his bedroom, and he took it all in greedily, as dry earth sucks in rain. The dead man was the girl's lover—he had come from Italy to see her; he had been lured, trapped, inveigled to that lonely spot in Richmond Park and there done to death. Now it was her business to find the murderer and hand him over to justice. And it was precisely at that point that Limmis grew shy—shy as a young horse at the first sight of a bridle. He wanted to do the handing over himself. And he said so.

" 'Tisn't as if I hadn't spent time and money on the job," observed Limmis. "The nights I've given to it! The money I've spent on this sort of thing—watching, waiting! I ain't disposed to go shares in what I should get if I laid hands on the fellow—alone."

"But I can help!" said the girl, eagerly. "I know

you have some secret—I watched you at the inquest and in the police court—and I knew, I felt that you didn't tell all that you could. Don't you see, if you told me what you can tell, I might supply just the little thing, the tiny touch——"

"How do I know that you wouldn't go straight to the police?" asked Limmis, still suspicious.

"My word of honour!" answered the girl, with a flash of her black eyes. "That, at any rate, cannot be broken."

Limmis rubbed his chin. This answer was quite in the best style; it was precisely what the heroine of a romance would have said. He drank a further glass of the wine, which was of a much more generous nature than he knew, and he smiled the smile of vanity.

"And you ain't really suspected—nobody?" he asked with a sudden weakening of his purpose.

"No one. But I know some of my countrymen in London," she answered, "and Ciappi may have known some of them, and if I had any clue—ah, why don't you tell me?"

Limmis sipped more wine and twiddled his thumbs. Again he smiled in the fashion in which all vain mortals smile when they know something.

"You'd leave it to me if you can suggest anything?" he asked. "You'd let me carry it on?"

"My honour!" exclaimed the girl. "Do you think I want any of the credit? All I want is to see that man hanged—hanged like a dog!"

She hissed the last few words through a set of pearl-like teeth, and Limmis felt that this, too, was in keeping, and that the girl was a coadjutor worth having. And suddenly the wine warmed all his soul, and he leaned forward across the table.

"There was something,"—he said, with a deepening of the vain smile. "There was—a shadow."

The girl leaned forward, too, until her warm breath and the scent of her hair were close upon her companion.

"A shadow?" she whispered. "Yes?"

Limmis let it all out. He had so often repeated the facts to himself that he was able to present them in short, telling fashion. The girl nodded her head at the end of every sentence.

"The shadow of what must have been a tall man, who wore a high-crowned, broad-brimmed hat, and whose moustaches projected past his cheeks!" She said. "Good! Good!"

"Know any fellow who'd answer to that?" asked Limmis.

"You see now how long you might have hunted around here!" she answered evasively. "It is so easy for a man to shave off his moustache and to give up wearing a hat of that sort; you might never have found him."

"I said—did you recognise anything in that description?" questioned Limmis.

"I know half a dozen men who might cast a shadow of that shape," she replied. "Was—was there nothing else? Come, already we are nearer. You will see how I can help you."

Limmis put a couple of fingers in a pocket of his vest. He bestowed a confidential wink on his companion.

"The police," he remarked, with a second wink, "think they're very clever. They searched all round that spot and found nothing. I did a bit of looking round too—eh? And I don't half do things when I do 'em. I found—this!"

Covertly he produced a small article, which he laid

on the table between them—a match box of white metal, much worn and scratched. On one side was an emblematic device, enamelled in the national colours of Italy—green, white, red. On the other was a monogram made out of two letters— A and P.

"Eh?" said Limmis with a chuckle. "What d'ye think of that, now? Good find: a little article belonging to—what is it?"

The girl, after one good look at the match box, one quick turning of it over, had sat back in her chair and seemed to be staring at something in the mirror behind her companion. And suddenly she looked around and up the length of the restaurant.

"There is a gentleman come in to whom I want to speak," she said. "The oldish gentleman just sitting down there at the end. Will you do me the favour to go and ask him if he will come here for a moment, where it is quiet, and speak to Miss Morelli?"

Limmis prided himself on his politeness to ladies. He slipped the match box into his pocket and rose.

"Anything about—this?" he said. "No letting out, now?"

"Nothing about this," answered the girl quietly. "At least, nothing of what we have said. I only want to ask him if a certain man is in London."

Limmis walked up the restaurant to the elderly gentleman—a stoutish, comfortable-looking person who was leisurely tucking a napkin under his double chin in anticipation. He bent down and delivered his message. The elderly man glanced at him in surprise.

"I don't know any Miss Morelli, sir," he remarked in excellent English. "You are mistaking me for somebody else."

"The young lady down there," said Limmis.

He turned and pointed to the quiet corner near the

street door. And as he pointed he let out a sudden exclamation. For the girl's chair was empty.

"Why—why," said Limmis, "she's—gone!"

The elderly gentleman sniffed, glanced Limmis up and down, and picked up a wine card. He evidenced a decided desire to ignore this interrupter, and Limmis, without a word, and a little open-mouthed, returned to his corner, and addressed a waiter who lingered near it.

"Where's that young lady I was talking to?" he asked.

The waiter glanced at the door.

"She go out—go away—when you walk up ze room," he answered. "She go off quick—at once."

Limmis paid his bill and went away in his turn. He lingered around the door of the restaurant for a good half hour. But Miss Morelli did not return, and at last Limmis went home to the quiet street at Kew.

When Limmis arose next morning he felt decidedly out of love with most things. The Italian wine had given him a touch of liver and a bad headache. Moreover, he had passed a wakeful night, and as he tossed and turned in his bed he had come to the conclusion that he had been tricked by the black-eyed damsel of the preceding evening. He had thought out a theory of his own about her, and it pleased him. According to that theory, the girl was the agent of the secret society whose emissary had murdered Ciappi, and she had been sent on to find out how much Limmis really knew. And there was no denying the fact that she had succeeded very well.

"Best thing I can do with my brains," mused Limmis bitterly, "is to take 'em out and butter 'em and give 'em to the dog! Honour, indeed! Fat lot of honour that wheedling young Jezebel had about her! And yours truly, 'Orris S. L., is an ass—'struth!"

Ass or not, Horace Sinclair Limmis had to go to the office. And on his way to the railway station he cast his moody eyes on the placards of the newspaper shop, and there he saw some staring letters which made those eyes open to their widest extent. The letters made up the words, "Another mysterious murder at Richmond."

Limmis was already by way of being late for his train, but he threw punctuality to the winds, darted into the shop and spent his halfpenny. Once outside he stood stock still on the pavement—trains, business, the manager's wrath, everything forgotten—and glued his eyes to the paper. This is what he read:

"Another mysterious murder took place at Richmond late last night, the victim again being a man of Italian nationality, and the circumstances of a somewhat similar nature to that of the recent murder of the man, Marco Ciappi, in Richmond Park. In both cases the murderer left no trace behind, and at present there seems as little likelihood of discovering the second assassin as there is of finding the first. In the case of last night, however, it is well established that the murderer was a young woman."

Limmis felt his mouth become very dry, and the sweat broke out on his forehead. But he took a firm grip of the newspaper, and read on.

"About half-past ten o'clock last night Mr. Antonio Porelli, an Italian who has lived some time in Richmond, where he had a business as a dealer in antiques, was having supper in company with his housekeeper in the parlour of his residence in Gunwalk Alley, when a sharp ring came at the front door bell. Mr. Porelli went to the door himself. According to the housekeeper, his opening of the door was immediately followed by three rapidly fired revolver shots. The housekeeper ran to the door and found her employer lying across the hall, dying, or probably dead already. With great presence of mind she at once sprang into the alley, and was in time to see a young and active woman, whom she positively asserts to be very dark of hair, rush away in the High Street. Unfortunately, although the reports of the shots at once attracted a crowd of people, the murderess got clear away, leaving no clue, and at the time of our going to press no arrest had been made."

Limmis deliberately folded up the newspaper and placed it carefully between the book and the packet of sandwiches which he was carrying. He saw everything now; he understood everything. The girl had spoken truly when she had said that her motive was revenge; she had lied brazenly when she had said she would not take revenge into her own hands. But that vexed Limmis no longer—he excused her. What sorely grieved him was the knowledge that the murderer of Ciappi had actually been, as it were, his own next-door neighbour for several weeks, and that he had wasted time searching for him in Soho, when there he was, close in hand, at Richmond.

"The chance of a lifetime!" mused Limmis, as he eventually boarded a train. "And clean chucked away! But what about her? No, I ain't going to move a finger in that direction—not me! What she's done, she's done out o' love—a love tragedy, that's what this is. An' I hope the bloomin' police never set eyes on her! Fact!"

If Limmis had only known it, there was no need for him to worry on the mysterious Miss Morelli's account. About the time that Limmis had meekly suffered a lecture from his manager and was settling to his work, a certain youthful-looking nun went away by the Continental Express from Victoria, and of all who saw her nobody suspected her of being anything but what she appeared to be.

VIII: BLIND GAP MOOR

CHAPTER I

ETHERINGTON, manager of the Old Bank at Leytonsdale, in Northshire, was in the first week of his annual month's holiday, and he was celebrating his freedom from the ordinary routine of life by staying in bed an hour longer than usual every morning. Consequently, on this particular—and as fate would have it, eventful—morning, it was 10 o'clock when he came down to breakfast in the coffee-room of the Grand Hotel at Scarborough, in which place he meant to stay a fortnight before going on for a similar period to Whitby. It would not have mattered to him if the hands of the clock had pointed to 11, for he had no plans for the day. His notion of a perfect holiday was to avoid plans of any sort, and to let things come. And something quite unexpected was coming to him at that moment—the hall-porter followed him into the room with a telegram.

"For you, sir," he said. "Come this very minute."

Etherington took the envelope and carried it to his usual seat near the window. He gave his order for breakfast before he opened it, but all the time he was talking to the waiter he was wondering what the message was about. He was a bachelor—his mother and sister who lived with him were such excellent administrators that he scouted the idea of any domestic catastrophe; neither of the two would have dreamed of bothering him for anything less than a fire or an explosion. His under-manager, Swale, was a thoroughly capable man, and all was in order at the bank, and likely to be so. Nor could he think of anyone who could have reason to wire him about business outside the bank affairs, nor about pleasure, nor about engagements. But just then the waiter retired, and Etherington opened the buff envelope, unfolded the flimsy sheet within, and read the message in one glance.

"Swale found shot on Blind Gap Moor at 6 o'clock this morning. Believed to be a case of murder. Police would like you to return. Please wire time arrival.—Lever."

It was characteristic of Etherington, always a calm, self-possessed man, that he folded up the message, put it carefully in his pocketbook, and ate steadily through his substantial breakfast before asking the waiter to get him a railway time-table. But he was thinking all the time he ate and drank.

Murder? who would wish to murder Swale? He mentally figured Swale—a quiet, inoffensive fellow of thirty, who had been in the service of the Leytonsdale Old Bank ever since his schooldays, and had lived the life of a mouse. And what could have taken Swale, a man of fixed habits, to a wild desolate spot like Blind Gap Moor before 6 o'clock of a May morning? He knew Swale and his habits very well and he had never heard that the sub-manager was fond of getting up to see the sun rise—and yet Blind Gap Moor was a good hour's walk from the town. Perhaps he had been shot during the night, or during the previous evening—in that case, what was he doing there? For Swale was not a fellow to take long, country walks—he was a bookworm, a bit of a scribbler, in an amateur fashion, given to writing essays and papers on the antiquities of the town, and he accordingly liked to spend his evenings and burn the midnight oil at home. Odd—the whole thing! But—murder? That was a serious business, murder! Still, no one who ever knew Swale would ever have dreamed of connecting him with suicide.

As for himself, he must act. He beckoned the head waiter to his side with a nod.

"You'll have to get me my bill," he said. "I am called home—unexpectedly. But first—a railway guide and a telegram form."

It was a long journey across country to Leytonsdale, involving three changes and two tedious waitings for connections, and 5 o'clock had struck before Etherington got out of the branch train at the little station of his small market town. Lever, the junior clerk who had wired to him that morning, was awaiting him; together they walked out into the road which led to the centre of the place.

"Well?" asked Etherington, in his usual laconic fashion. "Anything fresh since morning?"

"Nothing," replied Lever. "But the police are now certain it's a case of murder; they say there's no doubt about it."

"Give me the facts," said the manager. "Bare facts."

"One of Lord Selwater's gamekeepers found him," answered the clerk. "Just before six this morning. He was lying dead near that cairn of stones on the top of Blind Gap Moor—shot through the heart. The doctors say he would die at once, and that he was shot at close quarters. And—he'd been robbed."

Etherington made a little sound which denoted incredulity.

"Robbed!" he exclaimed. "Bless me! Why, what

could Swale have on him that would make anybody go to the length of murder?"

"His watch and chain were gone," began Lever, "and——"

"Worth three pounds at the outside!" interrupted Etherington.

"Yes; but he'd a lot of money on him," proceeded the clerk. "It turns out that for this last year or two he's collected the rents for those two farms up on the moor—Low Flatts and Quarry Hill. He'd been there last night. Marshall, the farmer at Low Flatts, says he paid him £56; Thomson, at Quarry Hill, paid him £48. So he'd have over £100 on him."

"All missing?" asked the manager.

"There wasn't anything on him but some coppers," replied Lever. "Watch, chain, purse, pocketbook—all gone. That ring, that he used to wear, was gone."

"How had those men paid him?" asked Etherington. "Cheque or cash?"

"Notes and gold," answered Lever.

The manager walked on in silence for a while. Certainly this seemed like murder preceding robbery.

"Do they suspect anybody?" he asked. Lever shook his head.

"They haven't said so to me if they do," he replied. "The superintendent wants to see you at once."

Etherington went straight to the police station. The superintendent shook his grizzled head at the sight of him.

"Bad business this, Mr. Etherington," he said as the manager sat down. "First murder case we've had in my thirty years' experience of this district."

"Are you sure it's murder?" asked Etherington quietly.

"What else?" demanded the superintendent. "If

it had been suicide the revolver that killed him would have been lying close by. No, sir—it's murder! And we haven't the shadow of a clue."

"I've heard the main facts from our clerk, Lever," remarked Etherington. "Is there anything you haven't told him?"

"There's precious little to tell, Mr. Etherington," answered the superintendent. "I've got at everything connected with his doings yesterday. He was at the bank all day, as usual. Nothing happened out of the common, according to your staff. He left the bank at 5 o'clock and went home to his lodgings. All was as usual there. His landlady says he had his dinner at 6 o'clock—just as usual. He went out at 7—didn't say anything. He called on Matthew Marshall at Low Flatts Farm at a quarter past 8. Marshall paid him half a year's rent. He was at James Thomson's, at Quarry Hill, just before 9; Thomson paid him a half year's rent, too. He stopped talking a bit with Thomson, and left there about 9:20. Thomson walked out to his gate with him, and saw him strike across the moor; it was getting darkish by that time, of course, but he saw him going towards that old cairn, near which he was found this morning. There was naught on him—he'd been robbed as well as murdered, sir."

"How far," asked Etherington, "is this place where he was found from these two farms?"

"A good mile from Quarry Hill—mile and a half from Low Flatts," replied the superintendent.

"Everything is very quiet on those moors at night," observed Etherington. "Did no one hear the sound of a shot?"

"I thought of that and inquired into it," answered the superintendent. "Nobody heard any shot. If somebody had heard a shot, you know, they'd only have thought it was one of Lord Selwater's keepers shooting at something. But so far I've heard of nobody who noticed aught of that sort. You see, except those two farms, there isn't a house on that part of the moors."

"There's Mr. Charlesworth's place—up above that cairn," suggested Etherington.

"Ay, but it's over the brow of the hill," said the superintendent. "That 'ud prevent the sound being heard there. I called at Charlesworth's; they'd heard nothing."

"Any suspicious characters about?" asked Etherington.

"My men haven't heard of any," answered the superintendent. "There were some gypsies in the neighbourhood a fortnight ago, but they cleared out."

"Poachers, now?" suggested the manager. "There are men in this town who poach on those moors."

"Just so. But we've no reason to suspect any particular one of 'em," said the superintendent. "I know of two men who do go up there after what they can get, but I've found out they were both safe in the town all yesterday evening and last night. No, sir, I think the whole thing'll go deeper than that."

"How?" asked Etherington.

"Somebody must have known Mr. Swale was going to collect those rents last night," said the superintendent meaningly. "He was laid in wait for. And yet, so far as I can make out, there wasn't a soul knew he collected them except Marshall and Thomson."

"I didn't know," remarked Etherington.

"Just so. According to the two farmers he's collected them ever since old Mr. Sellers died," continued the superintendent. "Those farms belong to Mrs. Hodgson, a London lady. Now, if somebody had got to know that Mr. Swale would have £100 in cash after he'd been to these farms last night—eh?"

"You don't suspect either of the two farmers?" asked the manager.

The superintendent shook his head firmly.

"No, sir; both decent, honest, straightforward fellows," he replied. "Oh, no! No, it's a deeper job than that, Mr. Etherington."

Etherington rose to go. After all, in this particular matter he could do nothing.

"Of course, there'll be an inquest?" he asked.

"To-morrow, at 10," answered the superintendent. "But, beyond what I've told you we've no evidence. It'll be a case of 'Wilful murder against some person or persons unknown,' you know, unless something comes out, and where it is to come from I don't know."

Nor did Etherington know, and he said so and went away. And after he had dined with his mother and sister, and discussed with them the tragic affair which had interrupted his holiday, he took his walking stick and set off out of town to the scene of the murder. And there, in the gathering dusk, he met Charlesworth, the man who lived at an old house called Hill Rise, on the edge of the moor, well above the cairn near which Swale's body had been found. Etherington knew Charlesworth well; he was an old customer of the bank, a man who did a big trade in timber. He was evidently on his way home at that moment, and was glancing inquisitively at the cairn when Etherington came up.

"Nothing to see," he remarked, as the manager advanced. "They were looking for footmarks all day, but they found none. The grass is too close and wiry for that."

"I didn't expect so see anything," said Etherington. "It's some years since I was up this way. I came now to look around, to try to make out how it was nobody heard that shot last night. I understand nothing was heard at your place?"

Charlesworth, a big, athletic man, turned and pointed to the top of the moor above him.

"My place is just three-quarters of a mile over there," he answered. "There's all this rise between it and us, and a thickish belt of wood between, too. We couldn't hear a pistol shot from here. We heard nothing."

"What about those farms?" asked the manager.

Charlesworth pointed in another direction.

"You can't see Low Flatts," he said. "It's down in that hollow yonder. And you can only see a chimney of Quarry Hill—that's it, peeping up behind that line in the moor. They'd hear nothing. It's an easy thing to try, as I told the police. Whoever killed Swale selected a good place. It isn't once in a month there's anybody about here o' nights—at this time of the year."

Etherington made no answer for the moment. He stood staring about him in the fast-gathering dusk. A wild and lonely place, indeed! Miles upon miles of ling and heather, and, beyond the chimney of Quarry Hill Farm, not a sign of human habitation.

"I wonder who did kill him?" he muttered absent-mindedly at last.

Charlesworth turned towards the hilltop with a nod of farewell.

"There's only one man living who knows that," he said; and went away.

CHAPTER II

No evidence was brought forward at the inquest on this unfortunate sub-manager's body which threw any light on the mystery of his murder or incriminating any person. Yet one small, possible clue was produced. A booking clerk from an obscure wayside station in a neighbouring dale came forward, and said that, at 5:30 o'clock on the morning of the discovery of the body, he, on going to his station to issue tickets for the first train, then about due, found walking up and down the platform a rough, sailor-like man, a perfect stranger, who presently took a ticket for Northport.

As he could give no very particular description of him, and as Northport was a town of some 250,000 inhabitants, the chances of finding this man were small. Nevertheless, there was the fact that such an individual, a stranger to the district, was within five miles of the cairn on Blind Gap Moor within a few hours of the time at which Swale was probably murdered.

Nothing came of this. Nothing came of anything that was brought forward in evidence. Only one matter seemed strange. The Leytonsdale Old Bank was one of the very few country banks which issued notes of their own; both the farmers had paid their rents to Swale in these local bank notes. At the end of a month none of these notes had reached the bank, where a careful lookout had been kept for them, each man having been able to furnish Etherington with particulars of their numbers.

And the manager came to the conclusion that the thief-murderer was a man sharp enough to know that there would be danger in dealing with those notes, and was making himself content with the small amount of gold, and the watch, chain and ring, which he had secured, or was so much more sharp as to change notes at some far-off place, whence they would reach the bank slowly and at long intervals.

Six weeks passed, and one day Etherington, entering the bank after his luncheon hour, asked Lever, now promoted to the sub-managership, if anything had happened during his absence.

"Nothing," replied Lever, "except that Mr. Charlesworth retired the first of those bills drawn on Folkingham & Greensedge. It was due next week. He said he'd take it up now, as he had cash of theirs in hand."

"That's the second time he's done that, isn't it?" asked Etherington, glancing at a memorandum which Lever put before him.

"Third," answered Lever. "He retired one in April and one in January. We hold three more yet. One August, October, December."

The manager made no further remark. He went into his own room and sat down to his desk. But he began to think, and his thoughts centred on a question. Why had Charlesworth got into a practice of taking up the bills of his drawn on Folkingham & Greensedge a few days before they were due for presentation? Why, as in the case of the last three, did he come to the bank and retire them by paying cash, instead of following the usual course of having them presented on maturity to their acceptors? Once in a way this might have been done without remark, but it was becoming a practice. Charlesworth was a timber merchant in a biggish way of business. He did a lot of business with a firm in Northport—Folkingham &

Greensedge, agents and exporters. For 12 or 15 years, to Etherington's knowledge, Charlesworth had been in the habit of drawing upon this firm for large amounts against consignments of timber. Up to about six months before this the bills so drawn had always been allowed to mature and to be presented in due course for payment, which had always been prompt. But, as Lever just said, Charlesworth had himself retired the last three before they could be presented. Why?

That question began to bother Etherington. Why should a man bother himself to retire a bill which would fully mature in a week, and would be promptly met? It was a strange couse—and since the New Year it had been repeated three times. Again—why?

Etherington waited until Lever had gone to his lunch, then he possessed himself of certain books and documents. He carried them into his own room, and jotted some dates and figures down on a slip of paper. In October of the previous year Charlesworth had brought in six acceptances of Folkingham & Greensedge's. They were of various terms as regards length; each one was for a considerable amount—the one, for instance, which Charlesworth had taken up that very day was for over £1,500. And the whole lot—representing a sum of about £7,000 to £8,000—had, of course, been discounted by Etherington as soon as they were paid in by their drawer. There was nothing unusual in that—Etherington had been discounting similar acceptances, drawn by Charlesworth, accepted by Folkingham & Greensedge, for many years. What was unusual—and in the manager's opinion, odd—was that, mostly, Charlesworth had taken up these bills before they became due. And for the third time Etherington asked himself the one pertinent question—why?

He took the books and papers back to their places presently, and got out a lot of bills which were waiting to mature. It was easy work to pick out the three of Charlesworth's to which Lever had referred as being still in their hands. He took them to his room and laid them on his desk, and examined each carefully. The first, due in August, was for £950; the second, due in October, for £800; the third, due in December, for £1,175. But Etherington was not concerned, he was not even faintly interested, in the amounts. What he was looking at was the signatures in each case. And presently remembering that he had letters of Folkingham & Greensedge's in his possession, he looked for and found them, and began to make a minute comparison, letter by letter, stroke by stroke, between the signatures on that firm's correspondence paper and those written across the face of the bills. It was a close, meticulously close, examination that he made—first with the naked eye, secondly with the aid of a magnifying glass. And, though he was no expert in caligraphy, he came to the conclusion, at the end of ten minutes' careful inspection, that the signature of Folkingham & Greensedge had in each case been carefully forged.

Etherington remained looking at those oblong slips of blue stamped paper for a long time. Then he put them, folded, into an envelope, in his pocketbook. And when Lever came back he went out to him.

"I must leave earlier than usual," he remarked. "There's nothing that needs my attention, I think. See that all's right. And be here at nine sharp in the morning, Lever; I want to see you then."

He walked quickly away to his own house, made ready for a short journey, and set off. It was only a two hours' run to Northport, and he must go there at once. Such a doubt as that which had arisen in his mind could not be allowed to await solution—he must settle it. If he was right in his belief that he had discovered a forgery, what might not arise out of it?

The Greensedge, who had given part of its name to the firm with which Charlesworth did such extensive business, had been dead some years; so had the original Folkingham. There was no Greensedge now—the entire business belonged to one Stephen Folkingham, a middle-aged man, who kept up the old style of the firm in spite of the fact that he was its sole proprietor. When Etherington arrived at his office in the famous shipping town, Stephen Folkingham had gone home. The bank manager followed him to his house outside the town, and was presently closeted with him in private.

"You are surprised to see me?" said Etherington.

"Frankly, yes!" replied Folkingham. "Something important of course."

"And as private as it is important—for the moment at any rate," said Etherington. He drew out his pocketbook, produced the three bills, and spread them on his host's desk. He pointed to the accepting signatures across the fronts. "Are these signatures yours?"

Folkingham started. He bent down, glanced at the dates, and let out a surprised exclamation.

"Good heavens, no!" he answered. "I haven't accepted a bill of Charlesworth's for—oh, eighteen months. I've dropped all trade with him for quite that time."

"Then, those signatures, to be plain, are forged?" said the manager.

Folkingham shrugged his shoulders.

"So far as I'm concerned, yes," he replied. "I know nothing whatever about them—nothing! I've dropped that particular line of trade—some time ago. You don't mean to say that Charlesworth——"

Etherington sat down and told Folkingham all about it. There had been six bills. Three had been retired. Probably the other three would have been similarly retired. And—nobody would have known of the forgery. The two men stared at each other when the story came to an end. Each was thinking. But Etherington was thinking of something that was not in the other man's thoughts—something worse than forgery.

"What's to be done?" asked Folkingham at last. "Or, rather, what do you intend to do?"

"I should be greatly obliged to you if you'd come over to Leytonsdale in the morning," answered the manager. "He must be confronted. And your denial to his face—is precisely what I do want."

"All right," agreed Folkingham, after thinking this proposal over. "I'll be with you by noon. Now stop and have some dinner—you can get a train back at 8:30. Dear, dear, this is extraordinary! What on earth's behind it?"

Etherington did not discuss that. He was still thinking of his other idea; he thought of it all the way home in the train; he thought of it during the night; he was thinking of it at nine o'clock next morning when he went to the bank and found Lever there and took him into his private room.

"Lever," he said, "you remember that last day that Swale was alive; just stir your memory. Can you remember anything special that he did—here? Anything relating to bank business? Think!"

Lever, a somewhat slow-going young man, thought for some time before he replied.

"I can't think of anything except that, during the afternoon, he got all the acceptances out and went through them," he answered. "There was nothing else, I'm sure, out of the ordinary."

"Did he make any remark to you about any of those acceptances?" asked Etherington.

"No," replied Lever. "None!"

Etherington nodded, intimating that he had no more to ask. But as soon as Lever had left the room he, himself, went out again and walked around to the police station.

CHAPTER III

ETHERINGTON remained closeted with Campbell, the superintendent of police, until after 10 o'clock. When he returned to the bank the doors had been opened to the public, and two or three customers had already entered. In one of them, a big, raw-boned countryman, the manager recognised Matthew Marshall, the tenant of Low Flatts Farm.

Marshall, who had evidently cashed a small cheque, was standing in front of the counter with a little pile of gold and silver between himself and Lever, who was leaning forward from the other side to look intently at something which the farmer held in his big hand.

"A' but doan't tell me!" Marshall was saying, in his broad vernacular, "I'm none one to forget owt o' t' sovereigns 'at I paid to poor Mestur Swale t' very neet 'at he wor done for—it is! I tell yer—'im an' me, an' my wife an' all, lewked at that theer mark."

Etherington went directly to the farmer's side and looked at the sovereign, on the upper side of which somebody had stamped two deeply incised letters—X. M. And Marshall turned to him with a wide smile.

"I'm tellin' Mestur Lever theer 'at this here sovereign is one——" he began.

"I heard what you said," interrupted Etherington, taking the coin and examining it. "Are you sure of what you say?"

"Ay, shure as I am 'at I'm speakin' to you, Mestur Etherington," answered the farmer promptly. "I'd noticed them letters on that coin afore iver I paid it away to Mestur Swale yon neet 'at t' poor feller was murdered. Him an' me had a bit o' talk about it. Oh, ay, that's t' very identical coin 'at I gev him! Now, isn't it queer 'at it should turn up at yor bank—what?"

"Leave it with me," said Etherington, putting the marked sovereign in his pocket. "Mr. Lever will give you another in its place, Marshall," he went on, leading the man towards the door; "don't say anything about this in the town this morning. Come back here for a few minutes at 12 o'clock."

The farmer opened his mouth, gave the manager a shrewd nod, and went off in silence; and Etherington went behind the counter to Lever.

"Did Charlesworth pay any of that money which he brought yesterday in gold?" he asked quietly.

"Twenty pounds or so," answered Lever. He, too, suddenly looked shrewdly at the manager, and his professional stolidity broke down. "Good heavens!" he exclaimed. "You don't think——"

"Hush!" said Etherington. "Listen! Charlesworth will be coming here just after 12. I've telephoned him. He won't suspect anything from my message. Bring him straight into the private room."

There was no one but Etherington in the private room when Charlesworth walked into it at a quarter past 12. And there was nothing remarkable in the manager's surroundings, except that on his blotting-pad lay a sovereign and a closed envelope.

"Just a question or two," said Etherington, in his calmest and iciest manner. "You paid some money in yesterday—to retire one of those acceptances. That sovereign was amongst others which you paid in."

"Well?" said Charlesworth. He glanced at the coin unconsciously; and the manager, watching him closely, failed to see any sign of alarm. "What of it?"

Etherington put the point of his pen to the coin.

"That sovereign," he said, "is marked. It's one which Marshall handed to Swale—the night Swale was murdered. How did it come into your possession?"

Charlesworth's face flushed a little at that, and he bent forward, looking at the coin.

"How on earth can I tell that?" he demanded. "You know how money changes hands!"

"I should like," remarked Etherington, "to know if that sovereign has changed hands more than once since Marshall gave it to Swale. But—here is another question. What did Swale tell you when you met him that night at Blind Gap Moor? Come!"

He rose to his feet as he spoke, picking up the envelope and beginning to take three strips of blue paper from it. And Charlesworth rose, too, and stepped back a little, staring almost incredulously at his questioner.

"Come!" repeated Etherington. "What's the use

of denial? Didn't Swale tell you that he had found out that the supposed signatures of Folkingham and Greensedge on your acceptances were—forgeries? And didn't you—eh? You know what you did then, Mr. Charlesworth, I think. But——"

He tapped a bell as he spoke, and the door of an inner room opened and revealed Folkingham and the police superintendent, and behind them the round, staring, amazed face of the farmer. Etherington laughed.

"You see?" he said, indicating Folkingham. "Hadn't you better confess and be done with it? Come——"

"Look at him!" shouted Campbell, as he sprang into the room. "The revolver! Look out!"

But the room was a big one, and Charlesworth was at the further side. And before any of them could reach him he had turned the revolver on himself and sent a bullet through his brain.

Etherington made a little, half-articulate sound of vexation.

"I hurried him too much!" he muttered. "But, then, I never thought he'd do that—!" He turned to the startled superintendent. "Get him taken away, will you?" he said quietly. "The affair is—over."

IX: ST. MORKIL'S ISLE

CHAPTER I

WHEN Geoffrey Hallam married Kitty Ellerslie he carried her off for their honeymoon to Barthwick, an isolated and lonely seaside village in an almost inaccessible corner of the northwest coast. Most of their friends said that they were foolish in choosing a quiet place wherein to set out on the great adventure of married life, but Geoffrey knew better.

His professional duties as a civil engineer had once taken him down to Barthwick for a day or two, and on his return he had painted such a picture of its beauties to his sweetheart that they had at once determined to go there for a month as soon as they were married. Barthwick, according to Geoffrey, had exceptional charms. It was a quaint and picturesque fishing village, far away from the world. There was scarcely a house or cottage in the place which was not old, there was an ancient inn which was as solidly comfortable as it was decidedly antique. The surrounding coast scenery was romantic, and the bride and bridegroom were enthusiastic amateur artists. And last, and best of all, right opposite Barthwick across a stretch of brown sand and gleaming water, lay St. Morkil's Isle, a great, gaunt mass of dark rock and grey cliff, on the extreme summit of which stood the ruins of an ancient religious house. Ever since he had first seen it, Geoffrey had been crazy to cross those sands and explore that island; he was all the more attracted to it because of the mysterious solitude which hung about its hoary headlands and surf-swept inlets. No human life was on that island; for many a century it had been given up to the sea-birds which tenanted it in thousands. Of it, the Barthwick folk told strange eerie stories; it was said to be haunted; there were tales of a headless monk, and of a dead viking, and of a golden-haired princess who wailed and sobbed amidst the ruins. If any of the Barthwick people had occasion to cross the sands to the island, or put in at it with their boats, they took care never to remain on its shores after twilight fell athwart the sea. All of which naturally made Geoffrey Hallam, in whom the spirit of adventure was strong, all the keener to explore St. Morkil's Isle from end to end, so that he might see what manner of spot it was which stirred up such feelings in the folk who looked out on its romantic shape whenever they set foot over the threshold or cast glance through window.

On the second evening after their arrival at Barthwick, the bride and bridegroom, hand in hand, stood on the beach a little way outside the village and looked across at the mysterious island. They had been looking at it a hundred times during that day, but it had never seemed so fascinating or appealing as in that hour of twilight and silence. The sun, a vast red globe, had just sunk beyond the far rim of a waveless sea; the western heavens were a mass of crimson and gold; against these vivid colourings the ruins on the peak of St. Morkil's Isle showed like black silhouettes; the island itself looked like a couchant lion, lifting its head in proud defiance. It was low tide just then; between mainland and island stretched a great waste of brown and yellow sand, with here and there a patch of water that gleamed blood-red in the sunset lights.

The whole scene was one to gaze at in silence, but Geoffrey Hallam suddenly spoke.

"We'll go across there to-morrow morning," he said. "We'll have a lunch basket packed, and we'll put in the whole day. I'll carry the basket and you can carry the sketch things. If we don't find something there that's out of the common, I'm a Dutchman!"

"If we could only paint it as it is now," said the bride.

"Too stiff for us—yet, anyway," answered Geoffrey. "We'll have to be content with same daylight effects. Look here, I'll show you how we go. Do you see that line of poles standing up at intervals across the sands?"

He half twisted his wife round and showed her where at the further end of the beach, a little way outside the extreme edge of the village, a line of tall, age-blackened timbers, planted firmly on the sands, began, continuing at intervals across the sands, until they reached the island two miles away.

"Those," said Geoffrey, "are guide posts to show you the path across. You notice they don't go in a dead straight line—they turn off at various angles here and there. We've got to keep close to those posts all the way over for fear of quicksands. Keep within a dozen yards of 'em, on either side, so the fishermen say, and one's all right. And if the tide should come up rather too suddenly one climbs up those refuges. See them? Two of them between here and the island; look like two platforms or pulpits, high up on stout timbers, and reached by ladders. If the tide should catch you, you climb up and wait till it goes down again."

"That would mean several hours," remarked Kitty. "A sad waste of time!"

"We'll be all right," answered Geoffrey. "It'll be low tide in the morning from 9 o'clock onwards. But we'll have to spend the whole day there until it's low tide again at night."

Then they both laughed, the same thought coming into the mind of each—it mattered little how many hours, or days, or months they spent on a deserted island, as long as they were together.

"And, of course, if we have plenty of food with us," said Geoffrey, adding a necessary word or two to the mutual thought. "But leave that to me, I'll see to the catering."

Next morning, then, saw these two blithely setting out across the sands, still wet and gleaming. And before long they made two discoveries—one, that the reputed two miles proved to be more like three; the other, that firm as the sands were on either side of the guide posts, it was more than once necessary to take off shoes and stockings and to wade through intervening channels in which the sea ran knee high. This tended to delay, and it was already past noon when they finally reached the island, climbed the headlands by a narrow path, and came to the ancient ruins.

"Lunch first and exploration second," declared Geoffrey, unslinging his knapsack in a shaded corner of what had once been part of the cloisters. "That tug over the sands has made me hungry. Let's unpack the things and eat what we want; we'd better leave one-half, though, for later in the afternoon, because we'll never get back before very late in the evening. I wish now——"

"What?" asked Kitty after a long pause, during which Geoffrey, mounting a mass of fallen masonry, made an inspection of their surroundings. "What do you wish?"

"I wish I'd arranged for a boat to fetch us at sundown," he answered. "I'm a bit of an ass after all! Of course, the turn of the tide'll be an hour later tonight Kitty, we'll never land back before 11 at the soonest!"

"Does it matter?" asked Kitty, who was unpacking the materials for lunch. "Even then it won't be quite dark, and as long as we can see those posts we shall be all right."

"I'm thinking about the people at the inn," replied Geoffrey. "I didn't tell the landlady where we were off to, and as everybody goes to bed at 10 o'clock in Barthwick, they'll think something's happened. However, it can't be helped now; and as long as you don't get tired——"

Kitty laughed carelessly. She was a strong and vigorous young woman of twenty and her notions of fatigue were vague.

"I shan't get tired," she answered. "What a lot they've given us to eat! and you've brought two thermos flasks. Why two?"

"We'll want 'em before night," said Geoffrey. "You'll see. I've been at this game before. Can't have too much with you when you don't exactly know what's before you. Now we'll eat and drink, and then, first thing, we'll have a look round these ruins. After that we'll try a sketch or two."

But there was to be no sketching that day.

CHAPTER II

WITH a mouthful of beef sandwich, eyes fixed lazily on the distant shore, where the red roofs and yellow walls of Barthwick glinted gaily in the June sunlight, and a mind entirely given up to the happiness of his present situation, Geoffrey Hallam had no thought of anything but the mere moment. And, therefore, he started a little nervously when his wife suddenly, but very quietly slipped her hand across to his wrist and whispered five significant words.

"Geoffrey," she said, "don't move! We're watched!"

Geoffrey had sufficient presence of mind to remain perfectly quiet. He went on munching, finished his mouthful and whispered back:

"Watched?" he said. "By whom? Where from? Anything suspicious?"

"Keep quiet; behave as if nothing was out of the common," murmured Kitty. "I saw a face just now at one of those holes in the wall just behind your left shoulder. A man—bearded, handsome, foreign looking, a cruel face. He didn't see me—I mean, he didn't see that I saw him; he was turning his face aside just then. I say, what shall we do?"

"Take no notice and go on with your lunch," counselled Geoffrey. "I daresay it's some tourist. Odd, though. We'll look round presently. Besides, what is there to be afraid of?"

Kitty shook her head,

"I don't know, but he has such strange, sinister eyes," she answered. "And this is about as lonely a place as one can imagine, isn't it? What are you going to do?"

Geoffrey had risen and was ostentatiously brushing crumbs from his garments. He gave his wife a meaning wink.

"Well, I'm going to prospect," he said in loud tones. "Put the things together, Kitty, while I see how the land lies, and then we'll get a move on."

He strolled away into the ruins of the old abbey, carelessly, saunteringly, looked up and down, round and about, went along one way, came back another, filling his pipe as if he had no thought in the world but the immediate enjoyment of tobacco.

"I see nothing and nobody," he announced. "You're sure?"

"Certain," replied Kitty. "And if there's no one there now, that makes it all the stranger."

"Let's leave the things here, on that ledge, and have another look round," said Geoffrey. "It certainly isn't a nice feeling to be cooped up on a desert island with people who suddenly appear and suddenly vanish. Come along outside the ruins to the point of that promontory."

He led his wife along a sharp spur of land which jutted out into the open sea, on the side of the island opposite to that which faced the mainland. And there, at the very edge of the cliff, both stopped surprised. Far down beneath them, in a little cove almost entirely shut in and hidden by the sea, by high curving cliffs, was a small rakish-looking steam yacht, on the sides of which men were as busy as bees. Kitty's untrained eyes failed to see the reason of their evident feverish industry, but Geoffrey, who had more experience of the world, started and exclaimed.

"By Gad!" he said. "Changing her colour! Do you see, those chaps are painting that craft sea-grey!"

Then Kitty noticed that one half of the graceful hull of the yacht gleamed white in the sun, the other was already of that nondescript tint which is usually associated with war craft.

"And—does that mean anything?" she asked.

"May mean nothing—may mean much," replied Geoffrey. "But look how rapidly they're working! You can almost see the thing being transformed before your eyes. Rather an odd thing for such a small craft as that to be run into a quiet harbourage like this, and changed from white and gold to a mere nondescript colour. And what a beautiful bit of stuff she is. Look at her lines. Heavens, I guess that yacht can do her twenty-six or seven knots an hour; she'll simply cut through the water. Of course, that chap you saw just now has something to do with her, but——"

He paused as Kitty suddenly clasped his arm. Her ears, quicker than his, had caught the sound of advancing footsteps. And the next instant three men came round the corner of the little headland beneath which she and her husband stood, one man walking a little in advance of the others. Kitty's grasp tightened on Geoffrey's sleeve.

"He's here," she whispered.

Geoffrey turned sharply to confront the mysterious stranger and his attendants. He was naturally quick to notice little details, and he saw at once that the two men who walked behind were foreigners of some nationality which he could not make out; he also saw that they carried revolvers strapped round their waists. So, too, did ther leader, a tall, bearded, handsome man, apparently of middle age, clad in irreproachable yachting costume, in whose steel-grey eyes, cold and resolute, Geoffrey was quick to see the cruel and sinister look of which Kitty had spoken. Unconsciously, he drew his wife a little close to him; unconsciously Kitty responded to the movement; together they turned inquiring looks on the stranger. And the stranger, never relaxing the cold, fixed gaze which had fastened on them at once, raised a bronzed hand and lifted his cap with studied politeness.

"You are looking at my yacht, sir," he said, calmly.

"A very beautiful one," answered Geoffrey. He

was already certain that here was some adventure which was out of the ordinary, and he endeavoured to keep cool and self-possessed. "Very fine lines. I was just remarking to my wife——"

"It is an unfortunate thing that you should have seen her," said the other, interrupting him without ceremony. "It is not convenient to me that she should be seen—here. You must excuse me if I ask you a few questions. You and your wife—your pardon, madame—are you all alone on this island, or are you merely two of some excursion or picnic party?"

Geoffrey's face flushed. Like all good young English men, he objected to being questioned, especially in this dictatorial manner, and his voice unconsciously showed his distaste.

"Really," he said, "I don't know why I should be asked such questions by a stranger, sir. But since you seem to attach some importance to it, I'll reply. We are alone. And we will bid you good-day."

But the tall man and his satellites barred the path, and the cold eyes grew colder and sterner.

"I am sorry that is scarcely possible," said the hard voice, "It is a pity, but you see you have hit on what I intended to be a secret. I know this island and this coast, and both are, as a rule, so deserted and lonely, and that little cove down there is so well hidden, that I thought I could come in and go away unobserved. As you are here I must trouble you to answer more questions."

Geoffrey's face grew hotter than ever, and his eyes flashed resentment.

"By what right——" he began fiercely.

"Geoffrey," whispered Kitty, "answer him, it will be far the best."

"Madame is right," said the imperious one. "It

will be far the best. Besides, you must answer my questions. You observe I have force on my side."

He pointed meaningly at his followers, and Geoffrey's colour changed from red to white, more from indignation than fear.

"What!" he exclaimed. "You threaten force to a woman and a defenceless man! That is——"

"Pooh!" said the other, sneeringly. "Mere words. My good sir, rather than have the venture on which I am engaged go wrong, I would cheerfully shoot you both! I can't stick at trifles. Now be sensible and answer my questions. I assure you it will be for the best. Who are you?"

"A London man staying for a while in the village across there," replied Geoffrey unwillingly.

"And you simply came across the sands to explore the island?" asked the questioner.

"Simply that!"

"Walked across the sands?"

"We walked across the sands."

"And you return—when and how?"

"We shall have to return the same way, and we can't until low tide—that will be between eight and nine o'clock this evening," muttered Geoffrey. "And what has all that to do with you?"

"It has everything to do with me, unfortunately," answered the other. "Well, I am obliged to you for answering my questions. But I shall have to detain you until to-morrow morning. You can't return until the tide is out, at nearly noon to-morrow. By that time I shall have had twelve hours start of you. I regret your inconvenience, but it cannot be helped."

"You mean to make us prisoners?" demanded Geoffrey. "It's an outrage!"

"It is—I agree with you. But it's got to be done.

The truth is—you see how frank I am with you?—I am a sort of modern pirate in a biggish way of business—that's the plain facts—and I have a very particular reason for wanting to get away unobserved. Now, I might ask you to give me your word of honour that you won't mention the fact of having seen me, and from what I see of you both, I dare say—nay, I am sure—you'd keep it. But the simple truth is, I dare not take the risk. I must be sure of things. And so, lest you should say what you have seen as soon as you get back to the mainland and before I am safely away, I've got to detain you until to-morrow morning's tide—just got to! No harm shall come to you. If you want food, you shall have the best we can send up from the yacht, but stay you must!"

"Of course we shall want food!" exclaimed Geoffrey angrily. "And you may send it up! You're not going to take us down there, then? And if not, where are we to be put? The whole thing is shameful, and—"

"It's no use exciting yourself," interrupted the self-constituted jailer. "These things have to be. I know this place very well; in fact, I've made considerable use of it in my time, for my irregular proceedings, and I've often hidden valuable property in these ruins, though, of course, now that you've found out the secret, I can never come here again. See how good I am to you; I could easily shoot both of you, and nobody would ever be any the wiser! But part of these ruins—the old tower of the gateway—is still habitable, and I propose to lock you up in there."

"Now?" demanded Geoffrey.

"Precisely!" said the other, with the first approach to a smile. "I daren't take the risk of having you roaming about. Please to come with me and this man; the other I will send down to the yacht for rugs, cushions, food and drink—cigars, too. You see how well I treat you?"

Geoffrey shook his head angrily, and made some inarticulate answer. The captor paid no attention. He pulled out a pocketbook and was scribbling in it; presently he tore out a page, gave it to one of his attendants, said a few words to him in a language which neither Geoffrey nor his wife had ever heard, and motioned him to go. Then he signed the two prisoners to march toward the old tower.

"You will like to pick up your belongings," he said, not unkindly. "I took the liberty of inspecting them when you strolled off, and I see you have materials for water-colour sketching. So you can pass your time in painting—you know—you'll get excellent views from the windows of the tower. And as 'tis summer you won't be subjected to any privation at night, the rugs and things I've sent for will keep you quite warm. Neither will you be strict prisoners after, say, midnight. We hope to get away by that time, and just before we go, the tower shall be unlocked. Then, when the tide's down again, to-morrow morning, you can depart. Really, I don't think I could be much more considerate. And if you knew what I have at stake—well, I think you'd agree with me that I couldn't do less than I am doing!"

Ten minutes later Geoffrey and his wife found themselves prisoners. An hour later the door of their prison was opened to admit their captor and the man whom he had sent to the yacht, the latter laden with rugs, cushions and a big basket of provisions. The self-accused pirate permitted himself to smile for the second time as the man set down his burdens.

"You see how thoughtful I am for your comfort," he said, and his eyes twinkled for a little as he glanced at Kitty. "I reflected that you could not paint without clear water; here is a bottle of the pure element. Now I leave you. Your door will be unlocked about 11 o'clock to-night. By the by, you can send a man over in a boat for those rugs and cushions. I make you a present of them."

Then, with a formal bow, he vanished, and the door was closed and locked.

CHAPTER III

THE bride and bridegroom, once safely incarcerated, turned to each other with inquiring looks. Then Geoffrey dug his hands into his pockets, stamped his foot and let loose one emphatic word.

"Damn!"

"Just so," agreed Kitty. "But then, Geoffrey, just think! It might have been so much worse. Geoffrey, I am certain that for quite a full minute that man had it in his mind to shoot us! And he didn't, and here we are together, and alive; and, after all, it's only for a few hours. Oh, it might have been infinitely worse!"

But Geoffrey was just then not inclined to consider comparative cases; he was fuming at the indignity of his position. To be deprived of your liberty, to be ordered about, to be treated as if you were a convict, especially when you have just attained the status of a full-blown married man——.

"Hang the fellow!" he exclaimed. "I wonder who he is, and what he's after? No good, of course. Sort of modern pirate, he called himself. Pirate indeed! As if there were such things nowadays! Plain thief, I should say. I guess I know what it is, Kitty. To use vulgar parlance, he's some fellow who's pinched that yacht, and now he's repainting her so that her own grandmother wouldn't know her! That's about it. You wouldn't notice, but I did—they were not only daubing grey paint on her beautiful white and gold sides, they were changing her rig. He's a thief, that chap."

"Thank heaven he isn't a murderer—of us!" said Kitty. She was already busying herself with the rugs and cushions and making their place of imprisonment habitable. "We might both be lying with our brains blown out and our toes turned up," she went on. "Instead of which we are quite alive and fairly comfortable. And there's a beautiful view from that window, Geoffrey. Look at it!"

Geoffrey looked up from the floor and glanced around him. They were in an ancient chamber at the very top of the tower, a chamber of bare walls of undressed stone. The floor was of cement, and the roof of dark timber; there was no fireplace and no furniture. But on one side of the room there was a recess going deep into the thick masonry of the wall, and in this was a long seat or couch of stone, on which Kitty had already arranged the rugs and cushions. Also, in one corner stood an old barrel or two and two or three ancient chests—these things, at any rate, would serve as chairs and tables, and Geoffrey began to move them to the window. In that window there was no glass, nor any sign that there ever had been any glass—it was merely a wide slit in the masonry, divided into two parts by a thick, much weather-beaten mullion of stone. From either side of this mullion husband and wife looked out on the island and the sea beyond. And all that they saw was literally island and sea. On the island itself there was not a human being in sight; on the sea there was not so much as the red sail of a fishing lugger. Of the mainland, they could, of course, see nothing, having their backs to it and no outlook in its direction. Up in that tower, perched high above the old ruins, the wind-swept, deserted headlands, the glittering, smooth, sailless sea, they were indeed in solitude, and each mutually recognised it.

"Geoffrey," said Kitty suddenly, "do you think this is how people feel when they're stuck in prison?"

"Bit of the same feeling, I should think," replied Geoffey laconically. "Sort of shut off from all and sundry, however close they may be. He's a clever chap, that thief man, you know. Do you see, we can't get a glimpse of that little cove and the yacht from here? And did you notice how that cove is hidden from the sea outside its mouth? I did—rather! You come into that cove from a narrow inlet, take a turn to your right in evidently deep water, and there you are! A hundred ships could steam or sail past this island and never know there was a vessel hidden in that cove. Clever gentleman! And I'd like to know who's yacht it is that he's stolen—for, of course, that's the whole explanation. I wonder, now," he went on, rubbing the tip of his nose—"I wonder what nationality that man is and what language it was that he used to those hard-bitten desperadoes who were with him? It was no European language, anyhow."

"I couldn't make head or tail of it, unless it's one of the South American Latin dialects—mixture of debased Latin and Portuguese," answered Kitty, who was a bit of a scholar. "But as for our pirate, I am very certain what he is."

"What, then?" demanded Geoffrey.

"A Brazilian who's knocked about the world a lot," answered Kitty. "I recognised his peculiarly cultured accent. Well, anyway, he's a polite pirate, and he's left us plenty to eat and drink, and he didn't forget such a little thing as the painting water. Geoffrey, I'm going to paint. Why don't you smoke one of the piratical cigars and do likewise?"

Geoffrey muttered something like a curse on the pirate and the cigars; he refilled his pipe, and continued to lean out of the window, staring at the sea, while his wife, much more philosophic and amenable to circumstances, settled down on one of the old chests and began to amuse herself with her brushes and colours. In her own secret and silent opinion there was little to grumble at, but Geoffrey, man-like, continued to chafe and murmur as he leaned out of their prison window.

"I'd give a lot to know what that chap's been up to—in strict reality," he said presently. "He's taking no risks anyway. Look here, he's posted a couple of sentries on points above that cove, where they can see on all sides of 'em!"

"What are they for?" she asked. "Is it to make sure that we can't escape?"

"Not a bit of it! We're safe enough!" growled Geoffrey. "It's to keep an eye on the land approach in our direction, and on the sea in all the other directions. I tell you, he's taking no risk. Now, if only——"

"If only what?" asked Kitty as he paused with a grim laugh.

"If only something in the shape of a lively piece of the British navy would come nosing round!" he answered. "Something with an inquisitive young commander and a business-like crew. Then we might see some fun. As it is I guess we'll stop here like rats in a cage, to be let out when the cynical devil pleases, and go home like a couple of whipped dogs while he sails off laughing at us!"

The afternoon wore on towards evening. Kitty remained placidly at work; Geoffrey alternately strode about the chamber, grumbling, or leaned out of the window, watching. And just as his wife was suggesting that they had better prepare an impromptu supper he started into excited activity.

"Kitty! Kitty! he shouted, "there's a ship! Come here, quick!"

Kitty leaned out of her half of the window staring in the direction which Geoffrey indicated wtih a trembling finger. Far away on the northwestern horizon she saw a wisp of smoke which was rapidly growing bigger and bigger. And even as she looked she saw a second and a third come up upon the dividing line of sea and sky, each increasing in size with every second.

"There's another and another!" cried Geoffrey. Three of 'em, all in a line, a mile or two apart and coming at a rare lick! Gad! What if they're after his lordship in the cove? For I don't know what they are—there's nothing else in the world can come along at the rate they're coming!"

"What, then?" asked Kitty.

"Destroyers!" said Geoffrey, with a grim smile. "Torpedo boat destroyers, my dear! There's nothing else could make that speed. Get the glasses out of the knapsack. Gad! What fun if they are really seeking that fellow! If only we could signal to them!"

Through Geoffrey's binoculars they soon made out the long, low hulls, the pugnacious-looking funnels of the three craft, from whose bows the sea was tearing away in white masses of foam and spray. Certainly they were coming along at a furious rate, as if in a great hurry to get somewhere and do something, and for a while husband and wife watched them in sheer fascination. Then Geoffrey groaned heavily.

"If we'd only a heliograph!" he said. "I know the trick of it! Then I could signal to those chaps. That nearest one, if it keeps its present line, will pass within a couple of miles. If we'd even a hand mirror!"

"Yes, and then our pirates would come up and put a bullet through our heads," remarked Kitty. "The passive spectator part is best for us, Geoffrey."

"Our pirate'll have something else to think about than us if one of those snaky things comes smelling around here," answered Geoffrey. "I guess he's aware of 'em now. Look at that sentry!"

The man posted on the knoll above the cove was making signals with a flag to the yacht far down beneath him. And before very long the two prisoners saw the tall, agile figure of their captor springing up the sides of the promonotory to join his outlook. They saw him unsling and adjust a telescope, and take a long look at the three destroyers; then he evidently gave some order to the sentry and went away. And the sentry dropped to a recumbent position, wriggled behind a pile of stones, and looked out over the sea, himself unseen.

"Look at the ships!" exclaimed Kitty. "They're spreading out!"

Geoffrey, who had kept his eyes on the pirate and the sentry, turned sharply. Certainly the destroyers were parting company. One, the furthest away, twisted in her course and went off to the southwest; the one in the middle kept straight ahead, the nearest one came direct for the island. And she was near enough now for Geoffrey to see through his binoculars that a keen lookout was being kept on her—from her bows, her bridge, her stern, glasses were being trained, and sharp eyes bent on every nook and cranny of the coast.

"She's seeking him!" declared Geoffrey with solemn emphasis. "Kitty, my girl, we're going to be in it. If we could only manage to signal to those chaps on the destroyers! Anyway, we can wave something out of the window."

"Wait," said Kitty. "If she's searching she will search. Wait, Geoffrey. Our part is to look on. And haven't we the stage box for this performance?"

Geoffrey almost danced with excitement as the destroyer came tearing along until she was abreast of the northern edge of St. Morkil's Isle. Suddenly she slackened speed and began to creep warily nearer and nearer to the shore. They could see right on to her narrow decks by that time, and as she came opposite the ruins Geoffrey's sharp eyes saw one of the officers on the bridge turn his glasses on their prison. And at that he threw all prudence to the winds, and snatching up a big white cloth which Kitty had just taken out of the provision basket, he waved frantically.

"Now you've done it, Geoffrey," said Kitty. "Those sentries will see that, and, of course, their master will come up and shoot us. Very well, let us have something to eat and drink before he comes."

Geoffrey laughed excitedly—not at his wife's humour but at something he had seen. The two sentries, both aware that the destroyer was now under the headlands scouting around the island, had risen to their feet and were running for the cove as fast as their legs could carry them. A moment later he laughed again. The destroyer's bows had come level with the narrow inlet of the cove, and the sharp crack of a light gun rang out across the sea, woke the thousand echoes of the cliffs, and sent thousands of sea birds circling wildly into the air.

"That's to call the other boats back," exclaimed Geoffrey. "The pirate's discovered. Look! This destroyer's stopping."

The long, low, black hull of the destroyer was motionless now. She had pulled up a little to the southward of the inlet and not more than half a mile from it, and Geoffrey knew that from where she lay her officers and men could see right into the cove. He could see, too, that, while one group was busily training a gun on the yacht, other groups were making two boats ready.

"They're going to board her!" he shouted, beating his fist impatiently on the mullion of the window. "Hanged if I don't believe they're going to fire on her first. There!"

A mighty bang suddenly rent the air and made Kitty clap her hands to her ears. Woman-like, she immediately thought of the damage to the fairy-like craft whose owner had made her prisoner.

"Oh, what a pity to fire on such a beautiful yacht!" she exclaimed. "Do you think they hit her, Geoffrey?"

"Pooh! That was merely to call her attention," answered Geoffrey, with lofty superiority. "They just fired to let her see that she'd got something to deal with that wouldn't stand any nonsense. Look! There's a couple of boats' crews coming into the cove. By Gad, I'd give a year's income to force that door and get out of this place! We shall miss all the fun. If only we could look down into the cove!"

He went over to the door and began to shake and rattle it, cursing its ancient timbers, which were as firm as when cut from some inland oak wood 500 years before. But Kitty continued to watch, and suddenly she screamed:

"Geoffrey! Geoffrey! The pirate! He's running away. Look!"

Geoffrey hurried to the window. Then he saw that, however bold and daring their captor might be in some matters, he had certainly no desire to face the business-like quality of a destroyer's boat crew. He had come up from the cove at the point where he had accosted Geoffrey and his wife and was now making his way at a rapid pace across the island, taking advantage of every bit of cover. And Geoffrey stared and at last laughed.

"Trapped," he said. "He's making for the path across the sands. And it won't be low tide for a couple of hours yet, and even then— Oh, Kitty, I do hope those chaps will come up here and let us out, so that we can have a look at things! It's beastly to be on the fringe of an adventure like this and not to get right into it."

But a good hour elapsed before their eager eyes saw a party of bluejackets, headed by an active and keen-looking young officer, emerge from the cove, look about with all its eyes, and then make for the ruins. It was well into twilight then, and the prisoners made violent use of their voices and the white cloth.

"They've seen us—they're coming!" sighed Kitty at last. "Geoffrey, promise you won't go trying to take the pirate."

"Promise nothing," retorted Geoffrey. "Let me get a chance at him, that's all! Hi—hi—hi!" he yelled at the advancing search party. "Hi! I say, come and let us out! Come on—quick! I've got something to tell you!"

The young officer hastened ahead and came up to the foot of the tower. He stared at Kitty and lifted his hand to his cap.

"Prisoners?" he asked laconically. "That man on the yacht locked you up there?"

"Hit it in once," replied Geoffrey. "And I don't know if he's left the key in the door, either. I say, send your men up to break the door in and let us out, then I'll tell you where the fellow is."

Three minutes later two excited young people stared into the calm and imperturable face of a boyish-looking person, who combined the dignity of an admiral with the concealed eagerness of a midshipman.

"See here!" exclaimed Geoffrey. "That chap who locked us up was a pirate, he told us so this afternoon. When your ship came he hooked it from his yacht and made tracks across the island. He's wanting the path over the sands to Barthwick there, on the mainland, and he can't get it till the tide's out, so he'll be hiding somewhere down here amongst the rocks. Come on! Come on! Let's go ferret him out! I've got an account to settle with him, though I don't know what you want him for."

The naval officer who had stared at Kitty with his eyes while he had kept his ears fully open, grinned widely.

"That's easy told," he said. "He is a pirate right enough, this chap, and a good 'un. Don't know if you ever heard of the Rajah of Bongolore? A big Indian potentate. Salute of 30 guns, don't you know, and that sort of thing. Well, he's scooting around a lot just now in this private yacht and this last fortnight has been on his way from New York to Liverpool. This pirate chap—heaven knows who he is!—ran up against the Rajah off the Mull of Galloway during last night, boarded him, robbed his highness of all his jewels, smashed his machinery so that his yacht couldn't move, and hooked it in the darkness. We came across the Rajah some hours after, drifting about, and so, of course, we stepped it lively after his pirateship. Made for these sands, you say, alone?"

"Alone! Come on," repeated Geoffrey. "Come on! I tell you he can't get away! Those sands are impassable until low tide, and there are no boats. He'll be lurking in some cave or hole down there. All right, Kitty, don't be afraid. I'm not going to get shot or anything, but I'm going to be in at the death!"

Guided by Geoffrey the naval men hurried down to the beach which faced Barthwick. And suddenly one man shouted and pointed. Then all stood and stared, and Geoffrey Hallam turned and exchanged a glance with his wife, who had kept up with the pursuers as eager as any of them. For they alone of all there knew the secret of those sands, and they saw that the pirate was hurrying to destruction. He had already started out, though the tide was still running a foot high, and, instead of keeping the zig-zag course of the posts, he was going straight across, occasionally leaving the posts well to the right or left of him. And in spite of the fact that the man was already a good half-mile away, Geoffrey lifted his hands to his mouth and shouted, shouted as if he would split his lungs in the effort.

"Keep to the posts," he roared. "You fool! Keep to the posts!"

But the warning, even if heard, was too late. As Geoffrey's last word was yelled to the light wind, Kitty Hallam screamed. For the tall figure suddenly swayed in the swirling waters, threw up his arms, fought with something, clutched at nothing, and disappeared. One second it was there, the next there was nothing but the tide running softly out, between the tall, black timbers. And Geoffrey drew his wife's arm within his own, and turned quickly to the astonished naval man.

"Quicksands," he said. "This channel's full of 'em. If you don't keep close to those posts you're a gone man. He's gone, anyway."

The youthful lieutenant shook his head.

"By jove, yes," he said quietly. "Poor beggar! And, I say, you know, the Rajah's jewels have gone with him!"

X: EXTRA-JUDICIAL

CHAPTER I

THIS was the first time that the judge, recently raised to the Bench, had ever pronounced the death sentence, and his voice trembled a little as he came to the final words. But he spoke them at last, and his accents became firmer as he added their complement.

". . . And may the Lord have mercy upon your soul."

"Amen!" said the chaplain, in a faint whisper.

The man in the dock, who had never taken his eyes off the judge during the couple of minutes during which the black square had rested on the grey wig, suddenly smiled—a cynical, half sneering smile. And, shrugging his shoulders as the warders on either side touched his elbows, he spoke—his voice as hard and steady as the judge's had been uncertain and faltering.

"If I get no better mercy from them above than I've had from them below I shall do badly!" he said. "However, there's none of you'll know what chances up yonder. Damn the lot of you!"

Then, with a harsh laugh that grated badly on at least one set of nerves, he turned and disappeared, and the judge, who had already risen from his seat, disappeared, too, behind the heavy curtains over which hung the insignia of Justice. He went slowly to his room and the high sheriff went with him, zealous in the performance of the duties of his office. A pompous and punctilious man, he shook his head as he and the judge looked at each other.

"A hardened sinner—a bad fellow!" said the high sheriff solemnly. "Sad—very sad, to hear such sentiments on such an occasion."

The judge took off his wig with a sigh of weariness. "I'm not at all satisfied about that case," he remarked. "Not at all!"

The high sheriff started. He himself was very well satisfied; in his opinion, the case had ended very properly.

"Not—satisfied?" he exclaimed. "I—ahem!— the evidence——"

"On the evidence," said the judge, quietly, "the jury could not possibly have found any other verdict, and the trial could not have come to any other end. But—I am not at all sure, in my own mind, that this unfortunate fellow is guilty."

"Dear me!" said the high sheriff. "Um! Oh, well, of course, I suppose we all have——"

"Our secret impressions!" broke in the judge, with a sly smile. "Just so. And, you see, that happens to be mine. In spite of—what has just happened—I am not satisfied. Judicially, of course, I am. But——"

"Oh, quite so, quite so!" said the high sheriff, who was not a brilliant man, and who called black black and white white. "I understand. But, of course, such things happen."

The judge slowly took off his robes and looked at his marshal with a whimsical smile.

"They happen," he said—"yes, they happen."

Then he began to talk of something else; and presently he drove away in state to the judge's lodgings outside the little town, and the high sheriff was glad to see the last of him for that day. Mr. Justice Machin had had a reputation for slight eccentricity and whimsicality before his elevation from bar to bench, and, in the high sheriff's opinion, he was bidding fair to deepen it.

"Not guilty, indeed!" mused the high sheriff, as he himself drove off to his country-seat. "God bless my soul! Why, the case was as plain as a pikestaff. Never heard clearer evidence in my life—Machin himself said so."

Mr. Justice Machin had certainly said so in his summing-up of the case, and his reminder to the jury that the evidence before them was purely circumstantial had not influenced them on the prisoner's behalf. Everything pointed to the prisoner's guilt, and as the judge slowly dressed for dinner that night he once more reviewed the whole testimony, point by point, and he knew that no conscientious jury could have arrived at any other conclusion. And yet——

"And after all," mused Mr. Justice Machin—"after all, there is such a thing as intuition. I suppose I possess a certain share of it, and my intuition, whatever it's worth, tells me that the poor fellow is innocent. Innocent! Yet found guilty on the strongest circumstantial evidence!"

For the evidence in what was known as the Muirdale case was strong enough. It was a somewhat sordid tragedy of primitive passions. In Muirdale, a lonely, far-away valley amongst the wild hills that shut in that side of the country in which Mr. Justice Machin was then holding the Spring Assize, two men, young farmers, were in love with the same girl, and the sad fact that one of them was now lying in a murdered man's grave, and the other sitting in his cell, awaiting execution for the murder, was largely due to another fact no less certain—that the girl had played fast and loose with each in turn. The mere details of the case, which had seemed so plain to the high sheriff—a good representative of popular opinion—were few. Michael Cruddas, a well-to-do young farmer, of Muirdale, cultivating his own land, had been engaged to the daughter of a neighbour, Avice Thormthwaite, who evidently had a reputation as the beauty of the district. Suddenly the engagement was broken off, and the girl immediately entered into another with James Garth, tenant of an adjacent farm. Michael Cruddas, undoubtedly a man of violent and ungovernable passions, had suspected Garth of underhand work, and, after a fierce quarrel with him at Highland Market, had publicly threatened to shoot him. Early next morning a shepherd, setting out across the hills from Muirdale, had found Garth's dead body lying in a lonely place near Michael Cruddas's farm, with half the head blown off. He had been dead some hours and had presumably been shot as he made his way home from market—shot, too, at close quarters. And close by the cottage was a cartridge which was new and had evidently been withdrawn from a fowling-piece as soon as it had been fired. Here had occurred a damning piece of evidence—Michael Cruddas was the only man in the neighbourhood who used that particular make of cartridge, and an examination of his gun by the police on the morning after the murder showed that it had been very recently discharged.

Considering the circumstances, and the savage threat made, said the witnesses, in apparent dead earnest, there seemed to be no reasonable doubt that Cruddas had been so obsessed by his passion for vengeance that, regardless of consequences, he had lain in wait for his successful rival and killed him.

But Michael Cruddas, promptly arrested, immediately declared his innocence. He said then what he afterwards said before the magistrates and at his trial.

He had certainly threatened to shoot Garth, and he meant to shoot him if he came across him. But he had not shot him. Confronted with the facts of the cartridge, of the recently-discharged gun, and the clear proof that no other gun in this district—a very thinly-populated one—could be used for such a cartridge, he merely replied that he knew nothing about the affair. He had returned from market somewhat the worse for drink; he had drunk heavily in his own house, and had gone to bed drunk. Of that night he remembered no more than that. But out of this the prosecution made much; Michael Cruddas, it urged, had been drunk when he shot James Garth in the lonely lane near his farm; he had gone home and drunk more; drunk so much, in fact, that his mind had become a blank. And, in the opinion of everybody in court, this theory was a correct one. No one doubted that Michael Cruddas was a murderer.

Nevertheless, Mr. Justice Machin doubted whether, in this case, justice was being done. He was unable to account to himself for his notions—they were vague, formless, but they were there. Something in the accused man's bitter, cynical, almost indifferent conduct in dock and witness-box had impressed him—the last remark, made with the death sentence still ringing in his ears, had convinced him that there was an element in the Muirdale case which so far had escaped notice. And late that night, as he smoked a last cigar in company with the smart young barrister—his nephew—who acted as his marshal, Mr. Justice Machin suddenly clenched a resolution that had been slowly forming.

"We shall finish all the business by noon to-morrow," he observed. "And we shall get away by an early afternoon train. And as I have no further duties for a week I am going—somewhere. The fact is I am going—keep the fact to yourself—to Muirdale."

The young man on the other side of the hearth glanced quickly at the keen face and watchful eyes.

"Muirdale!" he exclaimed. "The place of the murder?"

"Just so," replied Mr. Justice Machin. "The truth is—though I don't want it talked about—I am not satisfied about that case, and I propose to perform a little extra-judicial work upon it. I am going to Muirdale to have a look around."

"You'll be spotted—known," pointed out the marshal.

"I think not," said the judge. "If you remember, there were very few witnesses and persons concerned. Muirdale is one of the loneliest valleys in the North, I understand. Also I hear you can get a little fishing there. I shall put on an old tweed suit and take my rod. I don't think that the people who only saw me in court will recognise me in shabby mufti. Anyway, I am going."

When Mr. Justice Machin said he was going to do anything those who knew him best were well aware that he would do it, and his companion accordingly made no comment beyond remarking that the proposed excursion was rather unusual.

"I said I proposed to do a little extra-judicial work," answered the judge, with a dry smile. "I am not going to Muirdale in a professional capacity, but as, say, Mr. Maxwell, a quiet, elderly gentleman who wishes for a few days' rest amongst the hills. If anybody in the shape of, perhaps, police, recognises me—well, I dare say a quiet word will ensure silence,"

Then Mr. Justice Machin threw away his cigar and

went to bed, and before retiring he packed a knapsack and laid a fishing-rod at its side, and as he glanced at himself in the mirror he smiled to think what a difference a judge's wig and stately robes can make to a pleasant-faced, rather country-squire-looking gentleman.

"I don't believe anybody will know me from Adam!" he mused.

CHAPTER II

AT a late hour of the following afternoon an elderly gentleman in a well-worn suit of grey tweed, whose shoulders supported a small knapsack and whose left hand carried a fishing-rod, came to the head of a winding pass which zigzagged up a heath-clad hillside, and, pausing, looked down into a valley which lay, lost amongst the hills, far beneath him. And he laughed gently, but cynically, as he looked at the narrow streak of winding stream, the tiny spire of a little church, the cluster of stone-roofed cottages about a grey bridge, the sparsely dotted farmsteads on the hillsides and in the ravines which lay dipped in black shadow—this, according to the poets and painters, should be a haunt of idyllic peace.

"But, unfortunately," mused the judge, as he began to descend into the valley, "unfortunately the human passions run in as fierce tides in Arcadia as in Babylon. And if the spirit of Nature seems divine enough on the surface here in Muirdale I had enough proof yesterday that man's spirit is not appreciably different here among pastoral prettiness from what it is in Seven Dials or Whitechapel. Primitive! Primitive! I suppose my accommodation will also be primitive—if there is any."

He found accommodaton at a little wayside inn, whose landlord told him that he occasionally lodged chance tourists and strolling artists, and could give his visitors a decent room, clean sheets, plain food and a bit of fishing in the stream.

"Nothing better," said the judge, and went upstairs to wash away the dust of his journey.

He looked out of a tiny window on the lonely houses of the hillside, and wondered which of them was that across whose threshold Michael Cruddas would never again set foot—unless something extraordinary occurred to save him from the hangman. He wondered, too, in which of those patches of green standing out against the blue and purple of the hillsides James Garth had met his death. And before he went down to the little parlour to eat the bacon and eggs which he had ordered his mind was filled with wonder that, in such solitudes as these, men and women should so forget the impressiveness of the great silence, the far-stretching skies, the hush of the nights and glory of the sunsets, as to let their passions carry them to deeds of blood.

But the judge was soon to learn that the folk who live amongst the finer things of Nature are as much concerned with personalities as the people of towns. He sat in a shadowed corner of the little parlour that night and watched and listened. Men came and went—men passing along the dale who stayed a few minutes, men who sat down for half an hour over a pint of ale, men who stayed longer, sitting in accustomed places. And there was but one topic of conversation—the result of the local murder case. Also there was but one opinion upon it—James Garth had undoubtedly been shot by Michael Cruddas.

But there was a difference of opinion as to the state of Michael Cruddas's mind when the murder took place. The judge, although unused to the North Country dialect, easily made out what the difference was. One set of critics held that Michael Cruddas shot his victim in cold blood; the other set held that he was drunk when he did the deed, and never knew that he had done it. And they were arguing these differences, each side supporting its arguments by recalling interesting characteristics in Michael Cruddas, when a young man strode into the place, at sight of whom everybody became suddenly silent.

The observant watcher in the shadowy corner, seeing the effect which the newcomer's entrance had produced, looked at him with interest as he went up to the bar and demanded a glass of ale. He saw a tall, lumpish-looking fellow, heavy of face, cold of eye. His whole air and attitude showed a species of surly shyness, and when he looked around with a general not at the company his expression was furtive and almost suspicious. He was evidently in no mood for conversation, and he flushed awkwardly when one of the men sitting near the bar addressed him.

"Been a fair day for t' time o' year, Mr. Cruddas," he observed.

The newcomer turned away sullenly.

"Reight enough," he muttered.

He drank off his ale and strode quickly out without further word, and the men looked at each other.

"Allus short o' speech, is Marshall Cruddas," observed one. "Ye nivver can get much out of him."

"Happen he feels that a time like this it's best to say naught," remarked another man. "It's none a pleasant reflection to know that a relative's goin' to be hanged by t' neck till he's dead, now, is it?"

The landlord, who was leaning over the bar in his shirt sleeves, smiled and scratched his elbows.

"Well, it's an old saying that it's an ill wind that blows nobody any good," he remarked. "It's a bad thing for Michael Cruddas to come under t' hangman's hands, so to speak, but it's good thing for Marshall Cruddas younder. Marshall'll come in for all 'at Michael leaves."

There was a murmur of assent from the small company.

"Ay, that's right enough, that is," said an elderly man. "Land, at any rate. Marshall's all the man-relative that Michael's got. Oh, ay, he'll come in for a nice thing, will Marshall!"

"So you see 'at that old saying's right," observed the landlord. "T' wind's blowin' bad for Michael—he'll be hanged—but good for Marshall—he'll get what Michael leaves."

Then ten o'clock struck, and the two or three late sitters slumped away, and the landlord, having fastened the front door, returned to the parlour and looked at his guest. He was obviously inclined for a chat.

"Yon young feller that was in a bit since," he said, "is cousin to him that was sentenced to death at th' 'sizes yesterday. As them men were saying, he'll come in for all 'at t' poor chap leaves."

"And that," asked the judge, "is it much?"

"Niceish thing," answered the landlord. He supplied himself with a drink, and began to fill his pipe. "Michael's none badly off. There's happen 150 acres of land 'at's been in the Cruddas family many a hundred year; it's their own freehold, so it's bound to come to Marshall—him that was in just now. Then

I should think Michael has money put by. He's allus done well, and, though he drank heavy of late over this love affair, he wasn't a waster or a spender. And there's nobody much for it but Marshall, 'ceptin' an old aunt or two 'at he might leave a few pounds for."

"Were the two cousins on friendly terms?" asked the judge.

"Oh, they were right enough with each other!" replied the landlord. "Neither of 'em the sort for makin' much display o' family feelin', as you might say, but still the sort to reckon 'at blood's thicker than water."

"Live together?" inquired the judge.

"Nay, they didn't," said the landlord, "though single men both. No; Michael, his place is High Gill. You can see it from your bedroom window. Marshall, he runs a mill lower down in the valley. He'd be on his way home, would Marshall, when he called in just now."

"I read this case in the newspaper this morning," remarked the judge. "I suppose there is no doubt in the opinion of the people hereabouts that Michael was guilty?"

"None!" answered the landlord, with decision. "None whatever! But, as you heard to-night, there's some hold that Michael never knew he'd done it. Did it when he was drunk, they say."

"Is that possible?" said the judge, more to himself than his companion. "Could he really have shot this man and never known anything of it?"

"In my opinion he could," said the landlord calmly. "for I've known men do some queer things when they were in drink and have no recollection of doin' them when they grew sober. Anyway, they've found

Michael guilty, and I reckon he'll hang, and Marshall yonder'll step into his shoes."

"There was a girl mentioned in the case," said the judge.

The landlord nodded, and then shook his head.

"Avice Thormthwaite," he said. "Ay, just so! There gen'ally is a woman i' them cases, mister, isn't there?"

"What about this woman?" asked the judge.

"Why, she played fast and she played loose," answered the landlord. "She's a beauty—no denyin' that—but she's skittish. First she was on with Michael Cruddas, and then with Jim Garth; then she'd change about again. What drove Michael mad in the end was that he got it into his head that Jim Garth had tricked him. But what is likely is that what trickery was done was done by her. And," concluded the landlord, dropping his voice as he glanced round at his kitchen door, behind which sat his women folk—"and they do say—some of 'em—that Avice was tricking both of 'em, and that, instead of quarrelling over her, they'd ha' done well to ha' shaken hands and had no more to do wi' her. See, mister?"

"I see," said the judge.

Then he took his candle and went to bed; and as the murmur of the stream soothed him to sleep, he mused on the fact that when Michael Cruddas dropped into eternity through that gruesome hole in the floor of the scaffold, Marshall Cruddas would succeed to a very desirable bit of property, which would be none the less valuable because it had belonged to a murderer.

"That is," murmured the judge, sleepily—"that is, if Michael really is a murderer. Now, I wonder——"

But then sleep overcame him.

CHAPTER III

NEXT morning found Mr. Justice Machin, in his character of holiday-maker, exploring in the neighbourhood of High Gill. He came across an ancient woodman, who showed him where James Garth's body was found, and he was able to trace for himself all the details of the scene on which the sordid tragedy was enacted. And as he looked about him he formed a new opinion—that in cases like this it would be an excellent thing if judge and jury took the trouble to visit the scene of a crime and make a study of its geography.

The woodman was inclined to be talkative; it was seldom that he had a chance of playing the part of showman. From a slight eminence in the road on which the judge met him, he pointed out one place after another.

"Ay," he said, indicating a lonely farmstead in a deep dell just below, "yon's High Gill Farm, as belongs to Michael Cruddas, him as is to die for murderin' Jim Garth. Ye see yon little clump o' trees, master—there a' t' end o' the farm garden? That's where they say Michael laid i' wait to shoot him; that's where t'body was found, and that there cartridge that the lawyers made so much fuss about. Ye see, Jim Garth he were bound to pass that garden end on his way home—yon's his house, up t' hillside there. And yon cottage as ye see among t' trees in t' end o' this valley, that's where the lass lives 'at they quarrelled over—Avice Thormthwaite they call her."

"Is her father a farmer, too?" asked the judge.

The woodman laughed drily.

"It 'ud take a cleverer man nor me to tell you what

Thormthwaite is, master," he answered. "He reckons to be a game watcher, but there's them as would say he poaches a great deal more nor what he preserves. Queer lot is them Thormthwaites."

The judge made no reply to this. He was examining the landscape.

"Which is the way to the market town—Highdale?" he suddenly asked.

The woodman raised his hand and pointed.

"Go down this lane to t' corner of Cruddas's garden—where I told yer Jim Garth was shot," he said. "Turn there to your left and go straight over t' shoulder o' yon hill—ye'll see Highdale then. That," he added, "is t' way 'at Jim Garth walked to his death—he were coming back fro' market when Cruddas laid i' wait for him wi' t' gun."

Mr. Justice Machin gave his informant a shilling, and set out in the direction indicated. He paused a moment at the clump of trees by which Garth had met his death. Certainly that was a likely place for a murder. The trees made good cover, and the murderer could easily slip away amongst them when the deed was done. And the judge was conjuring up the scene for his own benefit when the hasp of a gate snapped close by, and out of the farm garden came two people in such close converse that they did not see the stranger until they were close upon him.

One of these two was the man whom the judge had seen in the little inn on the previous evening—Marshall Cruddas. The other was a tall, finely-developed, black-haired, black-eyed, bold-looking young woman, whose beauty blazed out in those Arcadian surroundings like a peony in a garden of quiet colour. Both looked up sharply as the stranger moved; Marshall Cruddas, recognising him as the visitor at the inn, dropped his eye and turned his head. The girl stared the judge through and through, and when he had passed her for some distance and purposely glanced back, she was still staring.

"Avice Thormthwaite, of course," murmured the judge, as he walked leisurely forward. "A bold beauty."

He went on his way, lounging about as a holiday-maker would, until he topped the shoulder of the hill pointed out by the woodman. There, two miles off, he saw Highdale, a cluster of grey houses around a square-towered church. But Mr. Justice Machin had no intention of going into the little town; the only people who would be likely to recognise him lived there. They were not many—a police official or two, a solicitor or two, two or three witnesses who had heard Michael Cruddas use the threatening words. Still, the judge had an object in his walk. In the map of the district which had been laid before him at the trial, there was marked, on the roadside leading from Highdale to High Gill, an inn called the Pigeon Pie. And he had a certain notion concerning that inn, and he went forward until he found it, a queer, half ramshackle old place standing lonely amidst pine and fir; and he went in and asked for a glass of ale from a landlord who had obviously little to do.

It was an easy thing to lure this man into talking of the murder; he, in fact, was reading of it in a day-old newspaper when the judge entered the house.

"I suppose," said the caller, "that you know all the parties concerned in this affair?"

The landlord shook his head with the knowingness of the man who believes himself unusually conversant with things.

"Know 'em, mister? Ay, all on 'em!" he answered.

"I weren't called as a witness, but I was one o' them that heerd Michael Cruddas use them threats to Jim Garth. In the Three Crowns at Highdale yonder it war—market day. Drunk, of course, was Michael —but not drunk enough to know nowt about what he said. 'Next time I come across yer when I've a gun in my hand,' he says, 'I'll shoot yer as I'd shoot a mad dog,' he says them words."

"I read the case," remarked the judge. "This house of yours would be on the way home for these men. Did Cruddas call here that night?"

"No, he didn't," replied the landlord. "I saw him go past, mutterin' and talkin' to hisself, just as it come dark, like. But Jim Garth come in—I've allus said, since, that I reckon I was the last he ever spok' to. An' I warned him agen Michael—'cause Michael had murder in him when he spok' them words—ye could see it."

"And what did Garth say?" said the judge.

"He said summat 'at I've puzzled and studied over ever since," answered the landlord, scratching his head. "It were this here—and he said it as he was sitting i' that very chair 'at you're in now. 'If Michael Cruddas knew t' truth,' he says, 'he'd be for shakin' hands wi' me, i'stead o' shootin' me.' 'Why don't you tell him t' truth, then?' I says. ''Cause he's one o' them 'at 'll listen to nowt when he's mad wi' rage an' drink,' says Garth. 'All t' same,' he says, 'it'll come out.'"

"What do you think he meant?" said the judge.

The landlord shook his head and stared at the smoke-blackened rafters.

"Don't know, mister," he said. "But—very—like —summat about yon lass. She played fast and loose wi' Jim, and she played t' same wi' Michael—and if she could do that wi' t' two on 'em, separate like, she could do it w' i' both put together."

"But you don't know anything?" suggested the judge.

"Nowt," said the landlord. "Nowt! All t' same, that were what Garth said, sittin' in' that chair an hour afore he met his end."

The judge said no more, and presently he rose to depart, and the landlord, following him to the door, looked critically at the lowering sky.

"There's goin' to be a heavy rain," he remarked. "It'll come within twelve hours. Stayin' i' these parts, mister?"

"For a day or two," answered the judge.

"Then ye'll see what ye've very like never seen afore," said the landlord. "When it rains here—it rains."

The judge went slowly back to Muirdale, thinking of anything but weather.

He was chiefly wondering if the evidence brought before men in his capacity is always as carefully prepared as it might be. If he had known of James Garth's remark to the landlord of the Pigeon Pie during the course of Michael Cruddas's short trial, he would have insisted on knowing more. But—of what—of whom?

"There is time yet, however," he mused.

He spent that afternoon in pottering around the neighbourhood of the inn; in the evening, after his simple meal, he once more repaired to the quiet corner of the parlour in which he had sat the previous night. And as he became accustomed to the gloom, he saw in another corner a strange face, which when he looked at it was fixed attentively on his own. Mr. Justice Machin knew when he saw that face that he had seen it before; he knew, too, that he had cause to remember it. But, in spite of an instant searching of memory, he could neither remember where he had seen it or when or why he preserved a recollection of it. It was a face that suggested gipsy blood—very dark, sinister, crafty; even in that dim light the judge could make out the black locks which framed it, and the gleam of the black eyes looking out from beneath shaggy eyebrows. And as he looked, it moved out of the shadow, and its owner, a wiry, muscular-looking fellow of middle age, clad in velveteens and whipcord, came across to him, pulling at his fur cap with an affectation of almost servile politeness.

"Begging your pardon, sir," said the man. "Gentleman as is stopping in the house, I think, sir?"

"Well?" said the judge, quietly.

"I hear as how you were after a bit o' fishing, sir," continued the other. "The landlord mentioned of it. If you like, sir, I can take you to a spot to-morrow, after the rain—it's coming to-night, sir—where you'll enjoy yourself. Grand spot, sir."

"Is it a place you have a right to fish in?" asked the judge.

"Oh, yes, sir; all right. Common fishing, sir—not preserved," answered the man, readily enough. "But," he added, with a knowing wink, "there ain't many as knows of it."

The judge reflected a moment.

"Very good," he said. "Come for me to-morrow when you think fit. It will rain to-night, you say?"

"Rain within half an hour, sir," replied the other, confidently. "To-morrow, then, sir? It'll be towards evening."

The judge nodded and the man, again pulling his forelock, moved off and presently left the inn. The landlord entered as he went out, and exchanged a word with him at the door.

"The man who has just gone out," remarked the judge presently, "is not, I think, a North Countryman?

"You're right, sir—he isn't," answered the landlord. "Comes from southern parts, though he's been here, game watching, these six or seven years. That's Thormthwaite. Father," he continued, drawing nearer to the judge and whispering, "of her that was talked of in the murder case."

"Ah, indeed," said the judge, indifferently. "He has promised to show me a bit of good fishing to-morrow. Will he be all right?"

The landlord laughed.

"Nobody better, sir," he answered. "Although he's not a native, there's nobody knows these parts better than Dan Thormthwaite. He'll take you where you can pull 'em out fast as you can throw in. There'll be good fishing after this rain—it's coming."

The rain came almost as the landlord finished speaking—came as it only can come in a mountainous country, with a suddenness of fury that swept all before it ere settling down into a steady, continuous, letting loose of the moisture that had been gathering all day around the hilltops in great masses of ominous cloud. It was still pouring down on roof and road when the judge went to bed; it was as heavy as ever when he woke in the night; the ceaseless rattle of it was there when he half woke in the grey dawn. Nor was there any sign of its cessation when he drew his blind at last and saw that the little river had already overflowed and that the meadow which flanked it had been transformed into a miniature lake.

All the morning and through half the afternoon the rain fell, never staying, and the valley resounded with the noise of many waters. Far up the dark hillsides the judge, staring out of the inn windows, saw long, white streaks come into being against the blackness of the rocks and the purple of the heather, and recognised them for newly-formed cascades pouring down from the moors above.

Now and then a soaked traveller came in and spoke of flooded and impassable ways. It seemed to the judge that he was being cut off from the outer world. And then, towards the close of the afternoon, the rain ceased as suddenly as it had begun, and a weak sun struggled out of the clouds and shot fitful gleams on the swirling brown waters in the valley. And presently, as the judge drank a cup of tea in the parlour, a dark face showed itself at the door, and Thormthwaite's voice hoped the gentleman was ready for his bit of sport.

"Is it possible to make one's way anywhere?" asked the judge, glancing at the window. "Aren't we water-locked?"

"Leave that to me, sir," answered Thormthwaite, knowingly. "If you'll follow me you shan't as much as wet your ankles."

The judge set out with demur. He had his good reasons for making this excursion. For one thing, he was a good sportsman and the adventure appealed to him; for another, he wanted to find out—quietly—where and when he had seen this man Thormthwaite before; and lastly, it was in his mind that during this excursion he might learn something which would throw some light on the business which had brought him to Muirdale. He would ask no questions, he would make no reference, but his nearly thirty years' legal experience would stand him in good stead if a dropped word, a mere phrase, came in his way.

Thormthwaite led the way out of the valley by a rocky path which ran along the side of the ravine over which High Gill Farm stood. Muirdale was filled with these ravines. They penetrated deeply into the hillsides, and when the trees were in full leaf, as they were at that time, they were black as night till unaccustomed eyes grew used to their gloom.

The judge looked curiously about him as they progressed. Below the shelving rock and loose boulders over which they scrambled, a swollen cataract poured down into the valley, carrying loose debris of plants and branches on its swirling waters. There was little prospect of successful fishing amidst such a tumult, and he pointed the fact out to his guide. But Thormthwaite pointed into the further recesses of the gloomy ravine, and the judge, straining his eyes, saw what looked like the ruins of an ancient water-mill.

"There's a pool behind those walls," said Thormthwaite, "where we shall find as many trout as I can carry. And there—it's quiet."

He led the way forward until they came up to the mill and to a door which stood in an angle of the wall. This he pushed open and stood aside, motioning his companion to enter. And the judge entered, and saw at once that he was in strange and curious surroundings.

The place he had walked into so unsuspectingly was a cavernous vault, formed by high, naked walls, open to the sky. Half-way up one of these walls water trickled freely through what was obviously a hatch, long unused; on the flagged floor on which the judge stood water stood in shallow pools. He was a man of remarkably quick perception and he saw instantly what this place was—the wheelhouse of a mill, from which the wheel itself had been removed. And he saw, too, that if the hatch in the wall above him gave way under the pressure of water in the dam behind it, the hole place would be submerged in a few minutes—or seconds.

All this Mr. Justice Machin recognised in an instant. And in the same instant he heard a mocking laugh and a hurried step on the wet stones. Then the door was slammed and a bolt shot into a socket without. He was alone—a prisoner.

"Now, I know that this man and I have met before," he said suddenly. "This is his revenge."

The immediate presence of what might be danger—might, indeed, be death—nerved the judge to an apparently imperturbable composure. And when Thormthwaite's face, sneering and evil, suddenly appeared in an opening high above him, he looked up steadily and even commandingly.

"My man," he said calmly, "you will come down and open that door at once!"

Thormthwaite laughed. He was leaning out of a ruinous trap-door in the side wall some twelve or fifteen feet above his prisoner, and he folded his arms on the ledge and sneered again as he watched he proud face below.

"You forget, Mr. Justice Machin, that I'm up and you're down this time," he said. "You're a good hand at forgetting. I ain't—I remember all that I want to remember. I remember you—knew you as soon as I set eyes on you last night. Hang me if I ever expected such luck—after all these years!"

The judge had been making a violent effort to exercise his memory to the full. And suddenly a certain day of the past came to him, and he nodded quietly.

"I remember you," he said. "You came before me at the quarter sessions at Malgrave—many years ago—when I was recorder. But your name was not Thormthwaite at that time."

"'Tain't now, for that matter," sneered the man, "but I'm the same chap. Yes, I did come before you, as you says, and you give me five years—five awful years! I wish I could keep you where you are now for five years. I would if I could!"

"And I also remember that you richly deserved your sentence," continued the judge, calmly. "You are evidently still inclined to wickedness. What are you intending to do now?"

"I'm intending to make an end of you," answered Thormthwaite, insolently. "You're going to drown—like a rat in a cage. I'm going to knock a timber or two out of that sluice up there presently, and give you a bath. Yu'll never want another. Look 'round; there's no getting out of where you are."

But the judge kept his keen eyes fixed on his captor.

"Let me point out to you," he said, as quietly as if he were arguing some legal quibble, "that you're putting a noose round your own neck. It is known that I am in Muirdale; the people at the inn also know that I have come out with you. If——"

"There's no 'if' about it," he said. "I reckoned it all out last night—especially after I saw what a lot o' rain we should have. My tale'll be straight enough to suit any crowner's jury, anyhow. You come out fishing with me—I show you a good place at back of the old mill, and I leave you there, fishing peaceable, while I go to get my supper. When I come back you've fallen into the mill-weir and drowned yourself. Eh?"

"I'm not in the mill-weir," said the judge.

Thormthwaite laughed once more; this time he seemed to be genuinely amused.

"You will be—when I find you," he said. "I tell you I've worked it all out. I shall watch you drown, and when you're done I shall let the water off by that sluice behind you—it only opens from the outside, so you needn't try it— and then I shall pull you out and put you in the weir. Plain and simple, eh? You fell in owing to the bank being rotten with the heavy rain. What d'y say to that?"

"I say you are a murderer," answered the judge, "and I hope you have no other murders on your conscience. But I doubt it!"

"You're a rotten liar!" said Thormthwaite. "I've none. And there'll be no murder done on you, only justice. I'd a wife and three youngsters to keep when you put me away for five years—all I'd left when I came out was the lass you saw this morning. And what—what," he suddenly burst out with a flash of ungovernable fury,—"what did you come spying around here for? A judge! You didn't come here by no accident, I'll warrant. Happen you think I killed Jim Garth?"

"I am begining to think it very possible," said the judge, coldly.

"Then you're wrong!" sneered Thormthwaite, laughing evilly. "For I didn't. All the same, as you're going where you can't tell secrets, I don't mind telling you that I know who did. And it wasn't Michael Cruddas!"

The judge's own danger was suddenly swept out of his mind. He turned a beseechingly eager face to his tormentor.

"Thormthwaite!" he cried. "Stop this foolishness! Take me out of this. Tell me who killed Garth, and I'll give you a thousand—two thousand pounds! I won't say a word about this business—it shall be secret between us. Cash, Thormthwaite—down in good gold! Come, man, be sensible, be—my God, what's that?"

High above both of them, high above the sluice to which Thormthwaite had kept pointing so threateningly a sudden cracking of the gaunt, bare wall showed itself, and a great spurt of brown water shot through, forming a gleaming arch, and hit the stone flags at the judge's feet. And before either man could cry out again the crack wavered, deepened, widened, the big wall seemed to be torn in two by giant hands, and, with a roar that startled the folk down in Muirdale, a mighty mass of seething water leaped out above them. The mill-weir had burst, and the judge just realised the horror of it as he was caught up, buffeted, crushed, swept away into stifling darkness amongst a whirling wreckage of wood and stone.

It seemed to him that he heard a human cry of shrill agony and he was vaguely wondering if it was his own, when a great blank rushed over him, and he knew no more. The blankness and blackness came so suddenly that he had scarcely time to wonder if death were also at hand.

When Mr. Justice Machin next knew anything, he found himself lying in a soft, warm bed, in a slightly darkened room. Near him he heard voices—hushed, murmuring. He lay still and listened.

"Bound to happen sooner or later," said a voice which had a professional ring in it. "The turning of that old mill-weir into a big fish-pond was a most foolish thing to do. I warned Sir Thomas myself of what might happen when an unusually heavy rain came—and here's the result! Half the village swept away, eight lives lost. Our patient here had a most lucky escape—and, by the by, when he comes round we must get to know who he really is."

The judge turned his head and spoke, and was frightened to hear the feebleness of his own voice.

"I will tell you that," he said, "if you will tell me how much I am damaged and when I can get about again."

The two doctors came forward and became busy, and the judge watched both.

"I must request an immediate and unequivocal answer," he said sharply. "Shall I be able to travel to London within a week? Yes or no?"

"No!" replied the elder doctor. "Certainly not! Nor within a fortnight."

"Thank you," said the judge. "Then I must trouble you to take down a telegraphic message for me, and I must ask you to personally see to its immediate transmission. The fact is, I am Sir Francis Machin, and the telegram is to the Home Secretary."

Two days later the Home Secretary sat in his private room listening to the report made to him by the very high official whom he had sent down to Muirdale on receipt of the judge's telegram. He smiled a little when the report came to an end.

"So it really comes to this," he said, rising and pacing the room. "On the strength of his own intuitive feeling in the matter, and on that chance remark of the man Thormthwaite, made to him just before the accident happened—that he, Thormthwaite, knew who murdered James Garth, and it was not Michael Cruddas—Machin wants me to stay execution in this case? That it?"

"That is it," answered the official. "What is more, I'm quite certain that he'll be in a fever until he knows that you've done what he wants. I never saw a man so earnest about anything in my life! He's confident that this man Michael Cruddas is innocent."

"And, pray, whom does he think is—or was—guilty?" asked the Home Secretary.

"His theory," answered the official, "is that the cousin, Marshall Cruddas, shot Garth, and that the girl Avice Thormthwaite was accessory, and possibly instigator."

"And those two, you say, are dead; drowned in the flood, as the girl's father also was?" said the Home Secretary.

"Marshall Cruddas and the girl were drowned together in Cruddas's house," replied the official. "The father was killed by falling masonry."

The Home Secretary smiled enigmatically.

"Machin," he observed, "was always a man of queer whims and fancies, but I don't think he's very likely to be wrong. Oh, well, send Machin a wire. A word will do. Send it now and set his mind at rest."

The official rose and moved to the door.

"The word?" he asked.

The Home Secretary had already reseated himself, and was absent-mindedly staring at the papers. He looked up, half vacantly.

"Eh?" he said. "Oh! Why, of course, there is only one—Reprieved."

XI: THE SECOND CAPSULE

CHAPTER I

THAT night a full moon rode high in the eastern heavens, and near it shone a great, coruscating star of peculiar brightness. Garthwaite, hanging over a parapet of London bridge, lifted his eyes from the quiet wash of the river to the still quieter skies, and took the radiance of star and moon as a good omen. All the evening he had felt in particularly good spirits; the splendour of the things overhead was rapidly lifting him from that state to an even better one; the silvery moonlight began to assume quite a roseate warmth. Around him the London clocks suddenly struck eleven strokes. When the last of them had died away, Garthwaite began to hum a gay tune. And while he hummed it he looked down at the steamer which, that very night—or, to be precise, at 5:30 next morning—was to carry him away from London and England on the first stage of a journey to another country and a new life.

A new life! That was the vision which made his spirits dance in sympathy with the little silver-tipped ripples on the brown river. Of the old one he had experienced enough; in future he meant everything to be new. And it gave him no concern when he looked in upon himself and remembered that he was, to all intents and purposes, a fugitive, an absconding official, carrying away with him, in one form or another, a vast amount of money which belonged to a far-off town wherein for many years he had been trusted as probably no public servant had ever been trusted before.

To have felt concern over a matter like that would have been to show compunction; and to compunction, remorse, consideration for anything or anybody but himself, Garthwaite was wholly a stranger. His one feeling, as he lounged and lingered on London Bridge that beautiful moonlighted night was of joy, delight, pleasure that his scheme had carried so admirably.

For many a long year—in fact, ever since he had entered their employ as a clerk—Garthwaite had meant to rob the Firminster Corporation, not in a small, mean, pettifogging fashion, but in a big, generous way. It was for that reason that he had been such a good clerk, toiling early and late, making and keeping himself thoroughly acquainted with the inner workings and details of the borough accountant's office. And in time his assiduity, his carefulness, his grasp of everything connected with his work, had led to his advancement. That advancement had been considerable—by big steps.

For two years previous to this particular night, Garthwaite had been not only borough accountant, but borough treasurer. Firminster was not a place of any great size, but an ancient borough of twelve thousand inhabitants has a considerable rateable value, and Garthwaite had had to deal with large sums of money. And at last, as the result of great care, forethought, skilful scheming and deep knowledge of exactly what he was doing, he had dealt with the town funds in such a fashion that before very long the town authorities would be looking for them in vain.

But not just yet. If there was anything that Garthwaite prided himself upon it was his attention to detail, and he had so worked and arranged matters that no one would find out anything until he was beyond all reach. He was entitled to a month's holiday every year; he had made his final dispositions just before leaving for that holiday. Then he proceeded openly, even ostentatiously, to Scarborough—to enjoy himself.

But on the very night of his arrival at Scarborough he had boarded the steamer which plies twice a week between Sunderland and London, and calls at Scarborough to pick up passengers. Once in London, he had booked a passage in one of the Batavier steamers which run from the Thames to Rotterdam; from Rotterdam he meant to make his way to Vienna, where he had already invested much money at call; from Vienna he was going to Trieste, on his way to South America.

It was all beautifully arranged, all splendidly conceived, and it was working out excellently. There, beneath his very feet, lay the steamer which was to carry him out of England; she was being loaded up at that moment with merchandise. At high water in the morning—5:30—she would drop down the Thames, and he would be well on the way to the new life concerning which he had formulated rare dreams. For Garthwaite was as yet a young man, as things go nowadays, and he had notions—notions of a luxurious existence in the tropics, of a life of ease and pleasure, vastly different to that which he lived in far-off, drab-coloured, sleepy old Firminster.

He laughed gently as he remembered how very cleverly he had done everything—laughed until he yawned. And when he yawned he turned away from the bridge towards his hotel. There, again, in making choice of his hotel for the night, he had shown his usual ability in concealment. Instead of going up West, or even to the Strand, or into the heart of the city, Garthwaite had deliberately sought out a riverside hostelry, old-fashioned, and of no great size, wherein to spend his last few hours in England. It stood almost under the shadow of the Monument; it was within five minutes' walk of the wharf whereat his steamer lay. He would have nothing to do but rise at five o'clock, pick up his suitcase and go aboard.

If he had cared to do so, he could have slept aboard, but a steward whom he had interviewed on that point had told him that the loading of goods went on all night, and Garthwaite was one of those careful individuals who are particular about getting at least four hours of sound slumber every time they lay heads on pillows. He went off to get that slumber now, and repaired straight to his bedroom. And he had scarcely entered it, and had not yet locked its door upon himself, when a tap, gentle yet assertive, sounded upon the panels.

Garthwaite's nerves were always in excellent order; he was neither startled nor surprised, and he bade whoever was without to enter. He expected to see chambermaid, or boots; instead, when the door opened and he looked up from the easy-chair into which he had just dropped in order to take off his shoes, he found himself confronting the slightly smiling face of one of his own clerks.

Garthwaite knew that face and that smile very well indeed. They belonged to a clerk named Tisdale, whose chief personal characteristics were a shock head of foxy hair, a pair of shifty, burrowing eyes and a perpetual grin, which would have been utterly fatuous if it had not been so maliciously sly and meaning. Garthwaite, in the bygone days, had ofen felt his hand literally itch to slap this fellow's face because of that smile; he now experienced a strong desire to sweep it out of his field of vision with something heavier. Instead, he put a sudden curb on his feelings and strove to suppress his intense surprise.

"Well?" he growled, "what are you doing here?"

Tisdale, who had carefully closed the bedroom door, leaned back against it and rubbed his hands together.

"Evening, Mr. Garthwaite," he said, softly. "This is—a little unexpected, I think, sir."

Garthwaite finished the taking-off of his shoes and put his feet into a pair of bedroom slippers. When he had finished that small task his mind was made up.

"Now, then," he said, "what brings you here, and what are you after? Out with it!"

Tisdale smiled more widely than ever and rubbed his hands again.

"After—you!" he answered. "And—there you are! Plain speaking, I think, Mr. Garthwaite."

"Let's have more of it," said Garthwaite. He quietly reached around to a hip pocket, drew out a revolver and let his visitor see it. "You've come into this room, Tisdale," he went on, "but you'll only go out with my permission. See this? For two pins I'll shoot you!"

"No occasion for violence, Mr. Garthwaite," remarked Tisdale, urbanely. "None whatever, sir. And I'm not afraid, not me! See here," he reached out, drew a chair to him and sat down. "I've a good deal to say, you know."

"Talk and be hanged to you," snapped Garthwaite. He saw that somehow or other Tisdale had got the whip hand of him and that he would have to submit. "What is it?" he snarled. "You've followed me?"

"Quite so, sir," replied Tisdale. "I'll explain. You see, Mr. Garthwaite," he went on, with another of his smiles which Garthwaite so much loathed, "you see, sir, you've been living in a fool's paradise, if you'll excuse the expression. You thought nobody suspected you. But I suspected you—and so did Mr. Earnshaw."

Garthwaite, in spite of his strong nerves, started at that. Earnshaw was a prominent member of the Firminster Corporation; he was chairman of the finance committee; a man of action. He had been a close personal friend, and to hear that he suspected him (Garthwaite) was a real surprise. Garthwaite could only stare at his informant.

"Well?" he said at last. "Well?"

"Just so," returned Tisdale. "The only difference between me and Mr. Earnshaw, however, was that he knew nothing, and I knew—something, eh?"

"How much?" asked Garthwaite, sullenly.

Tisdale drew his chair a little nearer his prisoner, taking care not to leave the immediate neighbourhood of the door.

"A lot!" he answered. "More than I could tell you just now. But—I know about the waterworks money, and the corporation debenture stock, and the——"

"That'll do," interrupted Garthwaite, curtly. "I'm not thirsting for more of your knowledge, confound you! About Earnshaw? You say he knows nothing?"

"Nothing certain—only suspects," replied Tisdale. "He's just getting to the dangerous stage. It was Earnshaw that set me on to you—that's why I'm here."

"How could Earnshaw set you on to me?" demanded Garthwaite. "You've been conspiring with him!"

"Honour bright, no!" affirmed Tisdale. "I'm a deal too clever, Mr. Garthwaite, to let anybody know what I know. I haven't said a word to Earnshaw or to a soul of what I've found out."

Garthwaite unconsciously heaved a sigh of relief. So long as Earnshaw did not actually know real facts—

"Well?" he said presently, "about this setting on?"

"Yes," replied Tisdale. "You see, that day you set off on your holiday to Scarborough—day before yesterday, of course—Earnshaw called me into his office, and, after binding me to secrecy, told me that he wanted me to go to Scarborough and keep an eye on you. If we met, I was furnished with a good excuse, —I'd exchanged holidays with Hopkinson, in the gas department. Of course, I set off for Scarborough at once—Earnshaw gave me plenty of money for expenses, in case I should want it. Of course, I soon spotted you, and I watched you board the steamer from Sunderland to London."

"You didn't surely get on it yourself!" exclaimed Garthwaite, wonderingly. "I never saw you."

Tisdale smiled evilly and tapped the side of his nose.

"No fear," he answered. "I know a trick worth three of that. I ain't a fool, Mr. Garthwaite. You see, it didn't take me five minutes to find out that the steamer didn't call anywhere between Scarborough and London, so you were safe once you'd got on board. I watched you sail and then I walked up to the station and took the next express for King's Cross, and I was in London and down here at the riverside—to meet you! And, of course, I met you and followed you up to this hotel and when you'd strolled out this evening I strolled in and booked the next room. Eh?"

"And—what next?" asked Garthwaite.

Tisdale rubbed his hands together and smiled. He made no answer, but he went on smiling.

"Does Earnshaw know of your movements?" asked Garthwaite, suddenly.

"No!" replied Tisdale, with alacrity. "He doesn't! Nobody knows. I'm playing my own game, not his."

"I can give your game a name, my lad," remarked Garthwaite, pinning the shifty eyes. "It's a name in one word—blackmail."

Tisdale laughed very softly.

"We've all of us a right to do what we can for ourselves, Mr. Garthwaite," he said. "That's common sense, sir. I'm out on my own. Never mind Earnshaw—hang Firminster! If you like to make it worth my while to—eh?"

"How much do you want?" asked Garthwaite. He had known it would come to this from the moment of Tisdale's entrance, and he had been thinking hard all the time under the superstructure of that assured knowledge. "Name your price! Not that I shall pay it, you know."

For a few minutes Tisdale appeared to be seeking inspiration from various points of the bedroom to which he turned his shifty eyes. And when his face was again projected in Garthwaite's direction the eyes were focussed on some spot above Garthwaite's head.

"Well, of course," answered Tisdale—"of course, out of those debentures alone you have made——"

"Hang the debentures!" exclaimed Garthwaite. He was playing a part and he meant to play it thoroughly. "Put it into plain language! How much do you want to hold your tongue?"

"Two thousand—cash down!" answered Tisdale, promptly.

Garthwaite got up and moved over to the far side of the bedroom, which was in shadow. On a table there stood a bottle of whisky, a syphon of mineral water and some clean glasses. He picked up the whisky, carried it back to the hearthrug and, taking a corkscrew from his waistcoat pocket, drew the cork under Tisdale's nose. He happened to know that the clerk was fond of a drink and he heard him sniff as the aroma of the spirit permeated the room.

"Now, if I give you a couple of thousand—in bank notes," he said, standing there with the bottle in one hand and the corkscrew in the other, "what will you do?"

"Not go back to Firminster, you bet!" replied Tisdale.

"I said 'what will you do?' " replied Garthwaite.

"I shall do what you're doing—hook it," said Tisdale. "Colonies—something of that sort."

"At once?"

"To-morrow morning. That is—if there's no bother about the notes. I could get them turned into gold —or as good, I suppose?"

"There will be no bother about the notes," said Garthwaite, with a dry laugh. "Not there." He moved back to the shadow, and began to play about with the glasses and the syphon. "All right," he said suddenly, "I'll give you that amount."

"Now?" said Tisdale.

"Just now," replied Garthwaite. "As I said, you can turn them into gold whenever you like. You're as safe as—as I am. That is—if you go off at once."

"Trust me!"' said Tisdale.

He watched the defaulter narrowly as he drew out

a bulky pocketbook and selected an envelope, which he tossed over the room to him with a curt order to count its contents. And engaged in that pleasant task, Tisdale did not see Garthwaite quietly abstract a small object from another compartment of the pocketbook, and drop it into the whisky, which he had just poured into one of the glasses.

"There's exactly two thousand in that envelope," said Garthwaite. "Twenty one-hundreds. Say when, Tisdale!"

He turned, holding the glass in one hand, the syphon in the other. But instead of looking at Tisdale he was watching a curious spreading of some substance in the whisky. Tisdale, across the room, could see nothing; but Garthwaite saw the substance melt, spread, mingle. He pressed the syphon, and the mineral water splashed loudly.

"Seventeen, eighteen, nineteen, twenty, all correct," said Tisdale, checking his notes. "I—that's enough, thank you. And—good luck, Mr. Garthwaite—to both of us."

Garthwaite made no answer. He handed the glass to his visitor, saw him take a deep drink, and turned away to mix another glass for himself. And already his own heart was beginning to thump, and his breath to feel hampered, and a big hammer was beating in his temple—for Death had come into that silent room.

Garthwaite, like many another man of busy life, had a hobby which absorbed all his spare time. He was a dabbler in experimental chemistry, and his labours had for some years been devoted to researches in poisons. In the pocketbook from which he had taken the bank notes he carried two tiny capsules, each filled with a highly concentrated poison. He carried them in case of a really desperate emergency—the really desperate emergency had arisen. He had made up his mind that the spy should never go out of that room alive; and now, as he stood there mixing his drink, waiting for a certain sound, he was reckoning on his own chances. They were good, they were sure, nothing could have been better. In his methodical way he tabulated them:

No one knew that Tisdale had tracked him.

None of the hotel people had seen him and Tisdale together.

He was certain that Tisdale had taken the utmost care to knock at his door unobserved.

It would be hours after his own departure that Tisdale's dead body would be found.

When Tisdale's dead body was found, there would be nothing to connect him (Garthwaite) with it.

No doctor or expert in the world could tell that Tisdale had been poisoned. Within an hour of his death all trace of that particular poison would have disappeared, and no post-mortem examination could possibly reveal or discover it.

He regained full control over his nerves as he came to the end of these conclusions, and his voice was steady enough when he presently spoke.

"Drink all right, Tisdale?" he asked.

Before Tisdale could answer, Tisdale died—died as he set down his empty glass on the dining-table at his side; died with a queer little murmuring sigh as Garthwaite darted forward and caught him, swaying back in his chair. And Garthwaite let him gently and cautiously downward to the floor, and thanked his own particular devil that the capsule had done its work so speedily.

CHAPTER II

But there was work for him to do now. There he was, alone in a small London hotel with a dead man's body, which he could not carry away as if it had been a parcel, which must inevitably be discovered, revealed to the police, to a coroner and his jury, with all the usual accompaniments of wonder and inquiry and speculation. The situation was one of peril; an ordinary man would have been frightened out of his wits by it. But Garthwaite was far from being an ordinary man, and he possessed coolness, resource, and fertility of conception beyond the average degree. The main thing was accomplished; all that remained now was to secure his own safety.

He went to work calmly and methodically. To begin with, he examined every pocket in the dead man's clothing. There were a few papers in Tisdale's possession, but Garthwaite carefully collected every scrap of them, tore them into small bits, and burned them in his grate. The dead man's purse, loose money, watch and chain, personal effects, he left on him; there was nothing in these things, not even an initial, that could lead to Tisdale's immediate identification.

Garthwaite's notion was that any identification should be delayed indefinitely. He saw clearly ahead —there would be the usual fuss about the body of an unknown man, and it would be days, perhaps longer, before Tisdale and Firminster came to be connected.

It was long after midnight before Garthwaite cautiously opened the door, stole out, locked it behind him, and went into the next room. He knew that was Tisdale's room, because the first object which he saw there was an overcoat, which he well knew to be the dead man's, thrown carelessly over the bed. Garthwaite went carefully through that coat, then through a small handbag which stood on the dressing-table. There was nothing in either of them that could reveal anything. He took some simple toilet articles out of the bag, and spread them on the dressing-table and washstand; then he hung the overcoat behind the door. And, that done, he turned out the light again, and went away, leaving the door wide open. The time had come for transferring the body from one room to the other.

Garthwaite stood for some time in the corridor, watching and listening. In one of the neighbouring rooms he heard a faint breathing; from another came a gentle, steady snoring. There was only the faintest glimmer of light around him; in that house they were evidently careful of the gas.

He had turned down his own light to a mere spark when he left his room, and it was in almost entire darkness that he presently carried Tisdale's body from one door to the next. He accomplished this swiftly and silently. It was with accelerated swiftness that he undressed the dead man, laid him in the bed, and covered him up in a natural position. There was a transom over the door. Some hours later, when no response could be got to repeated knocking, somebody would look through the glass of that transom, and Garthwaite desired that Tisdale should seem to be wrapped in heavy slumber. And as the body was still flexible, he disposed its limbs in a fashion which would suggest sleep rather than death.

"Careful attention to detail is the thing!" soliloquised Grathwaite. "Lucky for me that I have trained myself to it!"

In pursuance of this careful attention, he proceeded

to dispose the dead man's clothing about the room. He placed the purse under the pillow, the loose money on the dressing-table; by its side he laid the watch and chain, and he took care to wind up the watch; and finally—a master stroke this, in his opinion!—he deposited Tisdale's boots on the mat outside the door, took the key away, and retreated to his own room, where he immediately mixed himself a stiff drink.

The two thousand pounds' worth of bank notes which he had handed to Tisdale's suddenly nerveless grip, Garthwaite took up and restored to his pocket-book. Then he made everything ready for his departure at five o'clock. He had paid his bill overnight; there was nothing for him to do now but to take up his effects and walk to the steamer when the time came. And, all being ready, Garthwaite lay down, dressed as he was, and for three hours he slept as peacefully as if he were an innocent child. He woke to the required minute—a habit of his. Within five minutes—the exact time then being 4:50—he had left his room and the hotel, and was shivering a little in the street outside. And there, shivering too, but from quite another cause, a man came up to him—obviously a man who had made his bed on the embankment, or in some corner out of official sight.

"Carry your bag, guv'nor?" suggested this night-bird. "Give us a chance! Bin out all night, and ain't got a penny for a bite."

"No!" snapped Garthwaite, so decidedly that for a moment the man slunk off. But hunger was strong upon him, and he crept up again, and followed—followed across the street, and down another street, always entreating and begging, until the wharf came in sight, and with it the Rotterdam steamer.

It would have been well for Garthwaite if he had

tossed that man a shilling as soon as he accosted him —he would have gone way with it in quest of a coffee-stall, and left Garthwaite to pursue his flight unobserved. But Garthwaite had never given a penny in charity in his life, and he paid no further heed to the beseecher of it. He marched on to the wharf, while the man in his rear cursed him and slunk back to the hotel to look for less flinty people.

Garthwaite forgot all about that man as soon as he had turned his back upon him. Also he put Tisdale out of his mind, too. The last time he thought of Tisdale was when he went to the side of the steamer, took the key of Tisdale's bedroom from his waistcoat pocket, and dropped it into the river. That was as the steamer passed Greenwich. From that time Garthwaite became light-hearted, optimistic and appreciative of the pleasures to be derived from a long day's sailing over the North Sea.

That steamer was a slow moving affair and noon had passed, and Garthwaite, whose naturally good appetite improved with every mile, had eaten a heavy lunch before she came abreast of Margate. There, for a second, he allowed himself one brief thought of what might be going on at the hotel which he had quitted nine hours before. Of course, by that time they had discovered Tisdale's dead body. They had no doubt let him sleep on, undisturbed, until noon— there would be nothing odd about that. But about, or soon after noon, they would be suspicious, and the chambermaid would call the manageress, and the manageress would look through the transom above the door, and as Tisdale lay so motionless——

Garthwaite laughed. He pictured the hotel folks and their perplexity; he pictured the doctors who would be called in; he pictured the police——

"Hallo!" exclaimed a man who stood at Garthwaite's side on deck, staring towards Margate and its stone pier. "What's up? We're slowing down and there's a tug coming out to us!"

Garthwaite began to stare landward in company with everybody else. The steamer was certainly slackening in speed, and there, just as certainly, was a small tug puffing briskly in its direction. It was quite a small tug, but a very fast one, and before long those on board the steamer could see that it carried two or three men who were plainly not members of its small crew. And presently the man who stood at Garthwaite's side let out another exclamation, mingled with a sly laugh.

"Ha, ha!" he chuckled. "I see what this game is! Those chaps in plain clothes there on the tug are detectives—London men, too, I'll bet! But who's the fellow with them?"

Garthwaite, whose sight was not so good as the other man's, moved further along the deck. Detectives! And stopping the steamer! Could it be possible that——

The next instant Garthwaite knew what this unexpected development sprang from. There, on the deck of the tug, now close to the steamer, standing between two solid-looking men, was the night-bird, who had asked for the chance of earning a few coppers. He was looking up, and as he looked he saw Garthwaite looking down, and he touched one of his companions on the arm and pointed eagerly.

Garthwaite knew what had happened then. Everything had gone wrong. The hotel folk had found Tisdale earlier than he had allowed for. The discovery had got noised abroad. This confounded loafer had heard it, and remembered the man who came out of the hotel and boarded the Rotterdam steamer, and he had hastened to give his news. And the police had hurried down to Margate to intercept the steamer as she passed, and they had brought the man with them to identify him!

He walked quietly away to a corner of the deck and drew out his pocketbook. He had a sure and certain belief that if he once fell into the hands of the law he would never escape those hands, and for such a fate he had no appetite. And so he felt for the second of the terrible capsules. Everything within him was crying out that the game was up. Very well. He would take his own way.

The next instant Garthwaite jumped as if a hand had been laid on him. The capsule was not there! He searched frantically through the pocketbook; he even dropped some papers and notes, and gave no more heed to them than if they had been rubbish. He must have spilled that capsule on the table in his room when he took out the other! And if he had, and if it were found, and if it were analysed—why, then——

He turned suddenly as a commotion arose behind him. The men from the tug had come aboard, and as he twisted round on them and the steamer's officers the night-bird to whom he had grudged a sixpence raised a dirty finger and pointed at him for the second time.

Garthwaite, oddly enough, remembered that dirty finger and its queer, jerking movement most clearly of all his last memories when, some weeks later, a few men marched him out of a cell one morning, and made short work in hanging him.

XII: THE WAY TO JERICHO

CHAPTER I

THE tides of life were at low water mark with Melchior Rosenbaum. As he said to himself, he was up against it. There was no use in going through the farce of feeling in one pocket after another of his one suit of clothes in search of stray sixpences; all his pockets had been empty for three weary—and very hungry days. Nor was there any use in searching the chest of drawers in his bed-sitting-room in quest of coppers; sometimes when he had been comparatively flush of money, Melchior, with lordly indifference, had flung pence and halfpence amongst his socks and his collars, but he knew very well that there was not so much as a farthing there now. Yesterday had exhausted that particular mine. He had found twopence inside a folded shirt and had immediately fed his ravenous stomach with a penny roll and a penny glass of milk. Since then he had had nothing save the cup of tea and three slices—fortunately thick ones—of bread and butter which his long-suffering landlady doled out to him every morning. And it was now evening, and Melchior was desperately famished.

Like all sufferers in like case, Melchior thought rapidly over his chances of raising the wind. They were bad—hopelessly bad. Melchior had no settled employment. He was an inventor. He invented mechanical toys and games for children; there were several efforts of genius lying in a more or less unfinished state on his table at the moment. Sometimes he did pretty well—sometimes, as at present, he had awful turns of bad luck. But this was the worst, the very worst, he had ever known. He had been hard up for a month; almost penniless for a fortnight; utterly penniless since yesterday. He had nobody to turn to. It was useless to try to borrow half a crown from the landlady; he had not paid back the last shilling he had raised in that way, and he owed her a whole month's rent. It was useless to try to borrow from his cousin Isidore; he owed Isidore eighteen shillings, which, with interest, meant twenty. He had nothing to pawn—he had already pawned every single pawnable object.

Thinking of his uncle, the pawnbroker, made Melchior think of his real and proper uncle, Mr. Solomon Rosenbaum. It gave him a cold sweat to think of him, for Uncle Solly was a terrible old fellow when asked for money. He had money—lots of money. He was a man of property—house property. He was a bachelor, too. He lived in no style at all; he was housed in a little two-room flat near Gower Street station; his yearly expenses, all added together, could not amount to a hundred pounds, said Melchior. And he was taking in hundreds—hundreds!—a year in rents. What did he do with it? Why didn't he distribute it to his nephews? Miser!—that's what he was, old Uncle Solly, a miserable, grasping miser! Rolling in good red and yellow gold, the old skinflint, while he, Melchior, of his own flesh and blood, was wanting bread!

Walking about his room, hands thrust in his empty pockets, Melchior's troubled eyes suddenly encountered a cheap calender which hung above his fireless grate. September 29!—Quarter Day! The very day on which Uncle Solly collected his rents, always in person. The old man would have heaps of money that night; the very thought of it, gold, silver, cheques, banknotes, made Melchior utter frightful groans. Surely, surely, on a day when he had made so much himself, Uncle Solly would spare a little for one of his own tribe, were it but a few shillings now! But at the mere notion of asking for even a copper, Melchior felt the sweat break out on him again. He remembered how the old man had driven him out on the last occasion on which he had begged for five shillings.

At that moment something happened. Downstairs the landlady was cooking fresh herrings for another lodger's delectation and regalement; a whiff of them penetrated through the keyhole of Melchior's door. And, with something like a howl, Melchior snatched up his hat, tore from the room, took the stair in a succession of bounds and leaps, swept from the house, and vanished in the autumn twilight.

Melchior lodged in a drab and shabby street in the top end of Edgware Road. Being literally penniless when he rushed out of his lodging, there was nothing to do but to foot it to Uncle Solly. But Melchior knew every turn and twist of that part of London, and he made a direct cut across the outer portion of Lisson Grove towards the desired haven, walking at top speed in order to keep up his courage. On the way he frequently passed shops whereat they sold things to eat. He tried to keep his eye off these places, but once, as he drew near the end of his journey, he inadvertently caught sight of a dish of mutton pies at twopence each, and he growled like a famishing cur and sped onward at an accelerated pace. This time he would have money—were it but a shilling—out of

Uncle Solly; if need were, he would weep tears of blood to him.

Uncle Solly lived in a shabby tenement house in one of those dismal streets which are attached to the purlieus of Euston. Why a man of such affluence should reside in such a place was a puzzle to Melchior and Isidore, his nephews, who, had they possessed one-fourth of his means, would have tenanted a nice flat in Maida Vale. But there Uncle Solly lived—all alone—and had lived ever so many years; he had lived there before Melchior and Isidore were born. And except when he was rent collecting or pottering about his property, he was always at home.

Before entering the open door of the tenement house, Melchior took a careful look around. There was a light in the window of Uncle Solly's sitting-room, high up on the top floor. Melchior heaved one desperate sigh, and plunged up the dirty staircase. And from the street door to Uncle Solly's landing he did not meet, see or hear one single soul.

Before he actually reached it, Melchior saw that the door of Uncle Solly's sitting-room was slightly open, a good foot-breadth of yellow light shone through the opening. Everything was very quiet. No sound came from the room. And Melchior, whose footwear was necessarily of the thinnest, crept up the last few stairs as silently as a shadow, and with infinite precaution peeped into the parlour.

Empty! Not a soul to be seen. No Uncle Solly—nobody. But on the table, not two yards away from Melchior's straining eyes, lay—money! Gold, bank-notes, cheques, silver, copper! Melchior saw the meaning of the situation at a glance. The old man was reckoning up his quarter-day takings—there was his ledger with a pen lying across it—and he had interrupted his labours to go into his bedroom, but he must be there. How soon would he emerge, how soon?

It was all over in the twinkling of one of Melchior's bright black eyes. Noiselessly and swiftly he slipped through the door. Just as noiselessly, just as swiftly, one of his thin, long-fingered hands laid hold of a fistful of gold, while the other picked up a couple of coppers. With a similar swiftness he was out of the room again and down the stairs, unseen by mortal eye. And once outside that house he was round one corner, and making for another with the cunning and celerity of a fox. In less than three minutes Melchior had crossed Euston Road, plunged into the underground, and was slapping one of the stolen pennies down in exchange for a third single.

CHAPTER II

MELCHIOR came out of the underground at Edgware Road Station within ten minutes of his hurried flight from Uncle Solly's parlour. He had recovered his breath and his equanimity by that time. Already his sharp wits—further sharpened by hunger—assured him that he was safe. No one had seen him enter or leave the house. He was sure that Uncle Solly, who was very deaf, had not heard that cat-like tread in his parlour. And here he was a good mile away, almost at once. Luck! Why, was ever such luck before?

He stood for a moment to finally pull himself together and his eyes, wandering around in the murky streets caught sight of the back windows of Reggiori's Restaurant. The gleam of those windows made Melchior positively wolfish. He chinked the gold in his pockets. Well, why not, for once? Such places were above him as a rule, but not to-night. He rejoiced in the fact that his clothes and linen were quite good enough to ensure him admittance and attention at any good place of public resort. That was an advantage. Without further delay Melchior crossed the narrow street, slipped into the restaurant, and in another minute was studying the menu which an unsuspicious waiter handed to him with a polite bow.

It was a wonder to Melchior that he did not fall upon the bread basket and the cruet—he felt as if he could have eaten a mustard plaster. But he restrained himself admirably. Soup? Yes, he would have soup—a thick soup—and he would have his favourite dish—boiled chicken, with rice and mushrooms, and he would have a bottle—a bottle of burgundy—the best Beaune. Let the waiter bring that at once. And while the waiter shot off to fetch it Melchior laid hands on a hunk of bread, sprinkled a pinch of salt on a big nob of it, and began, at last, to appease his awful craving.

Melchior was no fool. He ate a goodly lump of bread before he put his lips to the red wine. But when at last he had slowly sipped a glassful he became conscious of new strength, new power, new ideas. Oh, what a stroke of luck—what a blessed, blessed stroke of luck! Could it really be? Was it, after all, a dream? Would he awake and find himself in his fireless room, and——

"S'elp me!" exclaimed a familiar voice. "If it ain't Melky! Here, what's the meaning of it?"

Melchior started and looked up from his soup to confront his cousin Isidore, a young gentleman of bold countenance, aggressive manner, and sharp eyes, dressed in something of sporting fashion, and wearing a horseshoe pin of imitation diamonds in his smart four-in-hand cravat. He was bending over the table and scrutinising Melchior as if he were a rare curiosity; from Melchior his eyes turned to the bottle of wine.

"S'elp me!" he exclaimed again. "A bottle!"

Melchior motioned Isidore to come into his corner, and, as a preliminary to pleasant conversation, drew out a sovereign and slipped it along the tablecloth.

"Your quid, Issy," he murmured. "Here, I'll stand you a dinner if you like!"

Isidore fingered the sovereign exactly for one-half second before he transferred it to his waistcoat pocket. Then he looked at Melchior with slowly widening eyes.

"May I never," he exclaimed. "What's it all about, Melky?"

Melchior lapped up his last drop of soup, and beckoned to the waiter.

"Oh, I just sold one of my inventions," he answered carelessly. "What you fancy, Issy? Order what you like. And what'll you drink? Give your order."

Isidore, who had entered the restaurant intent on an underdone beef steak and a pint of bitter ale, with accompaniments, made a careful inspection of the bill of fare.

"Give me a nice sole—a fat one," he commanded. "And after that I'll take jugged hare—mind there's plenty of thick gravy, and red currant jelly with it. And—what sort of wine's that, Melky—good?"

"Extra!" affirmed Melchior. "Try a glass."

The waiter brought a clean glass, and Isidore sampled, smacking his lips.

"That'll do," he said. "Bring another bottle." He rubbed his hands gleefully when the waiter had gone, and putting one of them under the tablecloth, squeezed his cousin's knee. "Melky, old sport," he whispered, "how much did it run to?"

But Melchior shook his curly head.

"No," he said firmly. " 'Tain't your business, Issy. You got your eighteen bob, and two bob interest, and you're going to get your dinner—and a good 'un, too, with wine. And I'll stand cigars and liqueurs, too, if you like. But I ain't going to tell my business to nobody. Nice bit, anyway."

"What was it?" asked Isidore.

"Model of machine gun—for kids," replied Melky, quite ready with a lie. "Shoots peas—cute notion!"

"Who's bought it?" inquired Issy, lifting his glass.

"Mendel," answered Melky thoughtlessly. "He'll do well out of it when Christmas comes around."

"Well, here's luck," said Issy, and drank more wine. "And hoping things'll still further improve, Melky. You always was a genius!"

"How's things with you?" demanded Melky. "Good?"

"Fair," replied Issy. "Backed three winners since Monday, and I'm doing a bit in the horse line. Just been up the road now to see a feller what's got a horse to sell, 'cause I know another feller as wants one. Cheerio! Melky—we ain't doing so dusty. But I say—take my tip. Don't you go a-selling of them inventions of yours right out! What you oughter do is to have so much down, and a royalty on every article sold. See?"

"Think so?" asked Melky. He was so thoroughly fed and warmed and restored by that time that he had forgotten all about Uncle Solly, and was almost convinced that his lies were truths. "Might be a good thing, that, too. I got a splendid invention now—it's at Fildridge's. They're considering of it—might hear about that any time. If they took it up and manufactured it properly, shooks! they'd sell thousands—tens o' thousands!"

"What 'ud it sell at?" asked Issy.

"Shilling—popular toy," answered Melky. "It's a sure thing—if taken up."

Issy's fat sole appeared just then, and for half an hour he and Melky gobbled and drank side by side in full contentment. They consumed much Italian pastry when the solid things were over, and they settled down to coffee and liqueurs and cigars, and to the discussion of money matters, and by the time Melky had paid the bill and presented the waiter with sixpence, they both felt that life should certainly show patches of gold—now and then.

Issy walked home with Melky to his lodgings, talking confidentially. Melky asked him in, and sent him upstairs, while he himself went down to the basement to pay his landlady and borrow an armful of wood wherewith to light his fire. When he joined Issy, Issy held up a letter.

"On your table," he said. "Melky, old man, it's from Fildridge's! There's their name on the flap."

Melky flung his dry wood into the grate and tore the letter open. He ran his eyes over the contents and let out a wild scream of joy.

"They're going to take it up!" he yelled. "I'm going there to-morrow morning and settle the terms. They suggest so much down and a royalty."

Issy threw his rakish billycock in the air. Then he seized Melky's arm.

"Hang the fire, Melky, old sport!" he shouted. "Come on! We'll go around to the best pub in the neighbourhood and drink your health. And s'elp me, I'll pay."

CHAPTER III

MELCHIOR woke next morning with a headache. He and Isidore had sought and found a select tavern in Maida Vale. They had drunk many healths and smoked several cigars, and the unwonted indulgence had produced evil effects on Melchior. At 9 o'clock his landlady, mollified in his favour by the settling up of the night before, brought him a breakfast of bacon and eggs. Melchior looked at the eggs with disgust and at the bacon with aversion. It was all he could do to nibble a bit of toast and sip a cup of tea.

And as he nibbled and tasted, he picked up the half-penny newspaper which was tucked in the toast rack and listlessly opened it to read the news. Suddenly his jaw dropped, the tea cup trembled in his hand and he let out a hollow groan. For this was what Melchior's eyes had fallen upon:

MYSTERIOUS ROBBERY NEAR EUSTON

"Late last night the police authorities were informed of a mysterious theft, which is believed to have taken place between a quarter to eight and 9 o'clock in the evening. The circumstances are of a peculiar nature. Mr. Solomon Rosenbaum, a property owner of that neighbourhood, who occupies a two-room flat in a house in Penkington Street, had, it being quarter-day, been collecting his rents yesterday afternoon and evening, and at half-past seven o'clock was entering the various particulars in his ledger. He had occasion to go into his bedroom, and when he did so he left on his table in the parlour a considerable sum of money in cheques, banknotes, gold and silver. Mr. Rosenbaum, who is very deaf, either fainted or had some sort of seizure on entering the bedroom, and he remained there, helpless and unconscious for some time; when he came to himself and was able to move back into the parlour it was a little after 9 o'clock. Upon examining the money which he had left on the table, Mr. Rosenbaum found that eleven pounds in gold were missing. He immediately sent for the police, but up to a late hour last evening no arrest had been made and no light thrown on the subject. No suspicious character was seen to enter or leave the house and we understand that Mr. Rosenbaum refuses to suspect any of the people who live in it. The extraordinary feature of the case is that the thief, whoever he was, might, had he liked, have carried off everything on the table, which, we are informed, represented a total of over two hundred pounds."

If Melchior had felt shaky before he had picked up that newspaper, he felt ten times more so when he let it drop from his hands. For everything was all wrong! Things were not turning out right. The course of events was not what he had designed. "Mr. Rosenbaum refuses to suspect any of the people in the house"—horror! Why, that was positively wicked of Uncle Solly! It was his duty to suspect the people who lived in the house—of course, it was! And if he didn't suspect them—why, he'd begin to suspect—ah, whom couldn't he begin to suspect? He might even be thoughtless enough to begin to suspect him, Melchior—which, of course, on any grounds open to Uncle Solly, would be utterly unreasonable.

Melchior thrust his hands into his pockets, fingered the considerable remains of the money, and reflected. And presently he got up and hid all but a few shillings in a safe place—to wit, within the body of one of his mechanical toys, amongst the wood and sawdust stuffing. You never know what mayn't happen, he said to himself, and the smartest detective would have to think for a long time before he hit on that place. He had just completed this task when the door opened and Melchior turned quickly to see a detective, an amateur one, Isidore.

Isidore, who was much more a man of the world than Melchior, showed no sign of his previous night's revel. He was dressed in his best; he was groomed and shaved; his clothes and hat were carefully brushed. He was looking fit enough—and his face was very grave. And in one hand he carried another copy of the newspaper which had just caused Melchior such pain, and with an accusing finger directed at it, he held it under his cousin's nose, and shook his head at him.

"Melky!" he said, in a low, tense voice. "That's you! You did that. Melky, you deep one! Don't lie and say you didn't—at least—not to me, 'cause it ain't no good, Melky. Not one scrap of good, Melky. 'Cause—I've been to Mendel's this morning."

These last words, spoken in a still lower, tenser tone, made Melchior Rosenbaum tremble all over. He collapsed on the edge of his bed, white and shivering.

"Yes," continued Issy, bending over him like an accusing angel. "I been at Mendel's just now. Oh, Melky, you're an awful liar, as well as a thief! You didn't sell no invention to Mendel—no, not for fifteen months. Ah, you can't get over your cousin Issy, Melky! Do you know what? I was up early this morning seeing after that horse deal, and I buy the halfpenny newspaper as I come home, and I see in it—that! And then," continued Issy, striking the side of his well-developed nose with his finger, "then I see something else! I see through you, Melky, my clever one! You popped into old Uncle Solly's room and took that money and then hurried to the restaurant to blue some of it on your proud stomach. Melky—and—Melky, where's the rest?"

Melky had recovered himself a little during this cousinly exhortation and he now glared sulkily at Issy.

"Don't I pay for your dinner last night?" he muttered. "Don't you eat and drink of the best—wine you drink and liqueurs, sixpenny cigars you smoke, and it's me—me!—what pays. Don't I give your eighteen bob back to you and two bob more for interest—one hundred and fifty per cent., s'elp me—and don't I stand whiskies and cigars again when we go to drink my health? And don't I pay my landlady what I owe her, too? Course I do! How much do you think I got when I pay all them moneys away, then?"

"About eight pound, Melky," answered Issy with promptitude. "That's as near as I can reckon it. Come on, now. You'll share with your cousin Issy, of course. Where is it, Melky?"

Melchior growled and shed a few tears, but he knew Isidore, and presently he rose and disembowelled the mechanical doll, and from the sawdust and stuffing he drew forth eight sovereigns wrapped in cotton wool. He held them out to his cousin in silence and Issy calmly appropriated five of them.

"That's kind of me, Melky," he said, hiding the gold away in some inner pocket of his sporting waistcoat. "I ain't taking half, you see—you had eleven. But, oh, Melky, what a fool you are! There was two hundred there according to the newspaper. Melky, why didn't you pinch the lot, when you'd such a chance? The chance of a lifetime, Melky. Why, you ain't fit to do no business for yourself, you ain't. And it's a fortunate thing for you that you have your cousin Issy to look after you; it is, indeed! Now Melky, a question. Do you think you're safe? Let's know all about it."

Melky gave a brief account of the visit to Uncle Solly's and Issy listened with alert ears. In the end he smiled and nodded with satisfaction.

"Good business!" he said. "I don't think no harm'll come to you, Melky. And now just wash and shave yourself and smarten yourself up, and then you and I are going out—what?"

"Of course, I'm going out," growled Melky. "Ain't I got a business appointment at Fildridge's about my invention?"

"And ain't I going with you to keep it?" said Issy. "'Cause I am, Melky, my son! You ain't no good at business, but your cousin Issy'll see you through. Hurry up, and we'll have a little refreshment on the way, that'll make you see things rosy-like, and—ah, you'll see what a bargain I'll make for you, Melky."

CHAPTER IV

THE man who had to do business with Melchior and Isidore Rosenbaum at Fildridge's came to the conclusion that of all the sharp and astute young men he had ever met these two were the very sharpest. It was useless for him to urge that the putting of a new mechanical toy on the market was a good deal of a lottery. Isidore, who did most of the talking, with occasional whispers to Melchior, first quietly assured himself that Fildridge's really wanted the thing, and then proceed to screw the buyer down to terms. Those terms were to be Isidore's terms and nobody else's. And at the end of an hour he and Melchior were out of Fildridge's, and Isidore had banknotes in one pocket and an agreement in another, and he led his cousin to a quiet corner in an adjacent saloon, and, after he had procured drinks and cigars, pulled out both.

"See what I done for you, Melky!" he said. "You wouldn't ha' done all that for yourself! One hundred pound on account, and a royalty of one penny on every blessed toy they sell. Melky, you're going to be a Rothschild. And I'll be your agent. Go on inventing them little things, Melky, and you and me'll make fortunes out of 'em!"

"Hand over the notes," said Melchior uneasily. "And less lip about you and me! Fat lot you got to do with it, Issy. Don't I invent that toy? Come on, now. I let you do the talking 'cause you gotta better gift of the gab than me, but ain't I the principal?"

"Commission, Melky, commission!" suggested Issy. "What you going to give me for my commission, now?" He retained a hold on the notes and kept them away from Melchior's itching fingers. "You oughter give me sixty per cent., Melky—that's the fair thing!"

Melchior grew pale with fury. He began to curse Issy under his breath. Thereupon Issy folded up the notes, put them in his pocket, felt for, and found, the five sovereigns which he had taken from Melky two hours earlier, and began to chink them.

"All right, Melky," he said. "Then I give you this five quid back, and I go straight to Uncle Solly, and tell him everything. And as you'll get twenty years in quod, Melky, and won't have no use for money there, I'll take care of this £100 until you come out. I'm sorry for you, Melky. I never thought a cousin of mine 'ud disgrace himself. And for eleven quid too, when he might ha' had two hundred of the best!"

Melky had to give in. Isidore let him off at fifty per cent. That agreed upon, he carefully counted out five £10 notes, and handed them to Melky with the agreement. After which he put the other five in his pocket and arose.

"Well, so long, Melky," he said. "I've got an engagement. You go home and begin inventing some things. "I'll come around in a day or two to see how you're getting on. Keep your head cool, Melky, and think hard. Maybe we get two hundred and a twopenny royalty next time."

With that he went away, and Melchior after swearing quietly for awhile in the loneliness of the corner wherein these cousinly confidences had taken place, went away, too, lamenting that Fildridge's letter had not reached him before he rushed away from the smell of the cooking herrings. For then he would not have gone to Uncle Solly's, and he would never have fallen, and he would never have met that shark, Issy, and——

CHAPTER V

ISIDORE ROSENBAUM, going away from this highly satisfactory bit of business, boarded a Cricklewood omnibus and went away up the Edgware Road to attempt another. He got off at a well-known depository for horses, and, with the help of his so-easily earned £50, did a bit of trade. He bought horse-flesh with that fifty, which, an hour later, he sold to another man for seventy—twenty pounds clear profit, chuckled Issy. And at the end of that transaction he blessed Melky for providing him with the means for carrying it out, but he had no thought of giving Melky any commission, not even a dinner. Instead, it being by that time two o'clock, Issy turned into the nearest good restaurant and proceeded to do himself very well indeed. He had great taste for the flesh pots, Issy, and for the wine jars, too, and having accomplished a most satisfactory morning's work, he thought that he had an indisputable right to enjoy himself. Wherefore, having eaten until he could eat no more, and having finished a bottle of generous wine, he lingered long in the restaurant, smoking a big cigar, and sipping Chartreuse, and he thought himself a clever fellow and promised himself that he would exploit Melky for all he was worth.

The liquor warmed Issy's already fertile brain to other schemes. He began to think about Uncle Solly Rosenbaum. Now, Issy knew men nearly as well as he knew horses—which is saying a good deal. He had studied Uncle Solly and he had arrived at certain conclusions about him. Uncle Solly, like nearly all well-to-do men, hated poor relations. He disliked having them about him. The mere knowledge of their poverty irritated him. He always looked at them frowningly, as if their very presence meant a sort of curt demand for money. And Issy, whenever he was hard up—as he often had been—always kept away from his rich relative's rooms, for he believed that Uncle Solly's big nose could actually scent poverty, as a mouse can smell cheese. But when he was flush of money, Issy liked to visit Uncle Solly, and to swagger around him a little. He knew very well that this old miser was much more likely to leave his shekels to a young man who could make money, than to one who couldn't. Issy had a firm conviction that in this world nothing is so certain as that to them that have shall be added, and from those who have not shall be subtracted.

A second glass of Charteuse and another sixpenny cigar warmed Issy to feelings of adventure. He would go around to see Uncle Solly, and condole with him on his sad loss of eleven quid; incidentally, he would let him know how well he himself was doing. He had no sooner thought of this than he acted upon the thought. Drinking off the last sips of his liqueur and setting his cigar in his full red lips, Issy cocked his hat at the proper angle, buttoned up his smart overcoat, and swaggered out of the restaurant, leaving twopence on the table for the waiter.

Uncle Solly, smoking his pipe by a bit of fire in his dreary-looking sitting-room, glanced suspiciously at his nephew when Issy blustered in. His face cleared, however, when he had taken stock of Issy's outer man. Prosperity was written largely over Issy, it was clear that he had not come there to borrow money. He allowed Issy to shake hands and clap him on the shoulder; he even graciously allowed him to sit down at his side.

"You doing well?" he asked, inclining his ear-trumpet to his visitor. "Making anything?"

"Extra!" shouted Issy. "Made £20 profit in half an hour this morning."

"What are you doing?" enquired Uncle Solly. "Peddling jewellery?"

Issy made a face of disgust and raised his voice.

"No!" he vociferated. "Horses! Buying and selling, Uncle Solly. See here. I buy nice horse this morning for fifty quid, and sell him for seventy quid, all within the hour, eh?"

"Where did you get the fifty quid?" demanded Uncle Solly.

"Saved it!" bawled Issy. "I ain't without money. Do you know what, I got a lotta money, in the savings bank. I'm a capitalist, I am. I ain't like that fellow Melky, living hand to mouth; soon I'll begin to buy property like you."

Uncle Solly twisted his patriarchal face round, and took another look at his nephew, musingly, and Uncle Solly began to think there was something in it.

"Umph!" he grunted. Then he gave Issy another sharp look. "You read in the newspapers this morning?" he asked. "You see that about me?"

"Yes!" shouted Issy. "Not till just this minute I don't see it, that's what I come for."

"What you come for then?" demanded Uncle Solly, alertly. "You don't know nothing about it, eh?"

"Come to offer my sympathy!" called Issy down the ear-trumpet. "Sorry to hear about it, you know. What you leave all them good moneys on your table for when you wasn't in the room, Uncle Solly?"

Uncle Solly made a face and groaned.

"I have a fainting fit," he answered. "I don't have my dinner till I reckon up my moneys, eh? Then I feel queer, and I go into my chamber to get me a little taste of rum, and I fall down by my bed, what? Then the thief, he put in his nose at my open door, and take my good money, what I can't afford to lose!"

"You should lock your door when you count your money," said Issy. "That's what I always do. Of course, some of your neighbours——"

Uncle Solly growled, and showed signs of displeasure.

"No," he said. "My neighbours are all honest people. D'ye think I'd live amongst people that wasn't honest—me?"

"Oh, well, £11 ain't nothing to you, Uncle Solly," said Issy as soothingly as his enforced loud tones would permit. "You ain't going to be broke for eleven quid, are you? Why you could throw eleven quid into the street."

Uncle Solly looked sideways at his nephew with unutterable disgust, and Issy saw that he had made a mistake. He hastened to repair it.

"What I mean is, you could throw eleven quid away without feeling it," he bawled. "A man what's got as many quid as you have——"

"You're a fool," snapped Uncle Solly rudely. "You ain't no wisdom. I couldn't throw eleven pennies away without feeling it. That wicked person what robbed me last night, has done me harm. I was going to invest a certain sum to-day; now I'm £12 short of it: I don't know where to get no £12. I shall lose my good investment, and it was such good interest, too. I'm a poor man; I don't go picking up no £12 in the street. I had to work hard before I buy my property."

Issy was suddenly struck by a brilliant idea. It was so brilliant, indeed, that it almost took his breath away. But he recovered his breath, and he smote Uncle Solly on the shoulder.

"Uncle Solly," he shouted. "Do you know what, I'll lend you £12 to take up your investment. I'll lend it to you till next quarter-day, and—and you don't have to pay me no interest, neither. What do you say, Uncle Solly?"

Uncle Solly gazed doubtingly at his nephew. But Issy nodded with eagerness, and Uncle Solly stretched out a dirty claw-like hand.

"You don't have it about you?" he asked in an avaricious whisper.

"This minute," responded Issy with alacrity. He drew out his pocketbook and carefully selected a ten-pound note, then he plunged his hand into the secret receptacle within his horsey waistcoat, wherein he had deposited the five sovereigns which Melky had withdrawn from their hiding-place inside the doll. He pulled two of the sovereigns out, laid them on the £10 note, and handed the lot over. "There you are, Uncle Solly," he said magnanimously. "Twelve quid till next quarter-day. And I don't take no interest from you."

Uncle Solly took the note and the sovereigns in dead silence. He held the note up to the light, he fingered it, he smelt it, he did everything but eat it. Then he examined the sovereigns, first with his fingers, then with his eyes. And then he got up out of his chair, and laid aside his ear-trumpet.

"I stand you a nice drink, Issy," he said. "What you like to drink, eh? Port wine, eh? I stand you a nice drink of port wine. You sit quiet a minute while I send for it. Very good port wine at the corner. I send for a nice bottle."

Uncle Solly shuffled out of the room and away down the stairs, and Issy sat back in his chair and laughed. Oh, what a clever fellow he was. What a stroke of good business! He had lifted himself miles high in Uncle Solly's estimation and good graces, and all by that little stroke of genius. What was twelve quid in comparison to all that property which Uncle Solly would be certain to leave him! He rubbed his hands and chuckled for sheer delight. And being alone, he fell into a day-dream as to what he would do when the property was indeed his.

Uncle Solly was away quite ten minutes. When his shuffling steps sounded at last on the stairs, they were accompanied by other steps. The sound of those steps made Issy jump; he knew that those steps belonged to policemen.

The door was pushed open, Uncle Solly appeared, the banknote and the two sovereigns still in his hands. And close upon his old heels came two very big policemen. Before those enquiring eyes, Isidore felt himself turning white and green, like Gorgonzola cheese. He rose from his chair, and his jaw began to drop.

"That's him!" screamed Uncle Solly, pointing a quivering and vindictive finger at Issy. "Take him! Handcuff him! Lock him up till the judge puts him away! Take him at once, hold him fast. Mind he doesn't jump through the window! Ah, the dirty sneak thief! Do you know what?" he went on, as the policemen lined up about Issy. "He come in here and offer to lend me £2—two of the very quid he pinched from me last night! These quid—look at them! Marked, I tell you, them quids are marked! Mr. Waters, one of my tenants, him what keeps the greengrocery store round the corner, he pay me them quids in his quarter's rent. They've marks on 'em both. I pointed 'em out to Mr. Waters. Mr. Waters, he laugh about 'em. 'You'll know 'em all the better, Mr. Rosenbaum,' he says—just so. Don't I know 'em—don't I know my own moneys? And he pulled one out of his pocket, the young thief, just now. Oh, shameless one! But you shall go before the judge. Take him away, misters; put the irons on him."

Issy backed away as one of the policemen beckoned him. But already he saw himself on the brink of the abyss into which the arm of the law was going to push him headlong. It was all up. Melky would naturally deny everything, and Issy knew that he couldn't prove anything against Melky. And he couldn't prove an alibi, either, for, as cruel luck would have it, he himself had been in Uncle Solly's neighbourhood the night before, ere proceeding to the restaurant. No, his luck was down and out.

"It's—it's a dreadful mistake!" he panted. "Them two quids——"

"Come on now," said one of the constables. He laid a hand on Issy, and turned him to his uncle. "You'll have to come and charge him, Mr. Rosenbaum," he said.

And at that, Uncle Solly picked up his hat, with alacrity, and, with Issy in its centre, the tragic procession set forth.

XIII: PATENT NO. 33

CHAPTER I

ALFRED PENNY, second-hand bookseller, was one of those people who somehow or other drift into the occupations for which they are naturally fitted. He had begun life as a grocer's apprentice, simply because his father and mother considered that to be a highly respectable trade. He had continued it as a grocer's assistant because that seemed the inevitable result. But during his apprenticeship and his assistantship, he had spent all his spare time in hanging round and about the old bookshops, of which there were many in Wolborough, and before he was twenty-five he knew more of the book trade—in its second-hand branches—than he did of his own. Grimes, proprietor of the shop which Penny most affected, said as much to him, and hinted that he would be much better and more fittingly employed in buying and selling books than in wrapping up packets of cheap tea. Penny thought as much himself, but he had been securely planted in his particular hole, and he saw no way of getting out of it. Old Grimes made a way for him—by departing this life. Grimes's one daughter had no mind to carry on her father's business; she had other views, which included leaving Wolborough altogether. So she offered Alfred Penny the entire business, stock, good-will, on the easiest terms. Alfred had managed to save a certain amount of money; he borrowed more from a sympathetic and believing friend; the combined results went into Miss Grimes's pocket, and Penny had a new sign painted to go over the shop front and the twopenny boxes. "Penny, late Grimes," became a new feature of Turnstile Passage, Wolborough.

Alfred Penny revelled in his new business. All his thoughts were devoted to it. The better sort of book-buyers in the town soon recognised him as a man who really had an interest in the books which he bought and sold. He became an expert on rare editions, scarce pamphlets, odds and ends of antiquarian literature; at the close of the first year of business he had completely forgotten all about the various sorts of rice and the difference between tea from China and tea from Ceylon. No adventurer sailing into unknown seas, or plunging into hitherto unexplored forests, ever set out with more zest for his enterprises than Alfred Penny felt when he attended the sale of some ancient country-house library or opened a parcel of books offered him in his shop. There was always the chance, even in a parcel of what looked like rubbish, of finding a first edition or a scarce tract. Consequently, Penny lived in an atmosphere of discovery, and—when his time permitted it, which was seldom—he wondered how he had lived through the ten years during which he wore a grocer's apron.

One winter morning, as Penny sat in his shop, busily engaged in turning over a number of catalogues just received from brother booksellers of distant towns, a soft and somewhat timid voice sounded close behind him.

"If you please, do you buy books?"

This seemed a superfluous question, for there was a sign outside the shop door which informed passers-by that books were bought within. But Penny was used to such inquiries, and he turned with alacrity—to find himself confronting a young, pretty, and shy girl, who he saw at once was dressed in mourning garments. He jumped to his feet.

"Yes, Miss!" he answered promptly. "In any quantity—from entire libraries to the smallest parcels. You have some books to sell?"

"My mother wants to sell some books that my father left," replied the girl. "Perhaps you would come and look at them?"

"With pleasure, Miss," answered Penny. "What sort of books might they be, now? And how many of them? Anything local?"

"I think they're chiefly technical books—engineering and mechanics," said the girl. "But there are some others—a good many. Two hundred, perhaps, altogether. If you could come to No. 12, Mayfield Terrace? Would it be to-day? We should be glad if you would, because we're going to remove the day after to-morrow."

"Three o'clock this afternoon, Miss," responded Penny, jotting down the address. "What name, please?"

"Mrs. Burland," replied the girl.

"Be there at three sharp," said Penny.

The girl went away quickly, and Penny, watching her slim figure as she passed through the door, was suddenly conscious of having seen her before. Of course—he remembered her now—she had been a customer at the grocer's shop; he had often seen her there with her mother—a comfortable, well-to-do woman of the superior artisan class, who always had plenty of money to spend. And just as suddenly he remembered something else.

"Burland—Burland!" he repeated. "Ah, of course, that'll be the daughter of that John Burland who was killed last year in the explosion at Ramsdale's. Of course, he was an engineer—that's why they'll be mostly technical books. Not much in my line—but there's always a chance of a find anywhere."

The house at which Penny presented himself that afternoon at three o'clock was one of a row of cottage-like dwellings which stood under the shadow of the Ramsdale's Machine Works—one of the biggest of the many big industrial concerns of Wolborough. It was the sort of house in which the better-class workmen lived, with a living-room and a parlour on the ground floor, but in this case the parlour, instead of being devoted to genteel uses, had obviously been used as a workroom by John Burland. There was a bench and a lathe on one side of it, a table with instruments and tools, all neatly laid out in the centre, a home-made bookcase in a recess. The widow, who obviously remembered Penny in his grocer days, waved her hand round the room as she led him in.

"Just as my husband left it," she said. "We've never touched a thing—except to put 'em straight. And shouldn't ha' touched 'em, very like, for it gives one a thought of him to come in here and see his things. But, you see, I can't afford to keep up this house any longer—we must go into a smaller one, me and my daughter—so I shall have to part with all that's in it here. There's a man coming to buy these tools and things to-night. And how much do you think you can afford me for the books now, mister?"

Penny was used to these appeals. Since he had succeeded old Grimes he had often been fetched to small houses to buy books which he knew at first glance to have no other proper designation than that of his twopenny-box placard. It was always distasteful to him, a soft-hearted young man, to have to explain to the sellers that their goods were of no great value. He knew by experience that his protestations were invariably taken as business, and that the people from whom he bought believed that he would presently get five shillings for what he had laid out fivepence upon. And he turned to Burland's collection hoping that he would find something commercially valuable in it, for he already had an idea that the widow and daughter wanted money.

"He spent a deal of good brass on them books, did my husband, one time or another," observed the mother as she and her daughter watched Penny go through shelf after shelf with practiced eye and hand. "He'd give as much as ten shillings for some of 'em. Said he couldn't do without 'em for the things he made. He was always inventing something or other in the way of machinery. Mr. Ramsdale, of course, he made most of the things my husband invented. He'd been inventing for more years nor I can remember, had Burland, when that explosion killed him."

"I hope you've profited by it," said Penny. "Inventions bring in a lot of money, don't they?"

"They haven't brought so much here, anyway," replied the widow, a little bitterly. "Taken more out o' this house than ever they brought in, I should say. Now and then there'd be an extra ten-pound note, or happen a bit more, from one or other thing; but naught bigger nor better. Of course, my husband always did talk of some grand machine that he was working his brains at—something that was going to make all our fortunes—but naught had come of it when he was taken. I'm afraid they're all alike, is these inventors—always living on hope."

"But you know, mother, that father told us his

big work was just about finished only the week before his death," said the girl. "If he'd only lived——"

Penny, who thought he saw something like tears in the girl's eyes, hastened to plunge into the matter-of-fact realms of business.

"Well, I'll tell you what," he said, "I'll make you a lump offer for the lot, and I couldn't offer it if this wasn't a town where such books as these are likely to be bought. A lot of 'em are out of date, some of 'em aren't worth anything to me. Twenty pounds for the lot, ma'am, and that's a good offer."

He saw that the girl was agreeably surprised; she evidently had some idea of the value of the goods, sold at second-hand. But the mother hesitated.

"Eh! Why, as I say, he'd give as much as half a sovereign for one book, sometimes," she said. "Of course, I'm sure you'd do right by us, young man. I used to see you when you were in the grocery line. You couldn't say more, now?"

"It'll be a long time before I get my money back at that figure," replied Penny. "Folks don't buy these technical books every day, you know. Shall I give you the money in notes, ma'am? I have them here."

"Well, twenty pounds is twenty pounds," said Mrs. Burland. "And I'm sure me and my daughter can do with it, for Burland he hadn't saved a deal, and though he'd worked at Ramsdale's all them years, Mr. Ramsdale he only allows us a pound a week, for a pension—like. And, of course, a pound a week and the bit o' money we have, it isn't enough to keep a house this size, so we're going to a smaller. Very well, then, mister, twenty pounds."

Penny counted out four five-pound notes and went to charter a handcart. He had a little conversation with the girl as he packed the books, and he thought of her a good deal as he walked back to his shop later on. A very nice young lady, decided Penny in his simplicity, and he felt very sorry for her. For it was evident to him that the father must have been a highly skilled workman, and perhaps if he had lived that big idea of his might have come off, and then—who knows? Like all men who have lived in the big industrial towns, Penny had been bred up on the stories and legends of what great good fortune may come to lucky inventors; and there were half a dozen instances of it in Wolborough itself. Why, at that very moment, wasn't half England—the manufacturing England, at any rate—talking about Ramsdale's Multiplex? A most wonderful machine which Ramsdale himself had lately invented, patented, and could not manufacture in sufficient quantity to supply the world demand for it. Of course, a lucky inventor was a millionaire in embryo, no doubt of that. And if Burland hadn't been killed by that explosion——

But Burland had been killed, and his widow and daughter were obliged to sell his small belongings. And that evening, Penny, after his custom, spread the books out on the big table in the shop, and began to sort them, separating the better sort from the inferior sort. A few of these books were really expensive books on machinery. These Penny carefully selected and set aside, hoping that he might find a speedy customer.

He opened one or two of the larger volumes, to look at the diagrams and folding plates, and suddenly, from one of them dropped a paper, on the back of which was an endorsement, in a stiff, rather laboured handwriting, the writing of a man who was obviously not greatly used to holding a pen. Penny glanced at that endorsement, and he started at what he read, for his thoughts of the afternoon, about the possible profits of inventors, were still with him. For there, on the back of the folded paper, were three lines, plainly written: "Memorandum about the invention of my machine, to be known as Burland Multiplex, October 6th, 1901. John Burland."

Penny stared at this endorsement during the whole of a moment's wondering silence. Then, glancing at the clock, he shut and fastened his shop door, turned down the lights, and, carrying the paper and book from which he had taken it with him, he went upstairs to the rooms in which he lived all by himself.

CHAPTER II

PENNY, creeping up his dark stairs to his little sitting-room, felt like a conspirator who has unexpectedly come into possession of a weighty secret. He was sure there was a secret, a mystery, in that paper which he so carefully grasped—there must be. Burland's Multiplex?—was it likely there could be two multiplex machines? Could it be that—— But the mere notion of a possibility which came into his mind filled him with a queer sort of moral sickness, and he made haste to light up his lamp.

It was very still in that little room; the silence seemed to Penny the fitting environment for what he was about to do—which was to read a message from a dead man, a message which, as fortune would have it, had come to none but him. He saw how things were—John Burland had written this paper and put it away in one of the folding plates of a book which he doubtless used constantly. And before he could take it out again his own death had come, by accident.

And no one had ever seen that paper until he, Alfred Penny, had chanced upon it.

He sat down at his table and opened the paper—a half-sheet of foolscap—before him. This is what he read, with wondering eyes and speculative brain:

"Mem. abt. my machine, to be called 'Burland Multiplex.'

First notion of this machine about seven years ago—probably in winter of 1894.

Worked at idea more or less regularly ever since.

Never mentioned it to a soul—not even to Mr. Ramsdale.

Began drawings in '98.

Finished drawings in 1900.

Made first model in 1900.

Broke it up 1900.

Began second model same year.

Broke that up as soon as finished.

Began third and final model, April, 1901.

Finished it September 29th, 1901.

Perfect. One of the most wonderful machines ever invented.

Lodged drawings and model with Mr. Ramsdale for his inspection and advice as to getting patents and putting machine on market this day, October 6th, 1901.

This will be my thirty-third patent. It will produce a fortune such as I scarce dare dream of.

JOHN BURLAND."

The discoverer of this document let it fall from his hands upon the table and gasped. He was a simple, honest soul, Penny, but he had imagination and penetration amongst his mental equipment, and it seemed to him that he was gazing into a vista, however. Surely, the whole affair was plain. Burland had given his drawings and his model to Ramsdale, his employer. Then Burland had been killed. Then Ramsdale, who probably knew that no one, not even Burland's wife and daughter, were aware of the existence of model and plans, had taken out this patent in his own name, had begun manufacturing the machine, had put it on the market; and was now reaping a colossal fortune out of it. Everybody in Wolborough knew of the success of Ramsdale's Multiplex. It could not be turned out fast enough. It had completely revolutionised the spinning industry. The wildest rumours were afloat concerning the enormous sums which Ramsdale had received from foreign manufacturers for the right to make it. It was said that Ramsdale, always a rich man, was now a multi-millionaire. Only recently, Penny, walking near Ramsdale's house one Sunday with a friend, had been told by that friend that it was said that Ramsdale was making thousands a week out of the multiplex.

"And he allows the real inventor's wife and daughter a miserable pound a week!" soliloquised Penny. "What a mean scoundrel! But——"

But what was to be done? Penny had seen enough of the dead man's widow to recognise that she was no more than a plain, womanly, working-class woman, who would certainly not know how to stand up for her just rights, and if she made any claim against Ramsdale, would probably take some trifling amount in satisfaction of it. The daughter, however, was of a superior sort; Penny, in that brief conversation with her, had found out that she was a school teacher and educated and of some ambition. She was a pretty girl, and a nice girl, and Penny had been rather more than a little struck with her. He had chivalric feelings, this little second-hand bookseller, and now he felt like a knight of old, and he smote his table with a big bang and swore that Burland's daughter should be righted. But—how? Who was he, poor Alfred Penny, to stand up and fight the great Ramsdale?

Imagination usually comes to people who urgently desire it, and it came to Penny. It came in the shape of a name—Mr. Wilmington. Mr. Wilmington was one of Penny's best customers. He was one of the few merchant princes of Wolborough who thought about things outside money and business. He bought books; he had a good trade in pictures. He was a very rich man, a powerful man, a magistrate, an alderman who had in his time been Mayor of Wolborough —and he was, withal, a very kindly-natured and easily approached man. Certainly Mr. Wilmington was the very man of whom to seek advice. And thereupon Penny cased himself in his overcoat, put the important document in his pocket, turned out his lamp, and set forth to get a tramcar to the residential quarter in which Mr. Wilmington lived.

Mr. Wilmington, a pleasant-faced, elderly gentleman, was alone in his comfortable library when Penny was shown to him. He smiled at the little bookseller as he motioned him to come to the fire.

"Hello, Penny!" he exclaimed. "What brings you here in such a hurry? Found something rare, eh? What is it—a Caxton?"

Penny sat down, got his breath, and stared fixedly at his host.

"I've found something stranger than any Caxton, sir," he answered. "Something that seems—well, terrible to me, Mr. Wilmington. You know—you know Ramsdale's Multiplex?"

Mr. Wilmington stared. There was no one in that neighbourhood who did not know Ramsdale's Multiplex. But—what did Penny know?

"Well?" he asked. "What of it?"

Penny bent forward and sank his voice to a whisper.

"He didn't invent it!" he murmured. "It isn't his, Mr. Wilmington—there's wrong being done!"

Mr. Wilmington stared harder than ever at his visitor. And Penny sat and nodded—the nod of complete assurance.

"You've got something to tell," said the elder man at last. "Begin at the beginning, my lad! And—be precise."

Penny drew a long breath and began his story—from the moment that the dead man's daughter entered the shop that afternoon. And his hearer heard—and his face grew graver and graver, and was very dark indeed when Penny, to conclude matters, placed the memorandum in his hands.

"Heaven bless my soul!" he exclaimed. "That's a strange story, Penny! And I'm afraid it's quite possible that your theory's a right one."

"Mr. Wilmington," said Penny solemnly, "it can't be anything else, sir. Look at the facts!"

"I'm going to look at several facts, my lad," said the old gentleman, who was carefully reading and re-reading the memorandum. "And we'll begin with one very pertinent one," he continued, as he rose from his chair and went over to a bookcase in which numerous large volumes were set. "It runs in my mind that this poor chap was killed just about the time that he wrote this paper. We'll turn up the account of that explosion in this file of the *Wolborough Observer*. Ay," he said presently, as he turned over the bound volume and put his finger on a certain column, headed by big black capitals, "here we are, that accident in which Burland lost his life was October 7th. The very day after he wrote this memorandum!"

"And the very day after he put his model in Ramsdale's hands!" muttered Penny.

Mr. Wilmington made no answer to that remark. He restored the newspaper file to its place, went to another part of his bookcase, and returned with a bundle of official-looking journals.

"We'll soon see when the patent office people advertised this machine," he said, as he sat down at his desk. "This is their official journal, Penny. You aren't conversant with the procedure in this sort of thing, eh? I am, having had to do with a good many in my time. What's done is this. The inventor must first of all file a provisional or a complete specification of his invention at the patent office. The examiner of the patent office then investigates it—to see if specification and drawings properly describe the invention. If he's satisfied, he advertises the specification in this official journal. Then two months elapse—for anybody interested to have a chance of opposing the grant of a patent. If no opposition comes forward within that two months, then the patent is sealed. Understand? Well, now let's see when Ramsdale's Multiplex was advertised—1901, eh? Here you are—there it is—December, 1901. So the patent would be sealed February this year. Since when, my lad, Ramsdale and the various folks to whom he sold licences and concessions have been turning out that machine as fast as ever they could make it! Penny, if Burland's memorandum is true, it's a bad, bad case!"

Alfred Penny sighed deeply. He could find no words—all he could do was to shake his head and reflect on the ease with which defenceless poor people can be robbed.

Mr. Wilmington shook his head, too.

"Ramsdale," he observed, "is not what I should ever call a scrupulous man. I've heard of other tricks that he's done. Taking unfair advantage of people, and so on. Some people call that sort of thing clever. I call it bad. In this case his procedure seems to have been pretty clear. Burland probably told Ramsdale that not a soul knew of this wonderful machine. When Burland was killed in that explosion, Ramsdale knew that he was in possession—sole possession—of the whole thing. He took immediate steps to patent the machine in his own name. And he satisfies his conscience—such as it is—by giving the widow and daughter a pound a week for life! Bad, Penny; very bad!"

"What's to be done, sir?" asked Penny.

Mr. Wilmington looked at his watch.

"Half-past eight," he said meditatively. "Plenty of time to do something to-night. Naught like taking a man unawares in a thing of this sort. But we'll have a bit more advice. Come on with me—we'll step around to Mr. Chelwick's and tell him all about it. He's a man of more influence than I am, and if he talks straight to Ramsdale, Ramsdale'll listen. And now's the time to make Ramsdale listen. Why? Because it's rumoured that Ramsdale's put in for a title—knighthood or baronetage, or some handle of that sort—and if this got out, Penny, my lad, good-bye to all his hopes of it!"

CHAPTER III

During the next hour, Penny, listening to a conversation carried on with great earnestness between Mr.

Wilmington and his neighbour, Mr. Chelwick, at the last-named gentleman's house, was not quite sure whether books were really as interesting as men. He already knew Mr. Wilmington pretty well; he had long known Mr. Chelwick by reputation as about the smartest lawyer in all Wolborough. And he sat in silent enjoyment as these two laid their heads together before him. For Chelwick, when he had heard everything and had read the memorandum, remarked that Martin Ramsdale was a cute and clever man and had probably evolved some deep means of protecting his own interest in this shabby matter. He might assert, protest, even swear in a Court of Justice that Burland had given him the invention. He might similarly protest that the invention was partly his own.

"The memorandum gives the lie to that," remarked Wilmington. "Burland distinctly says that he never mentioned it to a soul, not even to Mr. Ramsdale."

"Good; but Ramsdale may say that it wasn't perfected and that he himself perfected it," pointed out the lawyer. "If we only had the original drawings, the specification, the model.

"Ramsdale could be made to produce all," said Wilmington.

"Ramsdale is clever and ingenious enough to have had the drawings copied—probably to have copied them himself, being, as he is, a trained mechanical draughtsman," said Chelwick. "And as for the model, the difficulty would be to prove that it was made by Burland. This paper, undoubtedly in Burland's handwriting, speaks of a machine called the 'Multiplex,' which he says here he delivered a model of to Mr. Ramsdale, together with the drawings. What we have got to prove is that that is the identical machine in every respect which is now known as

'Ramsdale's Multiplex.' Personally, I haven't the least doubt that it is and that Martin Ramsdale is an unscrupulous thief! But how to prove it?"

Alfred Penny felt his sentimental heart swelling with so much indignation that it was like to burst his bosom. He thought of the defrauded mother and daughter; and, small person as he felt himself to be in the presence of these two great men, he ventured on a remark which sprang from his hatred of wrong and oppression.

"Wouldn't public opinion be on your side, sir?" he said, glancing at the lawyer. "I should say it would, sir; I should, indeed!"

Chelwick laughed good-humouredly and glanced at Wilmington.

"Ay, Mr. Penny," he answered. "I dare say it would; in fact, I've no doubt about it. But men like Martin Ramsdale don't care for public opinion—that sort of public opinion, anyhow. No, we've got to take a strong and bold line with Ramsdale. Wilmington, there's only one way. We must bluff him!"

"How, precisely?" asked Wilmington.

"Make him think that we're in possession of—well, of a much stronger case than we are in possession of," answered Chelwick. "Now listen. Mr. Penny, write down the address of Mrs. Burland. Thank you. I shall call on her first thing to-morrow morning. Now, I want you to call at my office at three o'clock sharp in the afternoon. Ramsdale will be there, or I'm no prophet. Then you'll take your cue from me. You'll neither of you say a word unless I call on you to speak. You're the two who know—well, more than you'll ever tell Ramsdale, eh? That's the only way—bluff—sheer bluff!"

"You think something'll come of it, sir?" asked

Penny a few minutes later, as Chelwick conducted his visitors to the door. "You think these two ladies will benefit?"

Chelwick winked over the little bookseller's shoulder at Wilmington. Then he clapped Penny on the back.

"You shall have the pleasure of carrying 'em whatever good news there is!" he said.

Then he shut his visitors out and went back to his study, and safely locked up John Burland's memorandum in a fireproof safe.

CHAPTER IV.

RAMSDALE, the proprietor of the world-famous engineering and machinery works which bore his name, was feeling more than pleased with himself next morning. The invention to which he had put his name was turning out a literal gold mine. He had been obliged to build new sheds and lay down new plant in order to make the machines; even then his workmen could not turn them out fast enough. He had issued licences and given concessions to other machine-makers in two continents; every machine made by these people brought into Ramsdale's coffers a handsome royalty. Ramsdale, in fact, was growing rich in such a speedy fashion that he sometimes dreamt that he was swimming in a sea of gold—a sea whose limits were beyond all sight. For the wonderful machine had revolutionised a staple trade, and manufacturers all over the world were clearing out their floor-space to make room for it. And Ramsdale knew that this sort of thing would go on for at least three years. By the end of that time he would be worth—he scarce knew what.

He had no compunction, no qualm of conscience—money, and what money would bring him, was the only god Ramsdale had ever thought it worth while to worship. All this affair was business—sharp business, if you like, but still nothing more, nothing less, than business. If John Burland had lived, Ramsdale would have bought that invention from him. He would have offered him a lump sum and Burland would have been satisfied. But Burland had been—providentially for Ramsdale—removed by that sudden explosion; therefore, Burland could not profit any more by any earthly thing. That was no reason why Ramsdale should not profit. But he was cute and careful in his doings. A few guarded inquiries convinced him that nobody knew anything about Burland's invention, not even the widow and daughter. Ramsdale was not the man to stick at points of honour; he would have been a fool in his own opinion if he had not taken this chance fortune offered. As for Burland's folks—why, who and what were they to command riches? A working woman and a girl who taught in a school! They wouldn't know what to do with money if they had it. A pound a week for life for 'em—ample and handsome. The girl was now twenty—suppose she lived to be seventy, she'd receive £2,600. Handsome, repeated Ramsdale—and quite sufficient.

On the morning after Alfred Penny's discovery, Ramsdale walked about his works glowing with satisfaction. He had good reason to feel set up. On his desk that morning he had found two letters which particularly pleased him. One was from a world-famous firm of machine-makers, which wrote to say that it wanted to make 10,000 machines, and offered £10 royalty on each machine—cash down on acceptance of the offer.

Ramsdale liked letters of that sort, there was £100,000 for no more trouble than signing a document and enclosing a letter with it. That was bit of good news number one. Number two was a private letter from the local Member of Parliament; it had nothing to do with machines. It was merely to tell Ramsdale privately that his name was safely down for a baronetcy in the forthcoming New Year's Honour List. Ramsdale scarcely knew which letter pleased him most. But he was not above a little day-dreaming, and he was scrawling Sir Martin Ramsdale, Bart., over and over again on a scrap of paper when one of his clerks entered the private office and handed him a letter.

"From Messrs. Chelwick & Radbourne, sir," said the clerk. "By hand. No answer, sir."

Ramsdale put the letter down and did not open it for a moment. He scrawled his name again in the same fashion, and, as an afterthought, added M.P. to it. But, upon reflection, he was not quite sure that he cared about Parliament—at least, about the House of Commons, for any Dick, Tom or Harry could get there nowadays. No, he would have a peerage. So he amused himself by scrawling Baron Ramsdale of Wolborough on the paper—after which, with a sly laugh at his own childishness, he tore it up, and cut the flap of Chelwick & Radbourne's letter.

Ramsdale rose from his desk a minute later, shaking like a man who has suddenly been smitten by palsy. His invariably cool and keen brain felt as if somebody had dealt it a crushing blow. Just as quickly as he had risen he dropped back into his chair—to stare again and again at the short, sharply-worded letter. And by degrees his brain began to clear and to recover from the mere physical shock. And, being a man who called a spade a spade, and who never lied to himself, whatever he did to other people, Ramsdale faced the truth. He was found out!

He sat there for a long time wondering. Found out! Yes, there was no doubt of it. He knew Chelwick, of Chelwick & Radbourne. Chelwick would never write a letter like that unless he knew. But—how had things been found out? By whom? When? Under what circumstances? So far as his busy mind could think, there was literally no living person who could have betrayed him. But Chelwick's letter showed that there was no surmise, no conjecture, no hitting out on the chance, in Chelwick's mind. There it was—Chelwick knew. And Chelwick summoned him—peremptorily—for three o'clock.

It was Ramsdale's daily custom to lunch at the Wolborough Club, a select institution where, at between one and three o'clock every day, most of the leading men of the town foregathered. Chelwick and Wilmington were there that day as usual, but Ramsdale was not. And the solicitor and ex-Mayor commented on this fact as they left the Club together at twenty minutes to three and walked to Chelwick & Radbourne's office, to find Penny meekly hanging about in the hall.

Chelwick, Wilmington and Penny sat in silent—and stern—conclave when Ramsdale was shown in just as the clock struck three. Ramsdale looked loweringly at all three. Knowing how things stood, he was prepared for Chelwick's sharp tone, for Wilmington's frigid and almost contemptuous nod. But who was the little man who sat in the background, staring at him in that queer fashion which somehow suggested something worse than contempt? He had an idea that he had seen that little man somewhere, some time, in the town, but he could not place him. Was it he who knew, or had discovered, the secret? Anyway, Ramsdale immediately became more afraid of Alfred Penny than of the other two; his very presence, inconspicuous as it was, was alarming. For Ramsdale knew something of unknown forces, and here was one. He did not know what that quiet-looking little chap might know and be able to tell, and so he feared him.

But Ramsdale meant to bluster, and he began to bluster. He began by throwing Chelwick's letter on Chelwick's desk, and demanding to know what it meant. And Chelwick picked up the letter and calmly threw it back, and he pointed Ramsdale to a chair with a look which made him take it.

"Now, Mr. Ramsdale," said Chelwick, "none of that in my office! The sooner you understand that you're at our mercy the better for you. You haven't come here to bluster, but to make amends. And if you don't make amends, then you'll see what happens. Do you hear that?"

"I hear you," growled Ramsdale sullenly.

"Then you shall hear more," continued Chelwick. "You shall hear what we know—know, mind!—and that all the world shall know unless you come tó your senses—as I fancy you will. The machine which you patented as your own invention is not your own invention at all. It never was, you never so much as invented a single spring in it! You never heard of it, never had an idea of it, until John Burland brought drawings and model to you the day before he was killed at your works. Then—when you thought you were safe—you stole it for your own benefit. Mr. Ramsdale, you'll never get that title you're fishing for, for we shall brand you and advertise you as a mean thief! Do you hear that?"

Ramsdale's eyes glittered and the veins on his forehead swelled. But—he knew Chelwick. And all that he managed to get out in answer to the lawyer's plain language was three words, hoarsely uttered:

"Where's your proof?"

The lawyer brought his hand down smartly on a folded document which lay before him, then he lifted it and pointed to Wilmington and Penny.

"The proof's here," he exclaimed, "and there, and there! Don't you make any mistake, Mr. Ramsdale. You know me. I know what I'm talking about if you don't. Now then, what is it going to be? Amends or absolute and complete exposure? Which? No trifling, sir! You'll answer that question here and now."

Ramsdale made a last effort to show some spirit.

"D'ye mean to tell me that you expect a man to answer a question like that off-hand?" he exclaimed, with an affectation of inquiry. "It takes some thinking, thinking about, and——"

"You've had a whole year to think about it," said Chelwick. "I said—here and now. Understand! I'm fully empowered by the widow and daughter to act on their behalf—you'll either make reparation on terms agreeable to me and Mr. Wilmington just now—or you'll take the consequences. I've a very accurate idea of the profits you've made and expect to make. I'm open to accept—for cash—a lump sum on behalf of the widow and daughter of the late John Burland in satisfaction of—everything. But I refuse to give you even ten minutes to think of anything. You'll decide now!"

Ramsdale looked from Chelwick to Wilmington, from Wilmington to Penny. And suddenly he lifted his finger and pointed at the bookseller.

"Who's that man?" he demanded. "What's he got to do with this?"

"Never mind who he is," retorted Chelwick. "You'll know quick enough if this gets into the law courts. Now, then—your answer!"

Ramsdale got up and looked significantly at the inner door.

"A word with you and Wilmington then, in private," he said.

Alfred Penny sat in a tremor of expectation while the three men stayed in that inner office. If this had been his own affair he could not have been more anxious. It seemed ages before the door opened and they came back, and he glanced inquiringly at all three. He fancied he saw satisfaction in Wilmington's face; he noticed that Chelwick held a folded slip of paper; he saw that Ramsdale's eyes had something closely resembling relief in them. And once more Ramsdale looked sharply and inquisitively at him—then he strode across the room and went away without a word.

Wilmington clapped Chelwick on the back.

"Well done!" he said. "Well done. And yet—he'll make an enormous fortune as it is!"

"Never mind," said Chelwick. He sat down, put a slip of paper in an envelope, wrote a name outside, and turned to Penny. "Now, Mr. Penny," he said briskly, "I promised you that you should carry whatever good news there was. So take that to Mrs. Burland. I had some talk with her and her daughter this morning, so she'll know what the bit of paper in the envelope means. Tell her to lock it up safely for to-night, and to come down with it to me to-morrow morning. Run! That's it, take a cab!"

Penny shot out of Chelwick & Radbourne's office

and fell into the first cab he encountered. It was some distance, and uphill, to Mayfield Terrace, and it seemed to him as if the cab would never get there. But at last it pulled up, and Penny, waving his envelope, darted into the little house. And although he had ridden, he was almost breathless.

"Here—here!" he exclaimed, thrusting the envelope into Mrs. Burland's hands. "From Mr. Chelwick! He says you'll know what it is. I—open it, ma'am!"

He and the pretty daughter pressed closely against Mrs. Burland's shoulder as she tore open the envelope, and drew out a cheque. She gave one look at it, screamed, and dropped it on the table. And Penny and the girl bent closer—and read:

"Pay Mrs. Sarah Burland or order two hundred and fifty thousand pounds.

"MARTIN RAMSDALE."

Then Alfred Penny did an extraordinary thing. By all rights he ought to have hugged the mother and kissed the pretty daughter. Instead, he let out a deep and terrible groan—and rushed headlong from the house. Nor did he cease his hurried flight until he had reached his shop, where he frightened his shop-boy by feverishly getting together all the books which Mrs. Burland had sold him the day before, and carefully packing them in neat parcels. For Penny was very sure that Mrs. and Miss Burland would now want to buy those books back again.

When Penny went to his parlour that night, he looked round its solitude, smote his forehead, and groaned.

"Separated!" he muttered. "Separated—on the

very threshold of love's blissful dream. Separated by a—a sum of sovereigns. What young woman who is heiress to a quarter of a million would ever look at poor Alfred Penny?"

But in that Alfred Penny was wrong. He had made up his mind that he would never go near Miss Burland again when, one morning, he met Miss Burland in the open street. Mr. Penny bowed and blushed, and would have passed miserably on; but Miss Burland—who also blushed—had other views.

"Mr. Penny," she said, with ingenuous directness, "why have you never been to see us since you brought the good news? Come, now—is it because of the money, Mr. Penny?"

Penny's cheeks grew redder and redder, and he wished the earth would swallow him. And he could not think of a single conventional excuse.

"Mr. Penny," said Miss Burland seriously, using her full battery of charms, "if you don't come and have tea with us on Sunday, I shall never——"

She paused, and Penny found strength to get out two words.

"Never—what?" he whispered.

But Miss Burland shook her head.

"No," she responded, "I won't say it—because you will come, won't you?"

So Penny became allied to vast wealth and a pretty wife. He sometimes passes Ramsdale in the streets of Wolborough, and they look at each other. And Ramsdale, on these occasions, always looks as if he badly wanted to ask Penny a question. But at sight of Ramsdale, Penny—who is now a collector of rare editions, instead of a seller of second-hand volumes—invariably assumes an expression which might have been copied from a statue of Virtuous Reproof.

XIV: THE SELCHESTER MISSAL

CHAPTER I

Mr. Guy Lampard, junior partner in the famous firm of Scriven, Lampard and Polkinghorne, of Lincoln's Inn Fields, solicitors, got out of an express at Selchester one autumn morning, wondering why he had been brought to that sleepy city. The cause of his coming there at all lay in his pocket in the shape of a telegram, and as he walked up Shoregate he took out and ran his eye over the wording for the twentieth time:

"Come here at once by next train. Most urgent and serious business.—Dean of Selchester."

The Dean of Selchester was well known to Scriven, Lampard and Polkinghorne. They had been his solicitors for many years, and his father's and his grandfather's. Consequently, Mr. Guy Lampard knew all about the Dean. One fact was that he had only attained to his present dignity within the past twelve months—previously to that he had been vicar of a certain fashionable parish in the heart of Belgravia. Another fact—and one that seemed to have a certain relation to the telegram—was that he was a somewhat nervous and excitable man, and apt to fuss about trifles. It might be a trifle that made him summon his solicitor to Selchester; that anything of a really urgent and serious nature could ever happen in that somnolent spot, which always looked to be lost in the last mist of antiquity, was beyond Mr. Guy Lampard's belief.

It was very quiet, very peaceful, very dignified in the ancient close into which Lampard presently turned through a vaulted gateway which had stood there, slowly crumbling since the days of the Plantagenets. He had been to Selchester before, several times, and the objects which he saw there were as familiar as well-known faces. There was the precentor's house, with its fine old architecture and its famous yew tree; there the canon's residence, first built in the days of Henry VII., and notable for its roofs and gables; there the embattled gateway of the bishop's palace. And here was the deanery with its fine lawns and shady gardens, and there, pacing toward him, his hands behind his back, his face bent earthwards, his whole attitude that of thought and perplexity, was the Dean himself. He looked up at the sound of Lampard's footsteps, and sighed with evident relief, and hurried forward with extended hand.

"Oh, it's you, Guy, is it?" he exclaimed. "I'm glad. I was rather afraid Polkinghorne might come. And this affair wants youth and energy—at least, I think so."

"What is it?" asked Lampard.

The Dean glanced at the windows of the house, and then motioned his visitor to follow him into a quiet tree-shaded walk. There beneath the shadow of beech and hawthorn, he turned to his visitor with a look of despair.

"The fact is," said he, in low, almost mysterious tones, "the fact is, the Selchester Missal has disappeared!"

Lampard let his mind go back to his last visit to Selchester. He remembered a pleasant afternoon spent in looking round the old cathedral; he particularly remembered an hour in the cathedral library, amongst the old books, deeds, parchments, the harvest of many a century. And he remembered the famous Selchester Missal, an illuminated manuscript of great age and value, which, in company with various other books of the same sort, was treasured in a glass-fronted case—to be looked at, but not handled. Antiquaries and bibliophiles came from all over Europe to look at that Missal; collectors from beyond the Atlantic came too, to envy the Dean and Chapter of Selchester their possession of it. And Lampard had a vague recollection of hearing that one of these American collectors had offered to buy the Missal, and to write out, there and then, a cheque for ten thousand pounds for it.

"The Selchester Missal!" he exclaimed. "Disappeared!"

"Stolen, I'm afraid," said the Dean mournfully. "It's all most mysterious and distressing. And, so far, we can't think how, or when, or by whom it was stolen—that is, exactly when or how. I'd better tell you all about it. That, of course, was why I sent for you."

"But my dear Mr. Dean," said Lampard, with a deprecating smile. "I'm not a detective, you know. Hadn't you better send for the police, or wire for a Scotland Yard man?"

"We don't want the police to know," answered the Dean. "We don't want a fuss, naturally. I sent for you, hoping you'd advise. You'll no doubt be able to suggest something."

"Well," assented Lampard, "the facts, then?"

"The facts are these," said the Dean. "To-day's Monday. Well. I saw the Missal myself on Saturday morning—I showed it to friends. In fact, I exercised my privilege and took it out of the glass case. I put it back with my own hands. Now, this morning —first thing, before breakfast—one of the vergers came hurrying here to tell me that the Missal had disappeared. I went over to the cathedral with him, and into the library. The case was locked, as usual. But the Missal was gone. There you are!"

"How many people know of the loss up to now?" asked Lampard.

"Nobody but this particular verger and myself," replied the Dean. "We haven't even told the Librarian, who is one of the minor canons. And, very fortunately, he's away from the city to-day. But the loss cannot be concealed long, you know. I've had the library locked up until you came. We'd better go across there."

"Wait a bit," said Lampard. "Let me hear all about Sunday. You say you yourself showed the Missal to some friends. Tell me about that."

"We had some people staying with us last week," replied the Dean, "several people. Some of them were old friends; two or three were friends of my daughter, whom I didn't know very well. My daughter, as you know, is an art student in London; these people I refer to were some of her artist friends."

"Men or women?" asked Lampard.

"Women—young women," answered the Dean a little impatiently. "Of course, there is no suspicion in that quarter; any friend of Margaret's would naturally be above suspicion. I'm merely telling you all this to account for Saturday morning's visit. I took the whole party round the cathedral, and, of course, into the library. As I said, I showed them the Missal —took it out and put it back myself. That was just before lunch—say, one o'clock. Now, according to Wilkins, the verger who shows people round, there were only two or three visitors to the choir and the library this particular Saturday, and he knew them in each case. One was Lord Freeborough—he wanted to consult something or other. Another was a young lady of the town, who is making a sketch of St. Hedwige's shrine. The third was a well-known London architect, Mr. Blatherwayte. So there you are!"

"What about yesterday—Sunday?" inquired Lampard.

"No one is shown round on Sundays," said the Dean. "The library is closed from five o'clock on Saturday until nine o'clock on Monday."

"How many people have access to that case besides yourself?" asked Lampard.

"Only two," answered the Dean. "The Bishop has a key, and the Librarian has a key."

"Perhaps one of them has removed the Missal?" suggested Lampard. "Have you made inquiry?"

"Might as easily suppose they'd remove the central tower," retorted the Dean. "No; that's no good. Besides, the Bishop is away—been away for a month. My dear fellow, the Missal's been stolen!"

"Well, then, we'd better do something," said Lampard. "Let me have a look at the library and the case in which the Missal was kept. You'll have to call in the police, you know."

The Dean led the way through the cloisters to the library, grumbling a good deal under his breath. It was such a nuisance, he said, calling in the police. The thing would get into the newspapers, and there would be scandal, and all sorts of unpleasantness. Let them see what they could do themselves—quickly—first. And, in order that everything should be quiet, he and

Lampard and the verger who admitted them to the library, locked themselves into that ancient building, so as to be free from interruption.

The Dean led the way to a glass-topped case which stood beneath a long, low window filled with coloured glass. He pointed to a vacant space amongst the old books, parchments, fragments of pottery, and time-worn relics with which the case was filled.

"That's where the Missal ought to be," he said lugubriously. "And where it isn't. I put it back in that very place with my own hands on Saturday at, I should say, a quarter to one. And, according to Wilkins here, the only person who entered the library after that was Lord Freeborough."

"Yes, sir; his lordship," replied Wilkins, pointing to a far corner of the library, "desired to consult our copy of Dugdale's Monasticon. I got it down for him from that tall case. I stood by while he examined it. His lordship merely wished to verify a reference, and he was only in the room a few minutes. After that we had no visitors in the library, and at five o'clock I locked it up, and it was never opened until I myself opened it at half-past eight this morning."

Lampard bent down to the case of exhibits and examined the lock.

"That's a patent lock, sir," remarked Wilkins. "There are only three keys."

"One of which Mr. Dean has in his possession," said Lampard. "Unlock the case, Mr. Dean; let us see how it works, and if——"

He paused and looked up suddenly as the Dean, who had been fumbling in one of his pockets, uttered a sharp exclamation.

"Bless me," he said in a tone of indignant vexation, "the key isn't there! I am as sure as one can be sure that I replaced it in that pocket on locking up that case. I certainly wore these clothes, and——"

He hastily turned out the contents of all his pockets, and his vexation and bewilderment increased as the process went on. But no key was forthcoming.

"Most extraordinary!" he exclaimed. "I could not possibly have put the key anywhere without recollecting the matter. Impossible! My memory is splendid."

"But you don't usually carry that particular key on you?" asked Lampard.

"No; certainly not," admitted the Dean. "I usually keep it in a certain corner of a particular drawer of my desk. But I am positive—absolutely positive—that, although I took it from that drawer on Saturday morning, I never put it back there. It should be in this pocket."

"Ah, but you must have returned it to its corner," said Lampard. "You've forgotten all about it."

The Dean frowned, fretted, grumbled, and finally hurried out of the library to search for the missing key. The verger turned to Lampard.

"I can get the Bishop's key, sir," he said. "His Lordship's away, but his chaplain will give it to me if I say the Dean wants it."

"Do," said Lampard, "it may save time."

Left alone, he bent over the glass top of the case, examining the ancient things within it. There was nothing there that was not hundreds of years old—books, scraps of vellum, bits of metal work, fragments of glass and stone—all were old. But suddenly Lampard caught sight of something half hidden by the edge of a crumpled parchment deed which was not old. That something was a bit of enamelled gold, a pendant such as those which hang from a woman's bracelet, and Lampard's sharp eyes knew that it was a modern bauble which had no rightful place amongst those hoary antiquities.

"Ah," he murmured, "now, how came that in there —that which more rightly belongs to Bond Street and a jeweller's shop than to this musty old spot? Dropped, of course! And—by whom?"

Wilkins was back within a few minutes—the episcopal palace of Selchester adjoins the cathedral. He handed a key to Lampard, who immediately made an excuse to get rid of him.

"Haven't you got a register of your visitors?" he asked. "Just let me look at it then. I'd like to see the recent entries."

Wilkins, who knew Lampard as the Dean's solicitor, went obediently away, and Lampard hastily opened the case, withdrew the bit of enamelled gold, and saw that a link which had evidently attached it to something else had snapped. He realised the significance of his discovery at once. Some thieving hand —a woman's without doubt—had purloined the Missal while no one was looking, and in the very act had dropped this tiny pendant from a bracelet.

CHAPTER II

THE Dean and the verger came back into the library together—the verger carrying a big book, the Dean hot and fidgety.

"Extraordinary!" he exclaimed. "I can't find that key anywhere. I've searched high and low. I must have dropped it, and in that case—oh, you've found it, eh?" he went on as Lampard, having pocketed the pendant, turned the Bishop's key in the lock. "I dropped it here, then?"

"No," answered Lampard, "this is the Bishop's. Wilkins borrowed it from his chaplain. But you've no doubt lost yours, and the thief must have picked it up and made use of it. Just let me glance at the register of visitors, and then——"

"But how could the thief get in here?" demanded the Dean. "The whole thing is more puzzling than before. Suppose——"

Lampard rapidly glanced at the last page of the register, and closed the book with a decisive bang.

"Mr. Dean," he said quietly, but emphatically, "we mustn't trifle with this. There is only one thing to do. You must come at once with me to the police."

The Dean being himself a man of authority, recognised that in this case he must yield obedience to his solicitor, and he accordingly accompanied Lampard across the cathedral square in the direction of the police station. But he made many faces of dislike, muttered more than once that there was nothing he disliked so much as the dragging of the affair into publicity.

"My notion was a quiet, unobtrusive inquiry," he said, as they turned in at the official portals. "If we could have recovered the Missal without letting the public know that it had ever been—er—appropriated, don't you know, eh?"

"Mr. Dean," said Lampard with professional severity, "the Selchester Missal is, so to speak, public property, though nominally, I suppose, it belongs to the Dean and Chapter. You can't afford to leave any stone unturned—and," he added, with dark significance, "you don't know what's afoot nor what machinations have been going on. This may be the work of an unscrupulous and designing gang."

The Dean and his companion found no difficulty in

procuring an immediate interview with the Chief Constable. They were ushered into his private office at once, and there, evidently in close consultation with him, was the great magnate of that neighbourhood, the Earl of Maxbury, chairman of the local bench of magistrates. He and the Dean exchanged nods, and the Earl, with a sharp glance at the ecclesiastic's countenance, at once brusquely asked what ailed him.

"The matter," answered the Dean, who had been prompted by Lampard, "is that my solicitor and I have come to report a most serious theft. The Selchester Missal has been stolen—at least it has disappeared under most mysterious circumstances. Mr. Lampard, here, says it must have been stolen. I suppose—yes, I suppose it really has been stolen."

The Earl and the Chief Constable exchanged glances; then the Earl turned sharply on the Dean.

"When was this?" he demanded.

"I should think Saturday," replied the Dean. "It appears to have been on Saturday. The circumstances are these," he went on, and gave his hearers a complete account.

"Between one o'clock on Saturday and early on Monday—to-day, anyway. The important fact is that it's gone. Do you think you can help me?" he concluded, turning to the Chief Constable. "The Missal is, of course, priceless."

The Earl and the Chief Constable once more looked at each other; then the Earl smote his hands together. He was a big bucolic sort of man, who looked very much like a respectable farmer, and his manners were vigorous.

"That settles it!" he exclaimed. "It's a regular put-up job; it's a gang! I was dead certain of that when I came in here. A London gang, of course, and deuced clever!"

"I don't understand," said the Dean feebly.

"Clear enough!" retorted the Earl. "You lost your old book on Saturday; I've lost my medal—Sunday! The famous Maxbury medal, you know; unique, world-famous. Given to one of my ancestors, either the eighth or ninth Earl—hanged if I remember which!—by a King of Spain—don't know which, either—for something or other the old boy did for him. Great feat, anyhow. King had a special gold medal struck for him; only one in existence, of course. Famous, that Maxbury medal. People used to ask for that when they came round sightseeing—used to ask for it first of all. Used to lend it out sometimes—police to guard it, don't you know, and all that sort of thing. Very well, it's gone! There last night, and gone this morning. Fact! And, of course, it's all a piece with your Missal. Gang of London thieves. Selchester Missal, Saturday; Maxbury medal, Sunday. Good haul, and deuced clever!"

The Dean, who had sat blinking his eyes and twiddling his thumbs during this speech, found his voice at last.

"Do I understand you to say that somebody has stolen the Maxbury medal?" he asked.

The Earl, who was calmly smoking a cigar, nodded and blew away a wisp of smoke.

"That's it," he answered. "Gone, vanished, faded away like that, only more so!"

"What are you going to do about it?" asked the Dean.

"Don't know; ask Kilburn, here," replied the Earl, waving a hand at the Chief Constable. "What would you do?" he went on, twisting round on Lampard.

"Lawyer, ain't you? Know your name, of course. What do you think about it? Rum business, eh?"

"I should like to know what your Lordship can tell about the circumstances under which the famous medal was stolen," answered Lampard.

"Circumstances, eh?" responded the Earl. "Oh, ah, well, very ordinary, I should think. That medal, now, was kept in a cabinet of curiosities in the south drawing-room at Maxbury. I saw it lateish last night myself. This morning, early, house steward comes to tell me—gone! And a window in the room open. That's all!"

"Was that cabinet locked, as a usual thing?" asked Lampard.

"Can't say," replied the Earl. "Don't believe it was, now I come to think of it. It wasn't locked last night, anyhow, because I took that medal out myself to show to some people."

"You have guests staying at Maxbury?" inquired Lampard.

"House full of 'em," said the Earl. "No thieves among those, anyhow; know every Jack and Jill of 'em. But I say," he exclaimed, his ruddy face suddenly lighting up with new interest—"I say, what an extraordinary thing that these people should go in for that old prayer-book and my medal! What value is there in a Missal and a medal the size of half-a-crown? None, so to speak. Deuced mysterious, what?"

"The Selchester Missal," observed the Dean gravely, "is worth many, many thousands of pounds. An American person of wealth—a man who traded, I believe, in preserved meats—offered my predecessor ten thousand pounds for it."

"Then your predecessor was an old ass for not

taking it." exclaimed the Earl, heartily and irreverently. "I wish somebody'd even offered me half of that for the Maxbury medal. But then," he added, relapsing into gloom, "I couldn't have sold it, don't you know. It's a beastly heirloom!"

The four men looked silently at each other for a minute; then the Dean brightened.

"I see it all!" he exclaimed. "At least, I think I see it. This is, no doubt, the work of a clever thief, or thieves, as Lord Maxbury suggests. I incline to the one-man theory. A thief with a penchant for valuable curiosities. Yes, I see it; oh, quite plainly!"

"Hanged if I do," muttered the Earl, with a wink at Lampard. "But I'm open to argument; always keep an open mind—best thing. What's the theory, then?"

The Dean balanced his eyeglasses and swung one leg over the other.

"This," he said. "The thief heard of these two objects—the famous Missal, the famous medal. He determined to acquire them—for what purpose, only his guilty conscience knows. He came here—he may probably have come attired as a gentleman, and put up at the Angel and Sceptre Hotel. He obtained access to the cathedral library. He was probably hidden there when I took my party round on Saturday morning; it would be easy to hide there. And I fear that he saw me drop my key. I must have dropped it on the floor of the library. And, of course, after that nothing could be easier for him than to abstract the Missal, make his way out of the cathedral at a convenient moment, and——"

"Hang round a bit, and then come on to Maxbury to lift my medal," broke in the Earl. "Good notion! Well," he continued, rising and turning to the Chief

Constable, as he prepared to lounge out, "same old game, I suppose, eh, Kilburn? Detectives—search for traces—finger-prints—and all the rest of it. Leave it to you, anyway."

With that, the Earl of Maxbury went off, and the Dean and his solicitor, after a little desultory conversation with the Chief Constable, also departed, and walked moodily back to the deanery.

"You're coming in to lunch, of course?" said the Dean. "Bless me, it's nearly two o'clock! We're late! Well, this is a sad, a terrible business. Perhaps some new idea may occur to us."

Lampard had no particular desire for new ideas. He had one already, and he kept it to himself—at any rate, until he had refreshed himself at the Dean's table. But when lunch was over he contrived to draw the Dean's daughter, Margaret, aside, and to lead her into a quiet corner of the deanery gardens. He and Margaret had known each other since their pinafore days, and there was the fellow feeling and confidence of youth between them.

"Look here," said Lampard, once they were safely hidden amongst the trees and shrubs, "you can keep a secret as well as anybody. This is a big secret. I've got something to show you. You're not to say a word of it until I give you leave. Look at this," he continued, as he drew out the bit of enamelled pendant and held it out to her on the palm of his hand. "Have you ever seen this before? Do you know to whom it belongs?"

He saw at once that the girl had seen and did know. Her cheeks flushed and her eyes sparkled.

"Why, where did you find that?" she exclaimed. "Of course I know it. It's a pendant which Mrs. Vanderkiste lost from a pet bracelet. She was looking for it all Saturday afternoon. Did you pick it up in the garden?"

"Who is Mrs. Vanderkiste?" demanded Lampard.

"She was staying here all last week," replied Margaret. "She is a woman we knew in London——"

"Has Mrs. Vanderkiste gone back to London?" asked Lampard.

"No; she left on Saturday evening for Maxbury," said Margaret. "She's gone there for a week. Lord Maxbury's got a big house-party for steeplechases to-morrow and Wednesday. Why all these questions?"

Lampard put the pendant in his pocket, and seized Margaret by the wrist. He gave her a dark and meaning look.

"Now, I will tell you all about it later on," he whispered. "There's a mystery. Gunpowder Plot was nothing to this. Meanwhile not a word, a look, a sigh. Utter silence—and confidence."

He left her then, and walking swiftly into the house, roused the Dean, who had retreated into his study and gone to sleep over the last number of the "Quarterly Review," with a handkerchief thrown over his head.

CHAPTER III

"Mr. Dean," said Lampard firmly, "you must come with me at once to Maxbury. I have just learned something very important, and you and I must see Lord Maxbury immediately. Now I'll order your motor car, and it will be at the door in five minutes. This is—urgent."

In the course of his six years' experience as a highly

respectable family solicitor, Guy Lampard had known some strange things and seen some queer spectacles. But he had never known or seen anything stranger or queerer than the effect on the Earl of Maxbury and the Dean of Selchester when, closeted with them in the Earl's own special sanctum—a small room, chiefly devoted to guns, fishing-rods, cricket bats, sporting literature, and choice French fiction—he told them all he had to tell, produced the pendant, and summed up his conclusion. Peer and cleric stared at him with open mouths and dropping jaws, and their faces expressed resentment and disapproval. And when they spoke they were unanimous in the opinion, if not in the choice of language.

"Rot!" exclaimed the Earl. "Letty Vanderkiste! Pooh! Known her for lord knows how long. She's straight enough—as things go. Come off it, dear boy. You're on the wrong horse."

The Dean rose from his chair, and shook his head gravely and with evident displeasure.

"My own sentiments," he said. "But, of course, in different phraseology. I quite agree with Lord Maxbury. It is utterly impossible that my dear friend Mrs. Vanderkiste could—oh, it is ridiculous! I have known Mrs. Vanderkiste ever since she was young. She was married by me. Since she lost her husband she has been a regular attendant at my old sphere of labour in London. Something, perhaps, of a rather worldly woman; the fact that she is fond of society and of—er——"

"Bridge!" interrupted Lampard, who had had another five minutes' talk with Margaret while the Dean's car was being pulled out. "And racing and theatre-going, and the latest fashions, and all the rest of the things which cost money. Very well. I have told you what I have discovered, and if you don't mean to pursue the matter further——"

He rose and walked towards the door.

"What then?" asked the Earl, while the Dean raised a supplicating hand. "What are you up to?"

"Then I shall go and tell the Chief Constable of Selchester," said Lampard. "It's my duty."

The Dean groaned miserably, and the Earl plunged his hands into his pockets and stretched his legs across the hearthrug.

"What a beastly nuisance!" he growled. "Of course, we'll have to ask her how it is that some of her property is found in that case at Selchester."

"You certainly will," replied Lampard. "Further," he added, with a look at the greatly disturbed Dean, "you'll have to ask her what she's done with your property!"

The Earl glanced at the lawyer with a new expression.

"Er—I say!" he remarked drily. "Ain't you rather condemning the lady before you've heard what she's got to say?"

"Yes, yes!" said the Dean hurriedly. "I, too, feel that. I—ah—um!—we shouldn't judge by appearances, you know. I——"

"I should be very glad to hear what Mrs. Vanderkiste has got to say," retorted Lampard. "If you will give her the opportunity of saying—anything, I should like to hear it. I think you both forget that this affair is really out of your hands. You have both been to the police. The police are already at work. So, if Mrs. Vanderkiste is at hand, why not speak quietly and gently to her? There is still a chance of recovering this stolen property, you know, if things are done with diplomacy."

The Earl looked at Lampard for a minute or two; then he silently rose and left the room. And Lampard turned to the window and looked out on the stately oaks and beeches of Maxbury Park, and the Dean marched up and down repeating one phrase:

"Distressing!—most distressing!"

The Earl returned in a few minutes, ushering in a smart, rather pretty vivacious-looking woman, still well under middle age, who started at the sight of Lampard, and paled when she turned from him to the Dean. And, after a swift glance at all three men, she involuntarily clasped her hands, and ejaculated four words:

"Oh, what is it?"

The Earl, who had carefully closed the door, pushed a chair forward.

"I say!" he said. "Of course, it's all right—sure to be all right, don't you know; but the fact is, this gentleman is the Dean's solicitor, and he wants to ask you a question or two. Do answer him, and let's have an end of it! You see, my ancestor's medal disappeared last night, and an old book was taken out of the cathedral library at Selchester on Saturday, and we've had to tell the police, and——"

Under Lampard's purposely cold eye, fixed implacably on her, the woman's own eyes fell, and her face grew paler than ever, despite the suspicion of rouge which ornamented it. And suddenly he plunged his hand in his pocket, and drew out the pendant, and held it before her.

"I know this is yours," he said quietly. "It's off your bracelet—that very bracelet. I found it—found it this morning in the case from which the Missal was abstracted. I think you'd better tell us how it came to be in that case."

There was a tense silence for a time; then the Earl, who was unusually fidgety, spoke nervously.

"Better say something, you know," he said. "Nothing to be frightened about—eh? So long as you say something or other, you know—what?"

Mrs. Vanderkiste suddenly turned on him.

"Nothing to be frightened about!" she exclaimed scornfully. "That's all you know. Nothing to be—— Good heavens, it's because I'm frightened out of my life that I took them!"

The Dean groaned sepulchrally; the Earl whistled.

"Whew!" he said as a final note of surprise. "So you did take 'em? Both?"

"Both!" replied Mrs. Vanderkiste.

"What on earth for?" demanded the Earl.

"Because I had to!" she retorted. "So would you, if you were fixed as I am."

"Fixed as—I wish you'd just say plainly how you are fixed," exclaimed the Earl. "Do! All amongst friends, don't you know?"

"I'll retire if Mrs. Vanderkiste wishes it," suggested Lampard.

He moved towards the door, but Mrs. Vanderkiste stopped him.

"No!" she said. "You're a lawyer, and you'll understand. Oh well, I'll tell you, and be done with it! The truth is, I'm completely in the power of somebody. A woman. You know her," she went on, turning to the Earl, "or you know of her. Leonie!"

"What! The woman who makes gowns!" vociferated the Earl.

"Gowns—yes; but she's two other businesses," answered Mrs. Vanderkiste. "She runs an establishment in which she sells antiques, curiosities, and so on—and she's also a registered moneylender."

"Tell us all about it," counselled Lampard.

"I owe her money—a pretty big lot," continued Mrs. Vanderkiste. "Dressmaker's bill to begin with. Then I borrowed money from her in her moneylending capacity and gave her bills, and of course I had to renew, constantly. And at last I got head over heels in debt with her. And then she suggested to me that, as I was constantly visiting country houses, I had admirable opportunities of picking up——"

"Missals and medals!" snorted the Earl, who had been vigorously punching one clenched hand into the palm of the other. "What a pity this infernal old nag is a woman! Lampard, of course, Mrs. Vanderkiste isn't the real culprit, don't you know. It's the other——"

"Where," asked Lampard quietly, turning to Mrs. Vanderkiste—"where are the Missal and the medal?"

Mrs. Vanderkiste shook her head.

"I sent them to her by registered parcel post this morning," she answered. "I sent them myself from the village post office here. Here's the receipt with her address on it."

Lampard took the scrap of paper and carefully put it away. Then he turned to the other men.

"That parcel won't be delivered until to-morrow morning," he said. "We must be at this woman's address when the postman arrives. There's no need for you to go up to town, Mr. Dean—I'll act for you. But you ought to go, Lord Maxbury."

"I'm going," said the Earl with great emphasis.

The numerous ultra-fashionable clients of Leonie et Cie. have never been able to understand why that clever lady suddenly closed her doors, broke up her establishment, and vanished into the unknown. Similarly, other people have wondered why a certain curiosity shop, which in its day was much patronised by collectors, was shut up at literally a moment's notice. Also a great many folk have never ceased speculating on the sudden wiping out of a quiet moneylending office and wondering why the money they had borrowed from it has never been demanded from them. But the Earl of Maxbury and Mr. Guy Lampard know very well why these affairs suddenly declined, and so does a certain lady, who, if she ever sees the names of these gentlemen in print, remembers a very bad quarter of an hour which she once had with them, and how they held an ultimatum at her head which left her no choice but to fall in with all their commands. The recollection of that little affair makes that lady feel morally ill and savagely vindictive, but whenever the Earl of Maxbury thinks of it, he shows his teeth from ear to ear, and chuckles with holy gratification.

XV: THE MURDER IN THE MAYOR'S PARLOUR

CHAPTER I

THE London express, stopping for a bare minute in the little station of Lyncaster, set down a single passenger, a quietly-dressed, middle-aged, spectacled man, whom casual observers, had they looked at him at all, would have taken for a member of the professional classes, a doctor, a solicitor, a chartered accountant. The few people on the platform paid no attention to him; within a moment of his arrival he had given up his ticket, passed through the booking-office, and was rapidly walking up the road to the town,—a collection of ancient houses set on the ridge of a low hill, from the crown of which two objects—the high roof of the old Moot Hall and the square tower of the parish church—stood out prominently against the glow of the December sunset. Within five minutes he was in the heart of the town—a market-place which looked, at first glance and in that uncertain light, as if nothing had altered in it since the Middle Ages. Gabled and timbered houses, diamond-paned windows, queer chimney-stacks, a pavement of cobble-stones, a pillared and canopied market cross, the old church at one end, the Moot Hall at the other—these things seemed to make up the whole of Lyncaster, save for a few narrow and equally ancient streets which opened out of the square at various unexpected angles. It needed but one sharp, shrewd glance on the part of the stranger to see that he was now in the midst of one of those antique English boroughs which are becoming rarer with every generation, and wherein life apparently still takes its tone and colour from the past.

But the man from London wasted no time in looking round. His quick eyes had at once fallen on two words painted on a projecting lamp, and thrown into prominence by the flare of a gas-jet. Those two words were Police Station—he made for the door beneath them, as a business-like man makes for the object which demands his immediate attention. The door was half open; within, in a barely furnished office, hung about with official-looking papers and bills, a sleepy-looking young constable was writing at a stand-up desk. He lifted his face—the face of a rustic promoted from the plough—and opened his mouth as if to signify that his ears were also open.

"Superintendent Sutton in?" asked the stranger. "Then tell him, if you please, that Detective-Sergeant Milgrave, from New Scotland Yard, is here."

The constable, awed to silence by this announcement, took one hasty glance at the London detective, and lumbered into an inner room. He muttered his news to some person who sat within, then turned and beckoned. Milgrave walked sharply forward, to be met by a big, burly man, who held out a stout fist, and showed unmistakable pleasure and relief at his visitor's coming.

"I'm right glad to see you, sir," he said, pulling forward an elbow-chair to the edge of a blazing fire. "We're not much used to this sort of thing in these parts, you know, and we want a Londoner to take a look in at this affair. I suppose," he went on, motioning Milgrave to seat himself—"I suppose you'll have heard the facts of the case—read 'em in the newspapers, of course?"

"No!" answered Milgrave. He set down his suitcase, unbuttoned his overcoat, and took a seat. "No! I know nothing, except that there's been a murder here, and that I'm sent down, at your request, to help to investigate it. I saw headlines in the papers, certainly, but I didn't read what was underneath them. I don't know anything. That's my way, superintendent —I like my facts at first hand. And so you'll perhaps tell me all about it, at once."

"You wouldn't like to take something, first?" asked the superintendent, with rural solicitude. "It's a long journey, and——"

"No, thank you—business first," responded Milgrave. "Let me know what's been done, and what's to be done, first of all. I'll see to myself when I'm posted up. Tell me all you can."

The superintendent, a bluff, hearty-looking individual, who obviously felt great interest in the personality of this man from the Criminal Investigation Department, drew his own chair to the fire, and shook his head as he dropped into it.

"It's a queer do—as we say in these parts," he remarked. "I never heard of a queerer, and I've been thirty and odd years in the force, Mr. Milgrave. Well, I'm a poor hand at telling a tale, but I'll put it to you in as good order as I can. Now, then, to be what we may term systematic about it, this is Thursday, December 10, 1914, isn't it? Very well, on the night of day before yesterday—Tuesday, December 8 —our young mayor, Mr. Guy Hannington, came into the Moot Hall by the front entrance, out of the market-place, and went up to the mayor's parlour. That was at half-past eight o'clock. The person—the only person—who saw him come in was the caretaker, Learoyd, a pensioned policeman. Learoyd and his wife live in the ground floor rooms of the Moot Hall—you can't enter at all from the front without passing their door and window, as I shall show you presently. Learoyd was standing at his door when his worship came in at the entry, and he asked him if there was aught he could do. His worship said no; he was only going up to the mayor's parlour to look at some papers. He went up, and Learoyd and his wife sat down to their supper.

"A good hour passed; Learoyd remarked to his missis that his worship was stopping upstairs a longish time. Then he went out into the entry and smoked his pipe a bit, expecting the mayor to come down. But he didn't come, and didn't come, and it got to be ten o'clock, which is Learoyd's time for locking all up. So, after a while, Learoyd got uneasy, and he went upstairs and listened at the door. He heard naught—no moving about, nothing. So at last he knocked—and got no answer. Then he opened the door. And he saw at once that something was wrong, for there was the poor young gentleman lying across the hearth-rug, between his desk and the fireplace, arms stretched out, and as still as could be!"

"Dead?" asked Milgrave.

"Dead as a door-nail, sir!" replied the superintendent. "There was no doubt of that. Learoyd just took one look at him—he was lying on his back, and the light was full on—and then he hurried down for his wife, and sent her for Dr. Winford, who lives in the market-place, and for me—I live just round the corner. Dr. Winford and me got there together. The doctor just looked him over and said he'd been dead quite an hour. And as to how he'd come by his death, he'd been stabbed!"

"Stabbed, eh?" remarked Milgrave. "Stabbed!"

"Stabbed through the heart," said the superintendent. "And," he continued, with a significant shake of the head, "from the back. Dr. Winford, he says that the mayor had been writing, or was writing, at his desk when the murderer drove a knife, or something of that sort, clean through his heart from behind. He says—the doctor—that he'd leap up, throw out his arms, twist round, and fall where he was found, on his back. He says, too, that death would be practically instantaneous."

"Learoyd never heard anything—no sound of a fall, or a cry?" asked Milgrave.

"Nothing! But you've got to remember that our Moot Hall is one of the very oldest buildings in England," answered the superintendent. "You'll see for yourself that the walls and floors are of a tremendous thickness—eight to twelve feet thick in places. No, Learoyd had heard nothing. And there were no signs of any struggle. Everything was in its place. His worship had begun a letter—written the date, and 'My dear sir.' That and an agenda-paper for the next council meeting were on his blotting-paper; his pen was on the floor. There wasn't a sign that anybody but himself had been in the room. And Learoyd had never seen or heard anybody go up there after the Mayor."

"Still, somebody could have gone up?" suggested Milgrave.

"Might have gone up while Learoyd and his wife were at their supper," assented the superintendent. "But it's unlikely—at least, at first sight—for, as you'll see, there's a big glass panel in their door, through which you can see the staircase, and Learoyd sat facing it while he was at table. We can't hear of anybody who saw a soul enter or leave between half-past eight and ten o'clock. Still, there must have been somebody—the murderer—because there's no other entrance."

"No back entrance?" observed Milgrave.

"Not at that hour. The back entrance is closed at six, when the clerks go away," replied the superintendent. "No; whoever did it must have slipped in very quietly, just when Learoyd happened to have his back turned, and have got out again in the same fashion."

"Suspect anyone?" asked Milgrave.

"Why," answered the superintendent, with a deprecating laugh, as if the suggestion was not worthy of mention, "there is some talk in the town about an Italian chap, a sort of showman, who got into trouble here some months since. Mr. Hannington was the magistrate who sent him to prison, and the fellow was understood to make a threat against him. Of course, we're trying to trace the man, but——"

"Just tell me about the mayor," interrupted Milgrave. "We'll leave the Italian. Who was the mayor? How long had he been mayor? Was he popular, or disliked? Had he any enemies in the town, or elsewhere? Give me any details of that sort."

"I should say a more popular young fellow never stepped," answered the superintendent, heartily. "Most popular, sir. Everybody liked him. Never heard a word against him from any quarter. His family's the principal family in the town; they've lived at the Manor Court since old Henry the Eighth's days. They're bankers—the principal bank belongs to them. This young Mr. Guy—his father died just as he was leaving Cambridge, so he became head of the family and chief proprietor of the bank at a very early age, only a couple of years ago. He soon showed that he was a very keen business man, and he began to take a strong interest in the borough affairs as soon as he settled down here. And this year he was elected mayor—been mayor just a month when he was murdered."

"Just a month!" soliloquised Milgrave. "Um—a keen business man—took a strong interest in municipal matters, eh? Was anybody against his election as mayor?"

"Not a soul, sir—unanimously elected," replied the superintendent. "Of course, both his father and his grandfather had been Mayors of Lyncaster in their time—ay, and their grandfathers before them. Our charter's a very old one, Mr. Milgrave—time of Edward the Third. We're an old community."

"So I observed from a mere glance round," said Milgrave. "Well, this is queer business, superintendent. You haven't a clue of any sort?"

"Not the ghost of one," replied the superintendent. "I don't believe in that Italian notion myself. This is a very small town. It's almost impossible that a foreigner could come in, or go out, without being observed. Besides, supposing this Italian did come back, how could he know that the mayor was to be found in his parlour at that particular hour? No, sir. And yet I can't think who—who could want to kill this poor young gentleman."

"Was Mr. Hannington married?" asked Milgrave.

"No; single—lived with his mother and two sisters," answered the superintendent. "A fine way they're in about him, too, poor things!"

"Do they know whether he had any enemies—anybody who had any reason for wanting to get rid of him?" suggested the detective. "On the very face of it, you know, there must have been some motive for the murder. I conclude, of course, that it wasn't robbery. Well, it may have been revenge. It may have been jealousy. Had Mr. Hannington any love affair?"

"Now, that's been speculated on," answered the superintendent; "but, according to his mother, he hadn't, and what's more, never had had."

"So far as she's aware, that is," observed Milgrave. He rose from his chair and buttoned his overcoat. "Well," he went on, "let's have a look around your Moot Hall, particularly the mayor's parlour."

The superintendent took his visitor out into the market-place, and across to the ancient building in which the affairs of the town had been conducted for so many centuries. Darkness had now fallen over Lyncaster, but Milgrave could make out the lines and general appearance of the Moot Hall by the light of the gas-lamps which flared from various stalls set up on the cobble-stones. That it was a place of great antiquity he saw at once. Without making any pretence to any deep knowledge of architecture, he knew that this old building had probably been looking down on Lyncaster market-place in, at any rate, the later Tudor days. But he was not just then so much interested in its antiquity as in its relation to the crime which he was charged to investigate, and he proceeded to look over the place in systematic and business-like fashion.

CHAPTER II

THE Moot Hall formed the centre of a group of ancient buildings which almost completely enclosed one side of the market-place. It was entered by an archway which led into a vaulted hall. On one side of this hall lay the rooms in which the caretaker and his wife lived. A glass-panelled door and a small window looked out of the living-room into the hall, and commanded a clear view of the wide stone staircase by which access was gained to the upper apartments. These apartments were few in number. On the first floor were the council-chamber, a committee-room, the town clerk's private office, and the mayor's parlour; on the second some smaller rooms, used chiefly as storehouses for the municipal archives. Above that was a vast attic, or lumber-room, in the high roof. All these various apartments and places were contained in the front of the building; through a door in the lobby of the first floor, entrance was obtained to a newer wing, in which the corporation offices were located. And, according to fixed rule, that door was locked and bolted by Learoyd at six o'clock every evening. It was, therefore, impossible for any person to enter the old, the front, part of the Moot Hall from the back after that hour.

"And Learoyd's positive," said the superintendent, "dead positive, that on that night he locked up just as usual, and hung the key in his parlour. So nobody could have got to the mayor in that way."

"There's the possibility that the murderer had hid himself somewhere in these old rooms before the mayor came," remarked Milgrave. "There's how it strikes me, anyhow. Hid himself, did his work, and sneaked out while Learoyd was busy with his supper. It wouldn't take him a second, you know, to slip out into the market-place."

They were standing on the threshold of the mayor's parlour just then, and Milgrave turned back into it and took another look around. The room had been left exactly as it was found when Learoyd made his terrifying discovery: the desk, the chair were precisely as the ill-fated young mayor had left them. There on the carpet and hearthrug was the terrible stain which signified so much. But Milgrave, who had already seen all this, did not look at it again. This time he was noting the antique beauty of the room—its groined roof, its vast fireplace, the mullioned windows, the fine oak panelling, black with age, the dusky oil-paintings of dead mayors and local celebrities, the fine old Queen Anne furnishings, the big oak chest. It was a fit scene for many things—for the deliberations of the town grey-beards, for the dispensing of that hospitality for which mayors are so famous—but not for a foul murder. He suddenly turned away, and, tapping his companion on the arm, went silently out of the room.

"Do you know what I'm wondering, superintendent?" he asked abruptly, when the elder man had locked the door, and they were going side by side down the wide stone stairs. "Can you guess?"

"Not at all, sir," replied the superintendent. "Something deep, eh?"

Milgrave laughed—a grim, slightly cynical laugh.

"Not so deep, perhaps," he answered. "No; I'm just wondering, not who it was that killed Mr. Hannington, but why he killed him—why? Motive, you know, superintendent, motive! If I could lay my mind on a motive—ah, I think I should soon lay my hand on a man. However, at present I'll get my bag, put myself up at the Lyncaster Arms yonder, eat my supper, and reflect."

Milgrave began to reflect as soon as he had quitted Superintendent Sutton's company, and he continued to reflect, and to surmise, and to speculate, and to invent theories, and to devise all manner of suggestions and possibilities during the next twenty-four hours—all without result. That evening, having installed himself at the old-fashioned hotel in the market-place and refreshed his inner man, he interviewed several people in Sutton's company. He interviewed more people next morning and at various intervals during the day. He got no light from anybody—no one had a single suggestion to make. The dead man's relatives could tell nothing beyond what Milgrave already knew; the great men of the town, aldermen, councillors, magistrates, were frankly puzzled. The corporation officials were utterly bewildered.

The inquest, held at noon on that second day, revealed nothing; the only fact that was beyond dispute was that someone evilly disposed had obtained access to the mayor's parlour, while the mayor was in it on that evening of December 8, and had stabbed him to death. How the person had obtained access did not seem a very important point. The hall of the Moot Hall was not over well lighted at night. Learoyd and his wife were at supper for some time; anyone having this murderous intention in his heart could easily have slipped up the stairs unobserved.

The only point raised at the inquest which interested Milgrave was the opinion of the doctor as to the nature of the weapon used by the murderer. The doctor said that that weapon must have been a stiletto or finely-pointed dagger; the rapier of other days would have caused such a wound. The mention of stilettos made those present think of the vindictive Italian who had muttered what had appeared to be threats against Hannington when sent to prison. But during that day a telegram informed Sutton that the Italian was pursuing his career as showman in a far-off part of the country, and had certainly not been within a hundred miles of Lyncaster on the night of the murder. And at nightfall, on the second day of his arrival in the town, Milgrave was as wise as ever. There was no clue; nobody had come under suspicion. The Lyncaster murder promised, in good sooth, to be one of those mysteries which are never solved.

Milgrave was sitting over a late supper that second night, wondering if the reason of the murder might not be found in some by-gone passage of young Hannington's life—some episode, say, of his college days—when Sutton came to the hotel, evidently primed with news. The superintendent closed the door of Milgrave's private sitting-room with great caution, and, in spite of their privacy, he dropped his voice to a whisper as he advanced to the detective's chair.

"Now then," he said, "I've heard something."

"Much?" asked Milgrave.

"Can't say whether it'll turn out to be much, little, or nothing; but it's something," answered the superintendent. "Did you notice, when you were at the inquest this morning, a queer-looking old chap that sat in a corner of the court—strange character in appearance?"

"No," replied Milgrave, "I never looked round the court at all. This old man, then——"

"Old chap of the name of Antony Mallalieu, but commonly called Snuffy Mallalieu, from a habit of his," answered Sutton. "He's one of the oldest men in Lyncaster, a regular patriarch, and one of the characters of the town. Keeps a queer odds-and-ends shop where he sells all sorts of old things. He's a bit of an antiquary and so on. I saw him in court to-day, and just now I got this from him."

He handed the detective a scrap of the whitey-brown paper which is used in small shops for wrapping up odds-and-ends. On it Milgrave saw a few words traced with what had evidently been the sediment of a very muddy bottle of cheap ink.

"Mr. Sutton.—If you like to come and see me to-night, and bring that London gentleman with you, it may be to your advantage.—Yours truly,

"A. MALLALIEU."

Milgrave smiled at the crabbed handwriting as he handed the scrap of paper back to his visitor.

"You think—what?" he asked.

"He's a deep 'un, is Snuffy Mallalieu," said Sutton. "He knows something. I noticed this morning how he was taking everything in at that inquest. We'd best go round and see him."

Milgrave had seen some strange places in his long experience, but never anything quite so extraordinary as the house and shop to which Sutton presently led him. The shop, which opened on a quiet alley behind the Moot Mall, was crammed from the floor to ceiling with what most people would have called rubbish—old furniture, old glass, old brass, old pictures—odds-and-ends of every description without order, arrangement, or sequence, thick and black with the accumulated dust of ages.

There was scarcely room to turn in it; there seemed to be less room in the gloomy house behind, where passages, stairs, every nook and corner was piled high with similar goods.

A shadowy figure piloted them from the half-lighted shop through a narrow passage to a parlour beyond, filled with strange things and permeated with an atmosphere of gin, onions, and strong tobacco. Then the shadowy figure turned up the wick of a lamp, and Milgrave found himself staring at the queerest old man he had ever seen in his life, the sort of man who might have been imagined by Dickens or drawn by Doré.

He was very old and dirty; his garments, of the style of the Regency, would have disgraced any scarecrow; there was a strong probability that he never took them off, and only put on a clean shirt once a year. Altogether, he was anything but nice to look at or be near, and Milgrave was thankful that he and Sutton were smoking strong cigars: But out of the old fellow's face, so wrinkled and scarred that it looked as if its skin—properly stretched—would have covered half a dozen human countenances, gleamed a pair of unusually, bright, knowing eyes, and one of them favoured the two men with a decided wink as a hand, that was suggestively like a bird's claw, pointed them to a dilapidated sofa—the only thing in the room on which a seat was available.

"All safe here," said the old man, in a much stronger and firmer voice than Milgrave expected to hear from such an ancient atomy. "I slipped the bolt in the shop door when you came in, Sutton, so we shan't be interrupted. Your servant, Mr. Man-from-London—you look a sharp 'un! Quiet and close and sharp—them's the sort—eh, Sutton? Well, well! but you must have a drop to drink. I drink gin myself, but I'll give you some whiskey that's been in bottle—ay, five-and-twenty years. I'll lay aught neither of you ever put lips to its like!"

Milgrave would have refused this offer of hospitality, but Sutton gave him a nudge and a look; he therefore remained quiescent while the queer old figure, bustling about in its strange surroundings, produced a sealed bottle and dexterously drew the cork.

"I bought two dozen of that whiskey at Lord Felbrough's sale twenty-five years ago," he said. "I had it all specially corked and sealed and I've seen to the renewing of the corks at proper times. Now, then, here's what you might be surprised to see in this den, Mr. Man-from-London—clean glasses and pure water. Best crystal in two respects, eh, Sutton? Now I'll help you, and then I'll help myself to a drop of my liqour—never touch aught but gin—and then we'll talk. A bit of talk—illuminative talk—is what you both want, eh?"

"Light—certainly," answered Milgrave.

"Ay, light!" exclaimed the old man, seating himself on a pile of leather-bound folios. "Light on darkness—what? You want to know who killed young Hannington, my lads, don't you?"

"Do you know?" asked Milgrave.

Snuffy Mallalieu's sharp eyes fastened themselves on the detective's with a shrewd twinkle. He suddenly bent forward and slapped Milgrave's knee with the claw-like hand.

"How old do you think I am, young man?" he asked.

"Eighty," replied Milgrave, promptly.

"You're wrong. I was an old fellow when Sutton there was a young man," retorted Snuffy Mallalieu. "I'm ninety-seven years old. If you doubt it, you can go and search the parish register. Ninety-seven! And sound in mind, body, and estate. Never wore glasses in my life, and still got the necessary teeth, and still as good of hearing as ever. I shall live to be well over a hundred."

"You're a marvel!" said Milgrave. He was wondering what all this was going to lead to, but he knew it was best to let the old fellow take things in his own way and at his own pace. "A marvel! Ninety-seven! A great age."

"Naturally, a man that's lived ninety-seven years in a place knows something about it," remarked the old man. "Sutton there can tell you that there's not much that I don't know about Lyncaster."

"Nobody knows more, I'll be bound!" assented Sutton heartily. "That's a certainty."

"Happen I know a bit more than I'm known to know," said Snuffy Mallalieu, with another glance at Milgrave. "Well, now, there's been a bit of doubt as to whether whoever it was that killed the young mayor went into the Moot Hall by the front—eh?"

The two listeners pricked their ears, this was something like coming to a point. But neither spoke, and the old man laughed with the slightly teasing glee of conscious knowledge. Then his face changed and became serious.

"Until this affair happened," he said, bending towards his visitors, "I believed that there wasn't a soul but me knew a secret about our Moot Hall. I thought I was the last to know it. Now I think—nay, I'm sure—somebody else knows it. It's this—there's a secret way into the old place!"

CHAPTER III

"WHAT!" exclaimed Sutton.

"That's so," said the old man. "My father, and his father, and his grandfather, lived in our Moot Hall, where Learoyd lives now. They all knew of this secret way, and they passed the knowledge down. It's a way that cuts through the walls, goes down below the market-place, and ends—where do you think?"

Milgrave made no answer. His sharp wits told him that the usually stolid man at his side was waking up under the influence of that crafty, wrinkled old face; there was a new atmosphere in those strange surroundings—he himself was falling under its spell. He kept silent. But Sutton's big form stirred uneasily.

"Well—where?" he asked, almost with a growl. "Where, then?"

Snuffy Mallalieu thrust his face still nearer to the two so intently bent on his own. He sank his voice to the ghost of a whisper.

"In a secret staircase in the Bank House!" he answered.

Milgrave felt the superintendent jump in his seat. Then he turned on his companion with a strange look, his back to the old man.

"What!" he exclaimed. "Mr. Leggett's! You don't say!"

"Sure," answered Snuffy Mallalieu.

He, too, relapsed into the same silence as the other when he had spoken that one word. Milgrave wondered what the silence meant—to the others, at any rate; to him it merely signified waiting. It seemed quite a long time before Sutton relieved his feelings with a big letting loose of his held-in breath, and a fervent exclamation.

"By Jove!" he said, in a tense whisper. "Who'd ha' thought it?"

"Just so," assented the old man. He pulled out an ancient snuff-box, took a hearty pinch, and looked at the superintendent. "You see what that means, Sutton?" he continued. "It's struck you! Mr. Man-from-London here doesn't see."

"Frankly, I don't," said Milgrave.

"Simple," remarked Snuffy Mallalieu. "Mr. Leggett, who lives at the Bank House, is a gentleman with a taste for antiquities and archæology. Also, he's for a good many years been manager of Hannington's Bank—trusted and responsible manager. Further, for ten years he's been borough treasurer. Eh?"

Sutton, who had been sitting open-mouthed, holding his glass in his hand, suddenly drank his whiskey and rose. He rapped the old man's shoulder.

"You can show us where this secret way is?" he said.

"Ay, for sure!" answered Snuffy Mallalieu. "And whenever ye like."

"Now, then," said Sutton. "Sooner the better. Come across with us."

The old man shook his head.

"Not till you're certain that we shall be by ourselves," he said. "You'd better go and arrange matters with Learoyd. Let him send his missis to bed at their usual time, and then let us in. I'll meet you outside there at just after ten. Mind you, Sutton, I don't want all the town to know that I've told you. It's been a family secret up to now, but—now——"

"What?" asked Sutton.

Snuffy Mallalieu laughed mirthlessly.

"Now I think Leggett's found it out," he replied. "Well, till ten, then."

Sutton took Milgrave out of the odds-and-ends shop and drew him into a quiet corner.

"Do you know what that means—may mean, mister?" he whispered. "You heard Leggett's name mentioned? Manager of the bank—borough treasurer—ay, but he's more than that—he's trustee for I don't know how many families in town! There's been a pile of brass entrusted to Leggett in this place of late years. A quiet, very respectable, smooth-tongued gentleman—universally respected, as the term is. Leggett! But by the living jingo—suppose—suppose——"

"I want to hear more before I suppose anything," said Milgrave. "You know more than I do. Suppose—what?"

"Young Hannington was a keen 'un about business matters," replied Sutton. "I know he was beginning to go into things. Supposing he'd found something out—wrong, eh, with money matters? Bank funds, borough funds—what? Now, do you see? And what's to be done?"

Milgrave's mind was already made up on that point.

"Have you two or three men that you can thoroughly depend upon?" he asked. "Men to whom you can tell a little and rely on fully?"

"Half a dozen," answered the Superintendent, promptly. "Good 'uns!"

"Two will do," said Milgrave. "Let those two keep a quiet eye on that Bank House, back and front, while you and I find out what this old man's got to show us. If it's as he says, and if it's as you think it might be, why then——"

He ended with an expressive shake of his head, and hurried the superintendent away in the direction of the police-station.

Milgrave, naturally quick to observe things, had noticed on the first night of his arrival in Lyncaster that the townsfolk were evidently in the habit of keeping early hours. By half-past nine the lights begun to be transferred from the lower to the upper windows, by ten the little town was wrapped in silence and in darkness, save for the two or three lamps left burning in the market-place. It was in this silence and semi-gloom that he and Sutton presently met Snuffy Mallalieu, who, buttoned to the chin in an old horseman's cloak, so ancient that it might have served some eighteenth-century highwayman, awaited them in a corner of the Moot Hall entrance. Silently the three were admitted by Learoyd; in silence they went up the stone stairs. At its head Sutton produced a couple of bull's-eye lanterns.

"There are three windows in the mayor's parlour that look out on the market-place," he said. "I don't want anybody to see any big light on in here, so we'll use these things. They'll be useful, too, if we're going to explore this passage that we've heard of."

He unlocked the door of the mayor's parlour as he spoke, and when they had entered he relocked it. Then he set the two lanterns on a centre table and turned to the old man.

"Now, then, Mr. Mallalieu," he said. "It's your turn. What's this that you've got to show us?"

Snuffy Mallalieu had moved over to the further end of the room, near the big fireplace, and was looking down at the stain on the carpet and hearthrug, which Milgrave had viewed, and made no comment on, at his first inspection. He looked up from it at the desk and the chair, and slowly nodded his head.

"Ay!" he said, reflectively. "Ay! Just as I expected it would be from what was said at the crowner's 'quest this morning—just! I see how it was done, my lads."

"How what was done?" asked Sutton.

"The murder, of course," answered the old man. "An easy job, though a clever one. Now, attend to me, both of you. As I told you, my father and grandfather were keepers—caretaker you call it now—of this Moot Hall, and their grandfather before them—ay, for two hundred years, as the town books'll show, Sutton. Consequently, there's not much about the old place that I don't know of. Now, then, you see this mayor's parlour? There's the front, looking on to the market-place, with three windows. Here's the side, overlooking Finkle Gate—it's two windows. By this last window, on this Finkle Gate side, young Hannington had his private desk placed. There it is—there's the chair he sat in when he was stabbed. What's behind that chair? You see—a fine old tapestry curtain, divided in the middle. What's behind that? Come and look."

The old man picked up one of the lanterns, and led his companions to the corner of the room to which he was pointing. Milgrave, who was following him with intense attention, at once perceived what he meant. In the middle of that side of the room a big, canopied fireplace projected well into the apartment; on either side of it there were, consequently, deep recesses. The recess behind the mayor's desk and chair was draped with an antique tapestry curtain. Old Snuffy tapped this with his finger as they advanced to it.

"Now take notice," he said. "When that chair is in its proper place, in front of the desk, its back is separated from this curtain by a space of about eighteen inches. Consequently, a man standing behind that curtain, where it divides—here—could easily reach a man sitting in that chair. And what happened, my lads, when the young mayor was killed, was this—the murderer stood, unknown, behind the curtain, waiting. When the mayor sat down in his chair at the desk and bent forward to do his bit of writing, the murderer put hand and arm through the divide in the curtain and drove his weapon straight into his back.

The mayor, as the doctor said, would jump up, twist round, and fall across there, where Learoyd found him. Now, then, where did the murderer go? Why, he went where he came from! Look here!"

Milgrave, closely following these details and suggestions, was impressed by the almost feverish interest, the intense delight with which the old man was making them. It was plain that Snuffy Mallalieu's passion for antiquities was aroused, and that what appealed to him more than anything was his pleasure in explaining to his companions how the secret architecture of that ancient building had furthered the murderer's nefarious designs. The claw-like hand trembled with eagerness as it drew aside the curtain; the crafty eyes glittered as they roved over the dark time-stained panelling of the recess.

"Bring that other lantern, Sutton," commanded the old man, as he swept aside the tapestry. "Shine it on here—here. Mr. Man-from-London, you hold this; I want both hands. Now, then, look—both of you. You see that this recess is panelled, just like all the rest of the room. Queen Anne stuff this, gentlemen, every inch of it! Good, solid oak that came out of Lyncaster Forest, sound as a bell yet. Now, you can look all this panelling over as closely as you like, and it'll take you a long time to find where the door is that I've told you of. But it's here! And I'll lay you all I've got in my shop to a cracked tea-pot that the man who's discovered the secret of this door and the passage beyond has taken good care to grease the hinges! Now look. You put a finger on that bit of carving there, you press this other bit of carving here—and there you are!"

Under the old man's trembling hands a narrow strip of panelling, five feet by two, slid away in the angle of the recess, and revealed a deep cavity in the solid masonry of the thick wall. And Snuffy Mallalieu, stepping into this, and beckoning the others to follow, took a lantern from one of them, and held it down to the dust of the floor on which they stood.

"What did I tell you?" he said, with a grim chuckle. "There you are—oil! You see, he's oiled the machinery, so that it 'ud open easy. Now do you see the trick of it?"

"What I want to know," said Milgrave, "is—first, does that panel open from this side?"

For answer the old man drew the panel into place, shut it tight, and demonstrated its opening. He looked at the detective with a grin of triumph.

"And second," continued Milgrave, "where does this passage lead to?"

"Ah!" answered Snuffy Mallalieu. "Now you're talking! That's the really important thing. Come on!"

The passage of which Milgrave had spoken, and into which Sutton was casting dubious and half-frightened glances, went off in the thickness of the masonry behind the built-out fireplace. It was about six feet in height, about two and a half in width. Cobweb hung from its roof, strange growths showed on its walls. But the dust that lay thick on its floor was dry enough, and the old man chuckled again as he held a lantern down to it.

CHAPTER IV

"Look there!" he said. "Footprints—plenty of 'em. Recent, all of 'em. Now, if you can pick out a nice, separate, distinct one, Mr. Man-from-London, and compare it with somebody's boot, eh?"

"I hope this is safe," remarked Sutton, looking uneasily about him. "No fear of it falling in, is there?"

"It's been safe for three hundred years and more," retorted Snuffy Mallalieu. He marched confidently forward, lantern in hand, until Milgrave had counted some fifteen paces. There a blank wall confronted them; at right angles to it appeared a narrow stairway, evidently cut through another wall. "Now, then," continued the old man, "do you know where we are, Sutton? That's the wall that runs down the side of the big staircase in the hall below. This stair's cut clean through it, right through the foundation, and into a passage, like this, that runs under the market-place. It goes right under Belford the butcher's cellars, and under the cellars of the next two shops, and then into another stair that cuts in the wall of the Bank House, which, I may tell you," he added, turning to Milgrave, "is an older building—the house part of it, anyway—than this Moot Hall. And in that house it comes out in another panel doorway that opens in Leggett's parlour, close by the fireside. There!"

The two men looked over the old fellow's shoulder into the black chasm of the stair. Sutton sniffed doubtfully at the cold, damp air which hung about them.

"Come back to the mayor's parlour," he said. "We'd best decide what's to be done."

It was at this stage that Milgrave took command. He had been thinking deeply while the old man made his revelations, and he had now decided on the course which he wished to pursue. Once out of the nearest door, and standing near the spot still stained by the dead man's blood, he spoke with decision.

"There's only one thing to do, superintendent," he said. "You and I must call on this Mr. Leggett at once. You must make the excuse that we want to ask him a few questions about Mr. Hannington. Don't frighten him at first, nor later, for that matter."

Sutton looked at Snuffy Mallalieu, and laughed cynically.

"It 'ud take a good deal to frighten Leggett," he observed. "He's as hard and cool a customer as ever I had to deal with."

"All the better," said Milgrave. "Now, then, this is my plan: You and I go straight there; we engage Leggett in what we'll call casual conversation—speculative talk about the murder. It's now twenty minutes to eleven o'clock. You, Mr. Mallalieu, go through this passage and make your way to the secret door in Leggett's house. You've a watch on you! Set it by mine. Good! Now, then, at precisely eleven o'clock you knock on that secret door. Knock loudly—once, twice, thrice—a second or so between each knock. See?

Sutton looked as if he did not quite see, but the old man nodded and chuckled gleefully.

"Good notion, my lad!" he answered. "I'll do my part; off you go. He's about certain to take you into that parlour; it's his sitting-room. But I'll knock in such a fashion that it'll be heard anywhere in the house. But keep your eyes open; he's one of those quiet chaps that might turn uncommon ugly, is Leggett."

"All right," said Milgrave. "Now, remember, eleven sharp!" He beckoned the superintendent to follow him out of the room, pausing on the stair outside to say a warning word or two to Learoyd. "Now, superintendent," he went on, as he and Sutton crossed the silent market-place, "is this Leggett a married man?"

"No; bachelor," answered Sutton.

"What household does he keep?" asked Milgrave.

"Couple of servants, middle-aged women. We've got to bear this in mind," continued Sutton abruptly. "If he's—what there seems to be a probability that he is, he'll be a dangerous man to tackle. There's two of my men there in that entry opposite the Bank House; hadn't I better tell 'em to keep handy?"

"No—wait," answered Milgrave. "I think you and I can tackle one man, at a pinch. We can watch him without seeming to do so, the thing is to be alert at eleven o'clock. Now, then, you ring, and do the first talking."

The bank manager himself opened the door of the house, a quaint old building at one side of which stood the modern bank premises. He remained for a moment framed in the doorway, a lamp in his hand, silently regarding his visitors. Milgrave, watching him closely, saw no sign of fear on his face, nor any surprise; all that he showed was a cold disapproval.

"Well," he said, acidly, "what is it, Sutton?"

"Sorry to disturb you, Mr. Leggett," answered the superintendent, apologetically; "but can you give me and Mr. Milgrave here a minute or two? There's one or two little matters that you might be able to help us in, sir; just a small detail or two, you know."

Leggett stood back, motioning them to enter.

"You come at a strange time," he observed coldly. "Was this the only time you could hit on? However, come this way."

He closed the street-door behind them, then turned and preceded them down the hall to a room which Milgrave at once took to be the parlour of which Snuffy Mallalieu had spoken. One glance at it, when Leggett had turned up the light, showed its great age. The floor concealed beneath the thick modern carpet was uneven; the big oak rafters which spanned the low ceiling were bent and twisted. It needed little knowledge to know that behind the panelling of the walls lay ancient stone walls raised by some mason-hand of many a century ago. Instinctively, Milgrave looked towards the fireplace and its surroundings, wondering whereabouts in the highly-polished oak the secret door was. There were evidences of the owner's antiquarian tastes on every hand—in the beautiful old furniture, the cabinets of china and glass, the rare objects displayed on the walls, the old prints and books. But the owner himself was of more interest —a thin, sparely built man, with a cold eye and un-sympathetic lips, keen, self-controlled—the sort of man who might not call forth affection, but would doubtless create trust and confidence.

"Sit down," said Leggett, still disapproving and acid. "What is it you want to know? It seems strange to me that you should expect me to be able to tell you anything. I should think everything that can be told was told at the inquest this morning."

He was looking at Milgrave as he spoke, and the detective was quick to take up the challenge.

"Just so," he answered. "But only on the surface. This affair, of course, is something that depends on more than mere surface information. My duty is to go down as deeply as I can. You haven't any theory of your own, I suppose?"

The bank manager had listened to this with a super-cilious smile. It was evident that he had no great idea of detective intelligence.

"If I have, I don't know that I'm bound to com-municate it to the police," he said half-musingly. "But, since you ask the question, I don't mind saying that, in my opinion, if you want to get at the secret of Hannington's murder, you'll have to go far back—as far back as you can in such a young man's life. I'm not going to suggest anything, but you must remember that our late mayor spent three years at Cambridge and two in London before he came down here to take up his father's place as head of this bank, and—he may have made enemies. Eh?"

"Quite so," replied Milgrave. "And you think that some enemy contrived a clever entrance to the Moot Hall at a particular moment—the particular moment?"

He was watching Leggett closely now, and he was not slow to see that Leggett was watching him. A subtle gleam of something—was it suspicion, doubt, fear?—stole into the cold, blue eyes, and, instead of an answer coming, a curious silence fell over the three. Milgrave waited a while, and broke it himself.

"Whoever made his way into the mayor's parlour," he said, in a quiet, even voice, "must surely have been remarkably well acquainted with Lyncaster Moot Hall. No stranger, for instance, would know how to time his entrance so well. The mayor did not usually go to his parlour at that hour every evening."

The thin lips smiled disagreeably.

"How do you know that Hannington hadn't made an appointment with his murderer?" they asked. "It's all nonsense, of course, about Learoyd not seeing anyone enter or leave. Learoyd was too busy with his supper to attend to things of that sort. A man could easily have slipped in and out; and as to getting away, why, it's not two minutes' walk to the outskirts and the open country from any point of this town, and——"

Milgrave, as if in a fit of absent-mindedness, drew

out his watch. It was already but a minute to eleven. He interrupted Leggett as if a chance idea had struck him.

"Of course," he said, indifferently—"of course, there may be means of obtaining entrance to your Moot Hall that I know nothing about. In these old places there are often such entrances—secret passages and such-like. And——"

He paused, looking at the bank manager as if for information. But even as he paused he saw that the shaft had gone home. A sudden twitch of the man's lips, a new light in his eye; but he laughed cynically, throwing up his head as if in contempt.

"Pshaw!" he said scornfully. "We don't live in the days of walled-up skeletons, and——"

With the first silvery chime of a clock that stood on the mantelpiece the first heavy knock sounded without the panelled oak by which the cynical voice was speaking; and, in spite of long years of training, Leggett sprang to his feet with a sharp cry, twisting round as he rose to stare at the wall whence came this strange summons. It came again, and the two watchers, who had also risen and were quietly moving nearer to him, saw great beads of sweat break out on his forehead. He reeled slightly, stretching out a hand; and as the third and more peremptory knock sounded, he uttered a queer, choking cry and dropped forward into Sutton's arms.

"Fainted!" muttered Milgrave. "Set him down there while I tell one of your men to call the doctor." He went out to the front door, and, returning a moment later, looked meaningly at the unconscious man. "That was a capital idea, superintendent," he said. "His nerve wasn't up to that. I shouldn't wonder if he fancied that was Hannington's ghost. Well, the next thing'll be to get at his motive. Financial, of course."

Milgrave stayed in Lyncaster long enough to have it proved to him, fully and abundantly, why Leggett killed the mayor. The borough accounts were all wrong—had been cooked and manipulated for many a year. The bank had been robbed, cleverly and systematically; numerous families had been defrauded. And the only thing that he ever wondered about, after Leggett had been safely hanged, was whether the murder would ever have been detected if Snuffy Mallalieu had not lived to his remarkable age in full possession of his remarkable faculties.

THE END

Lightning Source UK Ltd.
Milton Keynes UK
UKHW011348290720
367364UK00002B/653